Morkan's Quarry

A Novel by Steve Yates

To Rachel, who listens!

Steve Yates

Springfield, Missouri
2010

http://English.MissouriState.edu/moon_city_press.html

Text edited by Donald R. Holliday
Text layout by Angelia Northrip-Rivera
Cover design by Myriam Bloom, detail from *The Stone Breakers*, by
    Gustave Courbet

Library of Congress Cataloging-in-Publication Data

Yates, Steve B., 1968–
  Morkan's Quarry : a novel / by Steve Yates.
    p. cm.
  ISBN 978-0-913785-24-9
  1. United States—History—Civil War, 1861–1865—Fiction. I.
Title.
  PS3625.A76M67 2010
  813'.6—dc22
                              2010007357

This book is for my wife, Tammy, who has waited,
and for my father, Carl, who has waited even longer.

Book 1

This Town Won't Be in the United States

I

When the war was finally won and the Morkans reclaimed their quarry after a fashion, they did their best to forget the armies, the battles, and occupations. Still every limestone monument cut from their cliffs near downtown Springfield, Missouri—the markers for General Nathaniel Lyon, for the unknown Confederate dead—became more than memento moris set in meadows before the red mounds of graves. To the Morkans, each stone hardened the gray promise that the town they had known was gone, and the new city rising there would remain divided by the dead, by bleary memories, and by the fabulous inscriptions of the bereaved.

At the onset, on the morning of August 10, 1861, miners at the Morkan Quarry heard cannon, a sound like thunder before a summer storm. A strand of black smoke twisted and rose from the prairie southwest of town. Cadres of wagons bearing Federal Home Guards pounded past the quarry gates. In the quarry pit, the owner, Michael Morkan, and his son, Leighton Shea, loaded muskets and shotguns into a flat-bed wagon, and under these Morkan hid four casks of the quarry's black powder.

"Why?" Leighton asked once a foreman left him and his father alone. "It's safer here, ain't it?"

Morkan leaned so close to his son, his whiskers rasped Leighton's ear. "Everything you're sitting on just turned to gold. Close to the vest, lad."

Leighton brought the cock back on Morkan's favorite, a Belgian double shotgun, while Morkan went to the office for more. Leighton had turned fifteen in January, had quarried since he was eleven. The Rebel army, and he was sure that's what the cannon were, had been a long time coming. Cocking the gun left a painful dent in his thumb.

Leighton had watched the six thousand Federal troops drill in town. Many had dark blue, woolen uniforms. Others wore gray with stripes of yellow and bright red. Some swooped through drills in trousers as ragged as a scarecrow's. He'd heard among them the bark of numbers in German, and tongues as strange as the burbles of faeries in his childhood nightmares.

A rider trotted into the quarry gates, the bearded engineer Marcus Larue Heron, who was the liaison between the quarry and the Federals. He reminded Morkan of a mariner's purser, grasping and always a few thousand pounds ahead of his accounts.

Miners on the cliffs behind the Morkans shouted at him: "Hey, Captain? Who's won?" Only twelve miners and stonecutters arrived for work that morning and they were now limed so white they appeared as wraiths against the pulsating heat of the summer sky.

Morkan snapped canvas taut over the powder. Seeing his father's face harden, Leighton slowly set the shotgun down. Heron stopped his chestnut beside the wagon.

The Federal engineer bore a smile like a little boy's at play. "Do you seek now the safety of the Federal army?"

"I'm hoping that you all have settled the matter safely outside the city limits," Morkan said, fetching his own business smile. Under his straw hat, with his spectacles flashing like gold coins in the sun, Morkan could be a cipher. His red hair was limed and wild beneath the hat's rim.

Heron steadied his horse and leaned forward. "Lose hope, then." He remained smiling, then gave a wink as steely as a pistol hammer snapping down. "I come to tell you that in all likelihood what stone you've cut will be unclaimed." With his small, almost silver eyes he scanned the wagon bed. "And what you're doing looks like a fine idea. So long as it comes east with us."

He put out his hand, and Morkan took it without a moment's hesitation. "In another life you and I would have savored the long dance of commerce, Morkan. Alas, we become conquerors or conquered." He turned his horse and punched it to a gallop.

Morkan kicked at the wagon's wheel. Leighton waited for him to speak. The cannon intensified. Morkan cleared his throat, spat a thick clot of gray. "There aren't enough slaves in this town to fill a church hall, and over them a son-of-a-bitch like that is left in charge of all your business." He was forty, had been in America for twenty-five years, but his voice still bounced with the Irish accent Leighton worked diligently to overcome. Leighton chewed his lip and tasted the bitter lime. "Of weapons I have no fear. Of men like that, Leighton, I am sore afraid."

Morkan scanned the cliff. The miners shaded their eyes, pointed west, elbowed each other and argued. "If you can keep them working," Morkan said, "let's get at least a half day out of them. And then you and I need to get to the bank."

For the last month Morkan kept in the pocket of his coat his currency receipt for $2,500 in gold from the National Mineral Bank. The order the miners were finishing was for the ashlars to the grand courthouse that would anchor Springfield's square. Judging from the sounds of battle and Heron's visit, Morkan felt no assurance of payment.

Leighton cleared his throat to speak. Morkan nodded to him. "If this afternoon is all we got, let me use just a pop's worth of powder up there. I can chamber the holes deep." His voice rose as his father's face reddened. "If we have to feather and wedge, we won't finish, not with twelve men."

Morkan's eyes darkened. "No powder. Not a peep of it." He glanced to the gate. "We're damn lucky Heron didn't take all we had now. He's no fool." After a moment, he reached for Leighton's hand. There a gray callus from exposure to the lime rumpled the boy's palm. Leighton's face warmed—the men might be watching. His father's touch, so reassuring with the clatter of battle outside, was a reminder that Leighton was yet a boy. Morkan kneaded that callus. "Leighton, this is an ugly time. You'll have to bear with me."

Head down, Leighton trudged the ox path to the cliff where the miners waited. The Morkans had powder enough to blast for months—fearing shortages, Morkan had gone on a buying spree before Sumter and Camp Jackson. Leighton sorely missed using powder. Deep down, he longed for the audacity of it, the great blap black powder made, the shot ringing over town, rattling windows and puncheons.

At the top of the cliffs, he gathered the miners. The water they had been slurping left streaks of tanned skin showing beneath the grit on their chins and necks. Leighton took his chuck, and the men shuffled, hesitating, their eyes blinking, brows furrowed.

The limestone he knelt on was as gray-blue as November moonlight, and just kneeling to the stone stilled his soul. Two tall drillers with sledges huddled around him. He breathed deeply, nodded, and the black shadows of the sledges lanced downward. The iron chuck rang in his hands, stung his palms, vibrated his elbows. His shoulder joints shook. The second sledge whammed against the chuck, and a shower of white dust pelted his legs and chest and covered the brogans of his two drillers. With a slosh, the water boy tipped his gourd at the hole.

As the sledge hammer rose, a driller's hands whispered on the wooden handle. Leighton knew not to follow the hammer with his eyes. One look at the down swing, and you'd be flinching all morning. Fossils in the limestone bit his knees as he knelt, hands on the humming chuck, arms outstretched. No prayer he remembered demanded such an arduously reverent position. No devotion was this punishing: even his teeth and the cavities of his sinuses reverberated with the rhythmic moan of the chuck sinking and ringing into the blue skin of the earth.

He stood and slapped dust from his jeans. The ringing in his ears now assumed a rhythm from a drill and chuck team four yards down the bluff. Across from the quarry lot, long rows of buildings on Summit Street shimmered in the August heat: the lime-washed railings of the Beloit Hotel; The Quarry Rand Saloon; the low shacks of a lumber yard; and a wide lot where an outlet of a wagon company displayed a row of new open-bedded wagons, the pine of their sideboards still amber in the noon sun.

He strained to hear the battle, but could not. He tensed and relaxed the muscles of his shoulders. Work here had made him barrel-chested and creased his arms with bundled lines like the fibers of an oak root. He ran a handkerchief across his forehead and over his hair. The drillers began to feather the stone, banging small holes in rows where it could be wedged and split. Down in the quarry pit near the office, Morkan and Correy were hitching the stock together and loading wagons. The miners paused and gawked at the train of oxen and horses. Leighton felt his hands tremble—the stock only moved in winter when the mine closed for the worst months. Somehow he had thought the dazzling war could come, and he might even fight in it, a battle or two, but overall things would just spool along. The quarry would be fine. The stone, with a Morkan quarrying on it, glittered in an everlasting white at his feet. Men like Heron were lackeys. Leighton grabbed a miner named Bristow by the suspenders. "Take my key. Get over to the boom shack and get me a cask of powder and a bucket of clay."

The miner squinted at him, then hustled down the trail.

Leighton turned to the drillers. "Make little bells, gents. Deep. We'll pop this off."

The drillers ceased turning the bits, and the feather holes began widening at their deepest points to hold an extra charge of powder. By packing the wadding loosely, the blast would be more diffuse and quieter. Bristow returned, handed Leighton the cask of powder and the clay.

Leighton glanced down at his father and Correy, who were absorbed in loading the quarry's records onto the wagons. After opening the cask, he ladled powder into each beveled hole. The powder scrambled down with hardly a crackle, fine and perfect, black as coal. He wormed the fuses down in the holes, packed them with less clay than he normally used. Curving the fuses together, he crimped the ends of each to a long length of the powder-soaked fusing. The miners crept back from the ledge of rock and crouched; twelve of them, Leighton counted. The magnitude of what he was about to do, the danger of doing it while a battle raged outside of town struck him, and he dug his thumbnail into the wood of the match.

Before him, the shadow of their makeshift derrick loomed, casting a pattern like the bars of a prison window across the quarry basin. The Morkan's was the only steam derrick in town. The Mistress, Leighton's mother had called it, and the name stuck. To make the derrick, Morkan had purchased the boiler to an old utility engine, a rail hauler and straightener, which he left in Rolla. He brought the rest of the derrick together piece by piece over a summer, and in Rolla dismantled and brought by wagons every moving part to the derelict little engine. Then came a cold February when even rivers froze. Morkan mustered what idle, wintering miners would follow him, and dragged the boiler from the railhead through an ice storm, one more act that made him to Springfield's Scots Irish as alien as Eads was to St. Louis's Germans as he stalked the river bottom beneath his whiskey barrel and groped for treasure. Despite the boiler's compact size, the journey from the railhead at Rolla was the most dangerous task Leighton could remember—the oxen straining, he and a half dozen miners axing frozen limbs and downed trees along Telegraph Road, battling the cold, his father eyeing the blue ropes bearded with ice, the pitch of the sled. Morkan's face twisted with worry and insistence. But suddenly there in March was the Mistress, an assembled fact on the ground, belching black smoke, chugging, swinging stone down from the bluff on howling pulleys. For months farmboys gawked and local merchants scowled.

Now Leighton knew he jeopardized the derrick, the railway for the ore carts, the kilns, the mill, everything in the most mechanized quarry west of the St. Francois Mountains. Even so, with the lumps of the miners' heads ducking behind him, he'd feel a fool if he did anything but pop the stone now. The powder was in the holes. And he was right to blast it: the quarry could fulfill its contract and receive payment despite shutting down, and maybe collect right after the battle. His father was never bold, always kept the noise and dust at the quarry to a minimum, was more concerned about keeping peace with neighbors than with reaping quantities of stone.

He didn't holler fire, but cut the match against the cliff and touched the flame to the fuse. He took five steps backwards, then lowered himself to lie flat, resting his chin on the rock, bending the brim of his slouch hat forward so that his eyes were shielded. Smoking and hissing, the fire divided into four crackling entities, then dove into the holes.

There was a pause, the supreme quiet that came before every blast. For just a second the world seemed suspended in glass, waiting to be shattered. Then, four tongues of dust flared at once, accompanied by a gruff thump. The whole stone, a rectangular slab, jolted as if startled, then with a crunch, settled free of the cliff.

Down in the pit, Morkan dropped a sheaf of billings and Federal vouchers of service. The slap of the powder against the cliffs hit him like a bolt to the back of the neck. Along the lip of the cliff, billows of white smoke obscured the miners. Morkan glanced frantically at the gate. The town was quiet. Cannon thumped far away. Correy stooped to recover the vouchers, some of which scuttled off in the wind. Morkan slammed his fist so hard into the wagon bed, the two drafts jolted forward, then stamped and rolled their necks.

"It's all right," Correy said. "Nobody's paying us any mind."

Morkan's glare silenced him.

Leighton cringed when he saw his father glowering up at him. To his horror, the miners cheered, and he felt his neck burn. They whooped, faced the sound of distant cannon, spun their caps, shook their hammers at the battle.

Taking a whiskbroom from his belt, he swished away the dust on top of the block, then crawled over the block onto the shelf. Twenty feet below, the teal pool in the quarry's pit shimmered in the sun. Up a rise from the pool sat a long shack, his father's office. A single ramp of railway led from the bluff to the mill and the two blackened chimneys of the kilns. When he flicked the bristles of the broom across the lime, there emerged patches of fossils in the gray-blue rock. Rods and coils, corkscrews, sheaves of scales, shells, cogs, the living clockwork of some vast, teaming ocean that stretched as wide as the sky and stars above it. The sun gleamed off the rock. Imagining Morkan stalking behind him, his fingers gripping his collar, Leighton shivered as the wind shook the back of his shirt.

At one o'clock Morkan rang the bell outside his office. The laughs and shouts of the approaching miners saddened him. For the five years he had owned the quarry, their boisterous clamor had been a comfort. It meant a day's labor finished and men, pleased to work, coming for their rightful wage. He counted cash into piles, the daily pay for his miners and Leighton. Before the war, he'd had sixty men working here. With the nearest railhead 150 miles away in Rolla, Missouri, his townspeople had no other major quarry at hand. For strapped customers, he would even cut sandstone and fieldstone. Occasionally he and Leighton still followed an order out to the building site and for a fee built the forge or the springhouse and fruit cellar. They could build dry stone walls tight as a mare's teeth or mortar a wall solid as the escarpments of Tyre. Scores in town met the Morkan name at the hearth every morning in the straight hewn edges of their stone chimneys. And then the courthouse began to rise, a glittering testimony to him and his son. But there would be no houses built, no families settled, no courthouse finished till the war ended. He logged the expenses on a temporary notepad. All the quarry's other records were stowed in a steamer trunk on the flat-bed wagon waiting outside.

The office door opened, and the miners crowded in, lime tumbling from them at every step. The white snowfalls of it were nothing like the gritty chaff he remembered from the granite quarries in the Mourn Mountains of Ireland. Here lime weighted his lungs as if he breathed lead all day.

The first miners in settled against the frames of the open slat windows. The drill foreman, Correy, was extolling the Federals' general, a red-headed man named Lyon. The foreman shouted down dissenters, sweeping his arms about. He had round cheeks circled by sandy, mutton-chop sideburns. "Lyon won't either," he said. "He's whupped them all."

Amidst a barrage of protest at Correy, Leighton stepped through the door. A quiet settled on the office, and Morkan felt his face darken, more with embarrassment than with anger. He rued that he would now have to discipline Leighton, to find some way to curb his brashness, his urge for expediency, the trait Morkan saw as the boy's real flaw. But Leighton was young, he told himself, and he tried to bring to mind that feeling of youth, when a boy is sure he has all the muscle and mind he needs to be a man, but older men force him to wait.

Every day the boy's face, the plump curve of his cheeks, the slight bulge of a second chin made him appear more like Charlotte, Morkan's late wife, who'd died two years ago of smallpox. The lime only intensified this, made the boy the walking ghost of his mother. Leighton had her eyes, pinched and bright blue, devious above such a sharp nose and full cheeks. This afternoon, he was gray-white even to the roots of his straight, black hair.

Leighton's entrance subdued the argument enough that the miller, A. C. Greevins, stepped forward and raised his bony hand. Miners, even Leighton, crossed their arms over their chests and waited for the miller to speak. "Now, granted, this Federal army was right impressive." The miller's teeth were dark gray and his pupils black behind a white mask of lime. He popped his chest, produced a shower of dust. "But I seen our Missouri State Guard a'drilling. They beat the Hessians back to St. Louis and the Kansans back to hell."

Applause and mutters broke out across the shack. The arguments continued, until finally someone shouted, "Let's hear a Morkan!"

They quieted. Their eyes stared from gray faces. Morkan shook his head. "You men know I got nothing to say on this."

"The boy'll say," someone shouted.

Correy smiled and strode to Leighton. "Why, the boy can name every Federal general in this town."

Greevins likewise pushed toward the boy. "And every State Guard general. Do it, boy! Let them hear you."

Leighton flinched from Correy's hand and shot a glance at his father. Sweat burned his brow. He cleared his throat. "Sweeny, Lyon, Price, Lane, McBride, Sigel."

The miners roared with laughter, the names being a jumble of commanders from both armies. But Morkan had heard the boy chant the names of all the generals of each army as he and Leighton rode to work mornings. Leighton knew not only names, but that Sweeny was a one-armed Irish hero of the Mexican War; McBride was handsome enough to attract the daughters of Missouri but spread envy among her sons. The boy knew more of the lives of warriors than Morkan could ever teach him of the Saints.

15

Morkan stood and raised his hand. The miners grew quiet, then lined to accept their pay. When he'd finished distributing cash, he held up his hand again. Twelve of them, powdered white, blinking.

"Ashcroft or Correy one will come around to the Quarry Rand Tuesday and tell anyone gathered when we'll work next," Morkan said. The men looked at each other, brows scrunching. "Until whatever this is blows over, I'm shutting the quarry."

Even Leighton's eyes were wide with surprise.

"God keep you good men," Morkan said.

Some of the men pulled caps from their heads and clutched them to their chests.

As the miners filed out, Morkan's chin stuck forward, eyes slightly lidded, as if the closing announcement had been routine. In the crisp muslin suit, he looked practical and proper. With his spectacles and thin face, he reminded Leighton of one of the Jesuits who'd taught him in St. Louis, an intense, lanky Frenchman who went mad over a boatwright's daughter, then drowned himself in the Salt River. When the last miner left, Morkan's shoulders sagged, and his face slumped in a frown. The change was so profound, Leighton wondered if the closing were not permanent, if they might leave the quarry behind.

Morkan opened a desk drawer and handed his son a suede satchel, the carrying case to a pepperbox pistol. Morkan strapped a Colt revolver to his own belt.

Leighton removed the pepperbox from the leather. The pistol was a cold knot of iron and ivory with a ring trigger.

Morkan grabbed his wrist, and Leighton froze, but held the pistol tight.

"I want you to think about the danger you put us in," Morkan said. "They can take everything around you. This is war, Leighton. There are no rules with men like Heron."

His chin trembled with anger, and Leighton held his breath.

"I've spent near a month keeping quiet on the powder, denying I had any, and what do you do but scream it across the whole damned town in the midst of a battle!" He released Leighton, then pinched the bridge of his nose. "Son, there were miners on that cliff who didn't know we had powder."

After a moment his shoulders fell. "Leighton, look, we've got to play everything tight from here on out. Please, come to me for even small decisions just for this little while. It's a bad time, son. It's no sleepy Saturday in August."

Shaking, Leighton dropped the pistol in the pocket of his coat. It bumped his chest, and its weight stretched his coat across his back. Guilt swept a noose around his ribs.

Roped in a train muzzle to butt, the six oxen, four mules and eight draft horses lowed and brayed behind the flat-beds. Morkan led his chestnut Walker while he arranged for Correy to meet with him Monday night at a crossroads southeast of town.

Locking the gates, Morkan nodded to Correy.

Morkan edged his horse next to Leighton's gray Walker and gently pulled his son's hand from the reins. "I'm going to be leaning on you, Leighton, sooner than I ever reckoned." His voice was a rough whisper Leighton had never heard from his father.

When Leighton bowed his head, there was Morkan's palm open beneath Leighton's small hand. There the yellow and gray callus that matched Leighton's spread rugged as a lizard's back.

Despite the hurry in Morkan's voice, they watched Correy head east on the Galway Road toward the James River, a covert route to the Morkan farm. Morkan fiddled with the looped reins so nervously that the Walker rolled its eyes. The canvas tarp over the muskets, the dusty hides of the stock all disappeared into the shadowed columns of oak.

II

BEFORE THEY REACHED THE SQUARE, A HORSE AND RIDER
neared them. Leighton recognized the rider as a teamster named
Peterson. Peterson's shirt was torn open, and his right sleeve was
ripped off at the shoulder. That fabric was wrapped in a bloody
wad around his right hand, and he reined the horse with his left.
He wore one of the dark blue, flat-topped caps Leighton had
seen on the Federal Regulars.

Steering his sweat-streaked horse over to the Morkans, he
muttered to himself, his eyes wide. Finally he spoke, his voice
hoarse. "In about two hours this town won't be in the United
States no more." Soot darkened his face, and his wide eyes were
blood shot.

"Rebels won?" Morkan asked, inching his horse closer to
Peterson.

"God damn Texas banshees killed near half our army."

Leighton extended a canteen of water to Peterson, who
nudged his horse forward to take it. The teamster's leg rose and
fell with the heaving sides of his horse. Peterson cradled the
canteen between his right arm and shoulder, and stuck the cap
toward Leighton.

"Uncork it, will you?"

As Leighton pulled the cork from the mouth of the canteen,
he smelled the stench of powder and salty blood on Peterson.
Peterson guzzled the water, choked a moment, then guzzled
more. He handed the canteen back to Leighton.

"Them Rebs was chucking bodies in sink holes before we
even cleared the field." He paused and frowned as if thinking.
"That general's dead, too. Lyon, the red-headed one from Connecticut."

"You've seen this?" Morkan asked.

18

Peterson nodded. "If you're a Union man, Morkan, and I don't mean nothing by supposing, but if you are, I'd pack up and follow the army to Rolla." He raised his bloodied hand as if it were a heavy weight. "I got to keep this hand at least long enough to pack my people up. It'll come off by evening."

Leighton lurched away from Peterson and stared at the black and crimson wad of cloth Peterson held up.

"God keep you," Morkan said, and he crossed himself. Leighton did likewise, a motion he hadn't made since his mother died.

Peterson pressed his heels into his horse's flanks and headed north. Leighton rode closer to his father now. He shivered at the thought of unwrapping that hand, the cloth sticking and tearing at the pulp. He wondered if Peterson had screamed when the ball or saber struck. Peterson might have to remove the hand himself, and Leighton imagined cutting, the bones cracking, separating the fingers that jerked and spread of their own and last accord. He shook his head violently to clear it.

Glancing down the row of houses where the widow Slade lived, Morkan pulled at his chin. Cora Slade was an unspoken presence between the Morkans. She had nursed in the smallpox camp where Charlotte died and it was she and a priest who came bearing the news of Charlotte's death.

Later, when her husband died at the quarry from falling drunk into the kiln, Morkan comforted her. Within a year he took to visiting an evening or two each month. Leighton knew this from Correy—Morkan tied his horse in Correy's yard two doors down from the Slade house so there would be no talk in town.

With Peterson still on his mind and the wild notion that the Federals were beaten, Leighton felt emboldened. He stepped his horse close to Morkan. "Let's go warn her."

"Do what?"

"The widow Slade. Let's tell her what Peterson said."

Beneath the lime-crusted slouch hat, Morkan's long face flattened with dismay.

At the hospital the Federals improvised on the western edge of town, Cora Slade cornered a wounded Iowan. Tracking the two knobs of his shoulders she inched forward. His eyes, she knew, were rolling like pebbles in a shoal, blood seeping down from his poorly bandaged head, and to top it he was decked out in a blazing yellow vest, pink frilled scarves, a red merino shirt, and a belt of bobcat skin. In his fist was the gory crimson bone saw he'd wrested from a surgeon. A steady, low cursing came from his lips, which never stopped moving—she tried to place the language: Dutch, Slavic, Hungarian.

Quite a morning this had been. The Yankees took over the White River Hotel and wounded arrived by ten a.m. Within an hour, the blood and entrails and limbs surpassed any train wreck or cyclone she ever worked. The soldiers were soaked wet from the night's rain, the heat of the battle, and their horrible injuries.

And here was this poor fop, out of his mind and wielding a bone saw.

"Darling," she said, "you have got to put that down and let me comfort you."

When his cursing stopped for an instant she extended a hand, but lowered a shoulder to be ready. There was an awful pool of quiet in the heat and mayhem around them. Surgery nearby stopped, nurses halted, even some patients lifted their heads blinking.

The Iowan asked her a question in his barbar. His eyes stilled and focused.

"Yes, dear," she risked. "We'll let you take a rest."

When he raised the blade back over his head, she rushed him with her lowered shoulder aiming to stun him against the hotel's massive fireplace. But he was quick and rolled with her force, cracking her noggin against the bricks. They both fell, her with arms now numb around his waist, him flailing the saw, raking her knuckles. Once her bottom hit the hardwood floor, her hands and arms awoke and she wrapped her bloody fingers around his neck and squeezed with all her might.

Gagging, he clanged the saw against the hearth and lost it. A surgeon finally jolted from his stupor and dove to pin the Iowan's arms.

When they lifted him off of her, a whirlwind of black and green stars swallowed her and she was floored.

She came to and the sun was high past noon and the place in an uproar, surgeons and nurses packing. General Lyon was dead, the Federals whipped, the hospital threatened, the army was running for St. Louis. She rose unsteady. When she straightened, her eyes met the one searing white stone in the fireplace that had nearly killed her—polished lime and the bold name: **MORKAN.** She breathed. Michael's hand, Michael Morkan. She let the force of that name there draw her together and settle her heart.

On her bed at home, she threw a cottage cloak, her mother's quilt, a stained pelisse and Spencer already ruined with calomel treatments and root work.

The knock at the door stiffened her. Parting her curtain, she spied Michael Morkan with his son on the doorstep.

She took stock—her calico dress bore the brown of blood and yellow of bile. Her red-brown hair she tied back and a shining, rosy welt mounded at her hairline. Bandages swaddled her left hand and there on her feet were a pair of Leighton's outgrown brogans once gray and hard as iron from lime, now black with blood.

She pulled the door wide to them. "I was just praying the Lord would send me two stone statues incapable of lifting a finger and setting an old widow woman to right."

Michael hesitated in his charcoal trousers, his prim suspenders and spectacles dotted with lime, the crusted black slouch hat on his head. Rumples creased his white shirt, its cuffs rolled and gray. Tall and erect, he looked like an angry scholar who had been muddied by an errant wagon. And this afternoon, for the first time, some strain on his face at the creases of his blue eyes made him look all of seven years her senior. His son, short and muscular, bore his mother's round, pale face and slanted eyes, one lazy so that he never appeared too bright. She read no accusation in them this afternoon, only shock at the sight of her. She cringed a little.

"Cora, what in the world?" Michael asked.

Cora, he said. And with his son right there to hear it.

21

"Come help me pack. The army's on the move."

"To St. Louis," Leighton said, stepping forward.

"As you two should be as well."

Michael took her bandaged hand. There in view of the public street as if war canceled all propriety. She looked him square in the eyes and hid her astonishment. "It has been treated." Her voice fell. "This was a rough morning's nursing."

"Do you really aim to go?"

"I ain't no Rebel belle, Michael Morkan." With too tender of a motion she plucked one of the funny gray cones the lime left on his collar and flicked this away. His jaw was stiff in his thin face, a stubble of red growing there. Leighton averted his gaze, a good lad, who likely understood too well what he was seeing.

She dropped her hand to her hip. "You're staying."

"Tell me how I can pack a quarry to St. Louis."

She backed up. "What a fine day August 10 has turned out to be. Show me whose Saint's day this is and I'll worm them at no charge."

Michael glanced at Leighton then cocked his head at the waiting horses. Once he was gone, Michael touched her forehead, then stroked her hair. "No need to stand here gassing about it. You have a decision to make. Best get on with it."

Gripping his suspender, she gave it a jerk. He was mocking her. Those were often her words to him. "No levity, Michael. Come with me to St. Louis. What if this goes on for years? Leighton will sure be caught up in it. Get him somewhere safe."

But she could see the icy resolve in his blue eyes. He gripped her waist and his lips, dry and hard, brushed her forehead. "Cora. Come to the house. You'll be safe."

She pushed him back with the heels of her hands. "You have not made me welcome there, war or not. And I daresay the priests are busy today with the dying."

His jaw buckled and his face grew grim. "The quarry is closed for now. But Correy will meet me in the week. Let him know what you have decided." He embraced her quickly. "You know where we'll be."

"I'm afraid I do. Are you asking me to stay?"

He hated to be forced free of middle ground. Scowling he said, "Yours to choose."

When he rejoined Leighton and the horses, his son was watching him with Charlotte's eyes. Morkan mounted and wrapped the Walker's reins in his hands and they started. "You've kept to yourself that you knew of my fondness for her," he said. "Does it bother you to see it as well as to know it?"

They urged the horses for the town square and Leighton glanced behind him to see Cora, thin, short, frazzled red-brown hair so curly, the bump on her head, blood on her dress, miner's boots on her feet, watching them go. Today she had been to war. On her face were matching smallpox scars, red, as if a babe with scalding hands had clasped her cheeks and singed them forever. He noticed them again only now, for when she blushed the marks vanished and she appeared rosy as an expectant mother. Leighton realized she had been blushing the entire time he was present. With a bandaged hand she gave him a timid wave goodbye, the first gesture between them since his mother's death. And it had been she who held him close weeping that day while the priest stayed with Morkan. "We have a lot yet to do," Leighton said. "But I worry she won't be safe."

Morkan nodded, clasped his arm. Then Morkan thanked him, though Leighton was unsure of exactly why.

Riding to the center of town, they passed the courthouse, Morkan stone thrust three stories into the sky. Blazing white, the stone was their best work by far and Morkan panged to see it sit unfinished. With such a long project to focus on, Leighton had honed his skill at masonry, his angles and bevels achieving a smoothness as if all that met his chisel and mallet were butter rather than the hard, bitter lime. The joints and lines of the walls met the plumb lines with grace as he mortared. Morkan knew the boy possessed talent well beyond his own. In a slurry of pride and envy he noted townspeople marveling when Leighton ran a shift on the courthouse worksite. Farmers and their wives and daughters in from the hills gawked from their tailgates. Judges, lawyers, and clerks whiled away lunches watching the boy stonemason. Leighton reveled in the attention, and if the audience were large, he would neglect the quarry and stay on site until Morkan fetched him.

The streets were lined with saloons and chandler and tack shops, stout wooden columns supporting the balconies. Some merchants and their families huddled on the balconies despite the heat that shimmered up from the road. People leaned against the columns and massed along the wooden boardwalk. The wagons of the Federal Greene County Home Guards were braked in front of shops, and the Guards formed lines leading from the shops to the back of the wagons. Troops passed goods hand-to-hand from the doors to the wagons where the teamsters stacked the goods. Bolts of cloth, kegs of molasses, corn in boxes, crates of whiskey, sacked flour, shirts, boots, shovels, axes, and from the National Mineral Bank bags of currency, stacked gold bars. The Home Guards worked with the urgency and order of ants moving a nest of eggs. As he and his father neared a general store, Leighton noticed the two flags—State and Federal—usually displayed prominently from the columns of the store, had been taken down.

Where the storefront met the bank's facade, a crowd gathered. Men and women were jostling and cursing. In the midst of a staunch circle of Home Guards, Claus Weitzer, one of the bank's trustees, stood purple faced and hollering. A tall German with a sharp goatee, he always wore a black woolen vest and round-tailed wool coat regardless of weather. "Major receipts! Major receipts! Please!" It was a plea, the words barely intelligible over the crowd's wrangling.

Morkan dismounted and gave Leighton the reins. "If there's trouble," he had to shout above the crowd, "head for that alley." He pointed at the alley between the store and a smithy.

Morkan elbowed his way into the knot of people. A farmer named Owen drew back a fist, but was pushed aside by two other men shoving forward. Morkan reached the front and caught Weitzer's eyes. The German continued shouting; he glanced at a receipt handed from the crowd, shook his head, handed the receipt to a Home Guard. The soldier grabbed the woman who had extended the receipt. As he led her away by the collar of her traveling dress, she screamed and kicked, white flounces pumping.

From his coat, Morkan withdrew his purple and gold embossed currency receipt and handed this to Weitzer. Morkan felt his jaw bind. Cash was no easy thing to come by. Some of his customers still paid in vegetables and fodder, or pennies a week. Most of this $2,500 he accrued working for the Kansas-Pacific surveying ahead of and around the rail lines, buying the choicest land and re-selling it at wonderful profit to speculators in St. Louis and Chicago. After witnessing the disappearance of wildcat banks that followed the lines, it took him years of studying Weitzer's bank before he trusted it with his money. Seeing the swirling crowd, the cavalry scouts coursing by, Morkan expected to feel a soldier's grip at his elbow the minute Weitzer read the receipt.

Still shouting for silence and civility, Weitzer tapped one of the soldiers on the back. Morkan clenched his fists. When the soldier turned, Weitzer flashed two fingers and pointed toward the bank. There, Home Guards were relaying the bank's gold to the wagons.

In the street, cavalry sprinted past, heading north. Some stopped, whistled shrilly and began forcing townspeople onto the wooden boardwalks.

Two Home Guards descended the steps of the bank, each cradling a canvas satchel. Morkan struggled, swimming to remove himself from the crowd. The Guards with the bags followed him to the horses.

Morkan took a satchel from one soldier and clumped it against the boardwalk. He knelt, undid the thongs. The bag was only full enough to hold three hundred, if that. Double eagles, eagles, even silver dollars were mixed with the little gold Indian heads, so Morkan could not tally exactly what they had brought. The other Home Guard plunked his bag down and walked away. Morkan looked up at the remaining Guard.

"The trustee's own money," the Guard said over the fracas.

"Piss on him. What's a trustee for?" Morkan extended his hand. "The receipt."

The Guard gave him the paper. "Lucky a Lutheran would give you a dime, mick."

Morkan buried the satchel beneath a raincoat he kept in his saddlebag. He wadded Leighton's rain gear and crammed the second satchel in Leighton's bag. He wanted to leave for Galway before the army arrived and clogged the street, but he could see they were too late. When he sawed his horse around, people scrambled aside.

From the south, dust rose off a column of riders. Morkan swung his horse into the alley between the general store and a blacksmith's and waved at Leighton to follow him. Once he was in, their horses stood jostling for a moment, then playfully nipped at each other's necks and halters.

"Is it the Rebels?" Leighton asked.

Morkan shrugged and put a finger to his lips. He wished he could draw his pistol and take the rest of his money, but so long as either army was around fresh from battle, he would do his best not to show a gun. A new, six-foot high fence bottled the back of the alley, and he cursed this; a week ago the alley had gone through to Jefferson Avenue. He wanted to tear down the tin water spout from the store, wrench the thing around and chuck it in the street. Leighton had blasted the stone, had risked everything in his rush, in his brashness. Claus Weitzer had forfeited $1,500 to the damned Federals. And now a defeated army was between him and home in Galway. Cavalry churned in the street.

"Do you see this, Leighton?"

Leighton bowed his head.

"More than half of what we saved is gone, and you may as well set that powder out in the damned street." He grabbed Leighton's elbow, nearly jerked him off the horse. "Look at me!"

Leighton did, fiercely, his close set eyes surly and dull. Morkan gave him a last shake and let him go. When he did, Leighton was tempted to urge his horse on, leave Morkan to the Rebels, or whomever Morkan feared.

People on a balcony across the street clustered to face south. A man in red suspenders was pouring amber liquor from a bottle into the cups of everyone gathered at the balcony's rail. Even the women did not refuse. Leighton remembered his mother drinking only on holidays, and then in extreme moderation. The railroads Morkan had worked for often held small holiday parties. Morkan was a surveyor, crew chief, and eventually a designer for the Baltimore and Ohio Railroad's western office and later the Kansas Pacific in St. Louis before buying the quarry at auction in 1856. At these parties, Charlotte drank sherry, and after two glasses she did not become loud or immoderate as Leighton had seen some women do. She became grave, inquisitive, would retire with her son to one of the hostess's side rooms as if Leighton were ill. Then, and only then did she tell Leighton of Ireland, of seeing his father in a dream on All Hallows, a tall man returning to his village wearing a coat embroidered like the veins of a leaf. In the dream, when the tall man extended his hands, they were raw and burned. She sipped the yellow Sherry as if it were medicine. Though they could hear Morkan laughing and chatting with the railroad men, mother and son did not emerge until sent for.

Across the dusty street, a woman in a purple traveling dress and matching hat finished an entire glass in one draw. Though he sat quite close to Morkan, he gripped his elbows and held himself, for the alley was suddenly very wide.

After cavalry and flag bearers, there came teams of sweat-smeared horses dragging artillery pieces. Two wagons passed, their canvasses ripped and pocked with singed holes. A troop of soldiers trudged into the sunlight. Their shirts were open, their light blue pants ripped. Blood and soot smeared their faces, and bandages swaddled their limbs. Some looked to be Leighton's age or younger.

"God Almighty," Morkan whispered.

Uniforms on the troopers changed from blue to simple workshirts, light blue, white, butternut. Some stumbled from the ranks to the doors of the shops, some into the arms of friends and family. They saw Asa Martin gather his wife and two daughters in his arms and herd them along with him. With his rifle stock dragging in the dust, Andrew Lohman, a young bank clerk, shook his head and frowned dismally at an older couple on the balcony. He shouted something to them, and waved both

27

hands north. Mounted officers dashed back and forth shouting orders, forcing men into rank with lunges from the horses.

Leighton could scarcely believe this was the army he'd seen bivouacked in the fields around town, stabbing bayonets on the square and marching. The pale, bloodied faces, the blackened, powder-streaked uniforms. Dark crescents clung under their eyes. Scores of wagons banged behind the troops. In the last cordon of wagons, men were stacked like logs, bloody limbs dangling over the sideboards. Behind these soldiers came a stumbling troop of badly wounded men, some groping for the tailgates only to be kicked at by other wounded and shoved off by orderlies jogging at the wheels. There was no way this army would be coming to the quarry to demand the powder. Leighton's shoulders rose, and for a moment he felt a guilty relief in watching a trooper hobble by using a musket for a crutch.

A trooper in blue bearing a comrade lurched into the alley. Leighton's horse snorted and backed away. The soldier slung his companion against the side of the store where the man slumped as if dead. Only the thigh remained of the man's right leg, and Leighton marveled at the black and crimson stump that jutted from his tattered trousers. The soldier who'd brought him swung a rifle off his shoulder and waved it at both Leighton and his father. The bayonet at the end of the rifle was jagged and black.

"Give him water," he said. Dark circles bulged beneath his eyes and his bottom lip was cracked and bloody.

Morkan edged his horse forward and extended his canteen. The soldier swung the muzzle at him. "And get down. I'm taking that horse."

With a flick of his wrist Morkan flung the canteen which struck the soldier in the face. The soldier winced and cursed, his rifle clattering to the ground. Morkan whipped the Colt from its holster, cocked it and leveled it at the soldier.

The soldier blinked. Leighton drew the pepper-box from his pocket. The soldier knelt slowly, his eyes darting from Leighton to Morkan. He reached for the strap of the canteen, and when he touched it, he snatched the canteen to his chest. He crouched before his friend. Watching the Morkans over his shoulder, he doled water to his companion until the wounded man choked and sat forward. The soldier jerked the canteen away, sealed it. With a last look at the Morkans, he plunged into the street.

Morkan holstered the revolver and nodded at Leighton to do the same.

The street cleared momentarily, and the billows of dust settled. Morkan edged his mount in front of Leighton's and peered south. There were still knots of cavalry dashing about and the crowd was growing, barefoot men in dingy shirts, hill people. Such a crowd might become a mob.

Leighton dismounted and knelt with his canteen to the wounded soldier. Unstopping the cork, he touched the wounded soldier's lips with the bottle. Water surged down the soldier's chin, and he lurched and grabbed Leighton's arm.

"It's water," Leighton said, struggling against him.

The soldier's eyes were yellowed. He released Leighton, and his mouth fell open with a dry smack. Leighton eased water past his lips, and the soldier gulped and choked. Leighton held the canteen back while the soldier recovered. Beneath his shoulder was a red band on which someone had embroidered **EMPORIA** in capital letters. A Kansan right here, a jayhawker, a killer's killer. Leighton shivered. The Kansan wore a thin brown goatee and bushy sideburns. His uniform was fairly clean and still buttoned and whole save for the trouser leg, which erupted in ooze. From this amputation came the strong stench of tar. Leighton swallowed and felt dizzy in the heat.

When he looked up, the soldier was blinking at him.

"Damn secesh," the soldier croaked.

"Get away from him," Morkan said, wheeling his horse toward them. When Leighton turned, he saw his father had the revolver drawn again. "Leave him the canteen."

Just after Leighton remounted, a crowd gathered and milled in front of the alley and blocked the street. Morkan recognized some of the men as southern sympathizers. One of them carried a flag, a circle of white stars on a field of blue bordered by three alternating red and white bars, about as big as a flour sack. The skew of the stars made the flag look as if a child had sown it.

A preacher in a white linen suit stood on a wagon bed before the crowd. "The Lord has risen up a new nation from the ashes of a depraved and dying one!" He raised a quavering hand in the air and gave a fiery talk about the South and Missouri's heroes, a more rousing sort of homily than any Leighton remembered from the St. Louis Cathedral. Leighton knew him as the Baptist minister, Reverend Overbo, and knew his father had quarreled with the protestant over Morkan's immortal soul and the price of white wash.

Morkan took his eyes off the southern approach to the city long enough to squint at Overbo. Fixing his specs lower on the bridge of his nose, he scowled at the preacher for a bit, then shook his head and whispered, "There's your grand South and Rebel Army, Leighton, that great float bladder seething up there."

Leighton frowned. Beyond the heads of the crowd, wagons loaded with chairs, big metal washtubs and dangling skillets and lanterns wobbled past. Mothers clutched children. Dogs hustled to follow. The crowd jeered at some of the wagons. Leighton looked to his father, then remembered Peterson's advice. These were the Union families following the army. He passed the time watching for Peterson.

As soon as wagon traffic decreased, Morkan made to move for home, but Heron, wearing a brown coat and carrying a bulging carpet bag, stopped in front of the alley and stared at the wounded soldier. Heron glanced at Leighton and his father, then back at the wounded soldier. Blood had made a dark clump of mud under the wounded soldier's stump. Heron knelt. He pulled a watch from his pocket and reached for the wounded soldier's wrist. He held the wrist for a moment, shifted it about, then let the unopened watch dangle from its chain while he held the wrist with two hands. Stuffing the watch back in its pocket, he brushed his coat off.

"Well, Michael Morkan, and the pup. You gentlemen responsible for this dead Kansan in any way?" Heron stooped to retrieve his carpet bag, then stared at Leighton and his father with his silver eyes.

Morkan looked Heron up and down and shifted in the saddle. "He was here when we rode up. I take it engineers can leap in and out of uniform in the Federal army?"

"Retreat, retreat," he said merrily, as if a call to chaos were as welcome as the bell to Easter dinner. "You like the Kansan's cap, son?"

Leighton shook his head and backed his horse away.

Over his shoulder Heron glanced at his army hobbling northeast behind him. He wrinkled his brow at Morkan. "Say. What happened with that powder you were loading?"

"What the hell do you mean?" Morkan said, so loudly his chestnut Walker minced. "A little wag from Wisconsin came and commandeered it in your name. It's with that mess." Morkan crooked a thumb at the army passing.

Heron snorted. "Well, I never took you for a fool, Morkan. I'll have your whole quarry one day if you let the world weasel you like that."

Heron set down his bag and stooped to pick up the dead soldier's rifle and the rifle the other Kansan had threatened the Morkans with. "You want this one here?" He held out the rifle with the jagged bayonet. "U.S. issue." He shrugged and propped the rifle against the wall of the blacksmith's shop. He lifted Leighton's canteen from the dead soldier's lap and examined the canteen as it twirled on its strap. "Now, see. Jayhawker didn't get this from any government save the sovereign state of Missourah." Heron held the canteen up for the Morkans' appraisal.

When Leighton sat forward and was about to speak, Heron tossed him the canteen. "You have the right idea, pup."

Leighton caught the canteen. Heron opened his carpet bag and stooped. Leighton fingered the wet nozzle of the canteen, which felt as if it no longer belonged to him. With deft twists of his thumb and fingers, Heron unbuttoned the dead soldier's shirt pockets. He removed the contents of each pocket, popping a tin of snuff and spectacles in the carpet bag, discarding a wad of letters in the dust of the alley.

"My God," Morkan said, nudging his horse forward. "You're an officer."

Without a noticeable pause in thieving, Heron produced a pistol from inside his brown coat and pointed it at Morkan. Leighton lurched in the saddle and retrieved his pepper-box, but the man swung the pistol on him.

Heron's slim eyebrows rose, and he flashed a smile full of blue-white teeth. "It's going to be a long, old war, gentlemen. You best get the hang of things."

Heron moved toward Leighton. Leighton raised the pepper-box, felt the moisture of his finger slipping against the ring trigger.

Heron halted. "Pup, for a minute, I thought you knew what you were doing." He extended his free hand, his fingers wriggling like a spider's legs. "Give that canteen over."

Leighton raised the canteen. Heron crouched, but Leighton saw the man's pupils cut a sideways glance at Morkan. "Easy, pup," Heron said. "Drop it."

Leighton complied, the canteen plunking in the dirt of the alley.

Heron knelt and drew the canteen toward him. He tipped his slouch hat. "You two Morkans have you a fine evening. I'll have this Kansan taken care of." Heron pulled at his belt and stuck his pistol there.

Morkan caught Leighton's eye and jerked his head toward the street. He nudged his horse and soon was pushing his horse's chest against the backs of the crowd.

"Free us up here!" Morkan yelled, holding the reins high.

Leighton raised his reins, his horse's eyes rolling white, its teeth bared. A bouncing group of young men surrounded him. They were leaping and dancing, arms locked at each other's waists. "We made the Hessians run and the Yankee Doodles, too, Missourah, Missourah, Missourah, true!" they sang.

Hands groped at his legs and saddle, the horse reared, and the coins arced skyward. In a melee, the young men dove for the coins. One boy, gray teeth snarling, scrambled up Leighton's leg. Leighton dug his heels in the horse's flank, and she rose high churning her front legs. A pistol fired, and Morkan plunged toward Leighton, Colt held above his head. The boys rushed away. More pistols cracked. Leighton yanked the reins down to steady the horse and buried his face in its mane. Morkan grabbed him by the back of the collar and pointed to an alley three buildings down.

Leighton reached behind him and held the saddle bag shut.

They gained the alley, cut to a back street, and galloped southeast along the dirt road behind the stores. Shutters were clamped on every window of the shops they flew past. The boardwalks and balconies were cleared. His father's heels butted against the haunches of his walker. Leighton urged his horse, and they pounded east, slowing only at the outskirts.

The horse's sides heaved against Leighton's legs. When they finally stopped, Morkan dismounted to secure Leighton's saddle bag.

"I'm sorry," Leighton said. "I mean for everything today."

Morkan glanced down the road behind them but still held the strap to the bag. After a second, he nodded.

"What will happen?" Leighton asked.

His father shook his head. "I have no idea." His eyes were pinched. Dust from the ride gathered in the creases around them, and Leighton saw his father for the first time as old, much older than forty years.

"We'll bury this at home and stay quiet," Morkan said. "We may not even know the quarry when we come back to it."

They rode in silence. The army was gone, another army coming. Twilight dimmed the eastern sky. Drunken boys mashed their back teeth on Morkan gold, laughed and whooped at the true indentations. The alley around the dead Kansan was dark now. Leighton imagined him still sitting, the blue inners of his pockets hanging like strangled tongues. All his weapons gone, and no priest to penny his eyes.

III

FOR SAFETY'S SAKE THE MORNING AFTER THE BATTLE, Morkan insisted all the Negro hands breakfast with him and Leighton at the long table in the dining room. He and Leighton sat at opposite ends. All but Judith sat at the table, and she served every man, bustling and sweating, her heavy body shaking as she hurried. She was nineteen or so, Morkan figured, the youngest of the hands. At the table, the five Negro men ate with their necks rigid, their faces hunched close to their plates. Their eyes traveled slowly between glances at each other and quick, sidelong looks at Morkan. No one but Morkan spoke, and he did so only when offering plates of sausage or ham, eggs, potatoes, greens, drop biscuits. The noise of eating rose unsubdued, chomping and smacking, the click and scrape of forks against crockware. Morkan had purchased Judith and her father Johnson Davis in St. Louis to help Charlotte after Leighton was born. The other four—Chester, Isaac, Bragg and Bundum—he bought along with the two hundred acre farm here in Galway. Morkan knew when a man was responsible for himself and the building of his life, he worked like he meant it. After Charlotte's death, he freed his six slaves, and they proved him correct by staying on as hired hands. Seated there, they made a powerful house of workmen, good with carpentry, adept in the fields. And the quarry had just begun to generate consistent cash. Even poor Judith was so well fed, with no one to boss her, her girth was growing formidable. It was a household to be vain about, but now chaos loomed.

When breakfast was finished, Morkan set the Negro hands to work. Then he led Leighton to the springhouse where they wormed their way around all the vegetable stock, the butter, milk and meat, back to the far wall. There Morkan showed him

34

the loose stone behind which, in a cubby hollowed in the rock, all the Morkan fortune rested in a strong box no bigger than a loaf of bread. This at least he could save for Leighton, and the haste of the Federal retreat and the mayhem in town made him hopeful that Leighton's use of the powder would be forgotten.

They knelt in the loamy dark, the tang of spring water opening their lungs, clearing their chests of the stiffness the lime dust brought. Morkan spat a lump on the floor.

Somewhere, far off, the crackle and roll of a single cannon sounded. In his excitement, Leighton was about to lunge for the door, but Morkan caught him. The boy held still. Morkan wanted to hold the boy's face to his chest, tell him he was still a lovely little troll, as his mother used to call him. He had grown so soon, as if the lime dust fed him. The cannon fired again. "It's just us, Leighton. It's you and me against that." He was quiet. In the back of the springhouse, a cricket sawed two quick notes, then froze. Morkan could sense the boy squirming. "Leighton, I have no idea how all this will go. But I want you to remember your mother and remember your name. Do nothing to sully them. You are a Morkan, one day to be the quarrymaster, Springfield's only quarrymaster. Keep that name dear as an army keeps its flag. And know that all you do affects that name and its bearing."

Leighton stilled and he returned his father's gaze without skepticism or rebellion. His eyes were two ice blue coins, cool and intent, and suddenly in the lantern light Morkan saw the eyes of his lost wife. "Sadly you don't have to serve in an army to fight in a war," Morkan said. "Do you understand?"

The boy clasped his father's arm and held it for a long while.

Outside Morkan took a long look at the house he had dreamed of for his wife, now gone, and Leighton. So much needed finishing: the pine steps were to be replaced by stone. The balconies were still only platforms with rough log railings. So much time he and Leighton had already invested. Evenings of that first year Leighton quarried, the two of them had hewn the stones for the foundation from a shelf of lime close by. Chester, Isaac, Bragg and Bundum watched mystified as he and the boy grooved the new cut ashlars, as each square of stone locked

35

into place, became a floor topped with the first weatherboard the Negroes had seen. When Morkan raised the first of the five white Doric columns of oak, the four new slaves hid. The house, its columns and gray stone now sat solid as a bluff. The thunk of the cannon were blasts against its very foundation.

For the next two days, running through their routines of milking, hoeing, and finish work on the house, the family wavered between trepidation and a kind of vertigo. The Federals were gone, but from what Morkan could gather, no new army occupied the town. No soldiers rode on the farm to demand food and water. The war had flared, then disappeared. The woods and roads were stifling hot and still. Grasshoppers rattled in the meadows, a sound like chain spooling loose between pulleys.

As Leighton and the hands hammered on the back balcony, Morkan paced beneath them or hollered instructions for tasks they had already completed. Judith brought them all water and paused behind Leighton to listen. When Morkan left, she cocked her head and stared at Leighton for a moment. Sun beaded sweat on the Negress's stout neck. On her round face, her full, dark lips moved as if ciphering Morkan's words.

"He say anything that mean anything?" Judith asked in a whisper.

Leighton was shocked, but a laugh escaped him.

She smiled. Though she was some years older than Leighton, the two had been steadfast playmates and confidantes since Leighton was a toddler in St. Louis. Now, she had grown so stout, he had trouble reckoning his wiry companion of old with the cumbersome Negress before him.

"My Judith, My Judith. Where you from?" Leighton asked. It was an old childhood game—she would answer My Leighton with a story from an African nation that did not exist: Moracambia where every tree flowers but only at night, a million on a million blossoms in the darkness.

She brushed sweat from her forehead and squinted at Leighton. "I'm from on this balcony. Once I'm off this, I'll be from the ground." Her tone was sharp, as if some of their games might never be played again.

Late that evening, Morkan and Leighton left to tell the foreman Correy the quarry would remain closed. As they rode, the sky turned pink in the west, tufts of cloud bearing crimson and gray. Leighton lurched in the saddle and felt for the pepperbox. The pistol thumped against his breast when he patted his coat pocket. He reined the gray horse for a moment, realizing he'd already grown so used to the pistol's feel that the alien lump of it was now part of him, unnoticeable. In the oaks, cicadas whirred like the treadles of spinning jennies. Fireflies rose in crescent arcs.

As arranged, they met Correy on the southeast outskirts of Springfield. The Morkans recognized the foreman by the white spots on the paint horse they'd sold him two years ago. Thousands of stars crowded the sky with an almost green hue. But even with these shining, Leighton could not see the drill foreman's face, just a dark shadow against the purple woods. Correy did not greet them. For a moment, only the horses communicated, the paint bumping the neck of Leighton's gray.

"What's doing in town?" Morkan asked.

Correy sat forward in the saddle. "Still as a crypt. There's hardly a sign of an army save for all the wounded in the hotels and churches. Man named Stevens came to my place on a horse, brought you a letter from that judge, McBride."

McBride of the Missouri State Guard, one of General Sterling Price's adjutants, was Morkan's attorney before becoming a judge and later a state senator. Morkan took the letter and folded it into his coat pocket, thanking Correy. Morkan explained that he wanted to wait to open the quarry, that they might meet again Friday night.

"Tell me," Morkan began, fingering his coat pocket, "did the Widow Slade leave with the Yanks?"

Correy hesitated, glanced at Leighton, who looked away. "Not that I know of. I saw her going with Doc Cole Sunday and she didn't take any baggage."

"I'll bet the poor woman is tending the wounded, then," Morkan said.

The foreman's saddle creaked as he shifted. "I don't mean to be rude, but I don't relish the ride back. The town's like a house

37

abandoned with fire in the hearth. You wonder if the bad's not still around."

Morkan offered to put the foreman up for the night. They rode home in silence, and Leighton marveled at the idea of fearing a town whose streets he knew by heart.

Mud and water stains darkened the letter's edges, but Mc-Bride's script was meticulous, even enviable. In fact, as he read the letter in the parlor with Correy and Leighton watching, Morkan recognized the scythe-like swoops topping the judge's *l*'s and *h*'s from some of the quarry's contracts. Apparently, Mc-Bride was once his own scrivener.

The letter opened with a brief reference to Morkan and Mc-Bride's business associations in the past. Then McBride burst into triumphant, even blustery statements about the magnitude and ramifications of the Confederate victory at what the adjutant called the Battle of Oak Hills. McBride referred so often to the Missouri State Guard, Morkan wondered for a moment if that body alone had won the battle entirely, without the help of the Texans the fleeing teamster had mentioned. The letter then praised Morkan's standing amongst the citizens of Springfield and Morkan's "ability and service as an engineer and master of the most productive mining in this corner of the state." McBride requested that Morkan come to meet the hero of Oak Hills, General Sterling Price, Tuesday, at the Douglas Farm on Pond Spring.

When Morkan finished the letter, he read it aloud to his son and Correy.

Correy picked up his coffee mug and drank from it. Leighton sat with his mouth open, eyes wide.

Morkan knew of two misconstruances in the letter. First, he was no more esteemed in Springfield than scrubby-dutch landlords were in St. Louis. Second, his quarry was a culvert compared to those he'd visited along the Mississippi, sites he was sure Senator McBride had seen. "So, what do you think, young man?" he asked Leighton.

Leighton sat forward in his chair. "Those are fine compliments."

Morkan set the letter aside, removed his glasses, and folded them in his right hand. "Compliments only come from a man in a better position than your own."

Leighton's brow furrowed.

From memory, Morkan recited the close of the letter, then paused. "Those words could well come from a man who needs something. Not compliments, then, but solicitations."

"What's he want?" Correy asked.

Morkan shrugged. "An engineer, maybe some blasters."

Correy set his mug down on the table, which separated his chair from Leighton's. "So will you go to him?"

"If he's going to run the town, I'll have to."

Correy stroked the tufts of sandy whiskers that had accumulated since Saturday.

Morkan rose and stepped toward a cabinet where two doors with small mullioned windows displayed decanters of amber and brown liquor. He opened the cabinet and withdrew a sterling tray with three glasses and a crystal decanter of whiskey. He poured whiskey in the glasses and set two glasses next to Correy and Leighton.

Correy's face was pale behind the scruff of whiskers. He was a staunch unionist, and Morkan was sure the foreman detested any association with the secessionists. And Correy was a foreman he could not lose. Leighton sat blinking, a frown on his face, despite the whiskey which usually brightened him. Morkan knew the boy admired the Missouri Guard. He wished he could dismiss Leighton's sentiments as the whims of youth and dismiss the Guard's cause as a surface shine Leighton succumbed to. But just those whims in the last few months had left many a man dead, and many fathers without sons.

Tuesday morning, Leighton and his father rode through Springfield on their way to the Rebel encampment. Buildings and homes on the outskirts were abandoned, their doors swinging open, their windows wide and curtainless. Windows to some of the shops were sloppily boarded. Two and three story buildings separated by muddy alleys clustered near the intersections to streets leading downtown. Springfield was founded as a crossroads merchant town and thrived on that premise. Hotels, saloons, vast dry goods and general stores: Jerzit's Confectioners, Smith and Vernon's, Cowherd's, Pearson's Tack, The National Exchange Bank where two men with rifles stood guard, though iron-barred inserts were fastened to the windows. The two guards struck Morkan as ridiculous, there being no currency in the bank, but then he imagined they were either there expecting pay for still working or had been asked to stay to prevent looting.

On the porch beneath the white columns and purple gables of the White River Hotel, wounded men lay clutching blankets, sheets, even canvas awnings. Two well-dressed women circled among the men and carried metal basins. With cloths, they dabbed at the soldier's foreheads. Many of the sheets were spattered dark red, brown and yellow, and when Leighton slowed the Walker, he heard the wounded groan and whisper. From every mouth there came a hoarse and awful lowing. In this muddle he heard harsh German, and the brogue his father spoke.

A woman in a lacy indigo and white dress stepped to the porch and clutched a column for support. She was decked out as if for a day of shopping. To her lips she held a handkerchief, and her shoulders heaved. She was gagging; a string of spit dangled from her white hanky and rainbowed brightly. She hid her face behind the column, but the noise of her retching made Leighton's throat pump and quiver.

A short woman in a stained calico dress came out on the porch bearing a dripping rag. Her arms were bare to the elbow and browned with offal, her hair tied in a scarf. It was Cora Slade. In her calm brogue, so like Morkan's, she comforted the retching woman.

"Cora Slade," Morkan called out.

Shielding her eyes with a sullied hand, she stepped to the edge of the porch. "You Morkans," she said, sharply. But then a smile curved her lips.

Leighton sensed then, when mirth touched her eyes, a happy spirit in her and that must have been what was attracting his father.

"Get on about your business now. Leave us women to ours, since you men have made such a mess of things."

Morkan tipped his hat and bowed in the saddle.

In the hotel's alley, a flat bed wagon sat hitched to two mules. A tarpaulin covered the bed of the wagon, but bodies and parts were piled higher than the tarp could cover. Blowflies whirled. Leighton gripped the saddle horn. In the alley three dogs sidled about with their tails held high and taut. They were dirty and pot-bellied. The mules rolled their eyes at the dogs now licking at the mud gathering from a drip under the wagon.

By the time they reached the far west side of town, Leighton was riding so close to Morkan that Morkan had to swerve away now and again. The Walkers jostled each other and bumped cheeks. Ever since the alleyway and the dead soldier there, Morkan rued taking his son anywhere with him. Still, he realized there was no shielding him from the war unless they abandoned Springfield.

After a long ride down a hot, dusty stretch of tan road, they came on a group of twenty some men lounged in a stretch of grass that led to a fenced vineyard. The men wore filthy work-shirts, trousers that were torn and patched. All were armed, but their guns ranged from U.S. issue Sharps rifles to squirrel rifles and shotguns. Most of the men sat mashing wild grapes into their mouths and spitting green seeds, watching the Morkans approach. In the midst of them, a standard was planted, the flag light blue with gold embroidered letters: M.S.G., Wingo Co. C. This alone among them was clean. These guardsmen were all ragged, badly armed. They could not be the victors. Surely they were a tag along company the army didn't want. But the men shortly explained that they were a picket for General Price's camp. They each gave confusing directions mapped in a tangle of landmarks, a cow with one horn, that tree with bees in it.

Finding Price's encampment took the remainder of the morning. With the August sun centered in the sky and the humidity congealing the air, the Walkers, especially Leighton's gray, were frothy and shining. They were used to just the short trip to and from the quarry and this outing was well beyond their conditioning. The trail to Price's encampment was rife with mud that sloshed and plopped beneath the horses' hooves. Both Walkers broke stride at the fatigue and now the slop. Mud climbed up the back legs of Morkan's horse from fetlocks to well above the gaskins. Even beneath the canopy of oaks, the humidity pressed Leighton; the smell of manure mixed with clay made his nose curl.

In a wide clearing, men and boys wearing soiled civilian clothes loitered around a central camp, some forty tents of all cuts in a range from whites to dingy ivory. Men bearing guns were drilling in rectangular formations that stretched fifty men long and three deep. A clot of these marched, then paused, one end of the column so near Leighton, he could smell the strong stench of the soldiers' sweat. The men wore filthy workshirts, trousers that were torn and patched, vests as baroque as a bordello's drapery, Sunday jackets, straw hats and farm clogs, daisy chains, galluses and rope belts, chaps and riding boots. Beholding the Missouri Guard drilling was like seeing an old trunk of clothing exploded to riot in the heat and dust of the hollow. A soldier, whose only martial distinction was a white strip of flannel tied at his arm, delivered a foul-mouthed critique of the company's easterly advance across the clearing. The shamed company then relinquished their shotguns and muskets to a second company, all of whom had been standing about chatting and spitting, hands crammed in pockets. This second group raised their standard. With many whoops and brandishes of borrowed guns, they began a meandering advance westward. There across the field another unarmed company waited.

All the Federals Leighton remembered had carried rifles. They had drilled in tight packs, their thrusts and parries as mechanical as the pistons on a steam train. These men looked no better than the sods that loitered outside his father's gate on winter mornings.

Leighton rode next to his father and leaned toward him. "Are these recruits?"

Morkan shrugged, but felt the same surprise his son expressed. These weren't the sort of men Morkan imagined as capable soldiers. He and Leighton steered toward a long tent where the blue flag of Missouri hung alongside the new flag, the circle of stars and three bars. Before this tent, a sentinel in a black slouch hat stiffened as they approached. He lowered his shotgun. Both Morkan and Leighton stopped, and after staring for a long time at the sentinel, Morkan cleared his throat.

The sentinel cradled the shotgun in his arm and, with his thumb, pushed the slouch's brim back from his eyes. "What?" he asked.

Morkan reached slowly for his coat pocket where he had McBride's letter, but then realized caution was unnecessary. The sentinel was engrossed in watching Leighton, and then some movement in the troops' drilling. Morkan flipped the letter out and held it up. "This letter is from General McBride. He requests to see me."

The sentinel stood on tiptoes and examined the letter as if he were peering over a wall at something dangerous. "Well, I'll see." He ducked into the long tent. Under the canvas was a long table, and with the tent flaps rolled up, Leighton could see muddied riding boots and gray britches.

The sentinel was gone only a moment when the tent flap parted and he stuck his head out again. He shouted, "You Avis Cawley?"

Morkan stepped the horse toward the tent. "Michael Morkan."

The man nodded and slipped under the tent. Leighton slumped in the saddle. He expected fanfare; the letter indicated something grand and important for his father. He glanced around him at the scattered tents, the men jogging in staggered lines, stragglers sleeping barefoot beneath the oaks.

A tall officer with dark curls and a broad square jaw emerged from the tent. The officer was clad all in gray with gold embroidery at his lapels and buttons. Leighton recognized him as Morkan's former attorney, James Haggin McBride.

Leighton noticed his father slouch in the saddle, his wrists draped over the saddle horn. Morkan smiled, though Leighton saw nothing around him as humorous.

McBride paused beneath Leighton's horse. The man was startlingly handsome, a face absolutely out of place in the grime and chaos of the camp. His eyes were heavy-lidded and a darker blue than Leighton's. Long, thin lips loaned him an air of haughtiness. His square chin and the knightly jut of his slim nose sealed the visage. Leighton felt he could have leapt from the horse and followed this officer even into the Valley of Death.

McBride reached up and grasped Leighton's hand. "You're a young man, now."

The general stepped toward Morkan and took his hand. "I'm so glad you could come, Michael. There's much to discuss."

McBride led them to the tent where they dismounted and the sentinel took their horses. Around a dining room table sat three uniformed men Morkan did not know. McBride offered a chair, one of walnut that did not match the battered table. There was no chair for Leighton, so he stood inside the tent flap.

Morkan did recognize Sterling Price, a former governor, at the head of the table. McBride seated Morkan next to the General. Price had a long face, a wide, uncreased forehead marked by tangled black eyebrows. He had a long plump nose, and low-hanging double chin. Thin gray sideburns led up to a cap of silver white hair that curled at the sides. So here they were, the burning heart of the war in Missouri. If he bore a revolver, Morkan reflected, he could have ended the hostilities in his state. Plug these blowhards, and the rabble outside would all go home.

McBride cleared his throat. "Major General Price, may I introduce to you Michael O'Naira Morkan and his son, Leighton Shea."

Morkan took Price's small hand, and the General blinked and winced when he shook it.

"An honor," the General said, his voice distinctly tainted with an accent Morkan had heard only from Virginians.

Morkan nodded. The tent became quiet.

Price cleared his throat. "Brigadier General McBride informs me that you own that fine quarry east of Springfield. I have much good news for men such as yourself." Price winced and touched his right side along his ribs. "These have no doubt been turbulent times for businessmen. But I wish to assure you, now that this corner of the state has been returned to the sovereign control of the duly elected government of Missouri, your army will insist that business resume as it had been before the start of this conflict."

"Good to hear it." Though nearly all the townsfolk ceased buying, the Federals bought powdered lime for their sewage ditches, crushed stone for roads to various camps, even small lots of dimension stone for rifle pits at prices he tripled, since the Federals had no other source nearby. Of course, when Morkan thought of the Federal I.O.U.'s the army had issued, receiving them as payment gave him little comfort now.

Price smiled, his gaze roving over each man at the table. His adjutants all nodded, their eyes gleaming for his attention. "Your army will give this state back to her citizens. What is more, it is our firm belief that once the Federal army is driven from St. Louis, our state will be left to abide in peace."

Morkan blinked at this, but did not answer.

The General placed both hands together as if in prayer and touched the tips of his index fingers to his plump lips. He closed his eyes. "I need not remind you that there came a time in this nation's revolution when great sacrifices were asked and greater sacrifices were made." He breathed deeply, and shut his eyes. "When Patrick Henry addressed the troops at Valley Forge he said rightly, 'Tyranny, like hell, is not easily conquered.'" He opened his eyes and his shoulders rose as if he'd conquered a vast divide in recalling this. "Just such a time has arisen again."

Morkan kept silent. When Price stared at the floor and Mc-Bride sat forward, Morkan knew the medicine jingle was over: McBride was about to deliver the cost.

"The army of Missouri needs engineers. Every rail in this state may eventually be destroyed to thwart the Federals, but all will be replaced." McBride smiled slightly. "Your expertise is ideal for everything we must do. Once we secure this state, we will rebuild."

Morkan struggled but refrained from speaking his mind. Price would have to win a dozen battles before rails mattered.

"Gentlemen," he finally said, raising his hand and wishing that gesture could halt them. "I mean no judgment on the right of your cause. But there at the tent flap stands what needs me." He pointed at Leighton. "If I do anything it's for him."

In the silence that followed, Price's adjutants cast glances between the quarry owner and their commander.

After a moment, Price gave McBride a barely perceptible nod. Morkan got the impression that the first ruse was finished. The two generals had requested something Morkan was meant to refuse. The second and most pressing request would then be harder to deny. If this were a railroad negotiation, the ruse and the bum deal to follow would be too evident. But these were politicians, hardly as sophisticated as the railroad aristocrats Morkan had worked for.

Price rubbed his broad chin and nodded at Morkan. "The army of Missouri appreciates your candor." He paused and frowned. "I must point out that the method of our request is indicative of our policies as an army and as the governing body of Missouri. We are not the dutch, nor are we jayhawkers. We do not tromp into fields and take. We are respectful of people and property."

Nods from all the generals. Whatever came next was going for the jugular, Morkan was sure, something beyond money but short of actual service.

Price sat forward again, gripping the table with his small hands. "Mr. Morkan, before the Battle of Oak Hills, I had among my ten thousand men near two thousand who were un-armed. They strode into battle with only the grim hope of gain-ing weaponry from the dead, so strong was their conviction."

Leighton stirred from the flap and stepped next to his fa-ther. His thigh touched the edge of the table.

Morkan glanced at his son, but quickly returned to Price.

McBride spoke instead. "If we are short on the armaments that define an army, imagine how short we are on heavy arma-ments." McBride raised his eyebrows. "Mr. Morkan, your quarry often uses explosives. Our army needs all you can spare."

Morkan's chest tightened. Explosives were something he could spare. Before Sumter, he figured trouble was ahead and or-dered 400 pounds of black powder. He knew some might grow stale before the quarry could use it, but at least he would have powder. The quarry produced kilned lime and crushed stone, both of which required blasting, and dimension stone, which required only drilling and splitting. In the last month the quar-ry uncovered a monstrous shelf of fine tight grained rock that polished white as milk and made pristine flagstone and stone for the courthouse. What frightened him was that once he gave these men the powder, he would be labeled a secessionist. There was no way to stop the town and whoever governed after these men from spreading this rumor. Yet he saw no way he could avoid giving the Rebels the powder. If he refused, they were likely to come to the quarry and take the stores, regardless of all their respect of property talk. He set his jaw, and stared at each man at the table, settling on Price, ending with McBride.

"A quarry without powder is an army without soldiers. To put weapons in your hands, I have to offer you the blood of my own?" He held his hands out palms up.

Adjutants bowed their heads slightly and even Price and McBride glanced away.

Leighton stared at his father. Possibly Morkan was overstating the case. Leighton knew the quarry would move along fine without the powder. They were in dimension stone now, seamed as if the face were bricks in a wall. His father did possess an astounding ability to judge what sort of lime would be found layer by layer. Maybe the next shelf was good for little but crushed stone.

Morkan clasped his hands together and touched the bridge of his nose with his knuckles. The adjutants fidgeted. In the distance, a company cheered above the nearby whir and pop of grasshoppers. A soldier stuck his head in the tent, but one of the adjutants waved him off.

Price tapped an index finger at the edge of the table and stared at Morkan. "We gather the Federals needed you. Did you not regularly contract with them?" He paused. Outside a cloud took the sun briefly and this flicker of light made the talk sinister. "It worries me that when your state needs you most, you are a man of divided loyalties."

The air thickened in the tent, humidity pressing on Morkan's forehead and chest. He wanted to storm out, but these assembled politicians turned warriors were, for the time being, Springfield's government.

Morkan spread his hands on the table. Letting his spectacles ride a touch down his nose, he stared over the wire tops of them at the General. It was a look Leighton knew well from his father's negotiations with contractors and local potentates. The look meant jockeying was passed. Next loomed the wire.

"I came to this country for naught but opportunity." In his voice there rose an edge Leighton had never heard before. Morkan hid nothing of his Irish accent and sat tall and erect and fierce, despite the angry eyes on him. "For every ounce of work and brains I gave to opportunity, I was rewarded tenfold."

Tempers were rising—even the pasty McBride colored so that now he appeared both haughty and indignant. In the withered grass beneath the canvas, a stray breeze slipped like a snake passing.

"I'll die for the right to pursue opportunity," Morkan said. He paused. "But I see none of it in what you're asking of me."

"See here." One of the generals slapped his gloves to the table. McBride rose from his seat and motioned for his colleague to be still.

A dark storm of color shadowed then released Price's face. The old politician managed a smile. At once Leighton thought him the most gracious man he ever encountered considering his father's railing. "Wasn't it Benjamin Franklin who said 'The wise man finds opportunity on both sides of a river'?"

"A fart on Benjamin Franklin," Morkan snapped. He pushed himself back from the table with such force that all but Price rose. Leighton touched the cold weight of the pepper-box in his coat.

"I'll give you what I have tomorrow," Morkan said with an amiable lilt in his voice. The generals lurched, mouths dropping. Morkan wished he could ask them to conceal the act if at all possible. But he knew such a supply would be made quite public by an army that needed the people's confidence and needed recruits. He felt as if he had handed these generals the key to not only his office and quarry, but also his farmhouse and every scrap he owned. "Be at Morkan Quarry at nine a.m."

After taking a breath, McBride smiled. Price scratched his plump cheek, blinking. "Why, that will be fine," the General said. "You will be helping not just the victorious, but the righteous."

Morkan pushed his chair under the table.

"So be it," McBride said, extending his hand.

Morkan shook McBride's hand. "Am I free to work without powder?"

Price stood. "We would have it no other way."

All the adjutants rose. Morkan shook their hands and frowned into each set of eyes.

Leighton and his father rode back. Watching his father's face, Leighton could see small waves of muscle binding and rolling along Morkan's cheek and jaw. Even when they turned away from the road toward Galway and headed north on State Street toward their quarry Leighton did not speak. He worried that his use of the powder Saturday had somehow tipped the Rebels off, or that one of the miners had sent word around. Something in him, though, was pleased that the powder would at least go to the better army.

Along the way, there were no signs of the Rebels or Missouri Guard. The normally bustling streets carried only occasional traffic. Every hotel front and some of the church yards were strewn with blankets covering wounded men. Dr. Rawlins, a local practitioner who often treated miners at the quarry, stumbled by. The doctor's coat was greasy and dark brown with offal, the bags under his eyes so large and black, they looked like separate organs. He did not even glance up from his stuporous walk.

At the quarry, Morkan unlocked the gate while Leighton held the two horses. They were sweating, their tongues lolling round the bit and flopping. Morkan glanced up and down the street and rubbed his temple. Finally he stared at his son as if he'd just realized Leighton was there. "Take the horses in."

Leighton bowed his head. "The powder. Saturday. Is that how they knew?"

Morkan frowned. "No, but if you hadn't used it." He shook his head. His voice quieted. "I could have told them I had none, and they might have bought it." His jaw buckled. "You've got to learn some sleight of hand, because I promise you, son, sleight of hand is all the rest of the world is showing you. Let's move."

Leighton walked the horses to the tie next to the office. His father did not open the office but headed for the mortared stone boom shack that held the powder. Leighton scuffed the cherty ground with the toe of his boot.

"Go hitch the horses to a stone wagon, will you?" Morkan asked.

The idea of hitching the Walkers to a stone wagon galled Leighton. At the livery not a minute's walk from here, there were draft horses to be hired. He led the horses to the quarry's small stable. It was a hollow shock to open. Straw littered the floor, but the stable, empty now for three days, was almost devoid of animal smells. The Walkers hesitated.

First, he led his own Walker into the harness and riggings of the stone wagon. The gray rolled her eyes and shook her head at the broad leather straps. When he had his father's Walker fastened, both horses began lunging and kicking at the wagon, hooves thudding when they connected. The wagon harness was too loose, so Leighton was forced to ride his own Walker in order to steer. Gritting his teeth, he looped the reins in his hands. After much thrashing and whinnying, the Walkers brought the wagon from the stable. They jerked and halted across the lot, stumbling in unnatural gaits, never having pulled a load.

Leighton reined them both at the tie in front of the boom shack. Morkan circled his index finger in the air, and Leighton swung the horses around to point the back end of the wagon at the shack. The horses heaved and minced, fussing at each lurch of the wagon. When he set the brake, they shivered in the harness and jolted if they caught even a glimpse of the riggings.

His father propped the boom shack door open and was setting casks of powder outside the shack. Morkan heaved a cask and set it inside the wagon, nodded at Leighton to do the same. They loaded the wagon with about half the explosives in the shack. Morkan surrounded the casks with hay from the barn, then hid the casks under a layer of loose, wet hay. He leaned on the sideboards, his face flushed and sweating.

"Is this for the Rebels?" Leighton asked.

His father scowled at him. "Taking it back to Galway."

"With the Walkers?"

"Look. We got hours maybe before that army takes the town. I want this home, and I don't want no one, especially no livery stable yammer-kin, knowing we hauled anything."

"You promised Price and McBride."

Morkan rubbed his temples. There was so much to explain, to teach the boy, but the war rumbled like a storm front on the horizon. "How are we going to quarry once they're gone?"

Leighton felt dizzied in the heat. He gripped the sideboard of the wagon and stared at his father. "Gone?"

Morkan mounted his Walker and leaned for the reins of Leighton's horse. "Trot along beside them." He pointed at the ground. He rode the jerking Walkers to the gate, which Leighton opened.

His father turned the horses east, away from the city onto the back route. The chert road twisted for miles and eventually met Galway. The horses had already put in a good thirty miles today—from the farm, through town to Price's camp, back through town to the quarry. The unfamiliar harness and load would double, if not triple their working, and they'd never pulled a wagon in their lives. Late afternoon sun burned Leighton's hands and neck. Hair matted on the back of his Walker's thigh and rump as her muscles buckled and shook.

The town ended, barns and sheds giving way to wide fields. His father rode, clucking at the horses when the riggings bunched and frightened them. The wagon wheels crackled on the gravel, but the axles only hissed holding such a light load. Morkan drove slowly, because of the explosives, but what worried Leighton and slowed them the most was the horses' stumbling in odd gaits. The two were the best Walkers Leighton could remember owning. They were too good, and as worn as they were today, they might very well work themselves dead.

Leighton glared at his father as they moved into a dense knot of forest. The road worsened, deep, dusty holes interspersed with the hatchet-like chert. His father bounced and lurched in the saddle, then finally steadied and turned to him.

"You tired?" he asked. "You want to ride?"

"You're burning these horses."

Morkan shook his head and freed a cinch in the riggings. "You best learn you'll kill a lot of horses in your lifetime."

Leighton still glared.

His father regarded him. "The army you saw today won't last a year. For that year, they're running the town. This way we give them powder quietly. The fewer know how much we done for either side in this the better." He shifted on the horse. Even as he spoke the words, though, he wished someone were there to convince him that he hadn't taken a terrible step, that the war had not already ruined him and his son.

Leighton loosened a bind on the harness where it was already chaffing the neck of his Walker. "What makes you so sure they'll be gone in a year?"

His father shrugged. "Understand, I'm just feeling my way through this. Two things Price said tell me so. First, he asked for explosives. *Asked.* You think Heron would have asked if he needed? Second, two thousand men he had with no weapons." He paused, shifted the reins in his hands. "What did that Federal army take: food, currency, whiskey, just goods; not rifles, I guarantee. You don't steal what you have plenty of."

Leighton recalled the confidence of the generals, and now was amazed at their smiles and proud upright shoulders. Their uniforms were polished and crisp, epaulettes glowing. Yet, the way his father talked, what they said was smoke and cover.

Morkan halted the horses and climbed down. He reached behind the wagon seat where Leighton had stowed the saddle-bags. He brought out a canteen, and they shared the water Judith had drawn that morning. Sunlight shifted through the wavering canopy of oaks and sycamores then masked the Walkers, the straw, and casks in a green gauze.

He noticed his father watching him, arms draped over the sideboards. Morkan extended the canteen to him and nodded at the horses.

Far back in the woods, leaves crackled as something picked its way across the forest floor. Leighton and his father ducked and glanced at each other. Morkan's eyes grew wide. If a Rebel scout were to come across them, how would he explain where the powder was going?

Morkan nodded to the horses. "Keep them quiet," he whispered.

Leighton stroked his gray Walker, pressed his cheek against the sticky warmth of her neck. Out in the forest, the crackling increased. Riders, maybe two or three, easing towards them, slowly. Morkan drew the Colt and stationed himself behind one of the wheels. He crouched and peered over the wagon rail, his eyes pinched behind his specs. Over his taut face, the forest cover threw a web of green shadow and yellow light. The horse could smell the water in Leighton's hand and it began to stamp and complain. With his heart pounding, Leighton snagged the horse's dry black lip between his thumb and fingers and twisted it hard, pulling the filly's head down. The horse froze, but Leighton cringed to torment it so. He whispered in its ear, which was stiff as boot leather.

The crackling halted. Slowly Morkan stood, then turned to Leighton and pointed at the woods with the Colt. "Damned deer," he said.

A trio of does burst from the woods, went leaping towards the river.

Taking the canteen again, Leighton cupped a hand and poured water in it. The horses tongues were dry and rough slopping at the water. Their eyes were glazed wide. Both slumped in the harness. Sweat matted even the hairs of their necks, and tremors coursed their flanks.

Leighton rode and Morkan walked. In the forest, vines thick as branches hung from towering oak and hickory. Cedar and hickory switches encroached and narrowed the trail, scraped against the sideboards. Morkan walked behind until the trail widened and the trees thinned. After a snaking curve, the trail joined cleared farmland along Rockbridge Road. They watered the horses again; his father's brown bled at the bit; his gray huffed and sputtered, each breath sounding watery.

Around them, all was quiet and for the first time that day Leighton felt free of the war. Still he kept his voice low. "Why did you put on such a show resisting . . . you had to know you were giving them the powder in the end?"

"Leighton, giving them powder is going to cost us. Maybe all we have. They had to be made to feel a price to what we were giving. Because after that, for however long they are in charge I aim to stick them for every penny I can drain out of them."

Leighton's Walker stumbled, sleeping in the riggings. She lifted a hoof then set it down tenderly in exhaustion. "Always that isn't there. The ring of coin."

Morkan scowled. "Other than love of you, there is little else, boy."

By dusk they reached the barn and stables at the farm. Leighton's horse was dragging its hooves, its head hung down. He unharnessed his gray first, and she stumbled sideways and slumped against the barn wall. Down the long row of stalls, horses and mules rose from sleep and nickered at the smell of hurt in the air. The brown listlessly pawed the ground as Leighton examined his gray. Morkan waited at the back of the wagon, his head lowered so that his forehead rested against his wrist.

Johnson Davis stepped into the barn, holding a lantern high. Morkan directed him to fetch Isaac and Chester. The Negro hung the lantern and left. The gray slid to its knees, then reclined with its head raised, sides heaving, a terrible sign. Leighton touched its neck, now hot and dry.

"Get the brown undone," his father said.

Leighton complied. Once in its stall, the brown plunked its mouth in the trough of water. It did not drink, only snorted, black water dripping at its muzzle.

Leighton returned to the gray, now completely down, her sides pulsing in small, quick breaths.

His father and the hands stored the powder. The gray's eyes bulged and her mouth gulped like that of a beached carp. His mother had given Leighton the horse as a gift for his twelfth birthday.

After a long time, Morkan's shadow loomed over Leighton. Leighton turned, and the Colt glinted in his father's hand.

His father's face looked pinched and yellow in the lantern light. Sweat held straw and grit across his forehead and cheeks. "Drag her outside," he said, voice dry as gravel.

With Johnson Davis and all the hands helping, they managed to drag the gray out of the barn and down the hill a bit. Out in the air, the horse struggled once to rise, but sank. Twilight deepened. Swift nighthawks dove and cried above them.

"I'm sorry about this, Leighton," his father said. Morkan paused, and in his silence the whirring calibrations of a host of insects commenced in the oaks around them. "I'm afraid we're bound to do a lot worse this year." Morkan raised the pistol and moved toward the horse.

Leighton intercepted him and wrenched the pistol from his hand. He stepped to the horse, felt his father catch his sleeve. But when Leighton bent for the horse's mane, his father released him. Leighton jerked the head of his gray up, burrowed the muzzle of the revolver down in her ear. The animal rolled her eyes. Leighton fired, and felt the hot of the horse's blood on his hand in her mane, a sound like the cracking of a melon, then absolute silence. The horse lurched to her knees, began to stand, then collapsed in a heap. Leighton turned to hand the pistol to his father. Morkan stood in the purple dark, palms dug in his eyes, fingers wrenching at the curls above his forehead.

IV

WHEN THEY RODE INTO SPRINGFIELD THE NEXT MORNING, Leighton and his father took the nags normally left to John- son Davis and Chester. In the streets a sleepy hen scuttled from them, lost from some abandoned coop. Out of the pre-dawn haze one of the dead wagons crawled, the mule pulling it tromp- ing, head down. As it passed, Leighton leaned on the reins and forced the horse to stare at the wagon. The wagon was topped with amputated arms and legs draped over the dead, bodies stiff, lying back to back, mostly naked, black hair and blue-pink skin. Leighton did not blink as he worked the reins and murmured to calm the horse.

In the cedars along the quarry cliffs, katydids hissed and rattled. Within half an hour a party of cavalry pounded into the lot. They bore an Arkansas flag whipping on a standard. Morkan craned his neck, surveyed the streets, found them still empty. The flags, the cavalry, were the kind of pomp he dreaded. Their uniforms were gray worsted. Sharp embroidery struck every but- ton-hole, and fine streaks of crimson cloth sashed their chests. One cavalryman, shorter and more decorated than the others, dismounted. He removed his hat and strode to the Morkans.

The officer shook Morkan's hand vigorously.

"Mr. Michael Nara Morkan." The man's nasal accent rang like glass breaking. "I bring you the hearty hale and warmest esteem of General Benjamin McCulloch, commander of the Confederate armies west of the Mississippi."

"A pleasure," Morkan said.

The man beamed, his teeth a tangle surrounded in well-kept brown whiskers. "General McCulloch wishes to congratulate you on your generous donation of armaments to the cause of your state, and her sister states of Texas, Arkansas, and Louisiana."

Morkan wondered for a moment if this posse were not here to claim the explosives for these sister states. Just to see McBride's face, he entertained the idea of giving everything to the Arkies.

The little officer snapped his heels together and gave Morkan a salute so sharp it made him jump. The officer remounted. His posse split at the gates and galloped down opposite roads. The two color guards and the officer, though, remained near the gate.

Later McBride arrived accompanied by two riders. The general spoke with the Arkansawyers. When he talked, he sat stiffly in the saddle, thrust his chin forward, and maintained three yards between him and the Arkansas officer. Snapping his horse away from the gate, McBride trotted quickly to the Morkans.

He greeted the Morkans with a wave and sudden smile. McBride wore the same gray uniform as before. The riders with him both wore white shirts and butternut vests. Though their trappings weren't consistent, they were at least clean, and both were grinning.

McBride reined his horse, a gray sorrel. "We've taken Springfield, Michael. The flag of Missouri again flies equal with the flags of her sister states."

Morkan nodded. "You have a wagon on the way?"

McBride's cheeks reddened an instant. "We counted on the loan of one of yours."

Morkan whistled and shook his head. "Yankees bought every one I had."

Leighton looked up at this. There was still one wagon in the quarry stable.

"Bought?" McBride asked.

Morkan nodded. He leaned closer to McBride. "Scoundrels said they were taking pains to preserve the trust of the people."

"Lord, it's the first I've heard," McBride said. "Folks are saying the Federals *took* all they had."

Sweat itched at Leighton's back and he crossed his arms over his chest. He'd seen his father fudge gravel weights against particular contractors. But this was a lie told boldly, presented with his father's best business face. And it was a terrible risk—if the wagon were discovered wouldn't the Rebels suspect Morkan of hiding even more? He remembered the deer crackling in the forest, how the world was full of sleight of hand.

Morkan waved off McBride's comment and led them toward the boom shack. "Might be folks that want your sympathy are telling you that. I for one know I can level with you: I have your friendship, trust, and protection."

McBride swelled his chest a little, but his frown betrayed his lack of confidence. Still, he nodded. "Now, why didn't the Federals buy your powder?"

Morkan undid the padlock on the shack door. "That was a thunderous army you beat. I figure they got powder and whatever they need strung from here to Washington."

Both riders lost their grins at this. McBride squinted and shifted his weight in the saddle. "Do you mean they never asked?"

Morkan winked at him. "Thank God, no. They'd have cheated me as bad as they did on my wagons."

McBride relaxed. He scanned the floor of the boom shack, then leaned forward in his saddle peering deep into the shack.

"Enough to last us a summer," Morkan said. "Hope it holds you."

Frowning, McBride gave orders to one of the riders to fetch a wagon. The rider raised his eyebrows at McBride, then turned to leave.

"Since the Arkies know, you might ask them for a wagon," Morkan suggested.

McBride flushed. He cleared his throat. "We needn't bother them."

Morkan stared at McBride, eyes narrowing. After a pause, he explained how to judge qualities of powder. He opened a cask and burned a pinch on a white sheet of paper. McBride and the trooper lurched when the powder flared. "See there." Morkan turned the paper side to side. "Not a hole, not a scorch. If you get either, you're getting water in your powder. And pinch it."

After a moment's hesitation McBride and the cavalryman took a portion of powder between their thumbs and index fingers. Morkan held the pinch to McBride's ear. His eyebrows danced at McBride.

McBride's chin stiffened, and the cavalryman drew in close.

Keeping the powder to McBride's ear, Morkan rubbed his index finger and thumb together. "Would I blow the head off Brigadier General James Haggin McBride, my own and only protector?"

McBride squinted, then mimicked him, swirling the powder between his index finger and thumb. "I don't hear a thing."

Morkan swept his hands together. "If it crackles at all, the mix is off, and if you already bought it, you'll have some interesting times using it."

As Morkan continued to explain uses and behaviors of powder, McBride nodded often. To Leighton, it seemed Morkan was trying to sell the powder, but finally realized Morkan's advice was meant to feign openness and cooperation.

Morkan offered the soldier and general drinks in the office. McBride declined, but his companion, a trooper whose nose was mottled with sunburn, accepted. In the office, Leighton drank with them. The brandy was a thin, sharp syrup. As the trooper continued drinking, he grew more and more boastful of the size and prowess of the army of Missouri. Leighton's questions spurred the trooper into long descriptions of skies black with lead and smoke. He spoke in oaths so filthy that McBride shushed him. The soldier was silent for almost thirty minutes, then resumed without swearing. After some hours, the trooper added denigration toward the sister armies, especially the Arkansawyers, who held back at Oak Hills and did nothing in his esteem. The Federals he rated as top notch, save for the dutch. McBride began pacing.

Morkan's cheeks grew rosy; his tongue went numb. Now and again, he stretched and went to the window, watched the Arkansawyers heaving rocks into the lagoon at the bottom of the pit. They eventually rode away. The powder he was giving McBride cost him at least three weeks of uninterrupted mining.

Finally a wagon arrived drawn by two mules. It was a Conestoga, but only the single iron band of a rigging flying strips of canvas marked it as such. The trooper rode in front, his horse drooping.

The Morkans offered their help loading, but McBride refused.

From the window, Leighton watched McBride direct the wagon to the boom shack. Morkan joined his son. They both had to lean close at the small window, but Leighton avoided brushing his father.

The soldiers loaded bales of packing straw in the bottom of the wagon. Next they set casks of powder in the wagon and dribbled loose straw on these.

"Why's he putting straw beneath it?" Leighton asked.

Morkan shrugged. "He's a lawyer. What's he know of powder?"

McBride and his Guardsmen all mounted and started for the gate. The Arkansas color guard returned joined by most of the gray-uniformed riders from that morning. At the gate, McBride paused, and with his chest thrust forward, he gestured at the wagon of powder kegs raised and falsely multiplied by the bales beneath them.

"I'll be damned if he didn't salt the ore," said Morkan. The hay was there to make the wagon look full, and he guessed McBride and Price had boasted about the extent of local sympathy to the Arkansawyers.

The humidity in the office was stifling. Leighton felt sweat slime his armpits. His father was right. McBride made the wagon appear absolutely full. "As if you haven't salted *your* story." He couldn't resist saying it.

"Damn it, Leighton." His father turned to him. "Don't you understand what we've done? This may ruin us. I had to do it, but it may be our ruin." He shook. "I'm telling you, the worst thing to happen to this state is men like McBride. He may be a damn fine leader, but look where he's leading. Politicians turned generals will be the ruin of this place." Spit escaped his father's mouth, and he brushed the back of his hand to his lips. His face glared red. "You listen to four God damn hours of spume from a hooligan someone stole a gun for, and you think they're all heroes. Don't listen to what people say. Watch what they do.

Open up your eyes, boy! Not even Arkies believe in McBride nor want him."

"Lucky they believe you," Leighton muttered.

His father grabbed his shirt and suspenders. His jaw was a mashed fist quivering.

"God damn your mother's mouth on you," he growled. He released him.

They did not speak as they rode home, but drank brandy together from a flask they passed between them, Morkan muttering, his young son trembling, holding himself very still, then trembling again.

Before leaving Springfield that evening, they told Correy to gather what miners remained and meet at the quarry by ten a.m. When Leighton and his father arrived at the farm house, there was still light enough to work, but only Judith stood on the front porch snapping a table cloth free of crumbs.

"Where's my hands?" Morkan asked. He wavered in the saddle.

"Laying low, Mister Michael. They going to get stole for slaves."

Morkan snorted.

Judith folded the cloth. "Two riding soldiers from New Orleans somewhere come for water and directions. Chester say they slave nappers."

When Johnson Davis arrived Morkan told him to have the men working by first light tomorrow and to keep them working till dark. Abashed, Johnson took the horses to stable.

While serving a dinner of ham and boiled cabbage, Judith assured Morkan that she had the hands' papers, they'd be going nowhere. Morkan drank through dinner, then retired to the parlor.

Leighton sat on the front porch. Against the night sky, now dark blue with a silver tint at its western edge, gray twists of smoke hung in the humid air, cooking fires from Springfield's outskirts. For his town Leighton hoped there would come a time when he would cut the bright stone of grand buildings like those on the river front in St. Louis. That hope now seemed childish. The clomp of his father stumbling upstairs somehow con-

firmed this. Each defeated thud told Leighton the town might
be lost to them. The new army, like the old, would gradually take
anything useful that remained. Leighton shaded the front window with his hand, touched his nose to the glass, and squinted
through to the house's interior. Morkan's legs were long, his dark
brown pant legs dusted red. Sweat made a dark tongue down his
back, and his suspenders drooped. Bobbing, gripping the railing,
his father walked as if he grew heavier with each step.

Leighton looked at his own squat body, the small roll of
fat that rounded above his britches, his bulky chest and arms.
Only his hands were his father's: wide palms so gray and dried
that most of his lines were lost in callused serrations as rugged
as wounds in the bark of a hackberry. Kilned lime did this; his
mother told him so not a year after he started work. "They'll be
this way like your father's, all your life now." He remembered her
holding out her chin as if disapproving.

He heard the clanging of pots and skillets in the kitchen,
and he found Judith there working at the slops trough by lamplight, her hands dripping with water from washing. In one bucket she had boiled water, and in another she had cold rinse water.
He stepped behind her. She tensed for an instant, then relaxed.
She nudged him away with her hip. Warm water reeking of lye
stuck his shirt to his waist. Raised together like babes in the
same cradle, they attached to one another like magnets in a toy
set when left alone. But Judith had been a slave, forced to care
for Leighton. The black girl with her white play pretty. The only
time Charlotte bragged on Judith was in remembrance of that
pickaninny holding the hand of a toddler Leighton. Judith the
loyal, animal sister, then by slavery forced to leap over adoles-
cence into the role of big sister and finally servant.

"Father's gone to bed." Leighton said. "You can go on to
sleep."

Judith returned to scrubbing the skillet. "Mister Michael's
near with the dead. I seen him sleeping. He still clothed."

Her frown, the bluish bulge of her lips bore an intensity
beyond any concentration needed for the skillet. The heat of
the kitchen and the boiled water made her face shine, and her
cheeks stood out like glass baubles. Her eyes, he noticed, were

not on the skillet or the bucket of hot water, but focused on the edge of the trough. Was it Morkan she cared about? Surely not. She worried as any servant might, knowing the master is in deep, knowing she could be walking a dusty trail with no destination tomorrow.

As stealthily as he could, he plucked the gourd from the bucket of cold rinse water. Her hand swirled in the skillet, which was spotless by now, her eyes still lost in thought. He lifted a gourdful of water, was about to shock her by pouring the frigid water over her hands. He stopped. The skin of her palms and fingers was puckered and gray. He cleared his throat, and she glanced at him. When she raised her hand, he ran the water into the skillet. She nodded.

"You not going early tomorrow, I imagine." She set the skillet aside.

"It's been a terrible day," Leighton said, then stopped himself.

Her eyes widened. "What all went on?"

He shook his head. "You wouldn't understand. It would take too much explaining."

She faced him and crossed her arms over her chest. Beneath her arms, her dress bore a dark butterfly of dishwater where the calico had rubbed against the wet sides of the trough. "A day is a day, Leighton. And terrible's terrible." She paused. "Try me."

He turned his back to the trough and leaned against it. The stones of the floor held a gloss like the skin of pokeberries. "Things are pretty precarious. We can't know who's in charge, and I'm not sure when we're doing something right, or something that will get us killed." He whispered. "And between father and me. . . ." He stopped. "At the quarry, before all this, I knew I was helping, I understood him and everything we did. But now."

Judith's brow buckled. She cocked her head slightly.

"I'm not sure I want to help him. I'm not sure what he stands for." He sighed despite himself. "He seems to think everything is a story, something the generals or the soldiers or the Texans are trying to put over on us."

Judith lowered her gaze. Her chin puckered, her eyes winced a little. She pitied him, he thought, and coming from a Negro hand, her pity stung him.

"Damn it," he said, and stepped away from the trough. He could feel his elbows shaking against his sleeves.

She caught his arm and held it. Her hair was coarse. Her neck shimmered as if dusted with metal filings. She hesitated, then cupped the back of his head in her hand. On the back of his neck, her water-logged fingers felt like the scales of a snake. She drew his head forward to rest on her shoulder, held him there for a moment awkwardly. Then, she gripped his neck with such zeal that her fingers pained him. Her touch, their sudden closeness, reminded him of a time when they were both young in St. Louis, hiding in a closet from Charlotte after some mutual mischief, a lamp, a vase they'd broken at play. He pushed her away, but then patted her heavy arm. Looking at her face, he noticed for the first time a dark little mole, darker than all the rest of her. Around her neck were creases like the soft wrinkles crossing a woman's palm. In the summer, she kept her hair short as a hound's. Something about her stolid presence rebuilt him.

"I can't make any of this better," she said.

He nodded. "Go on to bed."

She fixed her bonnet on her head, and Leighton stepped out with her into the back lot. There the rear ell of the house made a quiet corner. Just around the house he knew the orange stars of the Rebel campfires glowed like the eyes of wolves.

"You are a good soul, Judith."

She snorted. "Don't forget that."

Her broad form receded into the night.

V

"Forts," Morkan said to Leighton. They drove the oxen, mules, and horses through town, a pack of children laughing and dancing behind them. All the little boys carried twig rifles and fired at one another between the heads and buttocks of the stock. Girls squealed when the big draft horses shat. "That's what we'll quarry for." He swallowed. The skin on the back of his neck was yellow. "One of these damned armies will build them. We'll make stone while we still have a quarry." Weaving in the saddle, he glanced at Leighton with a long face, made dark by the rings beneath his eyes. "While I'm still here to work it."

The dozen miners in the quarry office fell silent when Leighton and his father entered. Morkan sat behind the desk, and Leighton leaned against the wall. His father's eyes were very bloodshot, and on one side of his face capillaries erupted in zigzags like a map of a hundred tiny red rivers.

Some of the miners stared at their boss and his jaundiced face. They grumbled when he explained that after a certain time, if currency weren't made available, he would have to pay them in promissory notes.

"Look, now," Morkan said, holding up a hand at their murmurings, "we can either fold up our show, or work and make do. And of course, any are welcome to move on if my promises aren't good enough for you."

Leighton froze at this, but the men, even the most fractious among them, nodded.

After whiskeys all around, hand drills were clanging at the stone again. Dust flew. Leighton scanned the ridge and waited for more of the sharpened chucks. Once the pins rang and the Mistress grunted scooting the first blocks onto the ox sled, Leighton shivered with exhilaration. The oxen lowed and griped. The sled moved. From the smithy came the wagon-load of sharpened chucks, cold and slick with brine. The drillers and laborers gathered and hammers fell, chucks ringing high notes that deepened as they drove. The sounds, the rise and fall of the hammers, dust puffing around the oxen's hooves as they entered the cutting yard—the scene soothed him, as if life resumed a polished, level sense.

That next week, just as they were opening the gates, McBride arrived with four riders. His horse pranced a bit, and McBride threw his chest forward. A.C. Greevins removed his slouch hat and held it tightly to his chest in homage.

Morkan let McBride into his office, nodded to Leighton to fetch a chair.

McBride waved this off. "Michael O'Naira Morkan," he said, stiffening his shoulders. "In appreciation for your sympathy and service to the Missouri State Guard, I would like to present you first with five hundred dollars." He handed Morkan a stack of broad, gray bills.

Morkan squinted at them. Then he handed them to Leighton. The bills were printed in smudged gray ink. A bear grappled with a snake on each side of the number ten. SOVEREIGN STATE OF MISSOURI BOND OF CURRENCY PAYABLE IN FULL UPON THE VICTORY OF MISSOURI OVER HER ENEMIES was written below this.

"And second," McBride said, his voice rising, "to contract your mine and services for the Sovereign Governor of the State of Missouri." The adjutant handed Morkan a scroll bound with navy blue ribbon.

Morkan unrolled this, fixed his spectacles above his nose. He read with raised eyebrows, a smile, and finally a chuckle.

McBride stood blinking, jaw set, beads of sweat quivering at his hairline.

"I mean no offense," Morkan said, "but this is the fanciest order for tombstones I ever seen." He handed the scroll to Leighton.

The contract opened with an immense *W*, frilled with curlicues and circles, to start the word *Whereas*. The contract proceeded, in elegant calligraphy, to detail an order for four hundred pieces, 2' x 4' x 8", of dimension stone to be delivered to Holt Monument on Greer's Mill Road. All these frills for tomb-stones. It would be a more lucrative contract if the Morkans could also engrave the stones as they preferred to do.

Morkan stepped around the desk and shook McBride's hand. "I'm sorry, it struck me so. Our state's got a stenographer could make all the South jealous."

McBride's shoulders rose and he smiled. "My wife, in fact." He walked toward the door with Morkan. "She's awfully glad to be away from the hotels and the wounded." The smile left McBride's face. "She spent nearly a week at them. With theirs and ours."

Leighton remembered the woman retching from the porch of the White River Hotel. He ran his thumb over the ink of the calligraphy and imagined that woman, her dress scrubbed and returned to brilliant indigo, leaning back from this finished contract. The tight edges to the letters now struck him not as the pomp of Missouri's government on the run, but as the same leveling he yearned for and received each morning from the first flagstone scraping free of the shelf. She balanced herself, gained calm in every scrape of the pen, in each stipple of ink as the letters uncurled. He wanted to see that woman, hunched over parchment in a sunbathed parlor. He wanted to touch her arms as she wrote.

In the sweltering afternoon sun, the owner and barkeep of the Quarry Rand, strained to the office carrying two immense pails sloshing with beer. The miners, gathered on break in the slim shade of the office, cheered and called his name: "Shulty, Shulty!" The free beer, thin but bright tasting, was his newly brewed Grand Opening Under the Flag of Free Missouri Ale. Morkan stepped from the office, removed and folded his spec-tacles. Each of the men heaved the pails to their faces, drank in great sloshes that dribbled gray streaks down their limed chins and shirts.

That evening, Morkan divided daily wage in the Quarry Rand giving men a choice between his own promissory notes and the new Missouri Bills. Leighton knew his father still had a stock of V and X bills at home, nearly one hundred dollars, plus the near $1,000 dollars Weitzer had relinquished. He wondered at the fairness of this sleight of hand. The men all seemed to accept that the Morkans were out of the currency they'd been paying. More than half took the promissory notes. The rest proudly announced their wishes to be paid in the currency of the sovereign state of Missouri. Leighton took his pay in half of each. The men laughed and applauded. A Morkan paying a Morkan was an act they held ridiculously dear, and tonight's strange pay and Leighton's answer made them jeer him and swat him on the back.

Paid and blushing, Leighton led a group of them up to the bar. The Quarry Rand had not suffered any pilfering. The brass railing with its hundred thousand scratches still ran the length of the bar. The walls were cinder blocks from the quarry, and many of the pillars and cross braces in the low ceiling were rough ties as if the Quarry Rand were some sort of mine shaft.

A few customers Leighton recognized dotted the bar. But mostly there were men in uniforms, the sheaths of long cavalry swords scraping the dirt beneath their chairs. Almost every customer, Leighton noticed, wore a pistol. Before the war, Shulty had always made men disarm at the door.

Behind the bar on a tall slate, Shulty chalked prices. The list bore a second look tonight. The names of liquors were scrunched to allow for two sets of prices, one if paid in currency, another if paid in Missouri bills. Beneath these was a tangled conversion table that translated promissory notes from various local businesses, and bonds from Louisiana, Arkansas, and Texas into Missouri currency. The rate of exchange from Arkansas to Missouri would sober even the thirstiest Arkansawyer. Louisiana looked worth having.

"By damn, young Morkan," Greevins said. "Your promissory's worth more than any state west of the Mississippi. Buy us a round you Rebel tycoon!"

Laughing, Leighton spent most of his pay to set up two pitchers of stout and two bottles of whiskey. Greevins was right. His father's promissory notes were as good as Indian head dollars.

Much later many of the miners were gone home, and the barroom was dominated by soldiers and officers. Often, disputes over prices erupted at the bar, but officers, white sashes tied at their arms, jumped to stop anything that approached fisticuffs. Every time a new soldier arrived, officers of the Missouri Guard wasted no time in forcing a toast to General Sterling Price. If the drink came free, many toasted with the Guardsmen as often as possible.

An officer suited in an odd light blue ran a finger across Leighton's dusty suspender. He stared at the gob of gray on his fingertip. "What have you got all over you?" The man's accent sounded French, but not the French of St. Louis. This was a more dusky swirl.

"Lime," Leighton said.

The man smiled and stroked his beard. "How charming!" he said. "You will get me, then, a brandy."

The soldier frowned when he discovered Leighton was not a barman, but beamed when Leighton explained he was an actual miner. The man brought Leighton to a table of six men, Louisiana Pelican Rifles. They treated him to drinks, traded bills and promissory notes with him, examining each and squinting at Shulty's slate.

Amid the fervor of liquor and the heat, barkeeps and patrons alike accepted the confidence of myriad bank notes, flowing penmanship by senators from Shreveport, and the Mayor Protempore of Uther, Texas. Each bill Leighton saw traveling put on a polished face. Even the columns of some building or other in Little Rock, Arkansas made a dazzling printer's daydream of lines and shadow. His father sat hunched over a mug of stout, nodding and patting Correy's back. Maybe Morkan's own ability to pull off a sale, to hold a sly face kept him from being enthralled by this. Leighton remembered his father posturing with McBride. Twelve assorted colors of paper money spread on the bar before him, a homemade hand of cards whose value Shulty changed by the half hour.

Someone patted him on the sleeve, the Louisiana officer with the French accent. The man smiled broadly. "Show me another of these notes you have." He pointed at Shulty's board.

Leighton had no more Morkan promissories. He turned and pointed at his father. "You'll need to see that red-headed fellow. He's the quarry owner."

The Louisiana officer and Morkan shook hands for quite some time, Morkan warming up the broken French he learned in St. Louis. After a long talk, the officer returned and sat next to Leighton. He promised to buy him brandy all night for letting him meet such a fine man of business.

"With men like him," the Louisiana officer said, nodding with a haughty frown, "we win the war by winter, eh?"

Leighton nodded, but stuck to his stout and left the brandy untouched.

Within weeks, even the Morkan's promissories wavered at the Quarry Rand, and the scrip from other states became unacceptable.

Morkan lay with Cora in the fall twilight on the iron bed Sam Slade welded for the Slades when they married. With metals Sam Slade was a savant—all the wrought iron fence around the quarry he had fashioned, and this bed frame here would have been prized in a prince's chateau, its headboard bristling with acorns and oak leaves, its bedposts topped with beads of iron to create sprigs of wild muscadine. In the smithy he was a master; in life he was a drunken billy goat.

Morkan reclined on his back and Cora lay on her stomach, an arm on his chest, a hand stroking his hair. Sunset turned the room purple and cream in these sweet minutes before parting.

"I'm not getting any younger, Michael," she murmured.

He tucked a lock of her hair behind her ear. "Cora, we have a problem."

She planted her elbows in the mattress and raised her head. "If you'd have gone to Mass just once since Charlotte passed there'd be no problem. Father Brian's door is . . . ."

"It has nothing to do with Father Brian," he said.

Her face reddened and the smallpox scars on her cheeks dissipated in a glow of rose. On her chest and neck, her freckled skin was the color red berries leave in milk. He kneaded her shoulder.

"Cora, those Rebel generals cornered me. I had to give up our black powder."

Just as quickly as her color flared it subsided, and she paled. She touched his arm with her fingertips as if his skin were as delicate as a petal. "One of the Church busybodies said Michael Morkan's gone Secesh. I thought she was just farting in her bonnet."

He laughed quickly. "Would that she were."

She rubbed her brow, her forehead creasing. The welt from August was now just another dapple. "What will happen when the Yanks come back?"

"Nothing good."

They were quiet a long time. Outside a drummer boy practicing a snare rattled a tattoo as though to rally muster in the street.

Making a fist she socked him in the ribs. "Marry me anyway, damn you."

He caught her wrist and they wrestled a moment like children until his elbow bumped her breast.

"Mercy," she crowed, but grabbed both his ears in her fierce nails and pinned him flat. Glee was on her face. Her eyes, though, were watering.

"Why must you always be in the middle without a side?" she growled, her teeth clenched. "Not a Rebel. Not a Yank. Not married but in love."

He struggled halfheartedly at her wrists.

"You are in love, aren't you?" She tightened her hold. "Say so, or I'll stretch these ears long as an ass's."

He stopped fighting her and lay still. Her kinked hair was wild, her smile floating beneath tears. What a surprise she always was to him, swarthy of mouth, but never unkind, taut-muscled as a wolf from battling patients. What a comfort they had become to each other. What ruin he brought on them now.

"I do love you, Cora Slade," he said, his voice rough.

She released him warily. "You were almost too late with that." Bunching the sheet she dabbed her eyes.

"I must go," he said, sitting up on the bed.

71

As he dressed she raked his back with her nails. "I'm worried, Michael."

He stopped, but could not turn to her. "I am, too."

When he said nothing more, she fetched a housecoat and rose. He could hear her open a dresser drawer.

"I have something for you, and now's the right time."

She handed him a square tintype folded and nearly broken in two.

"I have only that one picture of me."

It was a novelty pose. In it she was done up as Marie Antoinette offering a silly piece of cake and with feathers and rhinestones in her hair. On the back, fat Sam Slade had piled into knickers and stockings, a tremendous powdered wig on his head. He sucked a prop pipe long as his arm.

"Poor old Sam Slade," Morkan whispered touching his dead blacksmith's image. "How'd you ever get him to sit still in those pajamas?"

"Bourbon, I'm sure," she quipped. Then she pinched her nose and wrinkled her brow to nudge him about the pun.

He flipped the portrait and there she was, having a grand time, probably just done laughing, for Sam Slade could garner a laugh at a baby's wake.

"I get a bad feeling we are going to be apart," she said.

His shoulders slumped. "This is no small matter. That powder's out there killing people. I rather wish the Yanks had took it. But a wish never fits in your money clip."

"Will you keep me with you?" she asked very softly, a joke at the picture, but when she pressed it to his chest her eyes glistened again.

"Can you wait for me?" he asked. "I will make this right, Cora Slade."

"Darling, I been waiting. Twill do me no harm."

He patted her hand as if driving it tight against his heart.

The Missouri State Guard marched north after Oak Hills. The Confederate army that fought alongside the guard returned to Arkansas. Price left a small body of troops, enough that Shulty's bar was never without near ten a night. In Shulty's, in the dry goods store, the blacksmith's, the livery, Price was discussed as if he were a miracle of weather, the inventor of the steam train, as if he'd risen from the White River itself to rule Missouri, a Merovingian sans beard, add sideburns. Around State Guardsmen and secessionist residents, Morkan bore himself happily, and it seemed that his contribution to Missouri's cause was right and wise.

"I must tell you, Mr. Henry, it was quite a sacrifice," Morkan said, sticking his tin cup beneath the spiggot of a keg of beer. Alabaster Henry, who had a son maimed fighting for Price, was buying mortar to rebuild a wall Yankees had torn down. The beer was barter. "But no man more than you understands that we have to give to preserve Missouri's sovereignty." Morkan raised the cup to him.

Alabaster Henry ran his wrist beneath his nose and began to blubber, and then proceeded to drink a great deal of the beer he brought for barter. The Henrys, one of the founding families, never had a word but contempt for the grubby micks at the lime pits. Morkan shut the office door, and let Alabaster drink himself into the staggers.

Every other Thursday, Leighton hitched four Morgans to each of the three stone wagons. Along with Greevins and another driller, he delivered the dimension stone to the Holt Monument company. There, Jacob Holt and his twin sons washed and polished the stones to a glaring white and carved either a name or one of three denominations on each: USA, CSA, or U if the cadaver's allegiance could not be determined. Recalling the rabble he had seen among the Missouri Guardsmen, the ragged Iowans, and the way the Kansan had been stripped, Leighton was not surprised these completely unidentifiable dead existed. Old Holt paid four Missouri dollars per tombstone.

While chiseling a name, one of the Holt twins stopped and stared at Leighton. The twins, Simon Peter and P.D., were impossible to tell apart, black-haired kids with pale skin and big pink ears. Leighton, like everyone save Old Holt, just called either twin Pete, and both would turn in unison and stutter when they answered.

73

"Did. . . ." Pete's jaw squirmed as if he were chewing honey-comb. "Didn't Joe Holcombe work at your mine in the winter?"

Leighton nodded.

Pete turned the stone up. The lime, scraping against the other stones on Pete's bench, sounded like an ice block scooted loose from its dark cave.

JOSEPH HOLCOMBE
M.S.G.

Holcombe was a heavy-set man, good with animals. He broke a sweat just breathing.

"If I knew," Pete paused, his eyes bulging, "I'd carve some-thing like **BELOVED BROTHER**." He touched his eyebrow with the back of his dusty hand. "But I don't know if he has kin around here any more."

Leighton shrugged. Pete's chisel bit the lime again, ticking like a clock as he lettered the next stone.

On the second delivery, Leighton halted on Greer's Mill Road. To his left rose mound after mound of new-spaded dirt. Single stones rested at the heads of the mounds closest to the road. Leighton climbed down from the wagon; Greevins fol-lowed him. All the gravestones faced south, and Greevins was quick to point out the victorious message inherent in this. A few of the stones Leighton saw did have names in small letters: Marcus Beasley, Lynn Brown. One said just Heinrich. Many bore only the markings CSA or USA. At first, the single U's troubled Leighton the most, though there were only a couple of them. At least the letters CSA and USA indicated something of the life they marked. Unknown, U. Name and cause polished to a white nothing in the lime.

Oaks, scorched after summer, let fine shafts of dusty light down from the eastern sky. There were forty-eight stones set here, the exact number of stones in the last delivery. Beyond these forty-eight, many more mounds rose up in groups dot-ting the ground beneath the oaks. Twenty-four stones lay flat in each stone wagon behind him. He touched the dirt of the mound, cold and dry. The Missouri scrip the stones represented was worth less and less each day. Possibly, the man beneath this mound had died for the government behind that scrip, for the senators turned generals. Leighton brushed his hand on his britches. He hoped the man beneath him had died for something permanent, and not just something his father would call a sleight of hand. On his knee, red clay mixed with white lime.

VI

ON A FRIDAY MORNING, LEIGHTON CUT STONE ON THE gang saw with Greevins. The mine's last two cutters, secessionists almost as adamant as Greevins, had not arrived to work. Rumors of an enormous Federal army descending from St. Louis were rampant. People spoke as if there were some thirty thousand, all led by a man they called the Pathfinder, a general named John C. Frémont. Leighton paid attention not to the name, but more to the notion that his father might soon be imprisoned. What Morkan predicted—the disappearance of the Rebel army— might come to pass. Watching his father train a new driller, he marveled that Morkan could calmly hold the chuck as the new man arced the sledge down, could point out that his swing need not lengthen, or needed a more steady rhythm even while an army was descending on Springfield, an army that might carry him away.

Stacked in fives with lathes between, only eighteen stones remained to fill the order from Holt. Even with the loss of laborers, the quarry finished the headstones in just over two months. It was now October 25th, and Leighton was impressed with their work. When he and Greevins finished, Leighton and three drillers loaded a stone wagon, and he left for the monument company.

On the way to Holt's lived a lass Leighton made a point to watch for, a buxom, stout, pensive girl he might never get an introduction to, he being Irish Catholic, and she Scots Irish and likely Presbyterian. At her front windows, instead of glass and curtains, at the busted sills the heads of six horses stabled inside the house nodded to Leighton's Morgans. The object of his affection, she was long gone. He used to dream how one day she would fall for him; her hero, he would save her from a runaway ice wagon. One more story he held dear overthrown.

In the streets, a pack of Rebel home guards caught up with him. The guards hurried past, hands cramming hats against their heads, guns and equipment clanging and snapping at their sides. Leighton waved to two of them, old acquaintances, who did not wave back. The two boys, younger than Leighton, ran in front of the company, shotguns wagging in the air. Three elderly men with white hair and whiskers skipped and whooped as they ran waving their pistols behind the young ones. Two very fat men— one Leighton recognized as the butcher's assistant—made the rear guard. They huffed and wiped their sleeves at their red foreheads. All wore clean white work shirts. He had never seen Home Guards run before. They preferred to stand in the shade and chat about Oak Hills. The sight tickled him, and he reined the two Morgans to watch the cavalcade pass.

From Greer's Mill Road, Leighton could see much of downtown, the white stone courthouse, wooden balconies and cupolas grimed with dust. Maintenance had grown slack since the Rebels arrived. Garbage, normally teamstered from downtown to a dump on the southern outskirts, rotted in the ditches. Men and women on errands rushed, clutching cloth strips to their mouths. By noon, he knew the stench would be rank, a thick, cheese-like odor with daily additions that never allowed a person to become acclimated. The Morgans ears flicked up and roved. He popped the reins against the Morgans' backs to urge them.

Two deer and a rabbit burst from the woods on the north side of the road. Neither deer paused on meeting the stone wagon. Both veered, eyes wide.

The town seemed diminished: some businesses still had boarded windows; he no longer saw women strut proudly under parasols. The people all rushed, glancing and shivering at the sight and smell of their refuse, and the awful stink that came from churches and hotels choked with the wounded. He wondered for a moment if the town could stand another invasion, another massive exodus of people and property. His father had lost half his miners, and now two more today, the cutter and a driller. Each stone now equaled one of Shulty's draw beers, amber, flat, and thin. Originally the four dollars of scrip bought two pitchers and a whiskey. What would any of the scrip mean if the Federals returned?

Leighton stopped the wagon. The woods north of Greer's Mill Road were thick and quiet save for the shufflings of squirrels and jays bantering. Then, above the whisper of oaks shedding leaves, he heard the popping of gunfire. The gunfire grew closer, and now the shouts of men stilled the forest completely. Hooves pounded, and far ahead of him, horses and riders burst from the trees, ducked between the buildings, the riders firing over their shoulders into the woods behind them. The Morgans' necks jerked and bobbed.

A boy thrashed free of a thicket, dropped his rifle and scrambled into the crook of an elm tree. He drew a knife and leaned from the crook as if waiting to snare the next rider to pass. He glanced at Leighton once, then resumed his vigil north.

The Morgans' heads shot upright and their ears tensed. The throng of oak and elm erupted: the neck, then the entire heaving body of an immense white horse lunged toward the boy's elm. Riding on the horse's back was a giant of a soldier, wool so blue it looked black, trimmed gold and white, a fire red ostrich feather shimmering from his black hat. He was bedecked and dandy enough to be a ringmaster. In his gloved hand, a saber flashed.

With a lurch in his gallop, the Federal's head jerked toward the boy waiting in ambuscade. Charging the elm, the Federal leaned forward in the saddle and held the saber low along his horse's flank. The boy flailed the knife, but the horseman ducked, then brought the saber in an arc that nearly clipped his mount's ear. The saber whapped the boy's skull and quivered. The Rebel boy dropped the knife and fell, but his foot caught in a crook of the elm. He tumbled and hung, yowling. The horseman wheeled his mount, switched his saber hand and charged. Leighton could see only horse and rider, but once they had passed, the boy's body hung kicking, blood plopping and gushing from the stump of its neck. It was a moment before Leighton could recognize the back of the boy's head crimsoned at the base of the tree.

Leighton patted his coat pocket. His heart pounded. It had been almost a month since he'd worn his pepper-box. The rider circled again, leveled his eyes on Leighton. With a lunge, his horse rushed forward. Leighton could see the man's jaw wagging as he leered. The blood-raked horse was almost on him, the Morgans heaving and rearing.

In the midst of a full, perfect beard, cherry red lips twisted in a white-toothed snarl, the eyes above the mouth glittering and hateful. Leighton hunched and covered his head.

The rider swerved, his mount's eyes rolling with the force of his motion. He pranced his horse around Leighton and the wagon, saber snapped at attention, tip against the horseman's right shoulder. The warrior drew close, and the Morgans slammed at the riggings. Leighton watched him over his shoulder, tried to keep himself absolutely still. He could smell the man's horse. Leaning forward, the horseman scanned Leighton's cargo. Soon an awful grin spread on the cherry lips. He nodded at Leighton and whirled his sword above his head, made the air whine and whoop. He spun his horse, and popped its rump, galloped toward town.

Leighton gave his entire body a shake, then buried his face in his hands for a moment, grinding his rough palms into his cheeks.

Gunfire drifted through the town behind him. The woods grew quiet. Finally a jay screeched and others joined. Leighton could not take his eyes off the hair matted on the back of the boy's head. He reached to set the brake, then groped frantically for the wooden handle only to find the brake already set. He stepped off the wagon and approached the body, avoided looking in the boy's face. He stepped behind the elm and heaved at the boy's bare foot until it cracked loose. The body thumped to the ground. On the opposite side of the tree, the boy's eyes met him, both locked in a wide upward glance, as if something in the top branches of the tree was frightfully interesting. The mouth was open, tongue bulging, skin covered in a goo of dark crimson, flecked with bark and dirt. Leighton gripped the tree for a moment, his mouth dry. He swallowed hard. The boy looked no older than Leighton, with the same blue eyes, thick black beard. It could have been Leighton.

After breathing to steady himself, he pulled out a handkerchief, then crouched to wipe the face. Lean, almost collapsed cheeks. A warm slurry of gore slopped over his thumb and fingers. Leighton jerked his hands back. He stood and, without thinking, tucked the sopping handkerchief in his coat pocket. Somewhere in the wagon was the stone the boy would be laid under. Leighton wished this were a face like none he had ever seen. He wished the boy would become only a marker, just the dim shadows of letters, so much easier to witness. Four Missouri dollars the boy fought for and lost upholding.

When he neared the quarry, dust rose at the trees near the quarry's eastern edge. He snapped the reins. Red dust rising clouded the road on which his father spent the Walkers. Leighton worried the invading Federals were here and were confiscating stock from the quarry. He pounded through the gates and found his father on the brown Walker holding the reins to Chester's horse. Morkan's face was red and sweating, though the air was still sharp and cool. The doors to the stable behind him were flung wide, and rows of hay and mud led across the quarry grounds toward the eastern road.

What to tell his father about the tombstones? He pulled next to Morkan and felt his chest tense, his throat go tight. Here he had hauled them back with nothing to show for it.

"Thank God," Morkan said, pulling a floppy straw hat on his head. He had changed into gray-streaked dungarees and a blue work shirt. "We heard the gunfire. All the others are dismissed save Correy and Greevins. They're helping us drive the stock home." He leaned forward, reached out to touch Leighton's coat sleeve. "Were you caught in that?"

Leighton nodded. He tied the horse to the back of the stone wagon.

"You hurt?" Morkan asked.

Leighton shook his head and climbed back onto the wagon seat.

"Sure?" His father thumbed the brim of his hat upward, his eyes searching Leighton's face. After a moment, he nudged the Walker, and they started forward. "How big an army?"

"Just cavalry. Big damn men, though. Dressed beautiful, gloves and hats." Leighton felt himself swallow.

"Lot of wounded?"

"Some," Leighton said. Morkan's jaw was tense his eyes batting in agitation. If the cavalryman had come across Morkan, would he have killed him?

Morkan did not press Leighton about the battle. The pallor of his son's face, the set of his jaw told him the boy had seen something horrible. Morkan cursed himself. Again the boy had been exposed to war and Morkan was helpless to prevent it. When the sound of gunfire had reached the office, it took little to surmise his son was in the midst of it. Morkan had been frantic ever since, and, though he'd rushed to mobilize the stock and gather his papers, Leighton's fate had been foremost in his mind. Each crack of a rifle made him fumble with the files and glance toward the quarry gates.

Leighton noticed his father's frown, the deep creases in his forehead. He was sure the next question would concern the contract. "I didn't make it to Holt."

His father dismounted and glanced at the back of the wagon. "Get down here, boy."

Hesitating, Leighton set the brake and slipped off the wagon seat. He steadied himself for a tongue-lashing.

Instead his father embraced him. With a lime-crusted hand, he tousled the back of the boy's hair. A great volley of gunfire spattered near the center of town and Morkan clutched the boy close. With his heart still pounding like hooves on a hard road, Leighton held tight to his father. "Brace up, now," Morkan said. He hooked two fingers in his mouth and gave a hunter's whistle for assistance. "These are for someone else, then, and thank God." He winked at the tombstones and ordered the miners to unload them.

Mounted again, he shook his head. "This war is getting to be a damn bit much." They reached the Walker road and ap-

81

proached the forest. "Federals take whatever you make, and the sowbellied Rebels take what you make it with."

On the leaves of the roadside trees—oranges and reds, stunning yellows—all had turned magnificently, and noticing this Morkan was completely disheartened. He mentally inventoried the quarry, opened a saddle bag and felt down in it to make sure he bore every contract or paper that might be incriminating, any dealings with the Missouri Guard.

Correy and Greevins stayed to dinner, and Morkan arranged a work stoppage. Correy and Greevins then argued over the quality of the army that had arrived. They were all seated in the front parlor drinking port.

Morkan worried that once the Federal army encamped, he would soon be jailed, but he kept this to himself. He asked again what Leighton had seen, and the boy said only that he imagined the riders were advance scouts.

"Oh, I believe outriders is a better term," Correy said. "In addition, the procession of the gunfire indicates a high order. This was the vanguard of the Pathfinder." Though Correy was young, not six years older then Leighton, he relished a fight with old man Greevins.

Greevins lit into him about the battle. They wrangled for many minutes, while Morkan stared at his son, and Leighton eyed the floor. The miller's face gained color as he spoke. He glanced at Leighton with wide eyes and sweeping gestures, as if he were telling Leighton the story of the battle also. When Greevins' tale ground to a halt, Leighton marveled that if he said nothing, if he never told his father of the beheaded boy, a whole part of his life would remain just a story to Morkan, something a miller had rattled.

Leighton fidgeted in his chair until he could no longer resist speaking. "Did either of you see this army?"

They shook their heads. There was silence. Windows poured evening's rose, a lingering dimness, long before lamps are called for. Leighton saw his father hide a grin behind his hand. Greevins and Correy sat and blinked, their postures stiff with surprise.

When he first spoke, Leighton had wanted to make fools of the two miners. He was witness to Death. He had seen history. But what could he tell them he had seen: a horseman, more trained and polished than any he had even read of, glean the head off a barefoot kid holding a buck knife? A kid no older than Leighton? Otherwise the same gunfire and shouts the miners had heard, Home Guards too fat for their uniforms. Just a dead boy, a victor with cherry red lips. A story not worth wasting afternoon light. This wasn't the war that appeared in the Memphis paper, battles involving hundreds, thousands of men, lasting all day, killing thousands on thousands. But here two men, whose work he respected, sat in the front parlor of his father's house and argued over the quality of uniformed and un-uniformed rabble they had not even seen. There was nothing more real and indisputable than the blood stain that had seeped into the lime hardened serrations of his hand, that was still present in the creases of his palm. Before, the war still had something grand to it, and Missouri's army won battle after glorious battle—Dry Fork, Oak Hills, Lexington. But now when he closed his eyes, he could hear the sword hissing through the air, could see the shocking gray bone and crimson of the Rebel boy's neck.

"I'm very sorry I interrupted," he said.

Both men waved this off.

He excused himself and walked the stairs to his room. The silence behind him made him cringe.

He crossed his bedroom and lit a lamp. He sat on the oversized bed and opened the drawer to the nightstand. Through the windows came a cold breeze, smelling of the first rotting leaves. In the drawer, he pushed aside Sir Walter Scott's *The Lady of the Lake* and a yellowed sheaf of his father's designs. Leighton regularly snitched these from the waste bin. They depicted bridge trusses, abutments, pilings. Beneath these, grit from iron pyrite covered everything. His father had brought him home a leather sack of fool's gold from which glitter was always escaping. Past the nub of a blessed candle, his fingers finally reached the suede pouch that held the pepper-box. He removed the pepper-box from its case. Its weight was a great comfort in his hand and that saddened him. He opened his coat, was pushing the pistol into his pocket when his knuckles scraped the stiff wad of the hand-kerchief. He removed the handkerchief, set the brown smeared ball of it on his knee.

On his night stand, Judith had set a bowl of well water, still cool, and a wash rag. Leighton wrung the rag and set it aside. He sank the blooded handkerchief in the bowl. The handkerchief bloomed, and soon minute strands of brown began swirling like red clay dust in the eddies of an alleyway. He kneaded the cloth. More brown rose in the bobbing water.

VII

No soldiers came. Mornings the Morkans ate cold biscuits and jerky. Morkan sometimes paused and watched the lane toward town for a long time. One night when Leighton retired early to his room, his bed was unmade, the sheets were dirty. Dungarees, handkerchiefs, a pair of brogans, three work shirts were strewn on his bed and across the floor. There was no wash rag, no bowl of water.

Morkan knocked, then entered holding a small lamp. He blinked and glanced around the room.

"Where's Judith gone?" Leighton asked.

His father's jaw tightened, hollows appearing at his cheeks in the candlelight. "I didn't want her here if Yankees came. Johnson got wind of them from Negroes in town. I had her stay away from the house down to Johnson's cabin. I don't trust the situation." He raised his eyebrows, shook his head. His voice fell. "And there's a part of me that doesn't want the farm hands to see the man of the house dragged off in shackles."

Vanity, Leighton thought, vanity he had never imagined from his father and yet it came combined with a touch of concern for Judith. "They'll know you been captured, one way or the other," Leighton said.

Morkan looked down for an instant. "It's seeing that matters. You must understand, Leighton, who we are in this town, what impression it takes for us to maintain what we do." He leaned on the doorframe, his brow furrowing. "We are a quiet force. No one need think of us, or pay us any mind, and it is better that they don't. Our work is dusty, loud, disruptive. But if we ourselves are quiet, if the only thing they see in us is a job finished, stones cut and laid, then we go on and on. Can you see why I hesitated with the powder? Because of it, I am stamped like wax with a traitor's signet. There is nothing I can do to remove that stamp from the mind of the town. And there is sure no need for it to remain on this house. There's no need for the hands to see that."

"They'll come, won't they?" he asked. "They'll take you."

After a moment, Morkan nodded.

"They may hang you, or shoot you."

Morkan cleared his throat. "No. I was coerced. They'll have mercy. I may be jailed, but. . . ."

When he stopped, Leighton was sure his father had no idea what might really happen if he were captured.

"Let's go south. We can go to Texas or Louisiana."

"No, Leighton."

"Why?"

Morkan bit his lip. "Leighton. You are innocent, and I am too old to start again. After I'm gone, if it be from war, or the hack, a fall, whatever, the quarry is yours." He held a finger up. "Not another family in this city has a thing like that to stay for." He waited. "This war will pass. It appears to me much of it has already been won. You may be fortunate enough to take a loyalty oath that absolves you. Absolves you of me. The Federals are granting some pardons."

"Maybe I don't want to be absolved of you."

Morkan was silent, but his eyes were creased with pain. The wick on his lamp sputtered like a moth flapping against a window. He turned it up, and the light rose around him. His chin stiffened as he looked at Leighton for a long while. "Rest yourself," he finally said.

Leighton remained sitting on the bed. The slim line of light vanished from the crack beneath the door.

When there was still no sign of the Federal army, Leighton and Morkan cut stone steps to replace the wooden ones leading into the mud room in the rear ell. Working with picks and shovels, they cleared the overburden from a long shelf of limestone on the northwestern side of the hill on which the house sat. Despite the cooling air, the overburden—great hunks of chert and sheets of moss that crackled and tore like fabric—proved a chore.

Beyond the gray pastures and stands of trees turned silver by dusk, the campfires of thousands of Federal troops made simplistic constellations, as if a man-made sky could know no better shapes. The orange dots dominated Springfield's southside and spread well into town. Morkan talked as if the war might be over, at least in Missouri. He talked of the British army in Ireland, of silent Masses held in groves and hovels. The fact that the Federals had not come to capture and punish him made him believe the issue, the war, was ended. The British army, if the war were still on, wouldn't have waited a day.

They lit a brief fire each morning, cooked quickly, then extinguished the stove. After feeding and milking, gathering eggs, they stood shivering at the windows, bundled and silent. Nights, they slept together on a rug in the root cellar, grimly clinging to each other for warmth. The fields and hollows, the gaping bays of their dark I-house were struck with calm. None of the Negro house servants came for work. "Like horses before a storm," Morkan said. "Bet they're far back in the barn."

At the windows again the next morning, Morkan spoke, but kept his eyes turned from Leighton. "If Federals come, you disown me." He dabbed his black scarf against his lips. "You tell them you hate your father, and you hate his God damn rebellion." He shifted the blanket higher on his back. "Leighton, beyond you I don't have anything in this world." His father appeared thin and his chin stuck out, red with stubble and shaking.

"Da," Leighton said. "Enough, now." But he gripped his hand, brittle and cold.

Late on the fourth of November, four cloaked apparitions darted from tree trunk to tree trunk, pausing at a gulley, where they fell to the ground. The Morkans were reading by lamplight, Leighton's chair facing the window. Engrossed in his favorite medicine show pamphlet adventure, Leighton watched until only two apparitions rose, rushed forward while the others crouched and aimed rifles. Horsemen emerged from the road and slithered through the trees.

Morkan grabbed his arm. "Go you to Johnson Davis's. Hide."

"What are they about?"

Morkan shoved him so hard Leighton stumbled. "Git."

87

Morkan heard the back door shut, and he ducked and peered from the window, hoped the house was not surrounded, cursed himself for sending the boy running. Running might get him shot.

There was a revolver near. He could shoot himself, or claim the Rebels . . . no. The wound would be too fresh, and the Rebels had been gone a long time. Twenty horsemen, weaving. More than a dozen foot soldiers, hooded pale faces. He decided to sit in plain view of the door in one of the high-backed velvet chairs. He took the medicine story, the pamphlet Leighton had been so absorbed in:

DOCTOR HARINGTON'S 40-KNOT SYCAMORE ELIXIR
presents
THE WIZARD IN THE WILDERNESS!

From Blackfly bites to Fantods,
Harington's *Smooth* Green Syrup of Colombian Morphine
and Arkansas Sycamore Extract will lead the Woods Man
through *ALL* Manner of Difficulty!!!

In a drawing, a happy yeoman and his mountain bride tilted 40-knot to their lips and looked all the wiser by the next frame. "They will see relief and happiness," said the advert, and then a great adventure began. Morkan heard iron-toed boots ringing on his stairs.

The door crackled as it burst open and four soldiers lunged into the room, leveled astonishingly long rifles on him. He peered at them over the pamphlet. The soldiers who piled in behind these four removed their flat-topped caps and gawked at the chandelier hanging above them.

Morkan raised both hands.

The soldiers under the chandelier snapped to attention. An enormous man in shining jackboots clomped across the entry-way. "You Michael Morkan?" The officer drew a revolver from his holster, bounced the butt and body of it in his hand twice.

Morkan watched the carbine glint. His arms ached holding them up. "I am," Morkan said.

The officer reared back, cracked him across the jaw with the revolver, and Morkan tumbled to the floor.

Johnson Davis opened his cabin door to Leighton's barreling figure, slipped the door shut, gripped him by the collar and ran him to a crook where he'd made a stand-up closet. There he shoved aside frozen summer clothes, and lifted a weatherboard panel set down to keep clothes off the dirt. Beneath was a hollow.

"Drop down in there. Lay flat as you can."

Leighton was breathing hard. He forced himself down in the cubby the panel hid, and Johnson pushed it shut over his head.

Above him, Johnson scooted the clothes back over the panel and sounds grew muffled. As he flattened himself, his forehead and fingertips brushed cinder blocks and mud. Walled off under the cabin with stolen masonry was a cool space in the earth about as big as a coffin. A clammy, tattered blanket padded the cubby's base. Immediately Leighton knew what the place could be—a hiding spot along the underground railroad. At once he felt concealed and comforted, dark in the earth he was always digging in, safe in the arms of the Negroes who kept the household living. Son-of-a-bitch, Johnson Davis, all this time abolition's captain in the shadows.

There came a pounding, and Leighton felt feet rush to it. Men shouted "nigger," and cabinets slammed. Boots tromped on the dirt floor. Something was pounded against the walls in Judith's room. Above him, the paneling Johnson Davis had shut thumped, and light struck its edges. Sweat balled at his brow, and he tucked his chin to his chest until his whiskers burned at his collarbone.

There was more shouting and pounding, a plea, Judith pleading, then silence. A long time passed. Then finally a scrabbling and the paneling rose, black fingers, Johnson's hand. All was quiet.

Leighton clutched Johnson's long john shirt. The Negro pried his hands off him.

"Where's my pa?"

"They took him." Johnson stood, adjusted his shirt.

89

"We got to go get him. They'll let him go. I'll tell them what happened."

Johnson frowned.

Leighton bowed his head. He felt his chest shudder, his eyes stinging.

Johnson pushed Leighton. "You better get on up." When Leighton looked up, Johnson was scowling. "House is yours, now." He nodded toward it.

"Hell of a risk hiding me," Leighton said. He touched the paneling. "And a risk showing me this." He held Johnson's arm. "How do I thank you?"

Scowling, Johnson brushed his hand away. "Survive. That's how."

November wind sent leaves skittering against the log wall. The crystal chandelier was dragged through the yard and left in a wad, trailing behind it a trench filled with flashing pieces as if an icy comet ran aground.

Mud spattered the steps of the entryway. Shards of glass from the chandelier sparkled in crevices between stones. Johnson waited on the porch. One of the velvet-covered chairs from the study rested on its back. A clock was missing from the wall. Above them was a void where chains dangled, where the chandelier once hung. Over on an end table, Morkan's black scarf hung like a snake skin.

Leighton picked up the scarf, then bent to fetch the medicine flyer he had been reading before the Federals came. The flyer was crumpled as if someone had squeezed it tightly in his fist.

Johnson stood before him. The Negro hadn't shaved in some time, and a couple of his whiskers were gray. "You got no time for this." Johnson squeezed his wrists. He nodded his chin toward the door. "What you reckon those soldiers going to say when they get back to camp? What you reckon they think?"

Leighton stared at him.

"I bet they be pretty impressed with this house, huh? Plenty for them here and no one to keep a hold of it."

"What do you care?" Leighton asked.

Johnson bent very close to his face. Leighton squirmed in his grip, until Johnson gave him a hard shake. "What you think I'm going to do if you lose everything? I ain't no slave. I ain't celebratin' 'mancipation.'"

Leighton pushed back from him. Then he nodded. "No," he said. "No, I bet you're not." After a moment, Leighton draped Morkan's scarf over his shoulders. "The stock," Leighton said. He looked toward the barn. His hands were shaking, and he tucked them in the pockets of his coat. In all the days at the quarry when he was in charge of a crew, he only carried out his father's orders. Now he was in complete charge of the family's holdings, and he felt as if he were treading in the midst of a swift wide river.

"Get me a fire started." Leighton looked at Johnson, who nodded. "Get some coffee going. Have some yourself. There's a lot to do." His voice was quiet, almost not his own as he gave the orders.

In the kitchen, Johnson brought in strips of cedar bark, laid them in the bottom of the stove. Leighton gripped the edge of the kitchen window and watched the side yard, his mind a jumble. If they came back, would the troops want the stock? At least the officers would. Morkan was on his way where? Rolla? St. Louis? The soldiers themselves would want food first. Then valuables. Judith? If Johnson knew so much, why didn't he just leave? What did he expect? The family was gone, dead, he was it, the last of the Morkans. He dried his eyes with the back of his hand.

Johnson fed a slim log into the growing fire.

"Feed the horses and oxen," Leighton said. He watched the edge of the woods for a moment, sure he had seen something move against the bare tree line. On the hillside around the house, all the leaves of fall spread like a brown rug beneath the black pillars of trees. He dismissed the movement as a trick of the wind. "During the day, spread the stock out all across the farm, in that gully by the cattle pond, down in the dry stream bed, out of the wind. Scatter them. At night we'll bring them in. And guard the barn, I guess."

Johnson nodded. Leighton took the Belgian shotgun, Morkan's favorite, from its hiding place under the mudroom bench. With his knife he scored the line at which he would saw it short. "I want to take all my mother's clothes, all dad's clothes and hang them in your cabin. There may be other things, but will you start there?"

"I'd hurry," Johnson said.

Leighton went to the pantry for a burlap sack. He could hear Johnson outside bringing wood to the back door. Leighton ascended the stairs to the master bedroom. There in a drawer in the sprawling walnut bureau was all his mother's jewelry.

The bureau was dusty, and the high oval mirror fastened to it was streaked. Leighton could remember when the bureau shone, though he had never seen inside of its drawers. He sat down, then squirmed for a moment on the short velvet-cushioned stool. Only in St. Louis when he was young had he seen his mother sit here before the bureau and arrange a pin or a clasp on her dresses. In Springfield, Charlotte rarely wore jewelry, entertained infrequently, and then only merchants and some local officials, always dressed in out-of-date, dusty suits, their wives outfitted as if they might be asked to help in the kitchen. He tried for a moment to recall her white face, her ink-black hair, whether she smiled or squinted and frowned when she sat here. It saddened him that he could not envision her, but remembered instead the meticulous and mechanical pinnings of her accessories. The blue void of evening glowed about his reflection in the mirror. Her arms were plump and pale as moonlight and how soft when they clasped him.

The middle drawer opened with an ease that made Leighton jump. Inside it lay strings of gold and several jeweled necklaces so that the bottom of the drawer sparkled like the surface of a creek. He gingerly extracted a massive pin which crackled against its neighbors as it rose. A cross spangled with bloodstone. The backing bore the minuscule inscription: Hoerkstroetter St. Louis. Leighton recognized none of the valuables, though he remembered keeping Indian heads and eagles in the long clasped boxes marked with the same German name, remembered seeing even more of the boxes once they'd left St. Louis.

He stared briefly at each piece before sending it snaking down the burlap sack at his knees.

Johnson came to the door. Leighton stood and swung the sack over his back. He told Johnson to take the clothes downstairs.

In the study, Leighton poured the contents of the sack into a metal strongbox, then lit a lamp, and descended into the cellar. The cellar had a mud floor, but the Morkans walled it with interlocking ashlars of lime. Against the northern wall, Morkan and Leighton built a wine rack, and rows of cool port rested there. Leighton emptied one of the racks, then hooked his fingers under the base of it. With a heave, the shelf smacked loose of the soil. Under its base was a dark hollow, a fine hiding spot. Leighton lowered the strong box into the hollow. A rectangle of black, the strong box rested like a babe's coffin in the oval of mud—everything valuable left of Charlotte Morkan. He knew of no way to save his father. Above him, he could hear Johnson's brogans clomping on the stones.

Morkan woke shivering, his face mashed against red grit he mistook as granite and he was sure he had stumbled off the carpentry at Bineran's Quarry and was laying in a crevasse of the mountain somewhere below the scaffolding. Inexplicably his hands were caught behind him in a sort of baling wire, or maybe fuse hemp. His jaw throbbed, another sign he'd fallen. A fall, especially one that left you blear-eyed, meant you were done, if not dead, done with quarrying granite.

"It's him, all right. God Damn." Strange accent near him. A Briton? He heard miners come shuffling around him, coughing, equipment clinking. Thank God they found him, but he prayed they were bright enough not to yank him to his feet to stand. He had come across accident victims whose rough saviors sent bones jagging through skin hoisting the wounded up in hopes they would walk off an injury.

He struggled to rise, but his jaw seared as if staked to the granite. The miners scuttled away, but a foreman, he figured, with very stout boots stopped beside him.

"Well, Morkan." A variation of the strange accent. "Where's your boy?"

His eyes focused abruptly on cobblestone and flickering torchlight, the sky silver above him. Missouri. A Federal stockade.

"Where's your boy, Michael Morkan?"

"Gone." When he spoke, his jaw burned as if a white-hot rivet corkscrewed to broil below his ear.

"You know where you are?"

He lay, afraid to shake his head or speak for the pain it might cause.

He heard scraping, and the man must have sat down behind him. He smelled the stink of wet wool and soil. "I suppose giving away your explosives made you one mighty proud Reb." The man sucked at a tooth.

Morkan pulled an instant at the bindings on his wrists, but these stung him. The man leaned forward and dug his elbows into Morkan's side. In the corner of his vision, Morkan could see the man's yellow fingers rolling a cigarette. Morkan was trapped in a brick structure with the roof torn off, starlight barely piercing the eddies of torchlight. Half a dozen other men with shackled feet were pitching nickels against the scorched brick wall. Silent, they shuffled forward and bent to reckon the distances.

"What's it like to give up everything for a losing cause? What do you think when you find yourself flat on your old face as it all comes undone?"

The man's elbows stabbed Morkan's sides as the soldier worked the tan paper. Bits of tobacco flaked from his twiddling fingers.

"Must be something, you're so quiet. I've heard micks are inhospitable and sulky, especially if they made a lot of money off decent folk."

Morkan rolled toward the man. His jaw stung so hard, it forced his eyes shut. He lay still for a moment. When he opened his eyes, the man was lifting the globe on a lantern, holding the metal hook, gingerly squinching his face forward to the orange light. Morkan imagined kicking the lantern, watching the globe skitter and break, reveling in the oil that would spatter the man's blue wool, his face, the flames catching and flaring.

His cheeks hollowed as he tugged on the cigarette. He wore a red wool hat, the peak of which slouched forward. What hair sprang from under it was slick and green-black. His eyebrows were a single wild tangle, his jaws lean and square and shaved smooth. A satisfied frown came over his face as the smoke curled from his nostrils.

"You know," he said, "you do make a fine listener." He inhaled and the cigarette glowed. He leered, and raised his bushy eyebrows. "What's your theory about purgatory?"

Morkan blinked at him. He felt sure he was being taunted. The man was surly, and he expected one of the soldier's superiors to arrive and cuff the bastard on the ear.

"No talking?" The soldier pinched the cigarette against his lips and squinted as he inhaled. "Father Jacques LaFontaine, Larkspur, Minnesota, taught us my theory. It says you commit a sin, say you tell an infamous story about a man. This story ruins him." He wet his thumb and fingertip and snuffed the remainder of the cigarette. "It makes him a pariah, a man nobody will have anything to do with."

He opened a pouch and dribbled the dregs of tobacco into it, leaving only the yellowed paper between his thumb and index finger. "Now, you can go to the Father, say bless me Father, for I have sinned through my own fault, yah dah dah, Hail Marys, Glory Be, all through. But that man you defamed is still out there paying, ain't he? And his son, his daughters, who can't marry. Your sin's growing like a crystal in a cave."

Morkan raised himself to his elbows. He was surprised that Father LaFontaine or whoever would use as an example the parable of sin based on a defamatory story. A monk in Ireland had talked about purgatory in a similar fashion—the sinner told a story about a good net-weaver girl who was then labeled a harlot.

"That brought you around," the soldier said. He smiled. "Nothing like sin for what it does to spark the heart. Anyhow, you done just this, but worse. You might as well have stood at the slaughter house door and given knives to any little boy

95

that wanted one. Run along, now! See just what it can cut!" He shooed a hand at Morkan as if scooting a child along. He bent very close, and Morkan could smell the tobacco on him. "And between here and Lexington, there's not a bridge you can crawl across."

Morkan opened his eyes. Only one bright star shone above the lamplight. The wall rose to a sort of peak where the roof once rested. He was freezing, and his eyes felt as if they had been pounded into his skull with a mallet.

"You know what's worse for you?" The soldier leaned forward, a new cigarette dangling from his lips. "We're going to find the only soul that gives a damn enough to pray for you, and send him to purgatory, too."

"Leighton. No part in it." Morkan felt himself tremble.

The soldier pulled the cigarette from his mouth. "We'll consider that a first confession. Three Our Father's, a Salve Regina, and the Apostle's Creed backwards." He strolled toward the other prisoners, who left their nickels and slunk away.

Morkan wondered if the soldier meant Leighton would literally be sent to purgatory, killed. What he would give to have followed the Federal army to St. Louis, to have left the quarry in the hands of any idiot! There was not a man in this town could run that mine and make profit without squandering himself or the lime. Maybe Heron could, God forbid it. The wet sulfur and lime in the mortar beneath him was a curse of greed and proprietorship and vanity. Vanity of vanities webbing every one of these cobbles together to bind him unto death. And his son. He heard the soldier's receding voice as if the words sank through a fever's delirium: "Amen, Everlasting Life and Body, thee of resurrection, the sins of forgiveness, the Saints of Communion. . . ."

Book 2

Leave Me Among My Countrymen

I

A RIDER TROTTED UP THE HILL FROM ROCKBRIDGE ROAD. It was Greevins, Leighton could tell by the way his long legs knobbed up beside the saddle. He wore a disheveled black coat Leighton had never seen and a straw hat with a drooping brim, the sort women wear to milk in during summer. Johnson and Leighton were loading furniture onto a stone wagon. Both stopped and watched Greevins as he walked his horse forward. He held the reins out with such solemnity that Leighton covered his smile.

"No washing here, lady," Leighton said, "but the dutch down the road are filthy."

Greevins scowled. He lifted the brim of the hat, which was so loose it covered his forehead to his eyebrows. His eyes met Leighton's, then fell to blinking at his horse's neck. "That sounded a lot like your pa."

"Where is he?"

"I got no sure idea, Leighton." Greevins handed his trace to Johnson, who still did not move to the barn. "They're holding some of them men in what's left of the Men's Academy. Surely they're going to have to move them."

"Can he escape?"

"This is all from hearing things. I can't get anywhere near there."

Leighton stood for a moment, his mind turning but unable to produce answers.

"Ain't you going to ask me in?"

Leighton glanced at the house. With its front doors thrown wide, the windows stripped of curtains, the house was a terrified face, mouth and eyes agape. He did not think of it yet as his. "Sure. If you want in. Sure." He nodded at Johnson, who frowned and tied the horse at the porch rail.

"We ain't got time for chit-chats," Johnson whispered to Leighton.

Greevins stuck his little finger in his ear and screwed it around. "Did I hear you right, nigger? Are you telling this young man what to do?" He stuck his long nose in Johnson's face.

Johnson said nothing, kept his eyes averted, but held his chin up facing Greevins.

Leighton touched their arms. "Maybe Johnson will get us some coffee on."

At the kitchen table, Johnson heated coffee in a tin pan over a bear oil lamp burning high, flames licking the pan bottom amid black smoke. The coffee was yesterday's, lukewarm and bitter as alum.

Only cane-bottomed chairs and Judith's stool remained in the kitchen. Leighton took Judith's stool, and the Negro and Greevins sat at the kitchen table.

Greevins shifted himself in the chair, faced away from the Negro. He told Leighton that Springfield was rampant with Federals, but they were motley and fussed publicly about their commanders while Kansans were out pillaging the countryside.

"Do you feel you're in danger?" Leighton asked.

Greevins nodded. "Why else would I dress like this?

Leighton grinned.

"Better question is what danger you put us in being here?" Johnson asked.

Greevins glared at the floor.

Leighton shifted on Judith's stool, waited for Greevins to answer. The miller's jaw buckled and he muttered something.

"Well, Greevins?" Leighton asked.

"You're in danger just setting here." Greevins' face began to redden. "What you think they're going to do, wait for Morkan to confess? If they don't come get you to testify, they'll come eventually and take this house apart." Greevins set his coffee down.

"All the more reason we shouldn't waste daylight a'talking," Johnson said.

Greevins hit the table with his fist then pointed at Johnson.

"Mister Greevins, I ain't thinking of nothing but the boy." Johnson kept his eye on the cup cradled in his hands as he spoke.

"And I'm after something else, am I?"

The Negro stiffened his neck, his back hunching in a quick shrug.

After a minute, Greevins faced Leighton. "Can he get something else to do somewhere?" He cocked his head at Johnson, but did not look at the Negro.

Johnson raised an eyebrow at Leighton, then placed his long hands on the filthy knees of his pants. "Mr. Leighton, I wouldn't dally." He rose and left the kitchen. Soon they could hear him thumping furniture onto the bed of the wagon.

Greevins leaned forward and his voice dropped. "I'm wanting to join the Guard." He watched Leighton closely, his eyes narrowing. "I got word they are just south in Arkansas, not much south of the border. Look, Leighton, everything's a loss here. I won't blow smoke in your eyes—your pa's gone." He gripped Leighton's wrist. "And if they take him to St. Louis, they're liable to kill him. There ain't no Irish left in St. Louis to vouch for him. Only the goll damned dutch."

Greevins released Leighton. "I want you to come with me, join with me. What those son-of-a-bitches are about to do to your pa!" He shook his head. "Only way to stop it is to join Price and kill them all the way to St. Louis."

Leighton rose from the stool, stood by the door to the mud room. The room needed Judith to douse it with lime water. A furry coat of moss was growing in the mud between the cobbles. When the wind blew against the house, the room smelled like a strange vegetable, despite the hint of cedar from the room's paneling. Leighton's stomach turned with hunger.

"You're sure you can find Price?"

"I'm sure."

The wood that comprised the benches in the mud room needed a coat of varnish. Tan cracks frayed the ends. He had held those boards while Morkan pounded the nails.

"Greevins, I can't leave here. I can't leave all this to the Federals." He turned.

Greevins stared at him. "They took your pa when you know he had to give Price what he did." Greevins stood. "Can you let them do that?"

"Let them? They already did."

"Leighton, I'm telling you. Your pa thought he could hide from this war. Did everything he could to keep out of it and keep from choosing sides. Well, there ain't no way to do that now. You can't keep the war from coming. There ain't no way to hide." He pulled at the brim of his straw hat.

"And so you think I should rush to it?"

Greevins frowned, his brow wrinkling, his eyes imploring Leighton.

Leighton spoke in a hushed voice. "My father told me, when the Federals come, I was to deny his name. Say I hated him and his rebellion."

Greevins blinked. "Well," he said. He pulled at his chin. "Well. That sure sounds like him." He raised an open palm to Leighton. "Not meaning any offense, but I never knew a man so careful in his own ways he couldn't see nobody else's like your father."

Greevins spoke of Morkan in the past tense, as if he were gone.

"All's I'm saying is I don't know any other way to keep you safe, but to keep you with me." His jaw stiffened; his face became stern.

Leighton paused, then grasped Greevin's forearm, knots of hard muscle beneath the old man's coat.

Greevins sank, and for a moment he held a hand to his eyes. Then he pushed the straw hat down on his head. "Then, I'm going to lay low for the winter, at least, if I can't find the Guard. Taney County." A pair of boots shuffled on the stone outside the kitchen. Greevins whispered. "Man named Thibodeaux. Cabin near Forsyth. The brewer in Forsyth can tell you where."

Johnson's shadow darkened the alcove.

Greevins squinted at Leighton. "You don't need to stay on his account. Or the negra's. They're like old barn cats. They'll do fine, even if there ain't a farmer around."

"I'm staying for the land and the quarry. It's what my pa asked me to do." He held Greevins eyes, wanted to show the miller all his determination. In addition, part of him wanted to hear the miller say he was right to stay, right to wait it out, and right to deny his father if he had to. Greevins did not turn as he rode to the gate. Down on the road, he looked every bit like a thin, old woman, bumping along south toward Ozark.

"You needed to stay, Mister Leighton," Johnson said. He tucked a bandanna under his slouch to keep the chill off his ears. "I don't mean him disrespect, but you doing the right thing."

Leighton dug his nails into his palms, an anger rising in him that he could not explain. "It's not really helpful to hear that from you."

When Johnson's jaw stiffened and the Negro turned away to lash down the wagon's load, Leighton wished he hadn't spoken. But Johnson was a Negro, Leighton figured, and was used to worse.

Johnson finished the wagonload, stowing the chairs. Earlier he and Leighton had loaded two of the bureaus from upstairs, even Charlotte's blue oval mirror cloaked in a buffalo robe. The velvet backings of the chairs had already picked up a dusting of lime off the stone-wagon's bed. They stowed flour, cornmeal, fatback, lard, all the easily moved foodstuffs in Johnson's cabin figuring the Federals might consider it already ransacked and not worth visiting again.

Johnson jerked a lashing tight. Leighton intended to store some of the furniture with Johnson, and the silver and china and meat in a cave on the property. Beyond that he had no idea of what needed to be done next. Through the ratty fabric across the back of Johnson's coat, Leighton could see the old Negro's shoulders working like plow blades, and this steadied him.

Turning, Johnson scowled. "I'm trying my very best to help you in this and you treat me to: 'I don't need to hear that from you!'" He hopped onto the wagon seat, held the reins out to Leighton. "You make me feel pretty damn low, Leighton Morkan. And I tell you something, that man may think I'm just a Negro." He pointed down the road where Greevins had disappeared. "But I brung even slaves to freedom right under you all's noses. And I can save you, too."

Hesitating, Leighton climbed onto the wagon and took the reins from him. "You might play that card on the quiet, Johnson." Morkan would never have taken this kind of insolence off Johnson. Leighton could almost recite what his father would have said at this point—"I'd like a lot less talk and a lot more doing right now." Leighton stared at Johnson's dark face, its pock marks and gray whiskers, the scar at his collar that ran deep blue and ridged like the tail of a worm, the yellow around his black pupils, a color like old newspaper on a wall. "You don't need to show me anything."

The sky was gray. A steadily falling mist clung to Leighton's beard, making his chin slick, his lips cold. Johnson's cabin was the original farmhouse, a three-pen log house with a loft and a lean-to kitchen on the back. The shutters were clamped tight and from a square hole in the roof, gray smoke crept skyward and hung over the clearing in a fog.

Leighton braked the wagon, and Isaac came out from the cabin.

"Where's Chester? And Bragg and Bundum?" Leighton asked.

Isaac hung his head. He was smaller than Johnson, his skin much darker. He wore three old flannel shirts of Morkan's, and his tiny wrists poked from enormous cuffs. "They gone find the Kansans."

An orange spark came whirling up from the hole in the roof. Despite the cold, a gloss of sweat darkened the bandanna at his forehead.

"They'll die trying," Leighton said. Finally he asked, "Why'd you stay?"

Isaac raised his head, and a smile began to curve his lips. "I kind a like the cabin all to myself." He meant the old slave cabin down the hill from Johnson's.

The mist fell in a gauze of silver. Without speaking, they began unlashing the wagon, unloading the trunks and chairs.

Together, he and Isaac shambled across the lot holding a bureau between them. Inside, they set the bureau down, pushed it against the farthest wall in the common room. Isaac headed for the door, but Leighton straightened his back slowly, glanced around the room. The floor was dirt, and in the midst of it was a square fire pit with iron riggings and a spit from which a small black kettle hung. A pallor of smoke obscured the air and made the cabin seem very cramped.

Johnson coughed at the door. "If it's too smoky, Mr. Leighton, Isaac and I be glad to finish for you."

Leighton glanced at him. "No. No." He waited. Only the smoke stirred in the cabin, hanging in the air like cream in well water.

Piece by piece, they stowed the furniture—the high backed velvet chairs, bureaus and end tables done in American Empire. The cabin became crowded. Leighton brought in his mother's oval mirror still wrapped in the buffalo robe bound in twine. He set this against the wall next to the partition of blankets. Judith moved chairs about. She wore a long calico dress; her hips and face seemed slimmer.

Lean, he thought. As the firelight played upon her sides, the world grew dingy and compressed. "Judith," he said.

She nodded at him, her frown so stern it tightened and pitted the nub of her chin.

"I'm sorry about the soldiers."

She snorted, but Johnson glared at her.

Leighton fetched two brass lamps with intricate globes. When he returned to the cabin, Judith removed the buffalo robe from the mirror. She stood before it, staring at her image, lifting the calico dress slightly. The fabric she stitched in to accommodate her girth in better times now folded like the collapsed sides of a fireplace bellows. Her eyes were glassy as if she had been sleeping.

Johnson ran a hand along the top of one of the velvet-backed chairs and watched Leighton. "We not supposed to sit in these?"

"I can't imagine you haven't sat in them before."

Isaac lowered himself into one of the chairs.

"I don't expect this all to sit here and you not use it, but this isn't permanent." Leighton glanced at Judith again, whose eyes gazed on him now from the mirror. Behind her image in the glass, stood a pale, bearded boy, beads of mist giving off a silver sheen along the brim of his hat.

He removed his hat, pulled his hand through his wet hair. "I appreciate what you're doing, Judith. Johnson. Isaac. I appreciate you staying."

On the easternmost edge of Morkan land, he and Johnson hid the dinner china and silver flatware far back in one of the caves formed in an exposed ridge of lime. Johnson worked quickly as if with renewed energy, and when they were finished he knelt beside Leighton and they both sipped handfuls of water they fetched from the stream that issued from the cave. Back in the half-light of the cave, stalactites oozed from the ceiling in yellow spikes. The walls were covered with the same fossils found at the quarry—cogs and wheels, teeth of sharks, the curled imprints of worms.

"Tight spaces trouble you?"

Johnson looked at him. "What's gone happen?" On his creased face, pits of worry gathered at his lips, around his eyes.

Leighton wiped his hands against his pantlegs. "I was hoping you could tell me, Johnson. Like old times." He climbed onto the seat of the empty wagon.

North of them the two domed hills that marked the middle of Morkan's land rose up stubbled with the whiskers of bare winter trees. Here and there, pines and squat cedars hunched in dark cones of green and blue green. A flight of crows swept the valley headed northeast toward town. Something excited them, for they burbled greedy conspiracies to one another.

Looking on these hills, knowing his father might never see their jagged red and tan again, the brown carpet of leaves beneath the bare oaks, Leighton felt the the hills, the soil draw him downward and claim him as lime will a cold spring. The columns, the unfinished balconies of their home, the quarry—Leighton saw his father's life and work as from above, a scaffolding, a toehold, an heroic start thrust from a cherty hillside. He would have to stay, or all his father loved would be lost.

II

SLEET PELTED THE PRISONERS' BACKS, AND WHEN THEY traversed a valley, snow whirled up and stung their faces. The pace was terrific, faster and farther the first day than Morkan had ever walked in his life. The bare trees that bearded the hills shimmered silver with a layer of ice in their upper branches. He was beyond shivering. The cold became an inch-deep ache down his arms and across his back. His feet fell like wooden clubs thumping the icy ground, and the rags they were swaddled in only amplified this hollow feeling. His cheeks and chin held a mask of ice and dirt. The rain-soaked days and frigid nights in the Men's Academy—a square of bricks, its roof gone in a fire—left him a cough deep in his chest.

Two wagons with teamsters and two other Federal soldiers accompanied the troop of twelve prisoners. One wagon was loaded with foodstuffs and supplies. The other bedded two more prisoners whose wounds did not allow them to walk. The Catholic guard, Sergeant Nimms, came along with them, and his presence heightened the veracity of the rumor that the entire Federal army was on its way to Rolla. The prisoners told Morkan to watch out for Nimms, but Morkan held no trust in them. In the nights at the Men's Academy, someone swiped his spectacles and his boots, and he never slept.

By the second day of marching, they saw no one and traveled in a world of close steep hills grown over with woolly scrub and a few towering pines, or a mass of tangled young oaks. The rises had an insular effect on the mind, as if the universe collapsed to nothing save the void between two round hills. The hills and scrub made the land seem ancient. For all the thousands of years Europe boasted its culture of high art and glorious warfare, this land staged its own brutal and secret history that

Morkan knew bits of from the shark's teeth and lizard skin in the limestone, but that only the hills remembered in full and kept to themselves. Rolls of gray clouds bleared the sky. Through his shirt pocket the tintype of Cora and Sam Slade chilled his skin, and he clasped it close.

Prisoners and guards, a strange and forlorn crew hobbling northeast, passed cabins and inns with boarded windows. Often the guards shucked their rifles into the wagons and, alongside the prisoners, pushed the wheels loose from snow drifts or mud that climbed to the axles. For hours the guards would not retrieve their rifles, the prisoners being too exhausted to escape. The prisoners had nowhere to run to, save into the teeth of the cold. Fearing bushwhackers, the guards wore nearly the same clothing as the prisoners—ragged cloaks, dungarees, the lice-ridden and grimy bed rolls. When the guards set their rifles aside, they were almost indistinguishable from the prisoners in the whirling snow.

That night they bedded under the wagons. A few of the prisoners had been Rebel guardsmen together and felt familial enough to sleep in a pile. Morkan sat apart from them, waiting for the men to hit a sound sleep before joining them.

Watching them rest, he remembered four Chinamen sleeping together in a railroad crew's tent. He had taken a guilty pleasure in their squalor, in the way the Chinamen seemed lost and expendable in the booming nation that embraced him. An aging Scotsman on the railroad, Otis Wing, gave Morkan his chance when Morkan took over a survey crew for a drunken Brit. Morkan soon discovered all the math mired in the Brit's survey logs—bench marks weren't tied back, elevations vaulted wildly, chains doubled or vanished. Wing never forgot the intervention, and insisted Morkan be chief surveyor, then engineer on every stretch under Wing's aegis. Even with the old Scotsman's fierce advocacy, the railroad commandants were prejudiced and snobbish at first when it came to using a mick. But it took only a perfect bridge truss finished in a day, or an abutment built of local stone saving miles of transport to make them smile on him. His mind and hands set him apart from the Chinamen, who were covered that night in a filth of ashen gray shale. After constant tutelage under the engineer at Bineran's quarry and then Wing, he found himself more in demand than even graduates from Munich or the *Ecole Polytechnique*. His own wage was reasonable and his engineering practices were frugal in the extreme. Now his own hands appeared frosted, the skin blue and flaking. Nothing his hands could build, nothing his mind could envision set him apart from the pile of Rebel soldiers. Under the wagon, all were prisoners, nothing more.

The reverend Overbo moved next to him. The first night, the prisoners were too wary of the guards to speak beyond grunts and monosyllables. Morkan knew Overbo was the reverend at the Baptist church, the church Greevins attended, a hotbed of secessionists. He vaguely remembered an embarrassing wrangle with Overbo over the price of whitewash for his church. The reverend had been much heavier. He was the loud sort of Protestant evangelist certain Americans revered for some reason. Lord, how the preacher yammered with the Rebels arriving. Now here he was, a lowly prisoner, wanting to bed down with a Catholic.

Overbo leaned back on his elbow and whispered, "You're the Irish quarrymaster?"

"Owner," Morkan said.

Overbo leaned his head closer. "Where's your boy? With A.C. Greevins, I hope." They both watched the guards sitting hunched by the fire, blankets draped over their backs. The guards looked like buzzards resting, their wings folded behind them in the dark. "Is he all right?"

Morkan stared at him. The reverend's eyes seemed to implore him. "I wish I knew," Morkan said.

"You must let me be a comfort to you, though we are of opposing faiths."

Morkan waved this off, then fell into a coughing fit. After spitting, he hung his head. Though his jaw stopped throbbing, he took no heart in its improvement. He wanted to lie flat against the frigid earth, let the cold take him.

Overbo's hand gripped his shoulder, so powerful it raised him.

"They may break our bodies," Overbo whispered, "but they must not break our spirits." He gave Morkan a slight shake.

"Saving a man's spirits is about the only thing I'm any good at, brother."

Glancing at the guards, Morkan pushed Overbo's hand from him. The reverend bowed his head. Morkan crawled beneath the wagon, and after coughing again, he wedged himself beside the sleeping Rebels. He rested his cheek on his forearm but watched Overbo. Frowning, the reverend piled leaves against the wagon wheel. He glanced at Morkan and the bunched soldiers, then sighed and lowered himself to his bed of dirt and leaves.

Walking, Morkan closed his eyes, envisioned the road as a ladder leading to another ladder. Or his mind turned on old remorses: he remembered stepping to the kiln where the fireman sat on a cord of wood while young Leighton, who had just started at the quarry, hove log after log into the furnace. Morkan grabbed Leighton's collar, yanked him clean off his feet, shouted at him about busting the back of the firewall. The fireman ducked his head and cowered off. Too late, it became obvious to Morkan that the fireman had egged Leighton on or just told him to heave wood with all his might. The boy did not protest, but the look in his slanted eyes was of such betrayal it made Morkan's ribs ache now to recall the incident. A dozen other such moments cropped up to trouble him, to make him pang for the boy. But opening his eyes and watching the road was even more maddening. At times, far off hills slithered away, inch by inch, promised never to be reached, and when they were reached they were replaced by more hills. The terrain gave Morkan the sensation of spiraling down and down and down.

Nimms slowed and moved beside him. "What do you think of to while the time away, Morkan? Bodies floating in a stream? Locomotives dashed into ravines? Lead sailing over Lexington?"

Morkan said nothing.

"Do help me here, for I am powerful bored."

Listening to his voice, Morkan entertained the notion that this might be true, that boredom made him so persistent. Glancing at him, though, Morkan noticed he walked leaning forward, almost on his toes. Overbo slowed and walked more closely to them.

"What do you watch when you close your eyes?" Nimms asked.

"The vanishing point in every man's landscape." Morkan brought his hand to his mouth but did not cough.

After a moment, Nimms grinned. "Maybe we'll make a citizen of you after all." He hurried his step and latched onto one of the wagons, hopped onto the seat.

"That man's mind is on evil continually," Overbo whispered.

"You may be right, reverend."

The wagon thumped and ratcheted side to side.

His cough grew worse until it sounded like feet marching through ice-bound rushes. Nimms refused him the wagon. He woke from dozing and found his arm draped on Overbo, the reverend staring resolutely forward into the hills. On a cable ferry, they crossed a wide, swift river. The big ferryman turning the crank sang a song about a church bell. Blocks of ice bobbed downstream, caused the ferry to wait, swaying on its wire in the current. Resuming, the ferry slunk towards a gravel bar, beyond which was a high limestone ridge topped by cedars, the sky gray as pewter. Curls of steam hovered on the water's surface. With the constant whisper of the water and the ridges bottling the river, even the horses stilled, their ears twitching. The ferryman's voice became the only living sound. Abruptly he sang a new song, and Morkan hung on every word as he might on sparks dying in wet tinder.

> Asleep in Jesus! Blessed Sleep,
> From which none ever wakes to weep;
> Guide us o'er the troubled deep;
> The Lord tonight our souls will keep.

The cable screeched. Morkan coughed and shuddered. From the back of his wagon a teamster glanced out. He waved to Nimms. Soon Nimms and the teamster dragged one of the invalid prisoners from the wagon and set him on the filthy deck of the ferry. His face was as white as the purlings of the river. His lips were blue.

The ferryman paused in his song. "Two bits and I have him buried."

Nimms began pulling the prisoner's effects from his pockets. He rolled them in the prisoner's butternut shirt. "I'll give you nothing and you'll bury him as you please."

Frowning, the ferryman hauled the crank around and did not sing.

Once on the opposite bank, the prisoners watched the ferry recede, the big ferryman rising and crouching with the crank, the white body stiffly waiting beside him.

They boarded a train in Rolla. No box cars were available so they rode in an open-bedded lumber car rigged with side railings. A guard stood watch while Nimms and the others remained warm in the caboose. The prisoners huddled under a sheet of canvas. Sparks pelted them, and smoke, pouring from the stack and scouring the car, blackened their faces. At night, the sparks swirled and dashed, caught in their hair, but no one moved to avoid them. They crossed fields silvered with moonlight. Morkan coughed himself to tears until his ribs ached and he thought they were splitting.

He woke in the night with Overbo hovering over him, loosening his coat. His throat felt as if he'd swallowed a hive of yellow jackets. Overbo tottered, then bent and scooped something from the bottom of the lumber car. He cupped his hands for a bit, said something Morkan could not hear over the bang of the rails. He touched his hands to Morkan's lips. His fingers were soft, tasted of pine tar. Water, salty and frigid, slipped between his lips. He felt his tongue broaden and give. Before he knew what he was doing, he latched both of Overbo's wrists in his hands, mashed the reverend's fingers against his cracked lips, suckling at the slush and water.

"There's more," Overbo yelled in his ear. "Let go."

Overbo bent and scooped more snow.

At dawn, the train approached the Meramec and was about to cross a bridge Morkan had built. Big tar-blackened pilings and struts swept down toward the river; it was a simple bridge with an almost imperceptible curve that allowed a locomotive to maintain speed while beginning the northeasterly turn toward downtown St. Louis. Morkan pulled himself up by the railing, pushed the canvas off his chest. The canvas flapped and woke Overbo. Morkan's throat quivered. What could he tell Overbo that would make any sense? He ran his hand under his eye, hoping his tears would be attributed to cold and wind rather than ridiculous sentiment over a structure. He pointed at the bridge just as the lumber car passed the first beam of the truss.

Overbo twisted and looked over the railing at the water. He turned to Morkan and shook his head. "You're too ill to swim," Overbo hollered.

In St. Louis, they de-trained at the downtown station. Where there had been barrels of beer and amber stacks of lumber, kegs of nails, smoked fish and whole hogs, there were now only ash and soot, stacks of rifles and canvas, cannon balls stacked like pyramids of grapes. A few onlookers from Market Street stopped and called to their fellows. Morkan smiled to see a three piece suit, a clean boiled shirt, a string tie.

Nimms lined them single file, forced them to clasp each other's shoulders with their right hands. He walked down the line of them, whispering. He came to Morkan, gripped his chin.

"We have a walk ahead of us. If you drop your hand from the man before you, you will be shot. If you speak to any of the crowd, you will be shot. Understand?"

Morkan nodded.

A crowd was gathering at the tracks. A Federal unit jogged beside the prisoners. Black boots picked up the brown dirt beside the tracks. Their uniforms were a dark blue, and all their buttons and stripes shone. Morkan coughed, bowed his head and felt his hand slipping from Overbo. When he looked up, Nimms drew his pistol and was smoking a cigarette, eyeing him. The troops formed a square around the prisoners, turned slightly to the side creating a fence of bayonets and rifles. They proceeded toward the center of town along Market.

The prisoners reached Fifth Street, marched away from the Riverfront to Myrtle and halted. Morkan coughed, leaned so close to Overbo, he thought of resting his head on the reverend's back.

"Prisoners!"

It was a new voice, and Morkan looked up to see a plump officer standing on top of a small raised platform.

"Welcome to your new home, the Myrtle Street Prison. I will now go over some of the very basic rules."

Soldiers in light blue shirts moved beside the prisoners. Each soldier dragged a chain and irons from which a small cannonball dangled.

Morkan squinted at a two story building laid out in cubicles like a cramped inn. The bottom floor was built partly underground, or swallowed in silt.

Morkan leaned forward. "Is there a sign above that building?"

Overbo nodded, "Says 'Billy Lynch: Auctioneer.'"

"Oh, Jesus," Morkan said. The plump officer rattled decrees from the same platform off which Morkan bought his first two slaves, Judith and Johnson Davis. The building before them was St. Louis's slave market, Lynch's Market as it was called. Morkan's hand was slipping down Overbo's back.

Nimms caught the hand with the muzzle of his revolver, raised Morkan's hand back to Overbo's shoulder, leaving the cool notch of the sight tingling on his palm. A Federal soldier knelt at his feet. The leg irons, when they clasped his ankles, were the coldest things Morkan ever felt on his skin.

They were marched inside the slave market, which was nothing but a row of cells topped by another row of cells. Each faced Myrtle Street, so that buyers could wander the windows and inspect the property before bidding Saturday afternoon. He remembered walking the bottom floor, peering in each reeking cell at the white-eyed, black-skinned folk behind the bars. The slaves all were shirtless, and their skin was oiled. The females' breasts hung in flat disks. Sometimes the males came directly to the bars. One explained something to Morkan at length in his native barbar. Morkan remembered watching the slave's chest and arm musculature as the slave gesticulated. Manfred Weeks, a contractor for the railroad, came with him and was prattling advice.

"That's a good buck, there. Ain't he charged up about something? Oh, look at that poor kid. I bet they've had her drink a fire wagon worth o' water all night. See how she's bloated. Them puffy arms give it away. Belly 'bout to pop. Lynch will do that. Thinks it makes them look healthy."

Johnson was the only slave that coolly looked Morkan over. Weeks was silent. The slave appeared fit, if wiry. His jaw sharp, his eyes clear and alert.

"That's trouble waiting," said Weeks. "I bet an eagle he's fractious."

Johnson held Morkan's eyes squarely for a long time. Morkan took no offense, though Weeks was bubbling at Johnson's insolence. The slave nodded, then popped his hip with his open hand twice as if calling for a dog.

A wee girl stepped from the shadows of the cell. She smiled at the two men. She had a baby boy's chest, a round face. She raised her hands to them, and cupped there was a toad. Morkan laughed aloud.

Now, two soldiers took him by the arm. Nimms followed them down the dingy narrow hallway to the door of a cell. They loosed the bolt, and Nimms called out: "Political Prisoner. Arms Merchant. Slave Owner. Rebel Sympathizer. A4."

The soldier pushed him into the cell. Morkan slumped against a wall of frigid earth. The soldier still stood at the door. In the flickerings of the lantern he held, he pointed to the chain and ball that remained just outside the door.

"Pull it in, A4."

Morkan gripped the cold chain now slick with muck that smelled of feces. When he pulled, the ball wobbled into the cell. The soldier popped the door shut, struck the bolt home, and the cell went entirely dark.

In his fever, Morkan could not sleep. When he closed his eyes, he felt the parallel lines of the rails zipping under his body. Rodents scuttled about. One leapt into the middle of his chest, and by the heft of its slick, reptilian tail, its body was at least two feet in length. He crammed himself against what he reckoned was the southernmost wall into a hollow of mud that accepted a body as if the silty depression had held many before him. His head swam, but still he fought off the rats, kicking his hands and feet, learning to listen to the inquisitive chitterings a rat makes as it weighs decisions. With his eyes closed, his aim grew so refined, he came to enjoy landing kicks that sent them screeching. Soon, he had his corner to himself save for the uninitiated and the most insistent.

Sometime, he imagined it was terribly late, maybe four a.m., the scuttling quit altogether. He opened his eyes, and they burned at a nothing of black so dark his mind began to supply flashes of blue and red where he thought the door should be. He coughed for a moment, then managed his breath tightly. The boarded window thumped as the wind shifted outside. When he swallowed, his spit tasted like brass.

Somewhere outside a bell was ringing, either the bell of a boat, or a fire bell, but as his mind tumbled down with fever and fatigue, the bell resounded and became Billy Lynch's bell that rang every Saturday afternoon calling the men to auction. In a panic he clutched at the tintype of Cora.

After many hours of the morning passed, Nimms took Morkan out and they sat together on a bench in a sunlit courtyard behind Billy Lynch's. It was the bench where the slave wardens used to sit and eat their noonday meal and their suppers later in the evening. Morkan could remember them all in a row, jawing over corned beef and smoked bream, corn cakes. His stomach knotted with hunger. Blinking and hardly able to see at first, Morkan trembled in the cold. Nimms brought him hot coffee and hardtack warmed to a mush in water.

"Let's cover your options. For one as extremely disloyal as you, there can be a trial and then a hanging," Nimms said. He flipped through a sort of notepad, a sheaf of parchments fastened with a leather thong binding two Morocco covers ripped off what must have once been a luxurious book. "Or there can be just a hanging."

"I see," Morkan said. The hardtack made his ribs ache. It was such a warm starchy goo, he fought moaning with pleasure when he swallowed. As his eyes focused, the high brick building that bottled the courtyard became visible. Across the courtyard, a guard dozed leaning against his rifle, which Morkan mistook for a broom.

"A third option is something new that General Halleck has thought up. An assessment. Cash."

Morkan's eyeballs itched and burned staring at Nimms. Some mornings, the sergeant's poor shaving practices made his jaw and neck seem dyed with indigo. And since he kept only a sparkling black moustache, Morkan wondered if he were part Dutch. "Take a good look at me, Sergeant. Money?" Morkan's voice crackled. He raised a hand, palm up, fingers curled as if he clutched a skull. "Alas, poor Halleck!"

Nimms frowned. "Ah, the legendary black humor of the Missouri puke." He jotted something in the Morocco-bound notepad. "With all the suffering we have afforded you, just think of the great literature that will one day spew from this shithole!"

"Much obliged, I'm sure."

Nimms snorted. "The assessment will be based upon your 1860 tax rolls. And I rather like this, very creative here. General Halleck will use the fine levied to fund the relief of the stinking refugees clogging the streets of St. Louis. Right Catholic that, eh?"

When Morkan did not react, Nimms sighed. "Oh, and after paying it, since you can't very well be banished to the real Confederacy and be expected to stay put with a son and a quarry waiting on you, you will be hanged. Fair enough?"

"All these options end rather similarly, don't you think? Where's the fun?"

Nimms bobbed his thick, single eyebrow. "I have for you a fourth option."

"What, this one starts with me hanging?"

Nimms pursed his blue lips. "You give me a cash assessment, since your real property is not so portable. Cash, as in you tell me how much you have stowed away right now back in Springfield. Where it is, kept in what, and so on."

Morkan stared, fully awake now.

"And I keep you alive." Nimms let this sink in. "Under some pretexts, of course. Say maybe the hope that you will break and tell us precisely what the traitor McBride told you." Nimms watched him. "What say you?"

117

"I think you have spoken your first honest sentences to me," Morkan said. He set the cup and plate aside. In the frigid air his chains sounded like brittle metal buckling. "I find them vile."

Nimms ran his clean, long fingers along the Morocco. "All right, then. A trial. What will your testimony be?" He fetched a cigarette from his thick coat.

"I was coerced. . . ." The hoarseness of his voice startled him and he paused. "Unless I gave black powder to the men who took over my town by force, they would have taken everything. Equally by force. What else is there to say?"

Nimms spit. "You Missourians and your 'coercions.' It's a miracle the Rebel army ever had time to drill with all the coercing it has accomplished." Nimms lit the cigarette. "Let me argue it this way. One could easily realize that, yes, the Rebels might come to one's mine and take everything. One could also rationalize that, though the Rebels had taken everything needed to mine, eventually they would be driven away, commerce could return to normal, and in a world crippled by war, the mine could rebuild itself at a pace almost equal to that needed by the town. Couldn't one?"

Morkan watched him, a little astonished at the clarity and perceptiveness Nimms exhibited. He coughed, bent double for a moment. Nimms held his own cup of coffee to him.

Morkan blinked at it, then drank. Wagons rattled by somewhere beyond the courtyard. A flock of pigeons arced upward in the sunny sky, their breasts as light blue as gypsum talc. He trembled to see them.

"Is that how I'll be treated in this trial?" Morkan sipped the coffee.

Nimms shrugged. "And then hanged, yes. Tell me, did you leave enough powder and currency for your son to quarry again?"

Morkan stared at him. "Depends. What've you all taken from him so far?"

"Morkan." He was quiet for a moment. His jaw was so tense, two oval shadows appeared beneath his cheekbones. "Take we might have. But, do you have enough *hidden* to begin again?"

Morkan slurped the coffee, closed his eyes.

"Come now. You are a sharp businessman, a wily mick and Catholic. Used to a bootload of shit from all comers." Nimms leaned in very close, his hazel eyes bright green and eager. "You can't tell me you haven't stowed plenty away."

Morkan drank coffee. "All gone in bribes. To the likes of you."

Nimms flushed, his thick eyebrows rising. "You tell lies as sure as a glassblower twists a bottle."

Morkan said nothing.

Nimms frowned. "When I look at you, Morkan, I think, Lord, what a waste! Here is a man of sharp faculties, enterprising, probably industrious. Yet like a highwayman or a confidence artist, he takes the gift God granted and he uses it for trickery and holds true to no creed or flag, but the flag of capital. You deeply try my faith in the choices God has made and the gifts He has given."

Morkan sat still. The whiteness of the sunlight stung his eyes.

Nimms stiffened. "Is there any morality in you Morkan? Even a fiber? Straddle the fence to Gehenna and the stink of it still gets all over you." He whistled for a guard. The guard sleeping on his rifle jolted awake. "Morkan, I have a great deal to say about when you go to trial. About whether you live or hang. You should see your way to tell me anything I need to know." He whispered, then, his lips very close to Morkan's ear, his words searing in their sudden warmth on Morkan's frozen ear lobe. "It's only money after all. *L'Argent de poche.* And a man like you, he can make it all again. But he must live to do that."

Nimms leaned back from his charge, hazel eyes assessing. "Take this one back to A4," Nimms hollered to the guard. "Bring the next!"

III

WEEKS PASSED. LEIGHTON COULD NO LONGER STAND WAITING for news. He felt sure any official he sought, even townspeople he knew, would turn him in were he to protest his father's capture. So he rode into town for the Phelps farm where he had heard the Yankees had encamped. He chose the scabbiest draft horse from the mine stock, and wrapped himself in a torn old coat of Johnson Davis's. He wore a slouch hat and kept a wool scarf bunched at his mouth.

Many residences were gutted, some burned. A black square and a scorched, smoldering chimney were all that remained of McBride's house. Leighton remembered delivering contracts there to the dark green slat porch.

The draft jarred him past the debris of McBride's fencing. These houses were sought out, and he thought of Galway for a moment, was thankful for the long ride, the secluded hillside.

He arrived at the gate and the long corridor of oaks that led to Phelps's farmhouse, where Greevins said the Federals were encamped. The gate hung open. In the clearing beyond the oaks, scraps of food and trash were being mulled over by scores of emaciated dogs, blue ticks and redbones starved. The black bowls of abandoned fire pits dotted the frosted mud, but there was no Federal army.

A Negro scooted out from the oaks. He wore a tattered shirt and no coat or shoes. He kicked one of the snarling hounds away from a heap of rubbish, then plucked a blackened hunk of something from the heap. He sat and began to gnaw at the hunk.

Leighton coaxed the draft through the gate and plodded up to the Negro. The man was tearing bits off the ribcage of a fowl, cracking the small bones and slurping at their ends. One eye remained cocked on two hounds that growled and circled, tails tucked. His other eye was clamped tight in a squint of effort and ecstasy. The Negro glanced up at Leighton, and swallowed.

"Colonel Phelps not around, sir," he said.

Leighton nodded. "And the army?"

"Price is coming, sir." The Negro resumed gnawing; he busted open a substantial bone, grunted and rocked as he sucked at it. His own ribs showed as black eels through holes in his shirt.

More Negroes were picking over the field, squabbling with the dogs. "Anybody in charge of you all?" Leighton asked.

The Negro wiped his mouth on his sleeve. "Mrs. Phelps freed me today, took a wagon full of food and bandages to find the Fed'rals. I got my papers here to show. They in effect tonight, eight sharp." He stood and began digging in his shirt pocket.

Leighton waved the papers away. "Fine. I'm glad for you."

"I ain't glad." The Negro blinked at him, his lips held in a tight, flat line. "They's no food in this whole place. And the wrong army's coming."

Leighton looked over the field that stood waist high in wheat that summer. In the shadow of the horse, the freed Negro was staring, lips curled at the hunk of bone and burnt flesh in his hand.

Leighton reached in his coat pocket and fetched one of the biscuits wrapped in a handkerchief that morning. The Negro looked up at him. He flipped the biscuit to the Negro, who caught it.

Leighton rode away before the freed Negro thanked him, and before any of the others begged him. The houses he passed were boarded. On a few porches, women sat, wool blankets wrapped about their legs, shotguns and varmint rifles cradled in their arms. No children were visible. The square was entirely deserted, though the Union flag still drooped above the unfinished courthouse.

At the burned shell of the men's academy Leighton paused. Rags and tattered clothes hunkered in frosty corners. There against the red brick walls and grimy puncheons his father had worn chains. Leighton fought the urge to dismount and touch the mortar he and his father had set. When the horse grew uneasy, Leighton turned it in a slow circle, its breath purling like milk entering water.

Correy lived down a back alley close to the quarry. The foreman's house looked dull and battered compared to what Leighton remembered. All the windows were shuttered, though there were slops steaming at the corner of the steps. He hesitated before reaching the steps. The town behind him was more quiet than he could ever remember, this intensified by the chill winter air. He pulled the scarf loose from his mouth and removed the hat. He could hear the creak and grind of a rocking chair down the street, a dog far away yelping. He glanced toward Cora's house and saw it dark.

He knocked. "Correy. It's Leighton."

There was shuffling behind the door, a sharp argument between two voices, one a female's. Correy opened the door. He wore a fine wool coat partially buttoned and beneath this a yellowed long john shirt. His eyes were solid red, almost bloody, save for the slim blue irises around wide pupils. He stank, like dregs at a winery, and stood blinking at Leighton. His lips were purple and swollen.

Correy glanced over Leighton's shoulder, scanned the street. What had been mutton chop sideburns spread to a scraggly beard across the foreman's sunken cheeks.

"Get in," Correy said, the words slurred between his puffed lips.

Leighton wondered what sort of fight the foreman suffered. He stepped through the door, and Correy snipped it shut behind him. One candle flickered in the middle of the floor. Leighton blinked his eyes to adjust. A small woman with kinks of red-brown hair stood in a corner with her head bowed, her arms folded at her waist. It took Leighton a moment to parse the situation and to believe it, as if the cold dulled him—Cora. It was Cora Slade standing there. Soiled clothes and spent wine bottles mounded on the floor. Correy sat on a creaking brass bed and took a bottle of port from his bedside table. He stuck the neck of the bottle at Leighton who shook his head. Correy poured the wine in a tin cup and cradled the cup in his hands.

"I saved some eagles and got Shulty to open up and sell a case."

Leighton's nose twitched at the house's stench. "When was this?" He could barely see Correy's bloodshot eyes blinking at him. The skin of his forearms bristled. The room was colder than the outside air.

Correy's breath roiled when he spoke. "Couple days back."

Leighton stared at the candle. "Where's the Federals?"

Correy choked for an instant, lowered the cup, then drank quickly. He breathed. "They didn't come for you all?" He slurped when he finished the sentence, his battered lips wet with spittle.

Leighton scratched his chin, glanced at Cora, who was staring at him. The gray light outside thickened and Correy's tiny room darkened as if a black spirit passed through the walls and rose up there to gloat and listen. "They come for you?" he asked Correy.

"No."

Leighton glanced at Cora whose head bowed a touch more. He felt betrayal all around, in the frigid air, in the stink of dregs, in the blue part that ran down the scalp of her red hair. The wind moaned at the stovepipe.

"Then how about your face?"

Correy cleared his throat and spat on the floor. The Federals likely tortured the foreman into revealing where all the quarry's powder had gone.

Correy swallowed. "Cora pulled 'em teeth so they can't conscript me."

"That is why I'm here, Leighton. Understand? That is why I'm here." Her voice grated like a stone cut free of its ledge.

Leighton sat on the bed. Correy opened his mouth. Squinting, Leighton could see a bead of horrible black pits in the gums Correy was baring. Without teeth, Correy couldn't bite the white paper cartridges full of ball and powder.

"Keeping drunk ever since." He wiped his sleeve across his lips. "A toothless old drunk now." He poured more port from the bottle, stuck the cork in it and rolled it across the floor to Cora. She stopped it with the toe of her boot, Leighton's old boots, but did not look up. Correy drank. He lay back on the bed.

Leighton tucked the scarf to rest above his lips. "Always thought you'd love to join the Federals."

Correy snorted. "The son bitches."

Cora uncorked the bottle, and the wine pinged sloshing against the sides when she raised it. Leighton had never known her to take a drink, for her dead husband Sam Slade was a souse and took keen sobriety to manage.

"Did they ask about the quarry?" Leighton pressed.

Correy stared at his hands for a long while. "Of course."

Leighton watched Correy's eyes. "About my father?"

Correy sat up. He leaned very close to Leighton. "Told them powder was a God damn rumor." He placed the back of his wrist against his wet lips. "And they shouldn't listen to rumors."

In the silence that followed, the house crackled in the wind. A smell of ash from the stove crept up Leighton's legs and hovered.

"They took him anyway," Leighton said.

Correy pounded the bed with his fist. "Beat the living light out of me, Leighton Morkan, and get gone. Now, damn it!"

Leighton got up from the bed. "I suppose in detaining people they worked their way up to you."

"He was the first they asked." Cora's voice was soft and changed, as if her mind were far away. "And the last they released."

"Shut up," Correy said.

She looked up at the foreman, closed her eyes. "And the only one to hold out. I pulled not even half them teeth. They knocked out the rest."

Correy's cup went sailing across the room and clanged against the wall above Cora's head. She shut her eyes again and tipped the bottle.

Correy sat rocking with his head in his hands. "Said they already had you. Said you confessed. They were looking for Morkan. And they'd come for him, anyway." The words slopped wetly and he swallowed after each sentence.

Leighton approached him. "And so you believed what they said, even though they were beating you. And you ended up telling them all they needed to know to keep my father." He was so close to Correy, he could taste the liquor on his breath.

Cora stood and pulled a black shawl around herself. When she touched Leighton, he swiped her hand away.

"Please, Leighton. Please," she whispered in his ear. "I been with him this whole time. Time's like these, neighbors got to band together. And that is how I have been to him. A neighbor, like the Lord said. Do you understand?" She took Leighton by the arm and tugged him toward the door.

"Elijah did his best. When they brought him back, he's real beat up. They told him when they let him go, they was considering conscripting him to ensure his loyalty. That's when I pulled the rest of them back teeth." She bowed her head. "I've saved a lot of good men that way lately."

Her eyes flickered in the candlelight, and in them Leighton saw brass reflected.

Correy shuddered and wrapped his arms tightly about his chest.

"Please get him sober," Leighton said.

She nodded. "Teeth take five days to heal." Looking at Correy, she bit her lip, which was chapped with white flecks of skin. "Leighton you have got to get Michael back. After what they done to Correy, I can only imagine," she whispered, her voice trailing off.

Watching her eyes, he felt the black spirit of the room enter him. "It rues me that you know what my father has done. I will not forget."

She froze and looked on him for the first time in fear, her eyes wide.

"Correy, the Federals are gone." Leighton said. "Price is coming back, or so the Negroes running loose all over the Phelps farm say."

Correy rose from the bed and swayed. "You lying at me?"

"Get sober," Leighton said. "I'll need you."

He left Correy gripping one of the bedposts. Cora watched after him, for a moment on the doorstep, then hung her head and retreated inside.

At home, his days assumed the dull sameness of winter, dense gray skies that only threatened but never snowed, biting winds, and then a stillness so thick it made walking the floor a startling activity. He worked the horses to keep them fresh, and did not hunt, though he was always armed with the sawed off shotgun. Nights he read out loud to no one from the last book they had been able to buy from New York, Vanderhauf's *New Principles of Steam.* When he finished a particularly intricate section, he would look up, a question on his lips, but he was alone. The lamp wavered. The wind sucked against the stove pipe, from which no smoke came.

One afternoon when Leighton returned from working the horses, Judith stood at the back door. Leighton reined Chester's old horse. Judith smiled, then bowed her head. Her dress hung loosely about her waist. Her cheeks, which had been two bubbles that summer, were far less rounded.

"I wondered, Mister Leighton, if you was needing anything."

"Needing?"

"Washing. You look like you need some washing."

"I can't start a fire for it. Why wash?"

"Cooking, then?"

Leighton snorted.

She frowned, bowed her head. "Mister Leighton, we ain't got much. We slaughtered one of them hogs, and the other ain't worth chasing." She took a deep breath. "I can smell it's going to be a bad winter." Her voice dropped. "I do just about anything for just about nothing."

In the trees, bare branches rattled against one another. Now that most of the leaves were down, he could see blue threads of cooking fires above Springfield, where the war was, where the slaves were free for the moment.

"Nothing is all I can give you, now. Except for food, and there's little of that."

Judith nodded, frowning.

He stood very near her, his shadow falling over her. "Why didn't you come around the house? Why'd you stay away when they took my father?"

She raised her chin. "Nothing I could do to stop that. I ain't doing no fighting to defend you all."

"A coward, then?"

She snorted. "I was damned afraid. And I don't owe you all nothing."

Her arms were bare in the old sack dress she wore, and her skin was knobby with gooseflesh in the cold. Slowly he took off Johnson's old coat, put it around her shoulders. "Judith," he said, "you and Johnson and Isaac are the only ones who don't seem to be lying to me." He led her into the house.

In the kitchen before supper, Judith scrubbed at the slops trough, while Leighton sat down with his back to her. Her scraping strokes grew louder.

"What you going do?"

He turned to her. She stayed bent but held the dark cloth against the trough. In the candlelight, the cloth appeared yellow and black with grime.

"Stay with the stock. Try to hold on to what my pa has. There's no getting him out that I can see yet."

She shook her head. "You all was like magic. Opened up the earth and money come pouring out."

"I can't say everything's going to be all right," he said.

After a while she nodded. The cloth resumed its whispering circles.

She arrived each day just before noon, and often she brought up beans or rabbit stew that she had cooked in her cabin so that no fire had to be risked in the house. If there was no work to be done with the hogs, cows, or chickens, he sat for long hours in the study, cocooned in blankets, but still shivering. By evening he acquiesced to a fire, and he and Johnson, Judith, and Isaac sat around the kitchen table to dinner by the warmth of the stove. Johnson held his head high and rattled advice at Leighton until Leighton squeezed his glass with white knuckles. Judith shot a glance at her father. Things settled and they discussed the condition of the stock, which Johnson rotated from the barn to the woods, to sloughs, and to lean-tos he and Leighton built. Had they any neighbors near who cared a whit about them, they could have counted on a warning that soldiers—Rebel or Federal—were coming. But there would be no warning, no time to do the heroic and storied, no time for hiding quilts in hollow trees, muzzling mules, stuffing grown men under dresses. When Leighton rationed the fodder, the milk dwindled. Watching the lanky cows trundle down their worn path to the barn, the winter clouds of evening spreading like a tide of iron across the sky, Leighton gripped the bailing twine, twisting it until the hemp bit deep violet lines into his palms. Every possession he had seemed as flimsy, as light and easy to lose as the strands of hay that twirled loose from the bail and vanished into the dark.

On a winter morning, Leighton woke early and built a fire. He knelt and warmed his hands. The coffee was gone, so he was about to make sassafras tea. As he dully listened for the simmerings of the water, a knock came at the back door, rattling the kitchen and echoing through the house. He did not expect Judith until noon. Johnson Davis would have knocked, then entered. Even Isaac would have announced himself. Leighton reached for the shelf above the hat pegs and took the shotgun down.

The knock came again. Leighton peered from the kitchen window, and in the violet of dawn he saw four horses, riders standing next to them. He squinted. The riders wore coats of four different cuts, not dark in color like the coats of Federals, but gray and brown in the misty light. Their bedrolls and saddlebags were not standardized, were likely from home.

Leighton opened the door and raised the shotgun. A bearded man drew a revolver, and from the yard came the cocking of weapons.

"Hell of a way to greet a person," the bearded man said. His breath steamed around his face, and Leighton could hear a smile in his voice. His accent was high and nasal, and Leighton guessed Arkansas or Texas. "That's no way to open a door either. Next time if you're worried about who it is," he wobbled the nose of his pistol as if directing Leighton, "open the door a little and shout."

Leighton remained still. If he raised the gun, the four of them would surely kill him before he could shoot. But if he lowered the gun, what would these men see in the purple fog of dawn? Truce or just movement?

"Well, shoot or drop dead, boy. Are you touched?" The bearded man put his hands to his hips. "Believe we got us a Mungoloid here, gentlemen."

Leighton cleared his throat. "I'm going to put the gun down."

The bearded man raised his pistol. Leighton crouched and set the shotgun next to the step. The bearded man nodded. "Right sharp, kid." He holstered the pistol and stepped forward so that the shaft of light from the door fell full on him. His black beard grew thick and long under his chin. The skin beneath his beard was dark, but Leighton could not determine if this was filth or sun. Under his gray coat, he bristled with the butts of pistols and knives. "You alone, boy?"

Leighton shook his head. "Three niggers on the property."

The bearded man hesitated, then came forward again. "We's wondering what breakfast is about."

"About gone," he said. "But you're welcome."

The four tied their horses to an oak, and soon they were seated at the kitchen table. They reeked mightily of sweat, horses, and musty wool. They peeled the remains of gloves from their hands. The bearded man's coat was the most decorated, but it also bore a tangle of threads where it had been patched with yellow muslin and black thread along his right arm. He introduced himself as Captain Harry Ferguson of the First Texas Cavalry Division and Liaison to Major General Price. The men with him were all young boys. Only one wore a beard as full as Leighton's, and it was sandy blond. The others bore patches of scraggly whiskers, which they pulled at as they lolled in their seats. None of them removed their hats.

"Pardon, but God damn my ass is sore," one of the boys said.

The other two chortled.

Ferguson scowled at them. They fell silent, and did not speak the entire breakfast though they gulped and smacked at the biscuits and hard, salt-cured ham. No one had raised the wick on the lamp, so the men ate in a dim flicker, their shadows thin and wavering on the floor and tablecloth.

When he finished, Ferguson reclined and gawked around the kitchen. Leighton cleared the dishes, then sat and watched the Rebels over a hot cup of sassafras. Ferguson noted every fixture, each brass handled cabinet, the size of the Evertz stove. He sucked at something caught in his teeth, and the noise was like the griping of a rat.

Ferguson raised his eyebrows. "This really your house?"

Leighton nodded.

"What the hell you do for a living, then?"

"Mine."

"Lead?"

"Lime."

A smile crackled beneath Ferguson's whiskers. The boys, too, were watching Ferguson. So many weapons bristled from their belts that the three squirmed in their seats for comfort, constantly readjusting their sloppy regalia.

"You the man gave the Missouri Guard all that powder?" Ferguson asked.

"Is he?" asked one of the boys.

"You really that man?" the sandy-bearded boy asked.

"Sure he is," Ferguson said, smiling. "He's just had the God damn Union on him all of autumn and won't say. It's all right. We understand."

Leighton stroked his beard, watched Ferguson's eyes. He wondered if his beard had the Texan fooled as to his age, or if the Texan were trying to be solicitous. "Forgive me," Leighton said. "I'm his son. I'm afraid my father's in prison. I would've told you, but it's hard to be trusting anymore."

Ferguson nodded and pulled a grave frown. "How can you be? We seen your town. It's a shame what they done."

The boys all nodded, but as the man spoke Leighton wondered what Ferguson would have done if he found more in town.

Ferguson leaned back in his chair and with a grand wave of his hand, he began a briefing for Leighton on the status of the war. "You see this maneuver is just winter distance," Ferguson said. "Our great victory at Lexington is but one of many triumphs." The Grand Army of the Potomac was routed and McClellan dead. Confederate mortars were pounding Washington.

A French fleet anchored off New Orleans. Texas conquered all of Mexico north of the equator. It was a confusing and beautiful picture, garnished with details like McClellan's zinc casket and color guard, the names of the French men-of-war, the streets and monuments in Washington that were devastated. It made Leighton tremble.

"Let me be real straight with you," Ferguson said, leaning forward as if there were someone eavesdropping. "My adjutments and I are looking for a place to winter. Now if you take us in, us four, you will have taken on the official emissary and cavalry advisory entourage from the state of Texas to the government of Missouri and Sterling Price."

The word *adjutments* puzzled Leighton. "And you four are all there is?"

Ferguson smiled. He nudged the boy next to him, who sat straighter and stared hard at Leighton. "Missouri," Ferguson said to his companions. "What I'm saying is, you take us in, and you'll not worry about any other foraging done on you."

"And if I don't?" Leighton asked.

Ferguson leaned back and pulled at his beard. "Then no hard feelings." He shrugged. "And I'll let the State Guard know the good man who give them powder is serving most meals at his house which I can lead folks right to."

One of the boys snorted and laughed, holding a hand to his mouth. The other two glanced at him, and he quieted but gripped his sides.

"How do I know you'll prevent other foraging?"

"You have my word as a Texan, and a gentleman of the South."

Leighton smiled and shook his head. "We'll see."

Ferguson glared and his hand moved to the butt of the pistol.

Deep in the stove, a log cracked like a detonation in a well.

"My family has been shat all over by this war so far."

"Oh? Do go on, son." Ferguson's black eyes twinkled.

"Missouri army left, and took with them what we needed to make money, and just last month the Federals took my father prisoner. I find it hard to trust either side in this."

131

"Well, boys." Ferguson glanced at each of his cohorts. All but the sandy-bearded one were wide-eyed and glancing between Leighton and Ferguson. The blond was regarding Leighton with a slight smile. "I ain't sure if I have a Secessionist, a Unionist, or some sort of hillbilly pacifist on my hands."

Leighton kept the most indifferent glance he could muster on Ferguson.

"Ain't you a cool-handed mick?" Ferguson asked. "Whose side are you for, then?"

One of the boys rubbed his thumb along his bottom lip. His thumb and the inside of his palm were stained deep rust. They had either poached an animal, or they had been killing. "I suppose I can do my part for those who help my state. If that's what you do."

"You just called me a liar."

"You could have killed me before you ate. That would have been honest."

Ferguson stared at him. "I don't need to kill you, boy."

"Good, then." Leighton felt his arm tremble. "You stay, and maybe you'll teach me again to believe in Southern promises."

Ferguson cocked his head back, a huge grin on his face. It was the grin of a man who was quite prepared to kill him, but found it wasn't necessary. Ferguson looked at each of the boys. "God damn," he said. "I be God damned!"

The Texans brought in their bedrolls, and by ten a.m. they were snoring on the parlor floor.

IV

SOON, MORKAN SLEPT AT EASE WITH RODENTS SCURRYING
over him. Only when they bit was he disturbed. His fever and
cough became something he lived with, learning nights to tight-
en his chest and hold his ribs still as if they were a glass orna-
ment, and then to draw sweet air through the dense phlegm.

He paced and waited, listened at the boarded window,
counted and tried to recall the voices and different footsteps he
heard coming and going. Food came through a slat in the door
twice a day, but the tin cup of water that tasted of moss and
rotten wood and was meant to last the entire day would not fit
and so the shackled Negro opened the door and left the cup inside. His cell door opened three mornings since Nimms extorted
him in Billy Lynch's courtyard. A saber of gray light marked
mornings; a square of light, the boarded window through which
he had examined slaves not ten years previous, marked daylight
hours. Mid-mornings, two guards stood near Morkan's window,
talked without fail about chewing tobacco and what gunboats
were entering portage. With evening the cell turned winter blue,
and then came darkness, awful and long.

He wondered if Johnson had listened that way at these
windows, had looked with any hope on the white faces that
purveyed him and his daughter. Surely the Morkan house on
Tenth and Bodley was better than the awful hull of a slaver
or this prison? But that was something he could never be sure
of. The humiliating irony of his situation was not lost on him.
The shackled, water-bearing Negro, the rodents, the night bells
he often thought of as missives Johnson left here for him. He
tumbled in his mind the paths that brought him to prison—he
purchased Johnson and Judith at auction for $955.00. There was
no morality to it. Purchasing slaves was legal and practical for

Morkan in 1846. Johnson could be immediate help to Charlotte, and the young Negress could be trained, maybe sold if not
needed. The only other maid he hired before cost him $2.00 a
week. These two Negros would pay for themselves in roughly
four-and-a-half-years. They were help for Charlotte and his
family just started, and to him, the preservation and happiness
of Charlotte and the boy was the only moral principle that made
any sense. It was a wondrous formula, like velocity equaling the
distance traveled divided by time. Every decision of life could be
examined through these fixed tenets: Charlotte, the boy, their
well being. He dismissed abolitionist pamphlets that jabbered
about cathauling and families busted apart. They were noise
to him. If slavery was practical and a majority supported it, it
would survive. If it damaged commerce, it would be eliminated.
Of course, he relinquished the powder based on the notion that
doing so might save his son, the only family left, and the quarry,
the only sustenance that family knew. Relinquishing the powder
had morality and sense behind it, even if his death were the
result. If Leighton could keep the quarry, it would all be set to
right in his mind.

Taking Johnson and Judith home that first day, Morkan was
skeptical about the basic premise that a slave would do work
despite the driver's reassurances. Even the most dunderheaded
whites could see through a bad arrangement and find ways to
avoid work entirely. He imagined a Negro might react similarly.
Johnson, though, was bought from a plantation that went under
in Arkansas, the driver said, and Judith came from the same
plantation. They both knew what work was according to the
driver.

"You understand what has happened?" he asked Johnson
that day, speaking loudly and slowly, wondering how Missourians born into this institution handled a new slave.

Johnson scanned the windows of the house on Bodley
then nodded. Glass, had the Negro ever seen it before then on
a house so small? His head was squat, and his broad forehead
always creased, as if he were deeply concerned about something.

"Good. This is my house. This is Mrs. Charlotte. She will
tell both of you what to do." Each statement rose like a question.

"Well, they look fine, Michael," Charlotte said. Her face was heavy then, with Leighton's birth approaching. She scowled at Judith, held the pickaninny's arms up. "She's a little 'un, but I bet she can lift the washing basket."

Judith's mouth dropped open. "Sure I lift a basket, Mrs."

Charlotte had died away from Morkan, quarantined in the smallpox camp outside of Springfield, her body taken from him, strangers washing it, and strangers sitting the night with it. Quarry men and church busybodies at her Mass and burial and no true friends to come for a wake. No last words, no final touch of fingertips. Riven, he cursed God and nearly throttled the dismayed Father Brian when he and Cora brought the news. After listless, sleepless, hollow weeks, he dreamt Charlotte came to him one last time. She wore a peasant cloak and no finery. Her hair was gray but shining, skin wrinkled, but healthy, unblemished. She bade him sit on the bench under the dogwoods at her grave. And said nothing, and Morkan could not speak lest he shatter the reverie. At last she took his hand. "St. Patrick was a slave, Michael," she said. He woke with a shout of agony, losing her again. Then he freed them, Judith, Johnson, Chester, Bragg, Bundum, Isaac.

Late that night, Morkan jolted from sleep. The stillness of the prison cell told him something was frightening the rats. A yellow lance of light sliced the floor and widened. He sat up. Two guards stepped in the door, one with a lantern. He shielded his eyes.

They hoisted a prisoner from where he rested against the door. With his feet dragging, they hauled him across the cell, plopped him in a heap in the corner. A second prisoner stepped in and sat across from Morkan. As if in farewell, he raised both shackled hands at the guards. They left without a glance at him.

The cell was silent after they shut the door, save for the labored breathing of the prisoner the guards had dragged in. Morkan held his own breath for a time, then cleared his throat. "I'm Morkan."

"Porter Moore."

Outside the window, voices murmured, and Morkan could hear chains slinking and thumping on the boardwalk.

"Listen at all them prisoners out there," Porter Moore said.

"Prisoners?"

"Hundreds. They're moving them in. That's why you got company."

"Where they from?"

"Probably from around Springfield was where they got caught, but they could be from anywhere around there or Boonville, or Newtonia."

"Are they all soldiers? Any civilians?"

"I'm sure a couple are civilians, but the most are soldiers."

Morkan paused. "You seem to answer things readily. Sounds like you're sure."

"Sergeant Nimms told me. I don't see where he'd lie."

"Why would a Federal sergeant tell a prisoner something like that?"

Porter Moore was silent, and Morkan wondered if the newcomer might be some kind of spy, someone Nimms sent.

"Well, I shouldn't say this, but I'm sort of a special case."

"That so?"

Outside, the feet on the boardwalk shuffled and clanked.

"Sergeant Nimms." Porter Moore's voice became quiet. "He's one of the best men this side of the river. He's keeping me from trial. They bring me up on the docket at the provost and Nimms goes there to represent me. I stay high and dry here. He's seen me through two dockets and convinced them I ain't nothing but a drunken dandy who got caught up with a bunch of Rebs without aiming to." Porter Moore snuffled, and Morkan worried that he was starting to weep.

"You know Sergeant Nimms?" Porter Moore asked.

"Would that I did," Morkan said.

Later that morning, the door opened and a guard lifted Morkan, tossed a sack over his head and yanked it tight at his neck.

Outside snow fell against his hands. A cold wind pushed the burlap bag flat against his neck. Guards tossed him in a wagon piled with other grumbling prisoners. For a long time they loped through the streets, wind whistling and snow stinging. Then he was yanked from the wagon and marched up a flight of stairs.

Someone whipped the bag off Morkan's head. The dimly lit room was high-ceilinged and octagonal. The floors were hardwood, and even above the onion odor clinging to his beard, Morkan caught the powerful smell of lye. The room reminded him of a lecture hall without chairs. Squat black stoves were arranged next to each of four columns, and the stoves were caged in a baroque arrangement of cast iron, as if scraps from ornate iron work were welded together. Guards directed prisoners to blankets rolled and stuffed against the walls.

Once they all took bedrolls, the guards made them face the center of the room. The stove nearest Morkan held a fire flickering through the black grate, and he could hardly keep his eyes off the orange warmth of it.

An officer stepped to the middle of the room, and the guards shouted for attention. Some of the prisoners actually stiffened their chests, locked their knees.

The plump officer raised both of his hands above his head, then began to speak. "I am Colonel J.W. Tuttle. There are rules you need to know." His voice carried in the room. "Unless eating, all prisoners are to keep their hands stabilized at their sides. No light save the light of a stove shall retain itself after sunset." He paused between sentences as if waiting to hear the echo. "No prisoner shall attempt to manipulate a stove or make water into the cage surrounding a stove. No prisoner may keep or hold coal or wood. Prisoners are positively forbidden to project their heads, arms or legs outside of the windows or to project spittle out of the windows, the sentinels being instructed to, after warning the offender, shoot the prisoner dead."

Tuttle paused, scanned the room. They were a ragged lot, red and brown with filth, clothes motley and bulky, slouch hats and bowlers, campaign hats, even a top hat on one fellow, rabbit fur, fox fur, a tattered buffalo robe, a woman's lace shawl thrown over one man's chest draped with all the dash of a cape Napoleon might have worn. Morkan estimated there were two hundred men in the room. "You will be joined by many," Tuttle continued. Morkan spotted Overbo by the slight bald spot on the back of the massive reverend's head. He kept his eyes focused there as if on a light.

"That is all. Sentinels, bed them down!"

Guards began grabbing men shoving them to the floor where they stood. Expecting to be shoved, Morkan lowered himself to sit and then lay flat. As Tuttle crossed the room, several prisoners reached out to him with complaints about their wounds or requests for water and food. He stopped before one who had both hands out, his fingers dandling like a babe's. The prisoner was no more than Leighton's age, if that.

"Stabilize your hands!" Tuttle shouted.

Cringing, the boy jerked his hands down at his sides.

That first night the sentinels walked aisles created by sleeping prisoners, corridors of human lumps visible in the room only by the orange glow of the stoves. They kicked any prisoner that stirred in a way they didn't appreciate.

Morkan stretched his legs a little, bumped another prisoner's head with his heel. The prisoner grunted. Despite the crowding, Morkan was glad to be warm, glad to have Overbo nearby. He gathered the ragged blanket close to him. It stunk of quinine. If he had to die, maybe he could tolerate it in a place like this.

He woke himself coughing. So many voices muttered around him, he wondered for a moment if he were still in a dream. In the sunlight pouring through the windows he could see gray and white clouds moving above the square brick boarding houses and roofs of the city. He sat up. Overbo scooted a tin cup to him and opened a handkerchief in which a gray clump quaked.

"You had to be awake for it," the reverend said. "I'll wake you next morning if I'm up. Will you wake me if I'm sleeping?"

Morkan nodded, drank from the cup. It was barrel water. His dried tongue spread open like a flower. He scooped his fingers in the gray mush, had no idea what it was, but finished all that Overbo had saved, then took a drink of the barrel water.

Men were crowded at the windows, pushing and nosing each other for better views while they kept their hands flat against their sides. With their grimy, whiskered faces turned to follow a white winter sun slanting down from the glass, they reminded Morkan of fish churning below a spillway,.

"Where are we?" Overbo asked.

Morkan looked around, shrugged.

138

"Thought you were from St. Louis?"

Morkan picked at the handkerchief, popped morsels of the gray mush into his mouth. He paused, looked up at the reverend. "How dirty is this?"

Overbo shrugged. "I rubbed it in some snow on the train."

Morkan nodded. Overbo blinked at him, then turned away. Morkan hunched, placed the handkerchief in his mouth and dragged it through his clenched teeth, sucking on it. His mouth filled with mush, grit, and a salty taste. He finished the water, trembling, his throat bobbing to keep the goo down.

Overbo nodded at the window. "Get some sun." He helped Morkan up. The windows were at least seven feet tall, arched at their peaks and barred with iron work. With Overbo's broad form plowing the path for them, they made their way through the crowd of prisoners who muttered and pushed against them.

Overbo turned his head but kept moving forward as they walked into the sun. "They brought in a trainload at dawn. That's why it's so awful crowded." The collar to Overbo's gray coat was turning greenish black.

Morkan recognized the street. Gratiot. Across from them were boarding houses where the surgery students stayed. This was the Surgeon's Academy and Medical College. Out in the cold, snow scuttled in eddies that sparkled blue and purple and searing white. "God," Morkan gasped.

Overbo glanced at him.

It was St. Louis, but the streets were nearly abandoned. The window looked over a business district, a barber shop, a tailor's, a medical supply warehouse, a carriage service all of which had operated on Gratiot and Eighth. No one was out. The streets were almost without carriage ruts. The snow in some alleys was pristine. This was once a bustling, scrappy River city. Here for the first time on these streets he had seen lime and cinder blocks, cut limestone in use, the stone that would become his vocation. The Cathedral seemed solid but barn-like, appropriate for the Irish who had worshipped in secret Mass in barns. He met Charlotte there, courted her by the River, watching steamboats chuff, their tall wheels whitening the water. A city of trade and change as constant as that of a sand bar on the River. Since the war began, he had grown accustomed to seeing Springfield abandoned, but to see St. Louis quieted this way stunned him.

Outside a column of gray and brown bundled prisoners marched for the college. Federals, their uniforms almost dark black, cordoned them.

The prisoners were from all across Missouri, and some were from Texas, Arkansas, Southern Illinois, Mississippi, Tennessee. They were infantrymen, mail carriers, bushwhackers, spies, deserters, arms dealers, and politicians, the fools and founders club of the Confederacy in the West.

Morkan and Overbo spent the morning by the largest stove where a drummer boy, a new comer, held court. His name was Horatio and he was oracular and spoke in the voices of the dead, his partners said. They were all from a unit that fought at Athens, Missouri, far north of St. Louis. Horatio sat cross-legged on the floor, and the interested prisoners did likewise. Horatio had a round yellow face and the dullest brown eyes Morkan had ever seen. His hair was black and curly, and he wore his tattered gray uniform with the top two collar buttons fastened, the rest loose. He sat, eyes glassy; then with no warning he began clucking like a chicken, his head bobbing. Settling again, he rattled a string of filthy invectives that set the prisoners roaring with laughter. Overbo turned so red, Morkan held his arm to keep him from leaving.

After a period of calm in which Horatio's partners again touted the boy's ability to contact the dead and speak their messages, Horatio began to shiver. His eyes rolled back in his head, and he slumped and jerked as if in a fantod. Then he sat up rod straight. Tendons, like taut cables, stood out along his neck, and his skin went fire red as he let loose of a scream that silenced the room and lasted for nearly half a minute. When he finished, the prisoners applauded, popping their palms against their legs.

Horatio glared at all of them for a long time.

Overbo turned to Morkan. "You reckon he's possessed?"

Morkan nodded. "Completely."

Horatio pointed at Morkan. At the stove, the guard was too engrossed to warn the boy against raising his hands above his waist. Horatio gurgled, then sat still and was clucking along again.

"Hey!" One of the prisoners stood and dusted himself off. "That it?"

Nimms crossed the crowd, weaving between prisoners. Under his arm, he carried the Morocco-bound notebook. Morkan stiffened.

Another prisoner was on his feet. "Yeah. I didn't set through that scream just to hear him make animal sounds. Set them dead people to talking."

Nimms knelt to a point just at Morkan's ear. "Were this not wartime, don't you imagine your state would have our dear drummer boy there licking salt peter in some quiet asylum? But here we have sent him to fight for the rebellion. War is good, eh?"

Nimms rose and strode to stand beside Horatio. Nimms addressed the gathering in a commanding, smooth voice. "The boy merely suffers from a form of St. Vitus's dance." The sergeant's brown hair appeared freshly washed, shining in the winter light. He raised his palm and the Morocco notebook beside Horatio's ear and ordered the boy to face the front. Horatio complied. Nimms brought his hand against the notebook right at the boy's ear creating a thunderous clap.

The boy gave what appeared to be a natural shudder, but then his shoulders bucked, and he collapsed, his head thrashing against his knees.

Nimms smirked at them all. He bowed slightly.

One of Horatio's partners blushed and covered his face.

Horatio sat upright, his jaw clenched. "I am the King of the Franks," he shouted in passable French. "What is the meaning of this? Where is the Pope?"

Some of the prisoners chuckled. The rest whispered that the dead spoke that way, that was their language for sure.

Morkan nudged Overbo. "Seems he's Charlemagne."

"*Où est le Pape?*" Horatio bounced as he said each word.

Morkan stood. Nimms raised his eyebrows.

When Morkan stepped forward, Horatio snapped to attention, his eyes on Morkan, his square chin jutting proudly. Morkan held his hands before him, the tips of his fingers pressed together and curved to make an oval crown. Nimms stepped back. The guard at the stove put a hand to his revolver, but Nimms waved him off.

Horatio swelled his chest, arched his back.

Morkan raised his hands in an oval high above Horatio's head. "I Pius the Nine, Bishop of Rome, crown thee, Charlemagne, King of the Franks, King of the Lombards, Duke of Saxony, Baron of Tuscany as *Carolus Romanus,* first Holy Roman Emperor, Horatio, Bold Protector."

He rested his hands on the curls of Horatio's head. Horatio closed his eyes, bowed his head slightly, pressed his palms together as if in prayer. The prisoners were silent behind him. Nimms' jaw buckled.

Morkan dropped his hands, made the sign of the cross above Horatio's bowed head. Then he knelt on one knee, bowed his head, but kept his gaze on Horatio. The boy's dull eyes watched him, but a smile hung on his lips. "Pope Adrian, you fool," Horatio whispered. He winked at Morkan, then pumped both fists in the air.

The prisoners whooped, threw their hats, clambered to their feet, shackles ringing. Several sentinels rushed over.

"Hands at your sides!" Nimms shouted. He smacked Horatio's arms.

Sentinels in the crowd thumped prisoners with cudgels. They scattered.

Overbo grabbed Morkan by the elbow, tried to pull him away. "What did you do that for?" he whispered in Morkan's ear.

Nimms stepped before Morkan. "You come with me."

Overbo held Morkan for a moment. Nimms cocked his head at the reverend, inserted the tip of a revolver between Overbo's fingers and Morkan's arm. Overbo released him.

As Nimms led Morkan from the room, sentinels were forcing the prisoners to lie flat against the floor, pushing cudgels and the butts of revolvers into their backs. Squalling, Horatio was lifted to his feet, then flattened against the floor, two sentinels cramming boots against him.

Nimms led Morkan across the crowded room. They reached a spiral staircase, tromped up the stairs. The ball strung to the shackles on his legs thumped as it hit each stair. After dragging it around so long, he had almost forgotten it, and he bent to pick it up. They reached a wide, bare alcove from which four hallways proceeded. Finally they stopped. Nimms flipped through the Morocco notebook and ushered Morkan into one of the rooms. Two large windows lit the room white, but frost crawled high on the glass, and he couldn't see the city. There was a large table, the wooden top of which was thick enough for a butcher's chopping block. On the walls hung wide floor-to-ceiling banners on which Morkan could see the outlines of human forms. Nimms set his notepad down and lit a lamp, placed the lamp in the midst of the table. As the light rose, the banners revealed full size paintings of nude cadavers with various body parts exposed, the flesh peeled back and pinned down.

"That was an act of genius," Nimms said. "An act of empathy like I would never have imagined of you."

Morkan stared at him.

"Of course it was a terrible disruption, and you better never do such a thing again." Nimms paced. "We can't have Tuttle discovering that you are a troublemaker. No. That will botch anything I do to delay your trial." He tapped his chin. "Do you need reminding you are a traitor, Morkan, a civilian insurgent? I have no way of exchanging you with the enemy. Now I have to explain outbursts such as this?"

"Kill me," Morkan said. "Hang me tonight." He cleared his throat, rested his hip against the wooden table's edge.

"That's it!" Nimms said. "Duress, the notion of the full confession you were about to make caused your aberrant behavior."

Morkan blinked at him. Nimms ran the tip of his tongue along his upper lip. He placed the notebook next to Morkan, pulled the steel pen from inside his coat. "Here, now. I want you to write out a full confession. Write out everything you have stored aside for your son, where it is stored, its relative value, and so on."

He extended the pen and an inkwell, but Morkan did not take them.

Nimms stiffened. "A confession will save you, and it may save your son."

"You have Leighton?"

Nimms nodded. "Just arrived in St. Louis." His face had lost some of its smile, and was flat and unemotive again, as if Leighton's arrival were no more important than the arrival of a skiff at the dock.

"May I see him?"

"Of course not."

"Then, why should I believe you?"

"I don't care if you do or not." Nimms busied himself arranging sheets of parchment and his pen on the table for Morkan. "You must understand, as a sympathizer, the only way you can come clean with me is to show me all you have, to show me that you can't do more damage. And if we release your son, assure us that he won't return home capable of aiding the Rebellion."

Morkan crossed his arms over his chest.

Nimms sighed. "From our chats, it seems to me that only two things matter to you in this world. The boy. And that quarry. I would say money, but money is but a match for any fire of life." Nimms smoothed his small fingers across the parchment. "Mr. Morkan, tell me. Do you have either of those things now? That quarry? The boy?"

The words hit Morkan like a blow. The prison was quiet, and yet with all the humanity crammed inside it there rose along its timbers a whisper, a churn of breathing and sighing and farting and weeping, snoring and dying.

"You do realize those are things you will never have nor hold again?" Nimms asked. "They are dead to you, as dead as you will soon be to them."

Morkan hugged his chest again, shut his eyes tightly. Nimms was right: the constants in the moral equation he used all along were likely gone. Leighton could be in prison, conscripted in the army, or dead.

Nimms bowed his head. "I leave you to your work. You have an hour. And the pen I must have back." He left.

Morkan stood before the diagram of the eviscerated body. Slowly he caught his breath, a struggle he had waited to endure until Nimms left. The man in the diagram was powerfully muscled. His bones were white; blue veins and red arteries crawled in and out of crimson flesh. One of his eyeballs was furiously exposed, cables of gristle attached to an egg that bulged into the agate of a pupil. Above him was a banner with the word *EXCISION* printed at the top, and beneath this were cross sections of limbs and joints and diagrams for the grafting and reattachment of appendages. Morkan fingered the banner, felt where water had puckered it. The eviscerated man was artfully drawn, like old Renaissance maps of the world. There were some lines and divergences to which Morkan could attach no significance, as if beneath the skin of man there were still some magical, inexplicable engines, sacs and organs the powers of which even yet escaped the reckoning of medicine and the mind.

If Leighton were in custody, then Morkan's moral equation changed. But he was still unsure of how to proceed. If he disclosed the money they salvaged from Weitzer, the stock from the quarry, what guarantee did he have that Leighton would be saved in any way? And if he saved Leighton after giving everything over to Nimms, where would Leighton be when the war ended? And why did Nimms care more about assets easily obtained by ransacking the house and yard? Because Nimms operated alone and beyond the pale. There would be no record of what Nimms would do. Prisoner shot while escaping, the old, official British lines in Ireland. Lamentably, prisoner took his own life.

Porter Moore thought he was a special case when Nimms saved him from trial. What did Nimms already have from Porter Moore? When the war was finally won, Nimms stood to be a very wealthy man indeed.

The thigh of the eviscerated man was a particularly grotesque explosion of vein and meat. What would Cora have thought of the drawing, veins she knew by rote?

Morkan took the pen and paper. The dissecting table was so scarred and rife with divots and pinholes that he had difficulty writing. He wrote out an exact description of what Price and McBride wanted, everything they said, of their intention to fight the Federals until the Federals left them alone, to beat the Federals all the way back to St. Louis, then take St. Louis.

The banner on the wall was so brightly colored that in the sunlight it cast a red patina over the room. He went on to describe McBride coming to pick up the powder. Then he wrote brief opinions of the two generals. It was a full confession. And it said nothing Nimms wanted.

Nimms returned. "Finished?"

Morkan extended the sheet to him.

Nimms took it, blinked at it, scanning it, his eyes darted back and forth.

"I see," Nimms said. He drew his revolver again, and Morkan tensed. Nimms took him by the arm. "There's someone here to see you, then." They walked the hallway, down stairs to a battered door, under which Morkan could feel the draught of winter groping. The wind paced back and forth, like a wildcat behind a menagerie's cage. Against his legs and the exposed parts of his feet, blue flecks of snow burned. Nimms opened the door and they descended a set of stairs so rotten the boards sagged beneath Morkan's bare soles. Two flights down and they were on the brick floor of a courtyard. The cat of winter howled, lifted Morkan's shoulders and shook them. Back against the courtyard walls were stacks of new pine coffins, piles of coal, dozens of molds for soap. A rime of snow and ice piled amongst the supplies.

In the midst of the courtyard were three telegraph poles sawed off to stand about eight feet high. Six feet up on each, two railroad spikes were hammered in. From the two poles on the outside hung prisoners, their arms bound together above their heads and tied at the wrists with whipcord. The railroad spikes held their wrists up. Heads bowed. Bodies limp. The blue of frost covered their tattered, motley clothes.

"Come," Nimms said. The sullenness of Nimms's voice, the red brick of the courtyard, the sound of the ball grinding along behind Morkan's ankle, the two prisoners frozen and unmoving filled Morkan with panic. For the first moment in all his captivity, real fear ran through him.

Nimms poked Morkan in the side with the revolver, then pressed Morkan's back against the pole.

Nimms glanced behind as if awaiting someone. He put his face very close to Morkan. Stooped from all the coughing and thinned from the rations, Morkan was still taller than Nimms, whose lips seemed to move now against Morkan's Adam's apple.

The sergeant whispered. "Look at these beside you, Morkan. They were healthy. You are ill. I know it." He gazed over Morkan's shoulder. When he did, Morkan saw windows, black squares on all the floors sweeping up from the courtyard, and at them the white ovals of faces watching. Nimms hid his lips so his words could not be divined.

When the wind hit the courtyard, the world shuddered. The cold beat tears from his eyes and froze the hairs in Morkan's nose so that they burned and stood on end.

Nimms awaited the wind's passing with the calm of long experience in this pit. When it abated, he whispered again. "This is the closet in which we come to pray to our God in secret. And Morkan, you'll pray. See the iron gate there?"

Across the courtyard was a tall, black, iron-barred gate, beyond it, blinding snow.

"Nod that you see the gate," Nimms insisted, pushing the muzzle of the revolver against him.

Morkan nodded.

"Good. Raise your hands, slowly. Place your wrists against the rail spikes behind your head there. That's it." Nimms watched Morkan's hands. "Cross your wrists. There. Exactly. Now imagine them tied." Nimms smiled. "They will not be."

"Through that gate there, Morkan, Satan will come striding. Across that courtyard, striding to see you." The silver of Nimms's breath purled at Morkan's collar, and was suddenly wet, warm, and disturbingly comforting. "When he comes, he'll assume you're secure, tied like these two poor Rebs here. You must not drop your wrists, lest he kill you in his surprise." Nimms' eyebrows bobbed. "And when he is finished, I feel certain you will want to tell me where all your funds are, every bit of treasure."

Nimms eased away, and Morkan felt the urge to call him back. "That is, unless you strangle him," Nimms said. He raised the Morocco notebook to hide his lips. "You are a free-willed creature. Stay very still, Morkan. Very still. Move not a hair."

Nimms turned. The wind again walloped the courtyard, throwing up whirling miasmas of snow in the sergeant's wake. The door shut, and the courtyard became silent.

Breathing cautiously, Morkan stilled himself. One of the prisoners next to him listed, the whipcords creaking. Very soon, his forehead tightened in the cold, and the spikes at his wrists became animate, like the jaws of two lampreys gnawing. The wind played tricks, threw steps out in the courtyard, iron-shod boots, a long shadow coming.

Morkan began to mutter over and over the old prayer of his mother's in the same rapid, manic whisper his mother used praying when all had fallen to naught and there was no more hope. "Now goeth sunne under wode. Me rueth, Mary, thy Son's fair rode. Now goeth sunne under tree. Me rueth, Mary, thy Son and thee."

The gates parted and across the courtyard walked a tall, black-bearded officer with silver eyes, a black hood pulled back to show rosy ears, boots shining beneath a dusting of snow and a spatter of horse dung. Heron.

Morkan jolted but then recalled he was not tied; he must stay still. Heron smiled showing just the tips of his white teeth.

"Morkan," Heron said as if tasting the name. "When I spoke with Sergeant Nimms, I could hardly believe." His eyes narrowed. "What things conjoin, collide in this universe! Here I am in St. Louis, arguing for a commission in Springfield to build forts from this fine quarry I know there. And I find the owner: why he has given powder to the Rebel Army, to Price," Heron hissed. "And he is in custody at Gratiot." The silver of Heron's eyes glinted like the barrel of a gun just blued. "And from the look of things he is not cooperating."

Morkan bit his lip. If he moved, Heron would know he was not tied.

Heron glanced along Morkan's arms and down to his waist. "And his son, the good sergeant says, in custody as well. So rather than assistance at this quarry—or worse resistance—from recalcitrant owners, I will find nothing but the lime, white as the flesh of a boiled cod."

Heron's teeth jutted slightly, and this pushed his lips forward. Their wetness made his lips gleam with hunger as if greed embrocated his palate. "Whatever made you think that you and your son and a business were more valuable than the lives of hundreds of boys from Missouri and Iowa?"

Morkan's fingers, completely numb now, began to curl downward. Holding still with his arms above his head took such a delicate balance of muscle that all along his back and neck little ruptures of pain cracked open and pulsed. Here was the ultimate negater of all ideals—pain, the force that made null any moral equation, that made even Christ cry unto God about forsaking him.

Heron circled the pole, walking with his head down. "You know, Morkan, this war some will say is about slavery and the abolition of it as an institution. Some will say it concerns states' rights. Some will even say it's economics. I say it is none of those."

Morkan slumped forward. His lower spine was an aching shaft. In his mind, he envisioned ore cars tumbling over a precipice, the rails disappearing, the bridge a smoldering wreck, and the locomotive charging into the void. Good, kill them, I hope thousands of you have died, he thought, watching the tips of Heron's shining boots.

"No. Slavery and state's rights are all parcels of the same problem: The Determination of Our Frontier, and I don't mean just the West. I mean humanity and its limits. What's the American credo? The will to push away from the civilized into the wilderness, away from the dreary and commonplace persecutions of town and gentry and into an infinity of possibilities. Freedom."

When the wind clapped the courtyard, Morkan nearly lunged.

"The war in the East some are trying to tout as the first of its kind: a war to set men free," Heron battled with a match for a minute, then managed to light it against the telegraph pole just behind Morkan's back. Morkan trembled. "Here in the West, I say we are fighting a war to ensure the end of that sort of freedom, an end to the freedom that only takes care of oneself and one's livelihood, the freedom that lets a lesser race languish in hard labor, ignorance, and squalor. The freedom that dictates to the educated and well-off that it is their right to be left alone to their decisions. This in the West is the real war and the only war, not the war of freedom, then, but the war to bring willful men to the rule of justice." Heron smiled. "When I walk, a conqueror, through the gates of what was once your quarry, justice will be served." He glanced at the two Rebels crumpled alongside Morkan. "If you have to endure this too often, you'll die of consumption, Morkan. I have seen it happen. Best tell Nimms anything he needs to know."

Morkan kept still, though he was fighting both his muscles and his heart. Heron gave him a smug salute and turned on his heels.

After what seemed an hour or more, Nimms returned. "Keep still now. Keep those hands up there." He approached, revolver drawn. "Morkan, it's so simple. And if you don't tell me, the likes of him will have all you've hidden and your quarry anyway."

"Hang me," Morkan said.

Nimms bowed his head. Then he stepped behind the pole. With a sigh, he began to tie the rope around Morkan's wrists for the first time. "You should have killed him when you had the chance. Now you'll suffer for it."

V

LEIGHTON'S STOVE BLAZED WARMLY EVERY DAY FOR A WEEK. Beside the front steps hung the flag of rebellion the Arkies had carried, but also a small red standard reading **1ST TEX CAV DIV**. The boys—Charley, Hoyt, and Bert, the sandy-haired one—slept in the parlor. Harry Ferguson settled in the master bedroom upstairs.

The quality of Johnson Davis's horse angered the Texans when they first saw the Negro riding it. Leighton stepped to the front porch one afternoon and found Johnson Davis and the gelding surrounded by the Texas boys. Ferguson shouted questions at the Negro from the steps. The horse rolled its eyes at the groping hands of the Texans. To keep the horse from kicking them, Johnson Davis leaned hard on the reins.

"Leave my hand be," Leighton shouted. Once he spoke, he felt as if he leapt off a cliff. His voice was loud, full of an authority far different than what he wielded at the quarry. His shout was an attempt at the sound of ownership and mastery. After hesitating a moment and glancing at Ferguson, the Texas boys withdrew from circling Johnson.

"Whose horse has he got?" Ferguson asked.

"His horse," Leighton said. After he spoke, his throat bound up as if someone were squeezing it.

Ferguson squinted at him, and when Leighton didn't flinch, Ferguson nodded. "Just promoting general welfare. Didn't look like his horse."

In the name of general welfare and the common defense, Ferguson took inventory of the Morkans' stock. As Ferguson wandered back from the barn, hawing at the three bony cows, Johnson leaned close to Leighton's ear.

"We going be lucky we don't all get killed by these fellows."

151

"Johnson," Leighton said, "we are lucky right now." His teeth were clenched and Johnson backed up when he saw this. "Let me tell you something. You've been strutting around here fathering me. It's got to quit. These dudes think I'm as good as my pa here. They think I'm in charge. I'm the son of the fellow that gave the Rebels powder and they think I own this place. Now, they got a very different way of thinking about how a Negro can act. There ain't a lot of freedmen in Texas." Ferguson had almost reached the gate from the barn. "You better start acting like a 'umble nigger real quick, or we will need more guns than luck."

Johnson stuck his jaw forward, watched the Texan approach. But Leighton could see pain in the corners of his eyes. "Yes, sir," he said to Leighton, just as the Texan took the front steps, boots scraping on the stairs. "Yes, sir, Mister Morkan, I do that."

Ferguson strode to them, took the cigar from his mouth.

Johnson removed his slouch hat, bowed his head. "Mister Ferguson, sir?"

"Yep."

"I apologize for my horse. I will endeavor to be more polite with him."

Ferguson blinked. "Be sure," he said.

Johnson bowed his head, backed away from Ferguson, and did not turn until he was almost inside the house, a move he executed with accomplished grace. Leighton was so amazed, he was hardly attentive to the fact that Ferguson was speaking.

"I said, 'At least you *do* get results out of them.'"

Leighton nodded.

"Did he say '*endeavor*?'" Ferguson wrinkled his brow at Leighton. "Jesus! You ain't one of those owners that teaches them things to read are you?" Ferguson asked.

"I think the girl can read some. But no, I wouldn't teach them to read."

"I knew a fellow once in Louisiana, crazy Catholic," Ferguson said. "He owned two dozen head, and taught them all to speak Latin. And worse, he made 'em speak it, would whup 'em if he heard anything else."

"What the hell for?"

"Something to pass time. You're rich. You know. Surely you got to find ways to piddle time?"

Leighton squinted at him. "They learned it?"

"Hell, yes," Ferguson said. "They're right smart. Learn anything if you whupped them enough. Pretty soon that fellow had a whole passle of niggers that'd just babble, and unless you knew that Latin, boy, you were lost. Answer the door with it even. And when they got in fights, them niggers would scream that stuff at each other. Even saw one of them cathauled, and when he was bellyaching afterwards: all Latin!"

"Well," Leighton said, "I reckon we have to be a little more practical up here."

Ferguson made his accent thick and muddy. "Yeah. Yore right. Up here we just give 'em better horses than most soldiers in the South will ever see." By the time he finished his sentence, his smile was gone and his eyes narrowed on Leighton.

The boys from Texas were hardly company. Though Leighton took a personal interest in entertaining them, he found they had no affinities for mechanics, nor reading, nor Missouri, which they'd seen from the Boston Mountains to the Missouri River. Ferguson and the boys held an immense pride about the former Republic of Texas. They began most sentences with, "Of course, in Texas..." followed with a summation of Texas sunsets or women or ham and beans, any of which by far exceeded what was available in Missouri. Leighton ended these conversations by reminding them what state had settled them, what state had won their Mexican War for them. They often complained of the lack of furniture in the house. Leighton told them he and his father hocked most of it.

Ferguson listened intently to Leighton's descriptions of quarrying.

"Of course, there was a time when we were working crushed and kilned lime and dimension stone," Leighton said.

Ferguson swallowed a big draw off his port. " 'Bout how long would you say you'd run like that?"

Leighton felt a little elated that a man of Ferguson's experience would care so much about what happened at a quarry. "Some seasons, seven months of it."

153

Judith walked through the room, gathered dishes and mugs from lunch.

Ferguson glanced at her, then looked back to Leighton. "And how much could you take in on a day with all that going on?"

Judith caught Leighton's eye. She raised her eyebrows quickly, widened her eyes.

Leighton paused, stroked his beard. He smiled. "It was good money."

"If it was so good, what you being cagey about?" Ferguson grinned stroked his own beard mocking Leighton.

"Judith, bring Captain Ferguson and me some more drinks, please."

Judith shuffled off. Outside the window to the study, Bert, the eldest of the boys was standing in the winter sunlight. He hollered something in a language Leighton thought might be Latin, he was not sure. He threw a knife at something beyond Leighton's sight, and from the astonished curses of Charley and Hoyt, Bert nailed his target.

How could he judge Ferguson? The Texan didn't pay any lengthy compliments that Morkan would call solicitations. His uniform and bearing were rough, but no more shocking than a lot of the rabble Leighton met at Shulty's when Price first held the town.

"Captain Ferguson, I can't let on that things are bad around the Negroes. It would bother them a great deal." He dropped his voice to a whisper, wrung his hands. "They really don't know how bad thing's have gotten. The Yankees took a hell of a lot."

"Hey, look, now," Ferguson said. His brow wrinkled. "You don't need to go into it. I seen plenty of folks got taken by them." He nodded. "I'll watch out for you."

The Texans came and went as they pleased, vanishing sometimes for days. Ferguson talked often of town and the necessity of constant contact with General Price, but there was no pattern to their trips, and they often came back drunk, replete with such goods as coffee, butter, even cinnamon. With their laughter, whooping, proclivity to belch and fart at any time and piss out the windows, off the balcony, chew tobacco and spit behind the drapes, they made Leighton feel like an inn keeper.

One December morning, a group of about forty soldiers came shambling up the trail in loose formation, rifles strapped at their backs. They hailed Ferguson on the porch. Leighton was standing with the Texas commander when the boys rampaged out of the house to have a dispute settled. Bert, Hoyt, and Charley halted their wrangling and assumed postures mimicking attention alongside Ferguson. A dozen soldiers approached the porch. Led by a soldier with a white bandanna knotted at his armpit, they were young boys mostly. Their pants were in tatters, their brogans strapped to their feet with leather thongs or with hemp so rotten it was black. Their rifles, though, were U.S. issue, the long-barreled sort Leighton had seen on Federal troops.

The commander with the knotted bandanna explained that the unit was from Newtonia, Missouri and was looking for forage, or a place to winter, most of the houses in town being already taken.

Ferguson took the cigar from his mouth. He had trimmed his beard and bathed. Leighton made all of them promise to bathe once every week now that the stove was going. Ferguson shook his head. "This house and the woods and fields are taken, I'm afraid. This here's for the Texas First." He pointed the cigar at the standard.

"How many men are we looking at?" the Newtonian commander asked.

"Forty-five. And twice that in horses."

"Forty-six," Bert said. "That boy from Texarkana came back to re-up."

Ferguson pulled his beard, nodded at Bert.

Men below the railings cursed, turned and began calling to their fellows. The Newtonian commander tipped his slouch hat. "Well, you can't fault a man for trying." He looked at Leighton. "It is sure good that you're putting cavalry up. They're a hard company for a whole winter."

Ferguson laughed, high and falsely, and the Newtonian commander grinned.

Leighton nodded. "I'm hoping we'll get by."

The commander smiled. "You've done a fine thing for this state. Without folks like yourself, this army would cease to be." He turned and followed his men toward town.

One soldier remained at the railing shivering and glancing at a silver watch in his hand. He looked at Leighton and held the watch up by its chain. "You all got a chicken or a blanket?" The watch twirled.

Leighton stared at him. The soldier's lips were blue, and the creases of his forehead and the skin under his eyes were dark green.

"It's a hell of a watch," the soldier said wearily.

"They ain't got nothing extra, Bub, so beat it home," Charley said.

The boy shrugged and turned away. The bottom of his left shoe popped against the sole of his foot as he walked, and when the sole opened, his foot was blue and black.

Once he was out of sight, Ferguson clapped Leighton on the back. "Who's helping Missouri today?"

Leighton shrugged the Texan's hand from him and gripped the porch rail. He was on the verge of calling the boy back, but one blanket might mean a dozen questions from the Newtonian commander. Ferguson's story would dissolve like gregory powders in water. "Did you want his watch?" He faced Ferguson. "I could call him back and get his watch for you. We got good, damn watches in Missouri."

Ferguson chewed his cigar and looked away.

Before dawn in mid-December, the Texans left for town. After tea, Leighton told Johnson Davis to fetch him at the quarry or in the square if the Texans returned to the house. Before leaving, he surveyed the parlor and rooms of the house, doing his best to memorize the location of clocks, lamps, books, stools, all the linens. He penciled a list of contents from two or three closets.

Outside Johnson Davis saddled Morkan's Walker.

"You may as well," Johnson said.

Wind scattered the light snow until only hard blue pellets remained beneath black twists of frozen grass in the meadows and lawns in town. The streets were rutted and bunched in waves. Smoke twisted from chimneys of all the houses still standing. In the yards of some homes, men in heavy coats were dismantling fences, stacking the wooden remains in their arms. Only men were in the street, some in gray coats taut with the bulk of layered garments beneath, others wearing the filthy regalia of farmers out milking in a blizzard. The light blue flags of Missouri regiments were stabbed beside houses.

No one questioned Leighton, though some soldiers stared at the Walker as he rode it over frozen ruts that swallowed animals' legs beyond the ankle and half up the cannon.

The chains at the quarry gate were cut and lay covered in a mound of snow and ice. The gate was roped shut, probably by Correy or Greevins. With effort, Leighton unwound the stiff hemp. Every lock was broken, every door hung loose. Something shuffled and chattered across the floor of the office when Leighton opened the door. The lamps were stolen, so Leighton propped open the slat windows for light. Once his eyes adjusted, he stood for some time shivering. Papers swirled in the wind from the slats. The ink well, pens, and all the paper weights from the desk were missing. Just this was enough to make him clutch his elbows.

Someone had shattered a crate of nails against the desk, and these dotted the wash of paper and debris. Old contracts and blast records were scattered among blank receipts and payroll tallies. Iodine dye was spilled across many of the papers. Viewing it all, he saw his father ruined. It took him quite some time to step across the office, to touch the desktop, rough and cracked now where water was scarring it.

He walked the ox trail from the stock barn to the cliffs, then inspected the rock where they cut the last tombstones. The cliffs bore little snow and only a few patches of ice where the outlets of springs froze into gray spikes. The cables on the arm of the Mistress were loosed and her arm had dropped into the snow. The boiler was undamaged.

On the edge of the cliff, the elevated rail launched toward the chimney of the kiln. He checked the crank and pulley, but found the ore car's draw rope was cast down and was now a frozen curlicue in the ice of the teal pool. Gray clouds rolled in from the northwest and a light snow began falling.

He turned the crank, and the pulley moaned but rolled with an ease he'd never felt. The ore car waited beneath the pulley, snow in its bottom turning gray with remnants of lime. This was why Morkan did not leave the town. The quarry, not the farmhouse or any attachment to Springfield, kept him from following the Parhams or the Weitzers to St. Louis and safety. He scooped a hunk of the snow and lime from a corner of the car and held it in his palm, melting the snow with his thumb to leave only the lime against his skin. The Morkans opened the skin of the earth and money poured out. Judith said that's what it meant to be named Morkan.

When Leighton approached the square, he heard gunfire, then whooping. A crowd of nearly one hundred soldiers and some civilians had gathered in front of Campbell's and Pearson's. Soldiers were waving the newspapers and dancing. General Price stood on the porch of Pearson's Tack. He lowered his scarves and removed his hat, and his corpulent face glowed red in the bitter wind. He held a newspaper high in the air. The men cheered, shouted his nickname, "Pap! Pap! Pap!"

Ferguson rode up beside Leighton and pulled his scarf below his chin. A grisly smile shone on his face. He handed Leighton a paper. "I was going to bring one home."

Leighton unfolded the paper. It was a Memphis paper from November 29. The topmost headlines concerned a confederate called the Swamp Fox and much discussion and illustration of an island in the Mississippi near Tennessee. In the bottom right corner was the headline:

MISSOURI OFFICIALLY ADMITTED INTO CONFEDERACY: CONFEDERATE CONGRESS VOTED THURSDAY AT THE BRAVE INSISTENCE OF THE STATE GOVERNOR, CLAIBORNE FOX JACKSON.

Leighton nodded to Ferguson, then edged as close to Price as the crowd would permit. The soldiers and civilians now gave Price their full attention.

"I will not speak long in this weather," he shouted. "This is the proudest day in the history of this state. The proudest day in the history of the finest army fighting for the South. You are now Confederates in a great and right cause."

More pistol fire, shouting and leaping. Citizens, many armed, were traipsing across the square toward the commotion.

Price raised a hand for quiet. "I have called for fifty thousand more men. You must call on your brothers, cousins in every burg and neighborhood to come now to this city, the Confederate Capitol of the Sovereign State of Missouri."

On hearing the recruiting call, some of the citizens tucked the newspaper under their arms, lowered their heads, and shuffled away. From a phaeton a Negro began to hand out bottles of amber liquor.

Ferguson moved his horse next to Leighton's. "Get you some of that free whiskey. This here's a big day for your state."

Leighton stared at him.

The Texan's eyes traveled Leighton from chin to boots. He smiled. "I bet your Pa would love for you to sign up with Price."

Leighton was about to tell Ferguson that signing up was the last thing he intended to do, but he paused a second. He even managed a smile. "I think he'd want me to open the quarry."

Ferguson shrugged. " 'Less you're mining lead, Missouri won't need you."

When he turned from Ferguson, he brightened to see Correy sitting across the road, hunched on the Paint and leaning very close to Greevins. He told Ferguson he would see him at home, then he rode to Greevins and Correy.

"Greevins," Leighton said. He stuck out his hand.

Greevins shook his head, bouncing as he shivered. Over his back he had thrown a dusty buffalo robe and several blankets. "Good to see you. I ain't taking my hands out."

Leighton laughed. "Correy! Among the living!"

"Laydon," Correy said.

Leighton squinted at the foreman. Above a scarf, Correy's face was pasty and tufts of red whiskers stabbed from the wool.

Correy blushed.

"From the looks of things we'll do good to sell anything but lime for the shithouses." Leighton nodded at trash heaped against the corner of Pearson's. "And it doesn't appear they're being all that cleanly."

Correy nodded.

"Greevins, Correy, can you manage it for me, in town business I mean?" Leighton said. "Don't take nothing but gold for lime. That is if they offer and don't just thieve it."

Greevins nodded again, but Correy moved his old Paint up against the Walker.

"After what's happened, you would let me touch anything of yours?" Correy asked. He stroked the neck of Morkan's Walker.

Greevins turned away, even took several steps into the wind.

"You're sober," Leighton said to Correy. "Where's Cora?"

Correy's face reddened. "She does fine. The doctors still have some cases."

"Do you see her?"

Correy stared at the muddy street flecked with snow. "I owe it to check on her. For Morkan and for me." He looked up. "She saved my life."

After a moment Leighton reached out and squeezed Correy's arm, so thin now in its coat. "Well, for me then, check on that quarry. I have trouble at home."

Correy nodded, his still lips sunken about his gums, which made him appear frightening, like an ancient soul in a young body. He clucked at the Paint and guided it toward Summit.

Flakes clung to the Walker's mane. He was neither impressed that Correy resisted, nor was he uncomfortable with his own inability to forgive. Smash an office; detain and beat men who know nothing of the actual war; toss the rope off the cliff rather than the ore car; burn a town. He felt a numbness drifting over him. It was just destruction. It was only mayhem. They were merely teeth after all. As the snow began to whirl, only his lack of surprise amazed him.

VI

FOR WEEKS OVERBO NURSED MORKAN, SAVING SLOPS
from the dishwashing, drinking only half his ration of water.
He gave Morkan his own blanket to sleep under and his coat
to wear, then stayed curled against him as they had seen the
Rebel soldiers do under the wagons. The lecture hall grew so
crowded that no matter where you stepped, you were on someone's bedding or tromping on a person's legs. The columns and
walls became dingy with soot and the grease of human contact.
Meals were rapid affairs in which successive groups of prisoners
were hustled into a dining hall and fed off the same plates as the
previous group. They ate by hand, not allowed utensils for fear
they might stab a guard or each other, or dig their way out with
a spoon. Many prisoners spent their evenings vulturing at the
slops trough for what the dishwashers threw out from dinner—
a gray and black sludge of crumbs and gravy, some beans, the
film off an evening's worth of plates. As a dishwasher, Overbo
claimed the sludge was considerably better if taken before it met
barrel water. He always saved Morkan some.

A Confederate surgeon found Morkan coughing and spitting in a corner. The surgeon tapped his chest and abdomen
and pronounced Morkan consumptive, brought on by cold and
abuse. After piddling in Morkan's sputum, the surgeon declared
that his lungs were producing chalk, and that this was a medical
miracle of extraordinary significance. It was a unique and slow
working consumption, with no prospects of galloping, unless
Morkan were continually exposed to dark, cold, wet places.

Morkan laughed himself into a coughing fit. "Look around
you, Doc."

The surgeon did so, then blushed.

When Overbo was at his washing duties, Horatio found Morkan and helped him struggle to the dining hall for the dinner meal. Dozing in the afternoons, Morkan was often interrupted by young prisoners who wanted to know what all was in the dungeon, how to resist every torture. Some became angry when Morkan would not tell them the story of how he overcame cruelties galore, for this was the way they heard it.

By early January, Morkan could walk unassisted, though his back was arched and his legs bowed. His fingers found feeling again and no longer went numb after dark.

One night, Morkan woke and found Overbo rising to a crouch in the blackness. Then the preacher walked on tip-toe over the prisoners around him.

"Overbo?" Morkan whispered.

Overbo froze. He turned to Morkan, his face a gray lump with coal black eyes in the darkness. Overbo stared at him for a long time, then waved him to come near. With great care, Morkan stepped over and around prisoners, wobbling now and again when his foot landed wrong or when the space between sleeping bodies proved too tight. Overbo took his elbow and they moved as quickly as he could across the hall, down wide stone steps, through a door, then carefully down a flight of wooden steps and into the kitchen. Near the back of the kitchen was a swinging door, and Overbo eased this aside.

He led Morkan by the hand, touching his palm to the metal edge of a long trough. Morkan smelled water and rust. They came to a wall, and in it, Morkan could just make out a square aperture covered by a panel framed in a hint of orange light.

Overbo squeezed his elbow. "I want you to swear to me that what you are about to see, you'll take to the grave."

Morkan stared at him.

"Can I count on you?"

The kitchen smelled of lard and the River, a strong fish and silt smell on wet air that clung to his forehead and ears. He nodded.

The door was hinged at the top, and when Overbo pulled it open, a waft of rotting garbage swept over them like a fog. Several roaches scurried from the hole.

Overbo squeezed himself inside the hinged door. From the inside he held the door up, reached and helped Morkan in.

"Hurry," Overbo urged him in a whisper. "Hurry, now."

They both ducked. The room was no larger than a coat closet. Beneath them was an iron trap door, freezing cold against the holes in the rags covering Morkan's feet. The trap door was layered with muck that smelled of sour milk and cabbage. He reasoned they were in some sort of garbage chute, or the shaft to a dumb waiter. In the wall of the small room, high along its roof, a student lamp flickered. There Morkan could see a hole through the brick, a hole wide enough to accommodate someone Overbo's size.

"What you are seeing, you are not seeing," Overbo said. "And what you're seeing will one day mean freedom."

Morkan squinted down the tunnel, but could see nothing. The tunnel angled downward from the hole, so there was no telling if it was occupied, or how long it was. Far down the tunnel, he heard a scraping, something like a rat scratching at a stud in a wall. He set the lamp to one side, peered down the hole. The scraping stopped and after a moment he heard a shuffling. Far down in the hole, which ran toward Eighth Street, there came a flurry of cursing followed by what seemed like the caws and clicks of a crow.

"Horatio," Morkan said. Overbo nodded.

Just beyond the lamp was a rope, and Overbo told him to pull on it. For a moment, the rope caught on some obstacle. Then after a yipe from Horatio, the rope bumped along in slow jerks, the weight attached to it increasing as it proceeded to the opening of the tunnel. An oval of metal attached to the opposite end of the rope came sliding and jolting up the incline toward the tunnel's entry. Cradled on the platter was a bulging burlap sack. Morkan handed Overbo the lamp, and pulled the sack from the hole. Noting the coiled rope on the ground, Morkan estimated the tunnel to be at least thirty feet long. Overbo untied the sack and emptied out brown mud and chert, then began smashing the dirt into the garbage with his feet. In his yellowed linen suit he looked like a strange dignitary at a wine festival. Holding back a grin, Morkan joined him, treading in the grainy

163

slop. At the mouth of the hole, Horatio's boots appeared; then the boy slithered out of the hole. His fingernails and hands were solid brown. He had a potato sack in each hand, and he opened these and dumped them on the iron floor.

In Horatio's tightly clamped jaw was a block of wood that looked as if it had been cut from a table leg. He shivered, frowning when he saw Morkan. Around the wood, he whispered something, then growled and shook. The boy took the wood from his mouth, then glared at Morkan. "You," he said. "You have betrayed Sparta."

Morkan smiled, raised his hands above his head.

Overbo held Horatio's arm, took the wooden table leg in his hands and popped it back in Horatio's mouth. Horatio ducked as if he thought he was going to be hit. Morkan held the wooden door out of the garbage chute open for the boy.

Horatio clambered through it, and was gone.

Morkan let the door drop. "Where is your tunnel leading?"

Overbo's forehead wrinkled. "We're hoping to come up in an alley, maybe in among some garbage." He grinned at the mess beneath his feet.

Morkan tapped his foot on the iron floor to the chute. "Does this not empty into an alley full of garbage?"

Rubbing his forehead, Overbo said, "Actually into a sort of loading dock set into the basement. And guards. It drops only in the day, and there's two sentries posted in the basement, day and night."

Morkan closed his eyes and tried to envision the arrangement. The tunnel must be moving East under Eighth Street. The dock had to face south to unload on Gratiot, thence down Gratiot to the river with the garbage.

"You haven't hit any water?"

Overbo shook his head. "Found what we think is a bracelet off an Indian."

"Are there more men than you and Horatio working on this?"

"You try digging in a hole alone night after night. You'd lose your mind."

Morkan snorted. "Reverend, I used to do it for a living."

"I knew you'd shine to this."

"I don't shine to it. You all could get shot or hung for this."

Overbo bowed his head, gave a slight nod. "That's why we work in shifts. Only one of us, at most two can be caught at once. And I know only the man who relieves me, the man I relieve, and Horatio. We wash in the troughs in the kitchen." He shrugged. "Hell, we're filthy anyway."

Morkan blinked. "How do you know when to work? What keeps four or five from arriving by mistake?"

Overbo hesitated, his lips twisting.

"The deed is done," Morkan said. "If I betray you, you're a dead man."

Overbo finally nodded. "We have Horatio go around in the morning and tell the tunnelers while he's reading their palms."

Morkan shook his head. "It's damn dangerous."

"Well, help us."

Morkan stared at his hands. They were ashen and so thin now, he could clearly see the exact outline of the bone beneath the skin of his thumb. Nothing in him stirred, though here a man valued his learning again for the first time since the war started. He thought of the Rebel soldiers sleeping under the wagon, and imagined, with strange anticipation, the warmth of Overbo's chest pressing the extra blanket and coat to his back, the way that Overbo breathed a smell like gravy down the collar of his coat all night.

"You're not doing this because they've sentenced you without my knowing? They're not going to hang you?" he asked Overbo.

Overbo shook his head. "I'll be here all through the war, though."

"It will end," Morkan said. "Why risk yourself in something this rash?"

Overbo narrowed his eyes at him, but after a moment his face softened. "I appreciate your concern. Understand, there is a lot I can do for our country on the outside," he whispered. "Here I can do nothing, and even if I survive all the years of this, where will I be then? What will be left of me? What will I be able to do for my country?"

"For your country? Is that what you're doing this for, a country that's not even a country? Overbo, we've both seen these two armies." He wheezed for a bit until he was able to bring up a solid, pleasing lump. He spat this onto the floor.

Overbo scowled, his face darkening. The wind outside popped and sucked at the iron door. In a lurch of lamplight, Morkan felt as if he were in a steerage compartment of a listing ship, the chute was so cramped and humid.

"Price's army, every time I saw it, they were more ratty, and desperate to please the people and the other Southern armies, because they were dwindling," Morkan said. "The Arkies didn't even want them." He dabbed his lip with his collar. "My point is you can do and do for sovereign Missouri, but I worry it's all going to naught."

"Maybe it is," Overbo said. "But it *is* right." His chin protruded, small ovals of muscle buckling along his jaw. "They can do this to you, and you wouldn't do anything to thwart them? They tied you to that pole." He snapped his gaze away from Morkan.

Morkan felt a well of warmth rise in his chest. Overbo was still a stout, imposing man. To see him argue, to see him on fire again as he had been in the streets in August, especially now when he stood haggard in muck in a suit stained and tattered to a yellow and green threadbare, this filled Morkan with a feeling very close to the love he felt for Leighton or for Charlotte.

"You truly care for me, Montgomery Overbo."

Overbo cocked an eyebrow at him and scowled. "What do you think the Gospel teaches? How could I not care for you? And our state?"

Morkan shook his head. "Most of what they have done to me so far is a result of me giving that powder to 'our state.' Why would I expect anything different? And what can either of us really do? Overbo, we are of no consequence here or out there. Sure you might inspire a boy to join Price. Or inspire a mother to carry on while her husband and sons are off dying in the wilds of Arkansas. But what have you really done? Nothing: and the war ruins you and it's over."

Overbo's face was red, his fists were pulling at the hem of his coat.

Morkan cleared his throat and went on. "You are a kind man. I am grateful beyond reparation for your kindness to me. Let me at least return some of it to convince you how needless a danger you're undertaking." Morkan paused, wetted his lips. "I don't want to be here with you gone."

"And I don't want to be here, period," Overbo whispered sharply. "I cannot stand this any longer. I'm glad I've been kind, but I tell you, kindness is requiring a great effort." He stopped, his face red and contorted. "I've never dealt with suffering like this. Everywhere: filth, blood, pus, and sores. I saw a man remove two of his own rotted teeth yesterday, then spend the rest of his afternoon trying to trade kids out of their mush for them. I'm losing my mind. I want to feel sun and wind. I want to see women and hear church bells. I want to smell horses."

Morkan touched his arm. "All that I can understand." The room was so close, he could feel the warmth off the paunch of Overbo's belly.

Overbo stood flushed and blinking. "There is no middle any more, Michael. You are occupying ground that's untenable. You have to decide. Come with us."

When Morkan was silent, Overbo lifted the lamp from the ground, returned it to the mouth of the hole. He stared at Morkan for a while, his fingers crumbling the fine brown soil. "You don't approve because Nimms has got you, hasn't he?"

"No," Morkan said. "And he'll never have me." Watching red clay stain Overbo's thick thumb and fingers Morkan saw clearly that even if Leighton and the quarry were gone, there was this man, Overbo, the reverend, whose hands held water to Morkan's lips and brought him food. What Morkan worried most was that Nimms would wring out of him the location of this tunnel and the names of the tunnelers.

Overbo cocked his head squinting at Morkan.

"I can't get in your tunnel," Morkan said. "You'll never get me out with my lungs like this. But I can show you how to build it and support it."

167

Overbo shook his head as if to clear it. "You'd show us how to build it and not come through it with us?"

Morkan nodded.

Overbo's fists were balled in the ragged pockets of his britches. "I took a grave risk in showing you this. Leave it to a Catholic to find an answer that is halfway there, but sounds like the Gospel."

Morkan reached out to Overbo, who patted him. Standing on tip toes, Morkan peered down the hole into the tunnel. "First," he said, "you've gone thirty or so feet. You're nearly under Eighth Street. I would turn immediately northwest. You may end up, then, in an alley by the medical supply. Right now, you're headed for the River and compacted soil under the street. You'll likely hit the water table. You may end up with the whole front of your tunnel submerged in water." He paused. Overbo's eyes were intent on Morkan. He nodded his head at each point.

"What sort of soil are you working through?"

Overbo shrugged. "We work in the dark, so I'm not sure."

"In the dark?"

"Horatio and one of his partners said that a tunnel like this that goes down won't get any air and a candle could burn it all up."

Morkan snorted. He imagined Horatio scrabbling in the earth, screaming and clucking and cursing in pitch blackness. He wasn't sure if he should laugh or weep. "Please take a candle down when you go next, and a compass. If the candle dims, then put it out and rest awhile. What are you digging with?"

Overbo pointed at the platter. Stooping, Morkan picked the platter up, examined the scuffed edges of it, how it was bowed slightly, looked almost like the shovel for scooping ashes from the quarry's kiln.

"You've dug thirty feet with this? In the dark?"

Overbo nodded. "We have."

"Incredible. Madness."

Overbo grinned. "Determination. Fortitude."

Somewhere down below them in the garbage bin and basement there was a clatter and a gonging as if a tin pot had been thrown to the floor. Overbo grabbed the lamp and doused it, then crouched with Morkan. They huddled there, their foreheads touching, the whispers of their breathing rising. Morkan could feel his heart racing even at the tip of his nose. They listened in a fury, until the night became a tangible thing to Morkan, a cold grease one parsed through to find a morsel or the worm.

After a long time, his forehead still against Overbo's, he whispered. "How high is your tunnel? Can you crawl on your knees?"

The oily circle of the reverend's forehead shuddered. "Horatio can."

"The kitchen stoves are wood, right?" He paused, listened, felt Overbo nodding. "Filch wood, and at any angle more than fifteen degrees, I want you to build. . . ." He halted. How to explain it to a man who probably had never seen anything more complex than a well dug? "Build a box around yourselves. Nothing fancy. Just a crate. I'll draw you one."

Overbo swallowed. His breath on Morkan, so measured and enviably easy, smelled as if dumplings could be made in it—he had eaten chicken and bread from somewhere. "Fifteen degrees?"

Below them was a rustling. With a jolt, Overbo grabbed Morkan's face, then pressed his fingertips to Morkan's lips.

They listened. Down through the iron, they heard a cat moan. They both breathed, moved apart from each other. Overbo lit the lamp, but neither of them stood. Dirty beads of sweat coursed clean streaks down the reverend's round face, which was bright now, smiling at Morkan.

Morkan swallowed. "Another use for the candle. With the candle straight up, you set her where the tunnel slants. If the wax drops but half your thumb away from the base of the candle, you've got a slope to contend with."

Overbo nodded slowly.

Morkan touched his arm, and beneath his fingers Overbo's old linen coat was crisp with filth. "Now listen. In this kind of soil, you'll have no warning of a collapse, least that you can hear. If you see cracks above your heads looking like horseshoes, then crate over that and for an arm's length on both sides of it."

Overbo nodded. "That's a lot of wood."

169

Morkan took the lamp and rose unsteadily to his feet. Setting the lamp in the tunnel's mouth, he ran his palm down the sides. Warm, grainy silt, Mississippi mud, a shard of chert. In the black hold of the tunnel's center it was hard to see freedom. Morkan cleared his throat, eased out of the passage. Overbo was looking admiringly at the tunnel now. "At least it's a temporary hole. If you have a choice of being buried in St. Louis dirt, or a Federal pine box, safety needn't be your primary concern. I'll draw up some plans, though."

Overbo stifled a laugh, gripping Morkan's arm. Then, delicately, he brushed silt off Morkan's coat sleeve. "I can't say that I really knew what sort of man you were before just now." For a long time, he was silent watching Morkan's eyes. The wind moaned at a space in the iron door. "Bless you, Brother Morkan."

Morkan hesitated a moment, then smiled. "An Irish rule of thumb about tunnels: don't bless me until you can do it in daylight."

But Overbo was not listening. Instead he was humming a hymn as he held the door for Morkan and led him past the steel troughs.

"Overbo," Morkan said. The reverend stopped. "I want you to understand. I am not doing this for sovereign Missouri. It's for you."

Overbo scowled but nodded. "We've been a little loud," he whispered, "so I want you to be careful on your walk back."

"You're going to stay and risk it still?"

Overbo nodded, then stooped at the kitchen door to listen at its other side.

Overbo clutched at Morkan's arm and pulled him forward. "All quiet," he whispered. He clutched Morkan's hand. "Daylight is coming, Brother Morkan." The kitchen door slipped shut and Morkan was in the dark hall.

Morkan moved through the night until he found the wooden steps. Groping, stumbling, he found his way to the lecture hall, where the tall windows let in a blue sheen from moonlight searing off the snow and ice outside. Gray lumps of men lay all across the floor, like a herd of sheep resting. It was too far to the spot he had vacated. He drew Overbo's coat around him. His foot found a space between the backs of two prisoners, men he had never seen before, probably new comers. He lowered himself to the floor, wormed himself down between them. The coat of the prisoner in front of him still smelled of the out-of-doors, of clean snow and soil, a little pond water. He was warm. Morkan held on to him, and did not even realize the volume and depth of the sigh of pleasure that rose from his own chest. The prisoner stirred. He muttered someone's name. Morkan drifted to sleep, hoping the prisoner had spoken the name of a sturdy, reliable woman. He imagined Cora, then, weaving brambles and dried clover into a wreath and striping the inside of her thigh with a perfume of crushed rose petals and apple brandy ready to welcome her prisoner home.

On the back of a tin plate, Morkan scratched a diagram of a crude support structure, with all the tongues and grooves and dimensions. Overbo took this down in the tunnel along with the candle and it became the plan every man followed. Morkan warned him that missing wood, more than anything else, might give the tunnel away.

A few days later, Overbo met him at the window. The reverend's face was red and his brows bunched. With the heel of his hand, he rubbed his bald head. He pulled Morkan from the window into a dark corner away from the crowd in the sunlight.

"We can't find the plate," Overbo said.

Morkan pulled his collar to his lips. "It's in the tunnel, right?"

Overbo shrugged.

"Why would it leave the tunnel?"

Overbo blushed and scowled.

He grabbed the front of Overbo's shirt, made sure that Overbo's back shielded his hands. "You can't work, then. They know."

"They would have destroyed the tunnel if they knew."

He shook Overbo. "They may wait to see who's working."

"Let us worry about that."

Morkan leaned into Overbo's face. "Worry about this. No one here could draw that diagram, save me. Nimms will know. Your missing plate may kill me."

Overbo squeezed his wrists. "We'll find it. I swear."

171

Nimms caught Morkan again seated before Horatio, who was speaking in what his partners claimed was Babylonian and revealing, as the spirit of one of Nebuchadnezzar's concubines, the dark inner secrets of the great king's harems. One of Horatio's partners translated. Once Nimms entered the circle of prisoners, Horatio and his translator quieted. Morkan stood stiffly when the two guards lifted him by the armpits. Overbo scowled at Nimms, but Morkan shook his head sharply.

Nimms and the guards led him up the same stairs and into another room on what must have been a floor of classrooms, one of which held the banners of the eviscerated man. In this new room narrow tables with polished wooden tops ranged in four parallel rows. Each table had a nook for a chair and near each nook there was a brass ringlet surrounding a little hole. The room smelled of alcohol, and all along the wall was a shelf of jars in which bobbed specimens—a babe with gill slits along its neck, a grasshopper large as any rat at Billy Lynch's, a Negro's hand, shriveled so greatly it appeared reptilian. On a wide shelf at the front of the room, dozens of jars were arranged, and in each there hovered a cat, the fur on their faces flattened, glares savage, legs stiff against the glass.

Morkan cleared his throat. "Lovely," he said.

Nimms set his Morocco notebook on a table. The back of the notebook was fattened with loose papers. For a moment, Morkan imagined all the other prisoners Nimms was harassing, all the hideous notations he kept. The guards stepped back.

Nimms paced. "Tuttle is not buying what I've produced."

"You have shown him what I wrote?"

"A useless piece of paper."

He cleared his throat, tasted lime and copper. "Tell me exactly what you want."

Nimms stopped. He rested his palms flat on the table. His dark eyebrows narrowed to a sharp *V*. "And if I tell you, will you then proceed with me or against me?"

Morkan weighed the two options. He knew in the end he would proceed against Nimms—either option ended in a hanging, or his eventual death by consumption. But in the tunnel somewhere, Overbo labored, his sweat dripping next to the flicker of the candle. "In the end, I will have to proceed with you," Morkan said.

Nimms nodded. For a long time, he stood with his eyes narrowed regarding Morkan. He stroked his chin. "There may be new items to discuss, something more of value you might know."

"Other than money."

Nimms leaned forward a little. "One may lead to the other." He opened the notebook. "For example, as a rail engineer, I imagine you tunneled."

"Not when it could be avoided."

Nimms raised his eyebrows. "Come now." He took one of the cats down, made a face at it. "I would say your home and holdings rival that of even some of our Confederate officers. You can't have earned all that cracking rocks."

Morkan's back began to ache, so he leaned on a table. He decided not to refute Nimms's skewed assessment of his wealth. The house he built himself, with help from Leighton and the slaves. The stone they quarried on site. At the quarry, a great deal of his business passed in barter, so the Morkan's could end a season replete with foodstuffs and fodder, but thin on cash to start rock work next spring. Most of his nest egg—the $2,500 in Claus Weitzer's Mineral Bank—he made surveying for the railroads, claiming the choicest lands and selling the plots to speculators in St. Louis and Chicago.

"Well, a great deal of capital toward the house did come from rail work, but a man doesn't make money digging holes. You make it surveying and land grabbing."

"Good. Good. Now we are being honest," Nimms said. "But you did dig tunnels?"

"Blasted some."

Nimms jotted something in the notebook. "Once you blast, what do you do?"

Morkan wrinkled his nose at Nimms. "Drive rail, man. What's left to do?"

Nimms wiggled his fingers in the air above his head. "Do tunnels just stay up? With great trains rattling through them?"

Crossing his arms over his chest, Morkan frowned. "No. There was a fellow behind me who would. . . ." He cleared his throat. "Who worked up the supports." He stared Nimms down. Along his arms, there was tightness, as if he touched the bare wire to the blasting battery. From Nimms' firm jaw, and bright hazel eyes, Morkan figured Nimms knew he was close to something. "Understand. I designed bridges, and turnouts and roundhouses, stations. Any fool can do what you're asking."

"So they did pay you well? They'd have to. Of course. What moneys were you able to save from the evacuation after Wilson's Creek?"

"The bank had no currency. The Federals had taken everything. I reckon you owe me somewhere around $2,500."

Nimms scrawled something with the steel pen. "You know a Claus Weitzer?"

Morkan nodded, worried he had misstepped.

Nimms flipped to the back of his book, drew out a purple receipt, undoubtedly from the National Mineral Bank. "This receipt, delivered to us by Weitzer upon the liquidation of the bank's currency, claims that you received $967.50 in currency from that bank, and that you retained currency receipts for the remainder of an account originally totaling $2,493." Nimms held the receipt up and frowned. "We know Claus Weitzer did not lie. They may not make soldiers, but the Dutch make superb citizens. Mr. Morkan, are you proceeding with me or against me?"

Morkan bowed his head. "The currency I received was absorbed in the daily operating expenses of the quarry."

Nimms pulled another sheet from the back of his notebook, this was yellowed, criss-crossed with smudged ink lines. Nimms handed it to Morkan.

Morkan held the paper close to his eyes. The top of it bore the imprint **MORKAN QUARRY, SUMMIT & STATE STREETS, SPRINGFIELD, MISSOURI**. In the right hand corner was the date 21 August 1861, the initials beneath that were his own. It was a sheet of ledger paper describing a payroll outlay. Beside the name of each miner was a figure—1.00 MS, 1.10 MS/N, 1.00 N. His mind raced: had he missed any more than this one? Had Nimms and the Federals sacked the house and turned up the quarry's records?

"What does *MS* indicate?" Nimms asked.

"Missouri Scrip."

"What is called Claibe Jackson money?"

Morkan nodded.

"What does *N* indicate by the name Correy?"

"A promissory note."

"I see some such notation beside every one of these names. This I know is an average day of your expenses during the Rebel occupation. I see roughly $48.00 in outlay here. Even if the quarry were open every day since the Federal departure of August 10th, you still could not have mounted payroll expenses of anything more than $350. And you had scrip coming in, and you were using scrip as pay."

Morkan shivered. The classroom walls and ceiling became very close, the air icy and thick.

"So you are telling me, then, that you spent $967.50 in currency in less than six days? On what?"

Morkan felt himself slump.

Nimms shook his head, paced slowly in front of Morkan. "You have nine hundred some odd dollars in currency rolling around—at that house, at the quarry, in a log, in a cave." Nimms stood on his tiptoes and put his nose close to Morkan's. "Tell me, and we will have taken a very significant step."

Morkan bowed his head.

After a moment, Nimms gathered his papers in the notebook, then drew his revolver. "Come with me then. We'll have you at pillory."

What was he protecting? Why endure his last days in pain? It was doubtful that Nimms would spare him the noose. The quarry was gone; Leighton was lost to him. It was only money. And Nimms might already know all he needed about Horatio and Overbo. He had asked about supports in tunnels. Maybe if he gave up his money Nimms would relent.

Morkan paused, took a deep breath. "I have some nine hundred dollars in coin hid in the springhouse on the farm," Morkan said. He wheezed, cleared his throat.

Nimms reached and touched Morkan's cheek. "And?"

"That's all."

"Stock at the quarry?"

"You have the records."

Nimms smiled. "Of course, but I want to hear you."

"Six oxen, four mules, eight draft horses, one Walker, and two buckskin geldings."

Nimms nodded. "Equipment of value at the quarry?"

"Gang saws. One steam derrick. One mill, two kilns. Two anvils. A forge." Morkan paused. "A hell of a lot of hammers." With each disclosure, he felt more and more that he lost everything. He was weak. "You know the rest of it. You have the records."

Nimms patted his cheek. "Is that all? Is there anything else of value, any asset you are not disclosing to us?"

"I can think of nothing else." Morkan spoke the words as if each were cast lead.

Nimms blinked, cocked his head. "We have gained ground. I had no records but the two documents I showed you. We couldn't get anything of value from your boy, and he's died at Billy Lynch's." Nimms stood before Morkan, arched his back.

Morkan gasped.

Nimms grinned. "Yes, but before that, who's in the tunnels?"

Morkan watched Nimms's eyes beneath their thick, black brow. "No one."

"Come now. These Rebels know who you are. Who asked for your help, Morkan?"

Morkan stood so still, one of the guards shook him.

Nimms stepped very close to him. "Do not hold out for men who do not matter."

Morkan said nothing.

"You best spend some time in the courtyard, then," Nimms said.

That evening, he woke with Overbo hovering near him. "They haven't stopped us," he whispered. He touched a tin cup of water to Morkan's lips.

"Plate," Morkan said.

"We'll find it, I swear." When he dabbed Morkan's brow, his cuff smelled of the River's mud.

VII

THE TEXANS DID NOT RETURN FOR DAYS. THEN LEIGHTON
awoke to them boiling real coffee. Judith served them all in the
front parlor. As she worked, Ferguson complimented Leighton
on the even temper of his slaves. There was a moment of stillness
and silence that passed between Leighton and Judith. Leighton
thanked him, and Judith continued serving. Ferguson sat stroking his beard watching Leighton.

Charley and Hoyt asked Leighton to read the Memphis
paper again and again. The newspaper contained an overview
of what it called the First Year of Confederacy with dozens of
battle maps. Oak Hills was included along with an illustration
depicting the death of General Lyon, the first Federal general to
die on this side of the Mississippi.

The Texans whooped at this, and Leighton stared at them.
He sipped his coffee. The more he watched Charley and Hoyt,
the more he was convinced they saw little of battle, and killed no
one. Bert was usually quiet, though a capable liar. His brown eyes
were alert and intent, but often they clouded and fell askance
when Leighton spoke, as if Bert were watching Leighton's chest
and arms for the words. Bert just might have killed someone.
He no longer wore the explosion of a beard that Ferguson kept.
Instead he wore a goatee, which Leighton admired and even
considered emulating.

Hoyt asked for Oak Hills again.

"Look, there's a whole set of other battles." Leighton waved
the paper at them. They followed the paper as if the newsprint
glittered with starlight.

Leighton read a long account of Manassas, pausing now and
again to make sure the troop numbers actually added correctly.

He sat back after a long paragraph concerning the army of the Potomac. "My God, that's a lot of people."

"You reckon it's accurate?" Bert asked.

"You can't fit that many people in a creek bed, can you?" Hoyt gazed all around the room for an answer.

"Oh, bullshit," Ferguson shouted. Everyone else jolted. "How could anyone see behind him and tell who was standing or who was squatting? That whole thing's a God damned lie. You can't see behind you in a battle no more than you can see down your own bunghole." He poked his cigar at Bert. "How much smoke was there at Lexington?"

"He's reading, Ferguson," Bert growled.

"No. Tell me, you bride's maid. How much could you see?"

"Just hay bales. Now, please."

"If that. God damn Easterners. Now see, they have one battle over there in a year, so they blow it full of puff and powder. I highly resent this. I will hear no more."

He remained seated with his arms crossed over his chest.

When Leighton finished the piece, Hoyt and Charley smacked each other on the knees and scuffled in happy excitement. Ferguson sat scowling so hard his expression raised his beard from his chest.

"That's more men dead than were even in the Federal army at Oak Hills." Leighton looked at Hoyt, then Ferguson. "That's a lot of dead men."

"Aw, let 'em rot. Easterners."

Before the war, the Morkans exchanged single gifts with each other, usually something handmade. Now it was the third Sunday of Advent. Leighton wandered about the sawbarn, doodling on this or that scrap in the cold. He was entertaining the idea of making something for his father to set aside for a homecoming, maybe a lathe-turned candle holder. But the moment he gathered the greasy fittings to the lathe and tested the foot pedal's tension, he grew despondent, and went to the house.

Christmas Day, he woke to find boughs of pine spread across the window ledges and end tables of the parlor. The Texans cleared away their bedrolls, and the smell of coffee, ham, and eggs drifted from the kitchen. Ferguson shared cornbread he said he bought from a woman in town, and this crunched rather than crumbled. Hoyt cried, and told them all a lament about how pretty West Texas was and how he hated snow.

Bert left the breakfast early and went upstairs. Leighton worried Bert was ill, and was surprised at himself for caring about the Texan. From breakfast, they all retired to the parlor for coffee. Soon footfalls came from the stairs. Bert descended wearing an astonishing gray coat with crimson cuffs, and golden epaulettes, tan riding britches with bright yellow stripes. A long peacock feather lolled from a scarlet band on his slouch hat. Hoyt sat up straight and solemn, while Ferguson smiled over his coffee. Bert held a crude wooden tray in his hands. His flushed cheeks were the only deviation from an eerily somber bearing.

"Bert and I wanted to wish you, our host, a Merry Christmas," Ferguson said. "And you, too, Hoyt. Charley."

The Texans exchanged gifts of cigars, chaw, and short, black daggers. Ferguson gave Leighton two big cigars and a decanter of whiskey he said was from New Orleans. The Texas boys passed their daggers around the room, and Leighton doled whiskey with the coffee. There was chatter and reveling, as if the five of them became a large party. Leighton noticed that Bert alone did not fully participate. The martial Father Christmas sat rod straight, his coat and pleated pants as crisp as if they were carved from wood.

After several rounds of whiskey, the coffee was gone. The room grew quiet. Charley and Hoyt's faces both glowed with the red numbness of young drunks. Leighton rose, then wavered a moment in front of the complicated brass samovar Charlotte kept on a bureau. He withdrew the set of keys trailing from a thin chain from his coat pocket. With the key, he opened a drawer, pulled out the basin of oil and a bag of Darjeeling. Leighton fetched water, frowned in concentration as he measured the leaves.

Ferguson was busy picking a divot in the end of a cigar. Every so often, though, Ferguson would glance up at Leighton and his work. From the cabinets, Leighton brought out the pewter service Charlotte used only on Christmas and Easter. After many minutes of hissing, the samovar finished. Leighton served tea into each of the five mugs, then carried the tray to the coffee table. He handed a mug to Charley, one to Hoyt. Ferguson's chin was against his chest, the cigar and pick still held before him, but he focused on Leighton and not the cigar.

"That's some teapot," Hoyt said.

Leighton handed Bert a cup. He smiled at Hoyt. "It's an old service my mother used only for the holidays."

Ferguson looked up from the cigar, raised his eyebrows. Leighton hesitated a moment when he met Ferguson's eyes. He handed Ferguson the cup.

By January the thought of more salt-drenched fatback made Leighton's eyes water and his throat ache with disgust. Johnson Davis and Isaac understandably avoided the farm house and woods, so his major source of fresh game was lost. Even the Texans' appetites decreased. Returning after a few days' absence, they often ate only half their normal fare. There were days when single rifle shots cracked and rippled from the hills, and sometimes Leighton spotted thin wisps of smoke above the woods. In the Texans' frequent trips to town, Ferguson reported catching and dispatching poaching soldiers from the land. The frequency of shots never seriously diminished though.

Bert stayed behind on these trips and read with Leighton. Bert embarrassed him with compliments about the Morkan library, though he mentioned that Homer, Horace, Marcus Aurelius, and Cato were dangerously under-represented. Bert's presence and the inactivity of winter made Leighton fidget. So the poachers' daily gunfire became an irritation, then an obsession.

The wind was bitter. He and Bert entered the leafless, snow-strewn woods. Leighton wore a heavy wool coat and four shirts. Bert sported the Christmas uniform so that they could identify themselves to the poaching Rebels rather than risking gunfire. Leighton even let Bert use Johnson Davis's horse. In his outfit, Bert looked like a colonel.

"Where'd you get that outfit?" Leighton asked. "It's a captain's, isn't it?"

"He was a lawyer from home. Near Uther, Texas. He taught me everything since I was a kid. Little Greek, lot of Latin, poems, not Whittier or Longfellow. You know amprabachs, heptameter?"

Leighton shrugged.

"Damn, is digging all you ever did?" Bert shook his head. "He was the captain I was assistant to." Bert's eyes narrowed. "Taught me about *eros* and *phulong*. You heard about *phulong*, Leighton?"

Leighton snorted. "Sounds like a dish for a Chinaman."

Bert smiled.

Leighton fought his horse for an instant. The horse was fitful, having been cooped too long. On January 12th, almost a foot of snow had fallen, and now, two weeks later, the snow had a crusting of ice pellets which crackled across its top.

"This snow's really fine," Bert said. "How long will it stay? Until March?"

Leighton shrugged. "What was Oak Hills like?"

Bert's forehead creased and he blinked at Leighton. "Not anything like Manassas."

"Why?"

Bert pulled his scarf closer to his nose. "That Manassas is so many soldiers, and so much about glory and honor and generals. No matter how much you write that a lot died, if you look at it that way, that 'standing like a wall,' it makes it all nothing but glory. Numbers run through a man reading like water through cheesecloth."

Leighton rode closer to him. "So what was Oak Hills like?"

Bert shook his head. "I don't know if I can explain. It doesn't make sense like Lexington." He halted the horse. "Cavalry from Uther, Texas were under Greer." He shrugged. "But that doesn't mean anything."

"Just say what you did."

"Cannon woke us up. We got half gathered, about fifty horses and men then got shot all to pieces from just four cannon up in the woods I couldn't see. So we just milled around and got shot at, and there was no one to tell us what to do."

"Then I saw these men in damn smart uniforms, beats this all to hell. Rode toward that creek again with them because they looked like they knew what they were doing." He stopped and

181

stared at Leighton. A sheen of frost circled Bert's scarf where his breath passed as he spoke.

Leighton nodded.

"Then we came up on this whole stack of people just chatting away in German and leaning on those four hot guns, and we killed every last one of them. They wouldn't ever shoot. Kept yelling '*Sie irrten sich!*' which is 'She ain't us!' We just killed them and killed them and killed them, and they had no idea in the world who we were."

Leighton swallowed. An acorn smacked the snow and rolled. Neither of the boys looked up. "Were you supposed to kill them?"

Bert shrugged, and despite all the bundling, Leighton saw his face quiver. "We sure carried on like we ought to."

They were silent.

Another acorn fell. Leighton gazed up the trunk of the immense oak they were under. He looked at Bert. Bert's eyes were downcast, his chin moving the scarf as if he were muttering.

"Squirrel up there," Leighton said. He nodded above them.

Bert snapped his eyes at Leighton and blinked. He dismounted and raised his rifle.

"You can't shoot him out of a tree."

Bert lowered the rifle and squinted at him. "You shoot up where you heard him and see."

"Waste of shot." He dismounted and stood beside Bert. "It'll hunker like a rabbit."

"City boy."

Leighton cocked the rifle, raised it and fired. The shot traveled the hills with great report, but only bark spattered from the tree.

"Shoot at that nest of leaves against the trunk."

Leighton tied his horse to an oak. Bert tied beside Leighton's horse. Leighton loaded, raised the rifle and fired at the wad of leaves Bert indicated. Amid screeching and rustling, a squirrel scooted from the nest, butt end dangling as it slipped down the branch. Bert raised his rifle, fired, and the squirrel spun and fell as Bert began loading.

"Load, city boy," Bert said, grinning.

They shot two more from the nest in the same manner. In the reports from their flurry of shots, Leighton thought he heard other rifle fire but dismissed the sounds as an echo. He was too intent on the squirrels Bert plugged with near mechanical precision.

"Damn." Leighton breathed in great silver bursts. "Damn!" He lifted one of the twitching rodents in his palm. The animal's mouth opened and closed, making rhythmic shrieks like a steam valve. Warm blood seeped through Leighton's gloves.

Bert plucked the other two up by their back legs and cracked their heads against the tree they'd fallen from.

Bert pulled his scarf below his chin and cocked his head. "You have hunted for yourself before, haven't you?" The smile that came over Bert's face was not the malicious one Leighton expected, but a quizzical, slight curving of the lips.

Far back in the woods, they both heard the crack of a rifle, the long roll of its report. Bert frowned, and his eyes grew pinched. His hand moved toward his belt where Leighton knew a pistol was holstered. His face darkened.

Leighton blinked at him. "It's just poachers, ain't it?"

Bert looked away, then knelt and gathered the squirrels in a circle. He removed his ratty gloves and pulled his black Christmas dagger from his belt.

Leighton knelt to the circle. Gray and silver of the fur and whiskers, eyes black and shining, half-lidded. The back leg of one pushed at the snow.

"It's Ferguson, ain't it," Leighton said. "He's the one out poaching."

Bert stabbed the knife in the ground, and his breath rushed out in a great pillow of white. He squinted at Leighton. "You just figured that out?" He shook his head, yet Leighton noticed Bert's eyes were watery.

After a moment, Bert plucked the knife from the ground, nipped the back of a squirrel with its tip and held the carcass up by the nape behind its neck. With its thick tail tucked stiffly between its legs, it dangled like a hung man.

Bert looked at Leighton, eyes wide and clear, his face as cold as the hardened snow. "You are dead right now where you set and have been dead since the moment he laid eyes on you. He ain't no Texan."

Slowly, Leighton took the squirrel by its middle, forced it down the blade of the knife. Its head folded forward, blood welling, then coursing down its white chest. When the bloody back of the carcass touched Bert's hand, he pushed it tight against Bert's skin.

Bert looked down at the snow, the red there, at the red crawling down his wrist. "Run from us, Leighton," he whispered. "I don't want this to happen."

"I'll die right here before I leave anyone my home.

Bert dropped the knife and squirrel. His face was a healthy pale after losing the filth of campaigning. The goatee ran a taut stripe down his chin and circled his mouth in a fine oval. His eyebrows were slim and dignified, chin strong though narrow, and his cheeks bore small flecks of rose. Leighton imagined how much richer life might have been with a brother like this. Bert's shoulders were broad, his chest bulky and strong. He would be a hell of a partner in a fight.

"Show me where they are," Leighton said.

They crossed the crest of the ridge, then spotted a sprig of smoke rising to the north. They halted well back from the cedar and oak that rimmed a hollow on the northwest corner of the property. There smoke wavered in a column above the hollow, then fanned out to form a still, violet canopy. The bare forest carried voices almost as well as it carried shots, and he recognized the laughter and banter of Charley and Hoyt arguing over who made what kill. Leighton dismounted and tied the horse, crept into the trees. From a part in the cedars, he could see Charley and Hoyt tossing their black daggers into the snow at their feet in some sort of game. Ferguson spraddled an enormous buck between two sycamores and was skinning it. Its entrails lay in a steaming pile. The snow crunched right behind Leighton. When his hand dove for the pepper-box, Bert caught his wrist and held it jerking.

"You ain't killin' no one with that whore popper." Bert whispered. His hunting rifle drooped down his arm and dangled on its strap.

Leighton glared at him.

In the hollow, Ferguson handed a dripping hunk of meat to Charley and Hoyt who skewered this on a flimsy spit and hoisted it over the fire where two posts were pounded. The boys jabbered and turned the spit at a whirling pace. Ferguson clapped Hoyt across the back of the head, told them both to shut up and roll the meat slowly. Leighton relaxed his arm, and Bert released him.

"All three them's got a revolver, loaded," Bert said. "You might get one, but Hoyt and Ferguson can flat shoot."

Leighton shook his head slightly, not at Bert, but at the situation.

"I'll tell you what'll get them," Bert said. He knelt. "Get back on your horse and ride right down there and act like you're happy as hell but sure sorry you ruined their surprise. Moon about how Texans are such kind folk to surprise their hosts this way and cook a deer to bring them."

Leighton suppressed a smile and stared at him. "That's pretty bright."

Bert shrugged. He cast his gaze toward his feet and adjusted his hat. A flush of color rose in his cheeks. "Don't let on I'm here."

Leighton mounted and went pounding down the hollow, burst through the cedars at such a rate that Charley fell to the ground and Hoyt and Ferguson drew their revolvers.

Leighton reined the horse well beyond them, spun the animal around and pulled down his scarf. He beamed at Ferguson, at the meat on the spit, at Hoyt and Charley. He hopped off the horse and held both hands to his blushing face. In the corner of his eye, he saw, obscured in the cedars, Bert's shadow rising and leveling his rifle on Ferguson.

"I thought I was coming on poachers and here you all are about to surprise me with a whole buck's worth of meat." Leighton strode toward Ferguson, who stood blinking, slowly holstering the revolver. "My God, you're good people."

Ferguson frowned beneath his beard. He wormed the toe of his boot into the ground. "Well, you ruined our surprise."

Leighton shook his head and put his hands on his hips. "You Texans." He bowed his head and wiped his eyes, teared from his rush through the cold.

"Shit," Charley hissed behind him.

Ferguson managed a smile. "Yeah, we thought we'd give you an honest to goodness feast."

Back in the trees, Bert's shadow disappeared.

After a string of awkward amenities in which the Texans strode right along with the surprise story, Leighton helped them strap the gutted buck on the back of his horse. He even removed a shirt to wrap the large roast once it had turned long enough on the spit under Ferguson's now unenthusiastic direction.

They strapped the deer and followed Leighton out of the hollow at a walking pace.

Judith was cooking at the stove, a gray whirl of smoke snaking up from the stovepipe, when they banged at the back door. Ferguson passed in holding up the great hunk of roast. He was beaming. Leighton followed him, fingers red with gore, a shank of venison in his hands. Hoyt and Charley followed with more meat.

"Lord!" Bert exclaimed, and the Texans and Leighton halted for a moment. Bert stood from a seat at the kitchen table. He had changed his clothes and was feigning to read from a picture book about steam trains. He looked at Leighton. "I thought you said we're having squirrel?"

Leighton looked away, disturbed to see Bert and Judith biding time in the kitchen as if Bert were part of the family.

Ferguson was still smiling, but the squint of his eyes on Bert was alarming. "Well you aren't!" he exclaimed, and plopped the suet soaked shirt on the table.

"Venison!" Bert touched the meat as if it were gold.

"Your pal nearly ruined our surprise," Ferguson said. "Get the stove to going. There's a whole buck to cook from the Texas First Cavalry."

Judith set out the greens, and Bert set out wine glasses. Standing in the corner of the dining room, hands clasped behind his back, Leighton watched. Bert and Judith worked in unison, but Judith's eyes were downcast, her jaw taut as they passed each other rounding the table. The others remained standing as Bert poured, Hoyt and Charley glancing to Ferguson who stood sweating with the family's fork and carving knife at the ready. When Judith left the room for her place at the counter in the kitchen, Leighton excused himself for a second.

Her eyes leapt when he met her. She backed away, but he held up a hand.

"I couldn't help showing him where things were," she whispered. "He drew a knife on me when I wouldn't show him how to set the table and where the wine was, all over the cellar, every inch of pantry, the two hutches. That ain't the silver or the china, but I never wanted him to see anything." She trembled. "He would have killed me. He's a killer. They's all killers."

Leighton touched Judith's hand. She sobbed once, her big form shaking. Then she took a deep breath.

"They're awful, Judith." He had never seen her so shaken. "If you want, you don't need to return till they're gone. But let's play calm for now." He looked around the kitchen. "Give me something to take in to them."

She pulled down a tray and set five crystal snifters on it, fetched a bottle of brandy from the pantry.

Leighton lifted the tray. "Maybe you want to get yourself some."

"Humph." Her frown softened for an instant.

Leighton stepped into the room, set the tray down on the table. The Texans were already wolfing down hunks of venison. Only a few stems were left of the first dish of greens. "Before we light in," Leighton said. They paused, wiped their hands on their britches, and blinked at him. He poured, popped glasses down in front of each of them. "To a band of men right with kindness: may your lives all be filled with those surprises we call blessings."

Ferguson nodded, and they drank.

"Did you want to say grace?" Ferguson asked Leighton.

The Texans bowed their heads. He spoke a prayer he remembered his mother saying the day the roof was finished on the house: "Visit, we beg You, O Lord, this dwelling, and drive from it all the snares of the enemy." He felt the room grow close, felt Hoyt tense next to him. "Let your holy angels dwell herein, to keep us in peace; and let your blessings be always upon us. In the name of the Father, and of the Son, and of the Holy Spirit. Amen." When he touched his left breast, he felt the lump of the pepper-box. Though Ferguson's chin rested on his chest, his eyes remained on Leighton.

"Now, there's a prayer against Yankees," Ferguson said, raising his chin. Bert frowned. Ferguson sliced more of the roast, which crumbled and gave. Plates were again handed around.

As the dinner progressed, Bert kept silent. Despite the joyous flavor of the meat, Leighton could not help watching Bert's quick bites. After each mouthful Bert tapped his lips with a napkin tucked in his right coat sleeve, then dove for food again. In his barbarity was function and grace. The Texans sweated though the room was not hot. Charley and Hoyt nodded often to Leighton after each drink, thanked him profusely for servings of the slimy greens, which Judith brought in to them.

Bert had lied to the Newtonian troops. He had invented a fib so keen that even Ferguson, a lord among liars, succumbed and relinquished a feast of venison. Bert swallowed, glanced at him, resumed eating.

To carry those voices, *she ain't us,* to hear them at every meal, in every fire and ripple of your own gun, and never to know if you had done right. To gorge now at the table of a man you may soon kill. For men like these, in the stink of a prison, or the void of a grave, his father was lost. Maybe he whispered their names—Charlotte, Leighton—soft as the sound of tintypes parting. Maybe he groped for their hands in the dark.

VIII

On Leighton's sixteenth birthday, A.C. Greevins knocked on the door and offered to take him into town for a drink at The Quarry Rand, but Leighton declined. Though the Texans had been gone for days, Leighton wanted to stay close to the house. He invited Greevins in and they sat in the library and sipped brandies from a stock Leighton had hidden. He told Greevins about the knife pulled on Judith, about the Texans' poaching.

Greevins brow wrinkled with concern. "Well, that don't sound like Confederate cavalry." He scratched the slim line of hair left above his ears, then rubbed the top of his bald head. He smiled. "This sure is good brandy."

"They're thieves, murderers. I'm pretty well stuck here."

"Well, they didn't exactly poach if they let you in on it."

Leighton snorted, but held himself back from saying anything cruel to Greevins.

After a moment, Greevins finished the brandy, and rose from his chair. "Well, I been with you Morkans long enough to know you don't change your minds unless you fall flat on your face." He fixed his hat on his head. "Let me come back in February."

Leighton showed him to the door.

The days before and after his birthday Leighton spent with Johnson Davis desperately trying to keep the stock fed. After so many weeks, even the tension of losing the animals disappeared—they would be lost eventually. Their ribs began showing like the hulls of boats under construction. They stared with dull, black eyes. Daily he busted his hands on ice in their troughs, and often sleet froze what little grain was left into a hard cake, inedible to them. The farmhouse became a monotony of tick-

189

ing clocks, eggs for breakfast and lunch, milking, chopping and stacking wood, warily watching the Texans come and go. Two weeks later, Greevins came again. The Texans left so early that morning that not even Johnson Davis saw them leave. Leighton let Greevins in and the old miller stood in the foyer, rain dripping from his coat onto the gray stones of the floor.

"Well, I checked with a friend of mine in the Guard," Greevins said, "and they are officially commissioned as cavalry attachés."

"What the hell is that: an ambassador to horses?"

"Leighton, you just don't understand the South."

Rain pockmarked the snow, but the wind held the slush in a limbo of staying and going. Piled against the houses, the drifts were red and brown with mud. Every tree and building dripped beads of water, and on some mud puddles there erupted a storm of noise. Mud spattered their horses' legs, and by the time they met the boarded shops of Ozark Road, mud clung to Leighton's shins and dotted his kneecaps.

Some troops were assembled on the square. Leighton could hear an officer shouting about the sovereignty of the state, of the warm embrace of the Confederate government. A heavy-loaded wagon marked C.S.A. MO was laboring south.

When they entered, the Quarry Rand was dark, and frigid. Correy sat at a table. He and Shulty and a barmaid Leighton did not recognize were the only people in the bar.

Leighton strode to the table. Correy stood and wiped the back of his hand along his lower lip that glistened even in the dingy light of Shulty's candles.

The three sat together and drank. Greevins asked Leighton his age, and they talked a long time in truths and inanities about the war putting years on them. Running a dry finger across the bare sockets of his gums, Correy produced a screech that made them all laugh and wince.

Shulty waved for the new barmaid, Danny, to fetch them drinks, and she hustled. He rose from the chair and followed her, left the three of them circled around the table.

The hollows in Correy's cheeks were so dark they bore shadows like bevels in wood. His arm shook. "Laydon," he asked, "what can I do to make up for what I done?" He swallowed hard, licking his lips after.

Leighton gripped the back of a chair and raised his open palm to Correy.

Correy sat with his chin stiff, the bevels in his face making him appear incensed.

"Do me one favor, Correy," Leighton said. His voice fell to a whisper. "Should the time come when you and me can go to St. Louis and get my pa or his body, say you will go with me."

Without hesitating Correy raised his whiskey bumper to Leighton, who then raised his. "There's times, Correy, when getting him back is all I think about."

Correy nodded. Then they all drank, but Leighton didn't smile.

They began to whisper war news of the extra activity Greevins and Leighton had witnessed on the way in. As they chatted small wisps of steam curled from their lips. In the waverings of the cheap candles, in their vines of black smoke, Greevin's lean face, and Correy's lips, sinking and puckering, the three of them appeared to be desperate men.

Though it was to be his birthday celebration, Leighton insisted on paying for everything in gold dollars, and the roll and shine of the little coins added light to all their faces. When Danny the barmaid returned with a pitcher and more toddies, Leighton noticed she parted the ratty fur wrap at her throat to reveal the rise of her tiny breasts salted with goose flesh.

Leighton rose and asked her to a table by the window. Though her babble nearly locked his eyes crossed, he sat with her touching her fingers and hoping for a kiss if Shulty wasn't looking and if she kept drinking. She gassed away about Kentucky and beaus and the swamp fox and her parents dead at his hands. When she hit that memory, she paused and her eyes went glassy. Leighton took his gaze off her chest, and realized then how young she was, how pretty, and how damaged.

"I sure am sorry," he whispered. He looked to the window so she could cry it out. Through the yellowed pane, the quarry appeared miniscule. Down Summit, intermittent groups of wagons and soldiers bustled south.

Leighton rode for home and Greevins accompanied him once it became obvious from the wagon traffic that the entire army was on the move. The square was clear and quiet. Garbage was heaped in every corner: scraps of canvas, bones, rotting beans. Even the carcasses of horses were neither buried nor dragged away. Bloated dogs picked at them, chewed thoughtfully, there being much to eat and much time.

The sun was just setting, and though the road was dark, the hills east of Galway glowed stubbly and yellow in the last of the light. Where the road became the trail to the house, they noticed the droppings of oxen, and deep hoof prints in the soft mud. He and Greevins galloped. The front door to the house hung open, and both barn doors were propped wide. A broad swath of mud rife with hoof prints issued from the barn. Hay lay strewn across the floor. Far in the back, one of the wagons slouched bereft of its front axle and hitch. Only the scabbiest of stock animals were in the barn, and even Leighton's horse lurched at this. Three oxen, two mules, four Morgans, Johnson Davis's horse, a flatbed wagon, all that was left of the hay, gone. A thousand dollars at least, and God knows what at war prices. Ferguson knew the stock, the hay, knew where the harness riggings were stowed, all the hemp. Nothing else in the barn appeared ransacked, save for the remaining wagon.

Leighton dismounted and moved in a daze from stall to stall. He peered at the empty, hay-flecked dirt of each, as if the animal that belonged there might be crouching, hiding. The remaining animals—two oxen, an old draft, a skewbald gelding, the milch cows—wagged their heads at him, their eyes wide and rolling as if there were a wolf about. Each breath was punched out of him with the blankness of every stall.

In the last stall, Bert lay with half his face mashed into the dirt, purple lips curled backward to reveal his white teeth jutting garishly from a broken jaw.

Leighton stepped into the stall. Greevins' saddle creaked and jingled. Leighton's horse snorted, and its noise burst and echoed as if the timbers of the barn roof cracked.

Bert's legs were twisted at impossible angles; his chest faced Leighton. From his jaw to his ear a purple swath ran cobwebbed with vessels of dark red, the imprint of a boot. In the dim light of the barn Leighton could see one of Bert's eyes was still open. Beneath the boy's tattered campaign coat, his shirt was soaked a dark brown. The fine officer's coat, the sharp riding breaches, where would they be? Divvied between Ferguson, Charley, Hoyt? Or still rolled in the bedding, strapped to the back of the scruffy Pinto Bert had ridden? Leighton heard Greevins' belt scrape past the stall door.

"And we got to bury one. God, I'm sorry, Leighton," Greevins said.

They stood over him a minute, and Leighton's chest sunk with every breath. He consoled himself that here lay a boy who had no idea of the necessity of extreme unction, who'd seen a world, knew it was beyond all he could imagine, and now was finished with it. The sick call set, gathering dust in some closet of the house, would have been a Byzantine tea service to Bert. Leighton imagined the crisp openings of the miniature doors, sliding out the gilded plate and the consecrated host, the crystalline finery of the phial of holy water, the silver cross glinting in the wavering light from the stubs of the blessed candles, probably the last two in the house. But even when Leighton saw this scene, Bert's face remained crushed into the barn's dirt, his body twisted. Leighton had to start at the beginning.

Quis creasti te? Leighton would ask him.

"Ferguson," Bert would answer.

If thou shouldst retain our iniquities, O Lord, Lord, who could sustain the weight?

"Ferguson. Hoyt. Charley. You micks. The dutch. The Republic of Texas."

"You reckon he was one who didn't want this to happen? You reckon he fought them?" Greevins asked Leighton.

"There's no doubt in my mind."

Greevins turned for the house, and, after a moment, Leighton followed.

When he caught up with Greevins, he tugged at the sleeve of his coat, then felt childish, but wanted to bury his face at the old man's breast. "Should I ride after them?"

Greevins shook his head, stepped slightly away from Leighton. "Oh, shit no, Leighton. Good way to get killed. Your stock's gone. No getting it back."

Lamps were missing from the front room. The wall clock was gone. Amid long swoops of mud, the chairs were moved and abandoned as if they proved too cumbersome.

"I'm lucky they didn't burn me out." Leighton searched a closet and found a soot-blackened old lamp with a slight wash of lard oil bobbing in it. He struggled with the dry wick awhile. Then it glowed to light.

The bedrooms were ransacked. Leighton's clothes were strewn all around. The few household rifles were gone. Two of Charlotte's empty jewelry drawers were smashed on the floor of the Morkan's bedroom.

Leighton wandered the house but touched nothing. Overturned, scattered, the belongings were entirely foreign to him. The house, frigid with its doors open, was hollow, stripped of residence as if the structure were borne here by flood waters, was none of his concern, yet held for him a terrible fascination. He shivered through the rooms.

Near the door to the cellar, small, white spheres dotted the stone floor. Leighton stared at them for a moment, thought the balls might be sleet blown in from outside. He gripped the cellar door when he recognized the pink and silver sheen to each sphere—they were pearls, hundreds of them.

Leighton opened the cellar door, and the sweet stink of port engulfed him. He went slowly down the stairs, and Greevins followed. The lamp revealed a floor red and reeking with wine. Shards of glass flashed green and yellow. Both wine racks were thrown to the floor. In the corner stabbed into the earth where the strong box and leather bags of jewelry should have been was one of the black daggers the Texans carried.

Leighton plucked the dagger from the ground. The blade wavered in his hand, and he breathed deeply to steady himself. A rumpled square of parchment was stuck at the haft of the blade. Leighton peeled this off. "**ONLY FOR THE HOLLADAYS**," was written there in a rough, jumpy hand.

Leighton dropped the dagger to the ground. He crumpled the note, his arms trembling. He knelt and lifted the wooden rack from the muck. He looked up at Greevins, whose head bowed. Wavering, Leighton stood.

"They took everything I had of my mother. All the pretty things pa gave her."

"Come here, boy." The old miller opened his arms to Leighton.

Leighton dropped his head to Greevins' chest, and Greevins clasped his back, drew Leighton to him. In his tears, the wool of Greevins' coat bit at his eyes.

"I'm so sorry, Leighton," Greevins whispered into the top of his head. His voice was rough. "They told me they was cavalry."

Leighton pushed away from him, wiped his eyes, recovered himself somewhat. "It's fine. We should have left. I should have made us leave town earlier."

Upstairs, Johnson Davis wiped his eyes and nose with the back of his hand. Morkan's favorite shotgun, the one Leighton had sawed off, he cradled in his arms. "Saved all them other quarry guns. They in the woods." He swallowed. Leighton held his arm, his own hand shaking. Johnson had been a father to him all through Morkan's absence, but in the trembling of the Negro, Leighton could feel that passing forever. "Start hunting us up some candles and lamps."

Working alone, each of them sifted through brogans, dungarees, cups, and books, held them up and inspected them by the wavering candlelight, tucked them in corners, piled shards of crock ware. They scuttled and crouched from room to room. Muttering to themselves, they lingered over scarred portraits and the shattered faces of clocks.

Without casket or prayers, they buried Bert the next morning near a stream where the ground was softened by a running spring. They stacked rocks to make up for soil. Leighton insisted they mark the grave with a heavy wooden stake. Of the Texans, he said, this might be the only one with relatives who cared to have what remained.

IX

MORKAN WATCHED HORATIO CIRCULATE AMONG THE prisoners, spotted a few palm readings with an earnest moment of concentration to them, ending in nervous laughter.

Horatio took the hand of a prisoner captured at Belmont, held it to his cheek, then stroked the lines in the prisoner's palm. Something passed there that Morkan could not catch. The prisoner's neck went rigid for an instant, and his eyes flashed to his palm as if Horatio were fixing a leech to him. The Belmont prisoner maintained his smile.

Horatio rose on his toes. "You'll meet a woman running a toll bridge for her uncle." He paused, then screamed, and the Belmont prisoner jolted and clutched his chest.

"Watch out for her," one of the onlookers said, spreading laughter all around.

The scheme made some sense. Horatio was too strange and theatrical for any guard to suspect he was actually accomplishing something.

Nights Morkan found Overbo gone, or spotted his broad form shuffling away. The time, or what he could judge of time from the moon and the pink and orange approach of dawn, was never consistent. Some nights, Overbo's chest and arms were tense behind Morkan, his breathing erratic. He was waiting for a guard to clear out of the hall or for others around him to sleep. Morkan imagined Horatio down in the pit, scraping all that wet soil around him, the sputtering candlelight. Any piece of chert bigger than a fist had to be a heartbreaking obstacle.

Nimms did not come back. The women of St. Louis were allowed to give the prisoners valentine cards—the bottoms of cigar boxes tinseled with foil. Colonel Tuttle opened every one of them and gave them his approval with the initials **JWT** on each.

Watching Overbo show his card around, Morkan felt a pang of guilt that he was not in the tunnel. The plate was still not found, though Overbo assured him it was either buried accidentally or long gone to the River with the garbage. Overbo still gave up his coat, though Morkan could walk now and his lungs improved. The reverend still brought Morkan a sludge of gravy and mush from the dishes, and handfuls of potato peelings, which they shared.

Waking one night and finding Overbo gone, Morkan rose, stood silently listening to the lecture hall sleep, a room filled with coughs and murmurs. He wrapped Overbo's coat around him and began to tip-toe his way to the kitchen. Tonight, he decided, he would join the workshift, find the plate himself if he had to.

Just before he reached the wooden stairs, he heard footsteps ascending and voices, two of them, one very deep, the other soft. It was Nimms. Morkan froze.

"We appreciate your visits, Father," Nimms said. "These may be Rebels, but I cannot abide the fact that they may die in mortal sin."

"It is no trouble," the soft voice said. "I must say, Sergeant, and I mean no disrespect, but there are a shocking number of deaths here."

They fell quiet, their feet thumping up the stairs.

Morkan hurried from the top of the stairs to a spot inside a doorframe where it was darker.

"And also, Sergeant, it greatly concerns me that the men are so thin, and seem to be dying of things that more warmth and cleanliness could alleviate." Before they reached the top of the stairs Morkan saw a candle bobbing. He pressed himself against the door. "In this modern age, with trains and ferries available to supply us, why are some of these men dying of what I perceive to be hunger?"

Like the bobbing yolk of an egg, candlelight clung to the walls. Nimms was delivering some kind of palaver about transferring men to Alton, Illinois. A hatch in the bottom of the door Morkan hid against opened, scraping his leg. Morkan stiffened.

A hand with dagger-like nails gripped his calf, yanked him toward the opening. "Break you fucking in half," grunted a voice behind the hatch.

The candlelight leapt, and Nimms stood before him, the muzzle of his revolver poked Morkan's ribs.

"Mr. Morkan," Nimms said. He kicked the hatch, smashing the groping hand in the door. There was a howl, and the hand vanished.

Nimms' eyes gleamed in the candlelight. "Father, do come here."

The priest stepped behind Nimms. The Father was a bald man save for a ring of hair above his ears; he had a thin face, little spectacles. He was fingering a very ornate crucifix Morkan spotted for German or French.

"You may wish, Father, to bless this one for he has sinned gravely and continually, and has *now* sinned mortally."

Another guard arrived fixing his hat. Nimms yanked him aside, began haranguing him for sleeping. The Father looked up at Morkan, and Morkan leaned forward squinting. It was Brother Guertín, a seminarian to the priesthood when Morkan was in St. Louis.

The Father's mouth dropped open. He gripped Morkan's arm. "Oh, Michael Morkan." He covered his mouth with his other hand, squeezed Morkan's arm. His eyes became wet.

Nimms returned to Morkan's side.

Father Guertín glared. "You must let this man free. He cannot be left to die."

Nimms stiffened. "Father, he supplied the Rebels with the powder that carried them through the whole summer of campaigning. More than any soldier in their army, death after death you may attribute to him."

Father Guertín blinked at Morkan, then bowed his head. He looked Morkan full in the eyes, stretched his small white hand out to a spot above Morkan's forehead. "Bless you in the name of the Father and the Son and the Holy Spirit, Amen." He made the sign of the cross over Morkan's forehead, then bowed his own head in prayer, touching his chin to his fingertips.

After a moment, he frowned at Nimms. "Take me from this place."

Nimms's face darkened, and he ordered the guard to take Father Guertín away. When the Father was gone, Nimms stuck his nose in Morkan's face. "May I ask you what it was you needed outside the lecture hall?"

Morkan was silent.

"Well, you have just condemned yourself to some lonely quarters." Nimms lit a cigarette with the candle. "I have kept my word. You are alive. And you treat me to this?" Morkan yawned without covering his mouth.

Nimms pursed his lips. When the other guard returned from escorting the Father, he and Nimms led Morkan down the corridor away from the wooden stairs and the lecture hall. They rounded a corner. Nimms opened a door, and the wavering sphere of his candle light bobbed on two rows of crates against the walls. The air stunk of urine and feces. In each crate, a man was crouched in the tight space. Some raised their heads, weakly. Others remained stooped, their legs and arms tangled in the crates.

One prisoner made an awful croaking sound, his eyes on Nimms. The prisoner's lips were so dry they appeared to be caked with flour.

The guard gripped Morkan's arms and kept them behind his back while Nimms opened one of the crates.

"Will you tell me what you needed in that hallway?"

Morkan was silent.

Nimms snorted. "It only goes to the kitchen and the morgue. Just tell me." When Morkan said nothing, Nimms shook his head. "Take his pants, Private."

The guard knelt, spun Morkan around to face him. He unsnapped Morkan's tattered dungarees, and they fell to his ankles with no struggle.

"Dag!" The guard exclaimed. "These Rebs stink worse every day."

The air was frigid on his balls and thighs. He shivered and collapsed to his knees.

"It won't be any warmer in the crate," Nimms said.

The door groaned, and a pair of boots came toward them, the new leather of them creaking. Morkan turned his head as much as he could, and saw a plump-faced officer striding. "Nimms," the officer called out.

Nimms snapped to attention. "Colonel Tuttle, sir."

The boots stopped before them, their leather so shiny black it was almost purple. The pants above them were blue and creased at the side. Two hands plucked at the knees of the pants. Then a plump, mustached face stooped to catch Morkan's eyes. "You're the cleanest puke in here, so I reckon your name is Michael Morkan."

Morkan affirmed this.

"Father Guertín rushed to my office, Sergeant Nimms. This is the first and only time I have had him advocate by name for one of these." Tuttle wrinkled his nose and told the guard to fetch Morkan a pair of pants. When the guard left, Tuttle came very close to Nimms, sticking his chin in Nimms's face. "This one one of your special cases? Mmm? You were going to lock him up with the incorrigibles? Mmm?"

"He is the traitor who gave Price and the Rebel Missouri Guard...."

"Yes, yes. I know." He looked Nimms over coldly. "I have some questions for you later. Stay where my orderly can get you, will you please, Sergeant?"

Nimms's jaw clenched as if he were chewing the bile of something he yet had to say.

"Dismissed," said Tuttle with such pleasant authority Morkan almost missed it.

The guard returned, held out a white pair of pants with a little draw string at the waist, the sort of pajamas Morkan had seen invalids wear. Holding tight to Tuttle's sleeve, moving languidly, as if all this were a pleasant dream, Morkan let the guard help him into the pants. He let go, drew the string tight, then braced himself leaning on Tuttle.

"Filthy!" one of the prisoners squawked. "I'm filthy. Can't you see this?"

Tuttle led Morkan through the door past the squalling prisoner. Tuttle's face remained unperturbed, plump cheeks, small gray mustache, eyes that appeared very red.

Tuttle helped him up a set of marble stairs, past the hallway where Nimms's interrogation rooms were, and on to a third floor. Morkan smelled coffee, and it made his knees weak.

A guard opened two tall walnut doors. Tuttle set Morkan down gingerly in a leather chair. Morkan dug his fingers into the cushioning, felt it give and rebound.

"Coffee," Tuttle said. "And biscuits."

The guard hustled off.

Papers and books covered Tuttle's desk. The mullioned windows behind the desk caught a clear dawn light high above any dust from the streets or fog along the river.

Tuttle sat behind his desk. He shuffled down into the stacks of papers. "Now, mind you, I listen to Father Guertín. But I know from experience the religious mind forgives often and tends toward hysteria." He lifted one stack and pulled out a bundle of parchment tied with a gray ribbon. He untied the ribbon. "Here we are. Yes. Nimms was to report to me on his progress at getting from you assessments of Price and McBride and the Missouri State Guard. After he had extracted everything, we were to hang you. Am I right?"

Morkan shrugged, shivering a little. That this was the warden, the man Nimms was to report to, the man not buying what Nimms was getting from Morkan, began to dawn on him. He gripped the arm of the chair, steadied himself. Though he had wanted to die just hours ago, the notion of a reprieve made his heart jog. He was too exhausted to dispute even a glimmer of hope.

The guard brought coffee and biscuits, set them on a table beside Morkan. When he took the cup, the gray and ingrained filth of his hands astonished him. Against the white china cup, his fingers looked like something a hound had unearthed.

"Sergeant Nimms has not exactly impressed me with what he has brought back."

Morkan sipped the coffee, held his chest and arms stiffly, forced his hands to be still. The coffee was rich, bitter.

"Is it because his prisoner is not forthcoming?" Tuttle asked.

"I told him." The coffee warmed and loosened his tight lungs. "Everything."

"Well, before we hang you," Tuttle said, "there are some theories I might posit with you. Father Guertín claims you have a concise, analytical mind."

Morkan tensed.

Tuttle sat back in his chair. He smiled, drank from his coffee. "It is my suspicion that Sergeant Nimms never really cared to obtain significant information for our army. Nor did he care to attempt the reform of Rebels into citizens, though he claimed this."

Morkan sat forward.

"Tell me, what would you say was the major thrust of Nimms's questioning? Confederate strategy? Clandestine operations? Codes?"

"Money," Morkan said. "All of his questions were after assets, their whereabouts, the amounts."

Tuttle's smile disappeared. His forehead wrinkled.

"I made a written confession of all my associations with Price and McBride," Morkan said. "It was thorough; I left nothing out. Yet, on seeing it, Sergeant Nimms proceeded with a line of questioning about my monies, what I had squirreled away."

Tuttle nodded, held up a finger, shuffled some items around on his desk. He dipped a pen in the inkwell. He scrawled something on notes he uncovered.

"Would you say that to an army your holdings represented significant booty?"

Morkan rubbed his temples with his thumb and index finger. "My holdings would not be significant to any army."

Tuttle nodded and wrote. "Significant, then, to an individual?"

"That individual will have all I need to open a quarry or to sell what I had for a pretty fair gain."

Tuttle stroked his mustache. "From what Nimms got out of you, do you imagine that he could easily locate these assets?"

Morkan nodded. "He claimed he wanted that information to break my will."

Tuttle glanced up from his notations. "Did he break your will?"

He weighed his answer like two handfuls of gravel. Tuttle's face was soft and round, the sort of man you wanted to buy tooth powders from. "Very nearly."

"Do you resent what happened?"

Morkan raised his eyebrows at him.

Tuttle scrawled.

"So his plan was what?" Morkan asked. "To hang me, then gather my goods once his commission was up."

Tuttle looked up. "Is that what you suspect?"

Morkan shrugged. "Should I?"

Tuttle put his pen down, rubbed beneath his eyes. He sat for a moment hunched. With the dawn now streaming down from the high mullioned windows, his dark coat suddenly made him appear like a spent priest Morkan had once seen recovering outside the drapes after a morning of hearing confessions. Tuttle's eyes squinted, and it seemed something very grave passed between him and Morkan.

Morkan was sure this was a way to damage Nimms, possibly ruin him. "He advocated sparing others, didn't he? Like Porter Moore?"

Tuttle nodded. "Moore Iron Boilers. Hell of a plant. Every steamboat out there runs off that boiler if it's a St. Louis boat. He was caught in that first group at Camp Jackson, and before that, he helped storm this building after the surgeons left. Rebs thought there were guns to take in the mansards."

"He was rich?"

"In the extreme."

"If this is happening why not sack Nimms? Put him on trial?"

Tuttle shook his head. He placed both hands on the table palms down. "Would you be pleased if Nimms were court-martialed?"

Morkan said nothing.

"Of course you would be. So would every man who's borne Nimms's interrogations. How do I know that you all aren't inventing this elaborate scheme and foisting it on me to get back at him?"

"My word is good. I was a loyal citizen of the Republic." Morkan sat back, raised his chin slightly and tried to appear affronted. "I was coerced into giving that powder."

Tuttle frowned. "Prove your loyalty, then."

"How?" Morkan asked.

Tuttle shrugged. "Tell me something I don't know about, be an insider for me. Tell about the lecture hall or the prisoners."

"I have to betray others to prove to you that I am loyal?"

Tuttle's lips were flat, his eyes unblinking. "It appears so."

Morkan stared at him. "What would be done to Nimms?"

"Court-martialed. Maybe."

Morkan nodded. Tuttle smiled.

Morkan bowed his head. The coffee had cooled, but still warmed his fingers and made his tongue ache and tingle. He coughed. In his memory he saw Nimms rolling a cigarette over him, saw the flecks of tobacco tumbling.

"I can't punish my own officer on your word alone." Tuttle said. His pug nose, covered with tiny black pits like pinholes, shone in the light from the window. Under his eyes, folds of blackened skin rumpled, and this led Morkan to think that he was likely a calculating man, and a poor sleeper. Tuttle paused a moment. "I want Nimms stopped, if he is doing what you say." Even the top of his hair shone a little, it was so well greased, gray and yellow and perfectly flat against his head.

Waiting, Tuttle poured himself a coffee. "Let me give you an example. You are known among the Rebels here. The quarry owner, an old railroad bridge engineer, who gave powder to the State Guard." Tuttle raised his eyebrows. "If they tunnel from here, would they not come to you?"

"You can't tunnel in this, not so near the river."

Tuttle sipped his coffee. "See. You teach me already."

Morkan felt genuinely warm for the first time since coming to Gratiot. Dread foamed in his stomach.

"You have already come to me," Tuttle said. He smiled. "Here you are." He leaned forward, ran his thumb along the edge of his desk. "Let's start simply. What were you doing in the hallway so late at night?"

Morkan tried to ease himself back into the chair and appear comfortable. "I'm embarrassed to say. It's demeaning."

"Please, Mr. Morkan," Tuttle said, his voice sneering, "I run a prison."

"I had wandered toward the kitchen. Sometimes prisoners who work there have leavings on their cuffs. You can sup at it when they sleep, if you're careful."

Tuttle pulled a frown, but raised his eyebrows. "Are there any dishwashers whose sleeves you find distasteful? Any particularly slick with Mississippi mud?" His eyes narrowed with each question.

Morkan's heart surged—he had failed. Trying to lie, he might have endangered Overbo. "No," Morkan said. "Not that I have found."

Tuttle stood, stretched his arms and yawned.

There was a flutter at the window. The shadow of wings beating obscured the light. Tuttle never looked up, kept his eyes on Morkan.

"Come now. Whose sleeves do you avoid?" He cocked his head.

In Overbo's hands, a pile of blue snow glistened. The water in them was frigid, salty. The rails banged against the trucks like a sledge driving pile.

"Mr. Morkan, I am far worse than Nimms," Tuttle said. "I have no vested interests, save that of the Union. And I don't care what you have hidden at home."

He came around the desk and leaned back against the desk-top. "You are a smart man, Morkan. I spent my life before the war cowing to smart men like you." He raised his eyebrows. "If you tell me who, I can separate you from a great deal of pain. I might even keep you from the gallows. And then, eventually you may return to your quarry, your son, your hidden wealth. And Nimms will occupy your crate among the incorrigibles."

He had already revealed too much. If he revealed a name, Horatio maybe, he might save himself. Then he remembered

Nimms's trickery, holding only two receipts, how the sergeant fished everything out of him with just a little pain.

"Morkan?"

"I am the only one tunneling. From the morgue, out onto Gratiot." He stared at Tuttle, and felt for the first time in himself the hot column of something solid and insuperable. "Not a soul in this place could succeed at it but me." It was a power like a jet of steam, like a cascade of water over a great wheel.

Tuttle crossed his arms over his chest. "Nimms is as poor a liar as you are. I'm sure you've understood by now that your son is alive. He was never in anyone's custody. Your land, your mine, they're all fine." He returned to his chair behind the desk. "Of course, Major Heron is there, mining for the Union. But what I might ought to do is just transfer Nimms. Say assign him to Springfield to interrogate prisoners there."

He flicked the cigar over the massive stack of papers. "But I'll make you a straight deal. Your neck and Nimms for the names of the tunnelers and where they are digging."

Morkan sat forward, his jaw set so fiercely it ached. Tuttle's round face was as placid as a pail of water.

After a long time, Tuttle took a bell from his desk drawer and rang it. Two guards stepped in. "Take Mr. Morkan outside to the poles. Let him stand at pillory a while."

The guards nodded, took Morkan by the arms.

"Nimms won't bother you again." Tuttle put his cigar out. "He'll be traveling."

The guards lifted him, hauled him through the door. They pushed through several swinging doors and finally down the stairs to the courtyard. There troopers waited beside the three sawed-off telegraph poles. The soldiers wore army blankets over their shoulders, their faces swaddled so that only their eyes stared out. They looked like grubby imitations of Bedouins in the cold. One trooper nodded when the two guards clicked their heels.

"He is to be pilloried, then rested."

The trooper's eyebrows rose. "I see. You know it ain't a pillory. It's a pole."

The guards snorted and left for the relative warmth indoors. With their breath smoking at their faces, ice crusting on the wool covering their mouths, the troopers positioned Morkan with his back to the pole then raised his arms above his head and slightly behind him.

"Hold your wrists up against these railroad spikes, Reb," one said. "That's it."

They roped his wrists together. Even through Overbo's coat and the decaying blanket wrapped at his shoulders, the steel of the spikes was frigid. He kept his back arched until one of the troopers pressed him flat against the pole.

"You're going to be out here for hours. Stand just so or you'll die of this."

They tested the rope. Straining, Morkan could see the head of the spike, silvery where some hammer had pounded it. Uncountable now the number of hours he had stared above him at these spikes and seen that hammer's terrible work. "You must be someone quite valuable. You either know a lot, or can get to know a lot, I imagine. You want some bourbon?"

Shivering, Morkan nodded. The trooper raised a canteen to Morkan's lips. Morkan drank, arching his neck up to swallow. His neck smarted as if a wire saw were caught in between his vertebrae. Then the trooper took the canteen away. Behind them, he glimpsed windows of the prison and the soiled ovals of faces there, prisoners watching.

The trooper whispered, barely moving his lips. "You know no country's worth what's about to happen. Speak now, and it stops."

Morkan closed his eyes.

Once they were done with him, they took him into the ward and made him lie down on a bed equipped with restraints. One of the guards coaxed him to drink a bitter fluid. It was laudanum, and he eagerly finished it. His stomach burned, but this passed, and the laudanum spread a warm shroud over his head and chest. If there was anything left of that core he'd been so proud of, it smoldered like an ashen stick in a fire.

Outside the ward's frosted window, he heard pigeons muttering. Somewhere tonight—cursing, caterwauling—Horatio was scrabbling in the pitch black, in the moist, River-stinking earth. Behind Horatio, the light, that tiny student lamp at the entrance to the tunnel, would shift, and he would crawl toward the light, expecting Overbo, delighted, screeching with excitement, the gnawed table leg growing wet in his lips.

He woke to someone shaking him. Tuttle was standing in the dark, a yellow halo of wavering light at his side. Morkan swallowed; the laudanum left an ache at the back of his throat, and though his lips were dry, his mouth seemed full of spit.

"I may have done you a great favor," Tuttle said. "Or you did yourself one."

Morkan blinked, thumped his wrist against the restraint, then remembered the straps, the bed, the poles, the freezing hours.

"It was the lunatic drummer that cracked and ratted on his fellows. We followed him on his way to the kitchen and caught him there, in your hallway, where you sup at the sleeves of dishwashers." Tuttle squinted at Morkan, touched his red wrists, his frostbitten knuckles. He whistled. "You never cracked. That's why you were out on the posts. I'd act nigh unto death when you're returned. That's my favor. They'll kill you otherwise."

"What happened to Horatio?" Morkan wanted desperately to rub his eyes. He was not sure whether this was a dream or not. His stomach wound tight with nausea.

Tuttle put a finger to his lips. He stepped back. "Rest," Tuttle said.

For a moment, Morkan's eyes gained focus. The yellow halo of light came from a brass student lamp, its base ringed with red-brown mud.

When the guards returned him to the lecture hall, Overbo and Horatio were both gone. The guards set him against one of the fences that screened the stoves from the prisoners. His head lolled back against the iron. Several boys hurried over, and soon the older prisoners began to gather.

"You're damn lucky to be alive," one boy said. "We saw you out there."

Morkan swung his head from where it rested, steadied himself to look at the boy.

"Look at his wrists," one of the others said.

"Come on, clear out and let him rest," said a burly man in a pair of rumpled trousers. He began to pull and push prisoners aside. Morkan recognized him as one of Horatio's partners from Athens.

When he had a space cleared around Morkan, he kneeled, tilted a cup of water to Morkan's lips. Morkan took the cup from his hands, watched him as he stood.

The prisoner from Athens cleared his throat. "We sure admire you, Mr. Morkan." He swallowed, raised his hand as if to remove his cap. "I wished we could have got to you to tell you not to hold out no more once they had Horatio." After a long pause, he said, "I sure am sorry. You didn't have to go through this."

"What happened?"

The prisoner from Athens frowned. "Don't trouble yourself no more. Rest."

Morkan eased himself forward, touched the prisoner's arm.

The prisoner held his hand. "Horatio lost his mind, what little he had of it, when they caught him, and one of them had to shoot him. It was sure a scuffle. I mean that Yankee *had* to shoot him. Horatio may have looked pale, but he had a lot of boy in him."

Morkan's hand trembled and he felt the water spill on his wrist and soak down into the cuff of Overbo's coat. He handed the cup to the prisoner. "Overbo?"

"We haven't seen him. He was with Horatio. He was in the tunnel and they caught Horatio going to him. Some say Horatio led them there on accident, then lost his mind when they wouldn't let him go."

There it was, the favor that Tuttle had promised. Or maybe it was the truth. The prisoner's cheeks tightened with pain, his brow wrinkled. Morkan considered for a moment shattering the lie and telling him that Horatio might not have failed them.

"Mr. Morkan, I am so sorry we couldn't think of any way to get a message to you." He patted Morkan's hand. "We feel responsible in this. We are in your debt."

Morkan put a hand up. The prisoner from Athens knelt, held out the cup again.

For weeks, prisoners helped Morkan up for breakfast, or saved aside a little of their porridge when he slept too long. The weather warmed, and the guards flung the tall windows open. When the prisoners touched the window ledges, guards warned them back with revolvers, and now and then, a prisoner was shot for disobeying. Morkan stood with his hands clasped behind him. Outside, a sales drummer worked by the gates trying to book officers for extra passage on one of the commissioned boats. As the drummer haggled, Morkan felt his chest buckle, his eyes sting. Wind stirred against his cheeks, lifted the filthy curls of his hair. There was the stuff of life, what Overbo had wanted, the wind, the River, the drummers and soldiers and ladies going about their business, green lacewings tumbling and rising in the sun.

Late in April, a pair of guards brought a stooped man into the lecture hall. His feet dragged behind him, bumping on loose puncheons. They flopped him in a corner by one of the tall windows. Morkan rose, and made it over to him, stared down a kid who was probably about to strip the man of his garments. The man's shirt was filthy brown, and he stunk powerfully of urine. The top of his head was bald, and two parallel lines of a red rash were ingrained across his scalp.

Struggling a little, Morkan knelt. The man jolted, slowly raised his head, his eyes ogling with effort. It was Overbo. His lips were swollen and cracked. His tongue was dotted with white, and his front teeth were gone.

"Git," Overbo said, his lips sliding about as if he had suffered some apoplexy.

"Do you want something? Can I get you water?" Morkan asked. He leaned very close to Overbo, his voice shaking. He put a hand on Overbo. Prisoners and guards gathered behind him.

"Git," Overbo said again, his voice rattling. He grabbed Morkan's knee with his hand, pushed him, his elbow quaking. "No more."

Morkan struggled to fetch him some water

When he returned, Overbo rose to his feet. Two alarmed guards cleared the prisoners away. Disheveled, his eyes drooping over black rings of skin, Overbo stood like a rabid bear, cornered, his dreadful eyes flashing from one guard to the other.

A wind blew in from the window and lifted Overbo's hair, which had dwindled to two feathers of gray. Morkan held out the cup.

Overbo turned to the window, stepped up to it. He glanced back at the guards, one of whom had drawn a revolver. Overbo looked for a long time at Morkan, his eyes as black and dull as charcoal, his face long, the skin loose and baggy. "Bless you, Brother," Overbo said.

Then he reached, grabbed the bars on the window, and shoved both of his arms far out into the sunlight.

"Overbo," Morkan said. A third guard had arrived and popped a hand in the middle of Morkan's chest to hold him back.

"Remove yourself from the window," the guard with the revolver shouted. The lecture hall went silent.

"You have one last opportunity to remove yourself from the window."

With a grunt, Overbo smashed his face against the bars, pushing out. His fingers, Morkan could see, wormed and clutched for the sun as if for the edge of a quilt.

Morkan pushed against the guard, who caught him in the stomach with an elbow.

The revolver fired, and Overbo's body bucked. In the back of his yellowed shirt there appeared a tiny hole surrounded by petals of red. His hands remained out the window, fingers erect and trembling. The revolver fired again, shattering his forehead out into the sun, leaving a red peony at the back of his head. His fingers drooped.

Dozens of guards pounded into the lecture hall, their boots booming on the puncheons. The cup dropped from Morkan's hand. The barrel water spread from it and darkened the wood floor for just a moment, and then the stain was gone.

A week after Overbo's death, two guards came into the hall, found Morkan staring at the sun through Overbo's window. The guards grabbed him by the arms and rushed him from the hall. Prisoners jeered at the guards, whistled and stamped. They took him up the stairs to the third floor, then to Tuttle's office. The colonel was hunched behind his desk, signing sheets of paper from one stack and laying them on another. He squinted over his square glasses at Morkan.

"Good," Tuttle said. "You look healthy."

Morkan said nothing.

"I wanted you to know that Nimms is traveling, but I can keep him in line. If I deem it necessary."

Morkan nodded.

Tuttle pulled his glasses off. "You've stopped a serious threat for us. I greatly appreciate that." When Morkan remained silent, Tuttle rose from the chair.

Morkan stared at him, then at the mullioned window. A cold front had passed through, and on the glass there remained beads of rain.

"There is more you can do for us."

Morkan watched his fat face.

"Periodically, I'll whisk you in here, as I did today. Now and again, I'll drape you on the poles outside. Just for show." He smiled. "Usually not, but such public penance will keep you safe. Then you can tell me who has started any underground engineering."

Morkan stared down at his hands, so filthy and hard-skinned, he had to imagine them attached to his body.

"If you don't tell us anything, well, we can have you caged awhile, like we did that preacher." Tuttle leaned forward and tried to catch Morkan's eye. "Morkan, you have already crossed the terrible line. You're ours now, a loyal citizen of your true country."

Morkan dabbed his lips with his collar, glanced up at Tuttle.

"Tell me. Are you with us, Mr. Morkan?"

"Take me back down," he said. "Leave me among my countrymen."

Tuttle frowned. "I'll be sure and tell Nimms of your decision."

For the remainder of the war, there were very few tunnels built out of Gratiot that reached more than ten yards before the perpetrators were caught. Morkan kept to himself and spoke to Cora's tintype.

No rumor Tuttle spread ever held. The flow of prisoners between Gratiot and other new prisons at Alton, Illinois and in Indiana became so rapid, that few men came to know anything but snatches of rumor about the gaunt red-headed man who stalked the halls and spent hours staring out the window onto Eighth Street. The flush of his face, the cough told men he was consumptive. Now and again, guards hauled him off in the night, then returned him. Rumor had it he was the inventor of a drill that could bore holes even in ironclads, or a device that operated on power from coal-oil for months at a filling. He would not tell the Federals anything, the rumors said, thus the abductions, the hours strapped to the poles in the courtyard. Often while he slept, young boys left him scraps of bread, a biscuit half, sometimes with notes under them smeared with soot, messages like

SIR: WHEN WE ARE ALL THROUGH WITH THIS I CAN HELP YOU TO FIND THAT UNDERWATER SHIP YOU SUNK TO HIDE IT FROM THESE DEVILS.

During the day, he kept the notes in his pocket, tearing them piece by piece. Nights he waited for a good breeze. Then, holding the bits up to Overbo's window, he set them loose, and they fluttered down to the street.

Book 3

More Than Watchmen for the Dawn

I

WHEN GREEVINS LEFT, HE SAID HE DESIRED TO FIND
Price's army and finally join him, even if all he did was cook for
them.

"I'd go with you if I thought that would get my pa back,"
Leighton said. Just off the porch, snow was falling so thickly
behind them the air hissed like a campfire doused with water.
"Do you think that will ever happen, Greevins?"

Greevins paused a moment, squinting hard, then he touched
Leighton's cheek. As Greevins loped off on his squat horse,
Leighton figured he would not see the miller again. He bowed
his head so that he wouldn't have to watch the old man vanish
in the snow.

A day later, a squad of black-clad horsemen veered from the
woods and coursed through the trees single file.

Leighton stepped out on the porch. The sun had risen and
lined the edge of the horizon silver. The wind blew down tufts
of snow that fell thumping like sacks of sand.

On seeing him one horseman whistled, and they tightened
into a crescent on the lawn. In the lower window of the house, a
shadow moved forward—Judith, just her face.

One of the soldiers drew a revolver. Leighton slowly raised
his hands. They were big men, and their black capes bore golden
buttons.

"You Leighton Morkan?"

Leighton nodded.

"You willing to come with us?"

"Sure. You're Union troops aren't you?"

They stared at him. One of the horses stamped.

"It's just there's been a lot of bandits," Leighton said.

The trooper with the revolver nodded. He waved the gun in front of him. "Get your horse." When Leighton returned riding Morkan's Walker, two troopers swung their mounts alongside so that he was pressed between them.

Federals escorted him toward town on roads vicious with mud and slush. The muck soaked his shins and made him grit his teeth against its cold. He worried they were taking him to retrieve his father's body. Shattered and empty windows stared, hollow, each facade a weathered skull. Soldiers, all blue-capped with black cloaks, were everywhere, stomping through the slush, jerking horses to course.

The cavalry passed through the quarry gates, which hung askew on their hinges. Dung littered the quarry yard, and near the office, a big brace of asses stood. About a dozen soldiers leaned on shovels, and behind them stood a tall officer with a long, black beard—Heron, the liaison Morkan had so distrusted, the scavenger from the alley. The Federals killed his father, he imagined, brought the body here to show Leighton. The cavalrymen halted and saluted Heron who stepped forward. His small eyes shone so light blue they seemed silver. When he looked at Leighton, a smile flickered over his face, and he gazed at something far away, as if Leighton were only half of what he expected.

"Hello again, pup." He squinted at the sky. "Your traitor father made some awfully poor decisions. For the time being I am in ownership of this fine quarry." He waved a hand at the cliffs as if shooing flies. "You know how to cut this?"

Leighton nodded.

"Fine. Fine." Heron nodded at the cavalrymen.

The two dismounted, pulled Leighton from the saddle, and stood him before Heron. Heron reached in his coat and held out a stack of papers bound in twine. He loosened the twine, pulled one sheaf from the bundle and held the sheaf before Leighton's eyes. The sheaf was the size of a playing card. The number 750 was written on it. Below the number was a very competent drawing of a grooved ashlar block with dimension specifications. Leighton took the card from him, stared, ran his fingers over the India ink, the indentations where the tip of the pen had pressed.

No. His father would have used minuscule cross-hatchings to indicate shadings. And the numbers were not precisely drawn enough to be Morkan's.

Heron was squinting at him. "Not clear?"

"It's a block," Leighton said.

Heron nodded.

This was a stone order. Heron handed him the stack. The next sheet depicted a quoins, the next angle stones, bevels, gablets. His father would negotiate this order. His father would diagram each stone and record a bid cost, slide a signed bid sheet across the desk to the customer, finish with brandy. His father was dead. Michael Morkan was dead. Otherwise, this bearded, squint-eyed bastard would not be here handing him cut guides.

"Can you do these?" Heron asked.

"Not without my father."

Heron frowned. "Your father said you'd know what you're doing."

"Where is he?" Disown me, Leighton remembered.

Heron pulled at his beard. "He's a traitor. Doesn't matter if he's in hell."

Leighton extended the bundle to him.

Heron waved it away. When he smiled, and his teeth were perfect and white. "I can kill a little of your father every day and bring a piece here to you while we wait for you to show us how to proceed."

Leighton's hand fell and the bundle twirled on its twine, binding his fingers.

"Now this is a moment I do like," Heron said. Leighton blinked at him. Heron's smile was a boy's smile, small and gleeful. "A trapped animal, say a lynx, will chew its foot off. In man, entrapment allows an ungodly trinity. Number one, the resignation of the stupid and docile of our race. Number two, the sulk of the Negroid and all lower races waiting to eat us alive. They will boy. Niggers are sulking in the trap."

"That's two," Leighton said. At least Morkan was alive. Unless this man was lying.

"Three is simple," Heron said. "The entrapped go stark raving mad. Squatting in a corner, eating-fly-legs mad. The trap disappears." He weaved again. He took a deep breath, then cupped his hands to his face. "Mad!" He shouted at the cliffs. The echo reverberated so suddenly it yowled meaningless, though the horses jerked at it. One of the soldiers cursed. Heron turned to Leighton. "This will be such a fine place to work. You should count your blessings." He scratched his beard. "The third will pick you," he said. "So which of the first two do you pick?"

"I'll need more men," Leighton said. "Men who at least have carpentered and used a sledge. Four dozen more. A blacksmith, too, for the drills. And oxen, and dray horses, or at least mules. I won't work with asses."

"Done."

Heron smiled at Leighton's horse, Morkan's brown Walker. "I tell you what. I'll get to the stablemaster's awful fast if I just take this here." He mounted the Walker, squared his stance. He smiled at Leighton, looped the reins in his hands. Heron rode through the quarry gates with his chin set proudly, as if he really had acquired ownership of the quarry.

Not one of them could wield a sledge without striking the side of the chuck, skewing it, and ripping Leighton's wrist.

He leaped from one mishap, stood cradling his hand against his chest and cursing. "Hit the thing square on or don't hit it."

Three soldiers stood around him laughing into their fists. The one who'd struck him blushed. The others clapped and hooted.

Leighton scowled at them. His hand throbbed. The sky was close and gray, and it would soon be too dark for work. None of the new men he requested had arrived. "One of you get down there." He pointed at the chuck.

They stared at their feet.

The mustached officer knelt, eyeing the other soldiers. He propped the chuck and nodded to Leighton.

Leighton took a sledge from a soldier. "It's an act of faith," he said to the officer. "Don't look at me or the hammer or else the chuck will drop and you'll waste stone."

He looked at each of the soldiers in turn, their black cloaks, stupid pale faces, hands that went red and blistered at half-a-minute's work. One idiot had tried to sledge wearing mittens.

Leighton rested the sledge on the square head of the drill. "You feel the head. It's one distance from you, always the same." He drew the sledge back, brought it down. It rang bell-like against the iron drill. The officer's eyes leapt wide, but he held. Leighton swung again. "You swing this." He struck. "Like you mean business. You mean it." He struck. "Mean it." Struck.

The drill began to sink. The officer shifted his knees.

The sledge hummed in Leighton's hands. Normally, the action became mindless, mechanical. But in front of these men—the like of which had wrecked the quarry office and imprisoned his father—he swung, and hated them. He struck. Hated them. He wished the officer's hand would rise, cover the head of the chuck. Down would come the sledge, the skin and bone would part, a red starburst, the ring of the chuck deadened.

Leighton looked away from the chuck for an instant, and saw the officer staring at him, eyes wide, lips set in a rigid line. Leighton jerked and stopped after striking. He'd never seen a driller who could watch the sledge and not flinch from the chuck. The man's mustache gleamed. His bottom lip protruded and was white from chaffing. A slight smile pulled at the corner of his mouth as if he recognized Leighton's awe.

"As the chuck travels, you'll feel a change." Leighton resumed, not wanting to appear too stunned. He struck. "It's not distance, only longer between strikes."

The officer continued to watch him. The chuck reached mark, and Leighton stopped. After he showed them how to jack the chuck, they picked another drill spot. The officer still held, and Leighton taught two soldiers to stagger their blows so that two sledges could work at once.

Down the cliff, four other soldiers set a third drill hole, too close to the first to be useful. Leighton almost stopped them, but when their chuck tilted, he saw what was coming, and so leaned on his sledge. The troops were whacking at the chuck, which barked and clanged across the cliff. The driller who had held the chuck screamed, stood. In the waning gray light, he gripped his wrist. The pulp of his hand jittered.

Leighton knelt at the first drill hole where lime dust was mounded in a small cone. The wounded soldier was howling, and two comrades held him to keep his writhing body from flailing off the cliff. Leighton scooped a handful of the soft, frigid dust. He stood before the wounded man.

"Hold him," he said. "I mean tight."

The men gripped the wounded man by the arms. Leighton took the gored hand and clasped the handful of dust over it. The wounded man flinched, but then ceased howling.

"Cold." The soldier sniffed.

Between Leighton's palms, splinters of bone shifted amid ragged gristle. He pressed slightly, spreading the powder. The wounded man's face tightened, his back arching. Men gathered around, their faces dark beneath the hoods. The light was gone from the sky, but there were no stars.

"This will stanch the blood." Leighton knelt and pressed more powder against what had been the man's palm.

As they were leading the wounded man down the ox trail to the office, Leighton fell back. He turned to the mustached officer. "Get him to a surgeon. In a couple minutes the limestone will be real painful, but it'll pucker that like alum."

The officer ordered one of the men to take the soldier. "This the way you treat your workers?"

"If I was working with that man, I'd have shown him the gate the minute he let the chuck angle."

"Here on, you tell them so, or we'll be stanching your hands."

At the office, the wounded man left moaning and clinging to the back of another cavalryman. The mustached officer ordered the troops to make a fire in the office stove.

Heron arrived and talked with the mustached officer for a moment. Leighton stood at the door watching the dark shadows of the soldiers crawl the floor in the orange light. Heron moved next to him. He drank from a tin flask.

"Why can't I stay at home?" Leighton asked.

"This is a fine home."

Leighton glared, but Heron seemed engrossed in the soldiers, their tusslings and grumblings.

"These men don't have any idea how to work here," Leighton said.

The boyish smile crossed Heron's face. It was small and be-mused, as if he were charmed. "Teach them."

"Why don't you find me just a dozen good ones instead of these clodhoppers?"

Heron blinked at him. "Let me teach you something, hill-billy. These are true Northerners, real Yankees, nothing like the last two armies through here." He smiled pleasantly, as if what he related were as benign as a play party guest list. "These men come from the land of the factory stacks. The cities. They are but spokes in a great wheel. And you will see me and that wheel transform you and your little craftsmen's guild of a quarry. Now teach them."

The smile so annoyed Leighton that he could not watch the man's lips. The soldiers crowded at the fire. They did not vie for Heron's attention as Leighton had seen Price's adjutants do. In fact, the Federals acted more lively than they had all day, grunting and hassling one another over space close to the stove. They were a lower sort of man than even the Texans had been: scrawny necks and faces, lice gray and gamboling in their hair. Heron's teeth glinted in the orange flames as he watched the soldiers scuffle.

Within a week, Heron sent horses, but they were neither Morgans nor any sort of horse Leighton knew, just ribs strung between four stilts.

Heron rapidly increased the number of men. It took no con-certed effort on Leighton's part for the soldiers to injure them-selves. The first ashlar finished claimed a foot. A soldier sunk a chisel in his thigh, and at the last of February, a soldier who'd followed Leighton to the ledge to set the feather holes for a bot-tom cut tried to purchase too much leverage with his boots at the very lip. His foot shot backwards and he vanished.

He made no noise when he hit the frozen surface of the teal pool. Leighton expected him to crawl and rise as he'd seen mules do. He lay like a flattened sack of sticks. With the others, Leigh-ton clambered from the cut and ran down the ox trail. When he reached the man, others crowded at the edge of the frozen pool. Only Leighton crossed the ice and knelt to him. The fallen soldier had green-brown eyes, and they were blinking rapidly.

Webs of white exploded in the ice around him. His limbs and torso appeared perfect, though impressed in the shattered ice. The eyes grew still. Leighton touched his forehead. A spoke off the great wheel.

He picked his way to shore. The mustached officer met him. Two soldiers wept, calling out Andy, Andy. Some of the troops tried to comfort them.

"Get the picks, and we'll get him out," Leighton said.

They brought the picks. At least half a dozen soldiers leaned on them. The mustached officer took a pick and stepped out on the ice with Leighton.

The officer handed Leighton the pick and nodded toward the dead soldier.

Leighton swallowed but could not speak. The spit in his mouth tasted of copper.

He stepped across the ice to where the dead soldier lay. But as he chipped along the soldier's sides, he resented working alone, hated the whistles and comments he heard.

"Swing her, mick."

He was not swinging the pick, only tapping at the ice, but now and again the pick bit into the soldier's woolen coat. Leighton's hands were numb with cold. Hairs in his nostrils stiffened in the wind that howled and eddied off the base of the cliffs.

The pick bit the back of the soldier's thigh. Leighton wormed the handle until it emerged, crimson. Leighton leaned his elbows against his knees, his breath steaming.

When he could move the body with the pick, he waved for the soldiers on the shore to step out. They were black shadows against the waning light of the sky.

The officer shouted, "Bring him here."

Leighton gaped at the officer. The men bobbed as they laughed. His stomach bound and churned, and hunger made him dizzy.

"Bring him," one shouted. "Pick him up, boy. You killed him."

The officer drew his revolver.

The dead soldier was taller than Leighton, and every bit as muscled. Leighton gripped the cadaver. The wool of his coat was abrasive and wet from where the body had melted the ice. Leighton heaved, felt the dead boy buckle and give as he rose from the shattered impression. Leighton slipped and landed on his ass. The soldiers shouted and laughed.

When Leighton stood, Morkan's horse with a bearded rider was trotting behind the men. Heron. He would have the good sense to relieve his quarry master from this.

Heron dismounted, and he and the officer talked. Heron shuffled across the ice, hands buried in the pockets of his coat. He stood over Leighton, chin pressed to his chest, beard protruding. His blue eyes blinked. "Drape him over your back and crawl." Heron nodded at the dead boy. "At least you won't fall on your ass."

Leighton felt his mouth drop open.

Heron raised his eyebrows. "It's just a damn body."

Leighton knelt to the dead boy again, heaved him from the hole. He held the body for a moment against his chest, dead arms splayed about his head; he stared at Heron.

Heron dug in his coat and withdrew a thong of leather from which a small watch dangled. "Put your hands on the ground."

Leighton's palms touched the frigid ice. Heron grunted and draped the dead boy's soggy arms around Leighton's neck. Heron bound the dead wrists together with the thong. Cold and ticking, the watch clung to Leighton's chin. "Onward," Heron said.

Leighton began to crawl. The arms weighed at his neck and made his head throb. The wool of the dead boy's coat raked and pulled Leighton's beard. His knees ached; his hands went numb. He could hear the men whooping above the watch's chitter.

"You know what you need?" Heron kicked a chunk of ice that went skittering across the teal. "With the coming freedom of the nigger, you need someone to work you just as hard as you and your traitor father worked them."

Leighton collapsed for an instant. When he rose again, Heron readjusted the body on his back. Leighton crawled.

His jaw ached from clenching, and the wool of the cadaver's sleeves crackled and yanked at his beard. His elbows popped, shifted; the ice appeared close and abrupt, but the shore stretched an eon away.

"You know," Heron said, "God did a great disfavor to man. He couched an eternal mind in a temporal body." His boots hissed on the ice. "Since this is war, I win this quarry. If this were not war, time would tell. And, alas, you'll know I've won forever."

The cadaver sloughed and jerked Leighton flat. Leighton raised himself, then twisted to right the cadaver.

Heron lifted the body, and Leighton felt its shattered weight assume the shape of his back. Cold singed Leighton's palms and rose in the bone's of his forearms. The watch hummed and ticked.

"Here comes the resurrected South," Heron hollered to the men on the shore. They laughed and shouted a gibberish of curses. "Here comes the nigger of the frontier to honor our dead with ceaseless toil." Whistles and applause.

The rest of the day, the soldiers were smug and silent around Leighton. When they listened to his directions, a shifting wariness came to their eyes, and they glanced at each other before complying. That night, as the office warmed, the stink of the soldiers was tremendous and made Leighton rub his sleeves and scratch at his neck. His skin felt soldered to his clothes. As he sat at Morkan's desk, a large chunk of callus on his right palm peeled off and left a burning circle. His palm pulsed whether he wetted it with his tongue, or blew air across it. The circle was red without lines or creases.

The gray hunk of callus that had fallen gave beneath his fingers. He pressed it against the desk, and water shone, then disappeared into the wood. A dead piece of him that defined him, that his mother rued, because the callus marked him as a common laborer rather than the son of a quarry owner. Heron and his kind made an orphaned son of him. Opening the bottom right desk drawer, he cupped his hand, scooped the callus across the desk. The dead skin ticked against the bottom of the drawer.

By early April, they'd cut enough stones to warrant a wagon, which came twice a day and hauled ashlars east on the road where Morkan had burned the Walker. From new troops,

Leighton learned of an immense battle in Arkansas. McCulloch was dead as were other Rebel generals; Price and the Missouri Guard disappeared into the mountains.

The troops who survived the quarrying became more proficient. Heron sent scads of them. The quarry never employed a work force this large. Soon Leighton saw the terrible logic of it: two hundred and fifty men cutting, pounding on the cliffs, chucks ringing. For whole afternoons, Leighton left most of them on the cliffs while he and the few others with steady hands stayed in the stone yard cutting. As the ashlar stacks grew, he dreamed that he would actually be paid for them, and this fantasy pleased him. He had never seen work completed so quickly. Even though he was sure it was out of the question, just imagining payment allowed him to sometimes forget how his coat and shirt were in rags, how the mustached officer let him wash his head and hands only after the soldiers turned the water in three huge tubs gray, frigid, and stinking, or how his father languished.

Remembering his father's ire over the powder blast the morning of Oak Hills, he pined for Morkan's guidance, his care and carefulness. His father worked quietly, turned when the wind was right to turn. Morkan taught him feathering with wooden wedges as he had learned in the Mourn Mountains in winter. They pounded the wedges down in the lime, left them overnight to expand. Unheard, in the dark of night, the stone split.

Summer came quickly, and the cliffs attained a glaring white by early afternoon. They were too hot to tolerate by two p.m. He ordered the troops to rise early and work the morning until noon, then break until evening. In June and July, twilight lingered for hours, pale orange and silver, then violet, and navy blue.

He felt steadied only when seated in his father's chair. When he drifted off, he sometimes felt the wool of the fallen soldier's sleeves itch at his whiskers, felt the soldier's dead arms drag and ache at his collarbone. The frigid circle those arms made, the torso's collapsed weight clutched him as tangibly as the imprint of a hat gone from the head. Gasping, he jolted, snatched at his shoulders. His gasps went unnoticed by all but the mustached officer, who noted the time, frequency, and intensity in a slim gray book with a leather clasp. Each morning before any fire was lit, the mustached officer presented this book to Heron for the engineer's perusal. Sometimes Heron kept this book most of the morning, wetting his thumb on his tongue and flipping the pages.

Heron arrived one afternoon in mid September wearing a new coat spangled with bright buttons and new stripes on his shoulder. He rode into the cutting yard on Morkan's chestnut Walker. It was glistening, heavier, its mane braded. Two mounted soldiers followed behind him. Their saddlebags bulged. Their rifles were drawn.

The ashlars and almost all the rest of the order were finished and the blocks were stacked in gleaming piles.

"Is work paid in wage per hour?" Heron asked. He was looking southwest at the town and its charred buildings. "Or are hours of work bought by blood and time?"

Men were filing into the cutting yard and gathering around the two mounted soldiers and their saddle bags.

"Wages per day, at this mine," Leighton answered.

"Do you not read your country's philosophers?" Heron frowned at him.

Behind Heron, Leighton saw the flash of gold being distributed.

"Blood and life," Heron said. "You pay life for each hour worked. That is why it is only acceptable to be the owner, never the slave. In the new order, all is equal. All pay to see that the wheel turns."

Leighton wished he could laugh at Heron. The sun emerged from the clouds, and long shafts of yellow knifed down between the gray.

"Your General Price got pounded down in Mississippi." He was looking directly at Leighton now. "There is no Rebel army left this side of the river."

The troops behind Heron were counting their handfuls of coins and wrangling. Leighton nodded to the ashlars. "There's a lot of stone to account for here."

Heron raised his eye brows at Leighton. "Don't act as if you don't care. Your army's gone. There was no one left on the field."

"There's nothing I could ever do about that."

Heron shook his head. "You've been doing it for over seven months now. The sins of the father are visited on the son. He's a traitor. You pay."

"Fine," Leighton said. "You've worked me like chattel. Now the whole lot is completed. That's 1500 blocks." He wanted more than anything to see in the man's eyes a hint of the magnitude of what the Federals were taking from him.

"Send the bill to General Sterling Price. He'll have some scrip written up for you right away."

"The Morkans have never given stone away."

"You just did." Heron clucked his horse. The shallows of the teal pool wavered and buckled with the wind. In the cliff was a long irregular scar where the soldiers worked. Judith said the Morkans conjured money from the skin of the earth. Then he was no longer a Morkan. He gripped the rough wooden fencing of the cutting yard, and the tender circle on his palm stung. Heron's blue woolen back sparkled in the September sun.

II

JUST FOR THE RATIONS, LEIGHTON SPENT A MONTH
on the crew that assembled Heron's rifle pits behind the quarry.
The Federals fed the workers twice a day—hardtack at breakfast, corn pone and bitter hash for supper, no dinner. From the
troops, he gathered that Heron had been sent south to lord over
a part of Arkansas.

One November evening after work instead of returning to
the quarry to sleep, Leighton walked under the full moon east
on the Walker's road toward the James River. The leaves were
down and the woods popped and rustled with the friskings of
animals. The craggy oak limbs, shorn of leaves, made a tangled
trellis over the road. One mile before the river, in a parting of
the trees, he saw the columns of the telegraph poles, wire strung
in lazy arcs shining silver in the moonlight. He tilted his head.
They were humming again between Springfield and St. Louis.
Like a cord jerked taut. His mind wandered the couplings and
poles all the way to the Riverfront, to the old railroad ferry, to
St. Louis, where his father waited or was dead. He followed the
scrubby corridor beneath the wire until it met the road to Galway.

The front doors to the house were open, and one hung askew.
When he stepped onto the stone floor, the entryway's bare ceiling surprised him until he remembered the chandelier gone.
Something banged in the kitchen, and he hollered Johnson Davis's name. For a long while he waited for the answer. Moonlight
filled the entryway. All the curtains were down. Along the wall
a field mouse scuttled.

When he could not find a lamp, he crossed the yard to the
springhouse. Standing outside its wooden door, he could hear
the crickets whirring inside. He opened the door, and they

230

ceased. Only the smell of wet moss and mud met him—the springhouse was cleared of vegetable goods. Leighton propped the door open. In the moonlight he saw the stone rim of the spring pool intact, the dirt around it slimy, but bare of tracks. He stepped behind the masonry pool. Cool, wet air seeped through the holes in his shirt. He felt along the back wall. Stone, mortar, stone, stone, then the gaps in the mortar that marked the strongbox's hiding place. He pulled the stone loose. When his fingers jammed against the strong box, when he lifted it and found it heavy with coin, he collapsed against the wall. Curling on the mud, clutching the box to him, he was asleep before the crickets resumed.

There was not even a broom in the house. He kicked debris out all morning, then battled mice, and snakes. The cots on the sleeping porches remained, and he spent the afternoon there repairing the yellowed netting on the windows. In the upstairs, he found one of his mother's lockets and opened it. The portraits Charlotte kept behind the crystal were now curled and shrunken at their edges, and fell easily into his palm. The portrait of Morkan that Charlotte saved appeared gray as if it had suffered water damage.

His father was a fool to make a life such as this out here. In St. Louis, every minute of every day made sense: the Brothers at the school were cruel, the sun shone, the smell of the River pervaded, Judith was his partner in mischief. Here, the Morkans were suddenly and precariously comfortable, and now they were nothing. Beneath the vacant walls of empty rooms, the blue limestone floor exuded a sharpness in the cold air. He worried his mother's locket like a stone between his fingers.

Days later, the house was awash in sunlight and the crackling of an enormous fire. Of wood there was plenty, though food was scarce. Leighton placed a hunk of choteau and a half dozen chisels on the dining room floor. Outside the wind swept against the house, and the ceiling breathed and rose like the top of a railroad car in motion.

There came a knock, a pause, then Judith entered the front door, but kept hold of it as if in an inner debate between coming and going. Her cheeks were even more thinned. Mud spattered and hardened the hem of her dress. Two oval blotches of red clay rode the fabric above her knees.

"You back?" she asked.

He held the chisel and mallet in his fists, spread his arms wide and turned a circle, his brogans crunching in the choteau dust.

She smiled, raised her eyebrows. "You need me for anything?"

He stared at her and felt suddenly cold. "It's only me here," he said. His voice sounded strange to him, he had been silent so long. "What do you imagine I need done?"

She shrugged, stepped inside the dining room. The house was clean as a gutted rib cage. Only a few leaves scrambled in, but otherwise the stone floor, the bare walls he kept scrubbed white. His coat was a weave of dark blue wool, one of his father's, tight across the back, cuffs rolled big as crescent rolls. His face was gaunt. He imagined he made quite a spectacle of fallen riches to her.

"You got money for it?"

He put the chisel down, eyed her. "You could start to work and find out."

She rested an arm over the back of the only chair in the house. "Look, I ain't got much to do. I wondered what you was doing."

"Just standing about wondering how I will ever manage." He resumed nipping at the stone with his mallet and chisel.

She smiled, and he felt an old adversarial warmth for her that he had felt only when they were young. "You are here, Judith, because neither of us can stand the terror of nothing. We aren't hermits."

She frowned and shook her head. "Damn. I forgot how you talk. Your brains must be like a hornet in a matchbox." She paused. "I do like hearing you." She tilted her eyes down at his sculpture. After a moment, she grinned, nodded at the head he was shaping. "Well, you carving yourself in stone."

He had not even discerned a pattern to what he was carving, and the face held no identity to him, though he hoped it would become his father's. It was just a face rising there, but now, she was right. It was his face.

She chuckled. When she rose to leave, he jolted and reached a hand to her. She took his hand, then rested in the chair.

"Stay," he said, and she stayed the morning and returned each day for the remainder of the month just to talk and wrangle with him.

To garner food, whiskey, and a horse, he joined the Federal Greene County Home Guards in mid-December. Five of the boys in his unit were younger than he. The other six men were in their forties. They carried garbage from the center of town, kept refugees from stealing logs from the forts or firewood from troops garrisoned in the houses. To Leighton, the Home Guards were a pack of sloppy deputies, and so he felt he made no major concessions to the Federals in joining the Guards. They met whenever his neighbor, Nathan Greer, came knocking at the door to tell Leighton where their muster point was. Most often it was at the livery stable near the quarry or at the unfinished courthouse.

After two weeks, the plump quartermaster who paid Leighton each day ordered him to report to the provost court. Leighton stood drinking mash in the frigid snow, holding bread under his arm. Fried eggs oozed a slick puddle of grease in his breast pocket. He was in a line of at least two dozen filthy townsmen, women, and Negroes waiting to enter the First Baptist Church, where Montgomery Overbo once preached. Some of the women wore trousers, and all but a few were grimy in the extreme.

Men crowded around him and asked after his father. Morelock Branson, Jason Jeffries, Dewey Greer (Nathan Greer's father) were all former customers at the quarry, and Leighton reflected that they were never particularly friendly before. Most of the men were clods Leighton didn't know by name. These seemed most concerned.

A man with dripping sties in both eyes pumped Leighton's hand so long Leighton dropped his bread. The man leaned close, and whispered, his breath rank with onions. "You tell your paw he'll be remembered in how he hept."

Shackled men packed the pews. Federal troopers sprawled drowsing with their rifles and bayonets lanced toward the ceiling. At the pulpit, the provost marshal sat behind a battered table along with a secretary and two standing guards. Leighton wondered if Morkan faced a court and what that court said. He hoped eventually that he might develop enough contacts in the Federal army to ask after his father.

"And the next," the provost marshal called, glancing wearily at his secretary, who was reading to him from a large tome.

After a long, whispered briefing from the secretary, the marshal began. "Leighton Shea Morkan, you are currently a member of Corvin Looney's Home Guards." He spoke very astutely, disdainfully, and sounded like an easterner. "Your father, Michael Morkan, provided the Rebel army with explosives of more than two thousand pounds."

Leighton blinked at the overstated figure. The church became quiet.

"You served in a work crew under Marcus Larue Heron." The marshal adjusted his spectacles and drank from a glass of water. "It is a risk to arm you, and foolish to issue you a horse and food." He looked at Leighton for the first time. "Why have you joined the Home Guards?"

Leighton wanted to take a drink or to smoke one of the bitter cigars the quartermaster issued. Disown me, Leighton remembered Morkan saying, and for a moment in the crowded church, he felt as if Morkan were there, watching him. He squared his shoulders. "To exonerate my father and my name. I want my father home from prison and will serve to save him."

The marshal held his fist to his mouth and cleared his throat. His hand was withered and appeared waxen in the lamplight. "That is by far the most honorable and literate answer I have heard in this town, a place which I imagine, young man, has forged a horrid influence on what might have been decent future citizens of our Union."

The secretary's eyebrows rose. The marshal called for the next case. The secretary wrote quickly all there was to write about Leighton Morkan.

234

Late that December, work on the fortifications stopped, and refugees spraddled lean-tos of brush and sheets against the stone fort by the quarry. Leighton and his Home Guard unit rarely left town. They still worked trash details, guarded the disintegrating forts, accepted bribes of game and whiskey for the right to pilfer the wood. Much of the army marched south, and the Home Guards received word that the last Rebel army in the West was destroyed near the Arkansas River. Leighton and a Guardsman named Shane Peale teamstered loads of garbage northwest of town. Once they unloaded, they sat on the wagon seat and shot their Enfield muskets at rats. Their horses flicked their ears.

When Leighton and Peale spent all their ammunition, they sat staring at the dump. They talked about the end of the war, about why the Rebels fought so long, almost two years now. Peale ran errands for the Federal telegraph office and knew more about the rest of the war than any townie. He discussed Antietam which happened, he said, in Delaware in October. Peale claimed this battle finished the Rebels in the East just as Prairie Grove finished them in the West.

The stores and hotels, saloons that Leighton remembered were charred ruins. Now ivory tents trembled in rows like exposed vertebrae in long spines. Around the bones, orderlies slipped in and out as if they were white and red-spattered carrion beetles. A hospital thriving with wounded from the Federals' Arkansas campaign. Churches, once bloodied with casualties, were now crammed with powder and cartridges, scrapped cannons stacked among families of gravestones.

On the first Wednesday in January, Nathan Greer woke him up to muster. Once the boy was gone, Leighton rode at a lope toward the tent city of Federal hospitals and encampments. With the sun not yet risen, the myriad dots of canvas appeared gray in the thin light. The frosted ground crackled under his horse's hooves. Leighton had spent a twenty-dollar piece from the strong box for the campaign coat he was wearing. Sewn inside the coat was a square embroidered with a girl's name and city—Anna Marie Van Syke, Manhattan—and the message: **"AVENGE OUR HOLY UNION."**

As he entered the first lot of tents, a portly man in long johns rushed past banging two skillets together. Leighton reined his horse. Blinking faces appeared at the tent flaps. Cowbells and triangles, bugles, whistles, shouts, men rushed shirtless, pulling up suspenders. They hollered for rifles.

Leighton heard the thunk and concussion of artillery. On the heights just north of Galway, four cannon issued curling puffs of smoke. Thunder followed. Asters of flame and noise boiled and faded deep within the tents. Gray specters scurried around the artillery pieces.

Leighton turned his horse for home, but was met by a cavalcade of Enrolled Militia riding hard into the tents. A burly little Federal officer was running with his sword shining high above his head: "We're the left! Left! Wheel, you bastards!" His face was crimson, legs pumping like pistons. But the horsemen continued their dash into the center of the tents, their faces pale, eyes wide and oblivious, horses lunging almost crushing the little man. The officer swiped his sword in a silver arc. Leighton jerked his leg aside, and the sword plunged between the ribs of his horse. The animal gasped and sunk. Leighton leapt free of the saddle, landed roughly, his knees and palms smarting in the cold. The little officer ran on swordless, screaming and waving his arms at his disappearing cavalry. Leighton stood and blinked. His horse lay grunting, pissing, steam rolling off the aortal spurts that shot from its girth.

The cannon wheeled and began firing across the tents at one of the forts and the roofless academy. Behind the cannon, in the growing light, Leighton saw horses circling, riders holding hats and rifles high. He saw no flag among them. They cut him off from home. He could chuck his coat and hat, but he still had the blue pantaloons with yellow stripes. Between cannon shots, he heard from the invaders a high trickle of sound. He shook his head, sure his ears were ringing.

Carefully he unhooked his rifle, worried the horse in the last fit of living might wale around and chomp at him. He paused a minute and the horse's white eyes bulged and rolled. He loaded the rifle, cringing at shell concussions. Then he burrowed the rifle in the horse's ear and finished him. Stooping, he tore his pantaloons at the cuff, cupped his hands in the horse's pooled blood. He smeared blood all up and down his calf. It clung warmly to his yellow underleggings. He shouldered his bag and saddle and headed for the hospital, affecting a limp whenever Iowa troops or Guardsmen crossed his path.

At the hospital more than a hundred men in ragged bedclothes and partial uniforms stood outside the compound. Some faces were green, some gray. A tall officer pushed the wounded into line, grabbed Leighton's arm and swung him to the end of the line. Two corporals issued cavalry pistols and Sharps rifles. The man next to Leighton faltered and grabbed Leighton. He stunk so strongly of quinine, Leighton gulped, his nose twitching. The Federals armed even the surgeons in their browned aprons. They marched the whole lot of them behind the log hexagon of one of the forts, formed them in a battle line, then rushed off shouting at each other and several of the wounded and ill.

Cloaked in ratty yellow, swaddled in bed sheets, blankets tied as capes about their necks, the patients manned what was called Fort Number 4 at the end of a long meadow on the western outskirts of town. A dense stand of oak darkened the westernmost end of the meadow. The cannon blasted away. To the east boiled a great melee of gunfire and horsemen. Some of the patients eased themselves to sit cross-legged, or laid down on the frigid dirt and loaded their black revolvers, the muzzles of which wavered like divining rods. The rifles lay in the dirt beside them. One man wandered behind a tree in the enclosure, pulled his pants down and squatted.

Leighton tamped his rifle, and stared at the forest. The log wall sheltered his body to the neck. Hollowed divots allowed soldiers to shoot standing, sitting, or lying flat. Like spots of fog across the hills a trail of wraith-like patients scuttled from the other convalescent hospitals across town. A company of near fifty arrived with bed pans strapped to their heads, crutches stabbing the frozen road, revolvers roped about their necks, bouncing against their bellies, several in wheel chairs, cussing and pointing as the nurses bumped them through the gates, amputees, men with gashes shaved bald on their scalps, a drooling boy missing much of his lower jaw, tongue squirming like a slug in salt.

Two wagons pounded into the fort, and on each of these, revolvers and rifles were mounded along with box after box of cartridges.

The cannon fired and shells yowled like saw blades through the air. The patients ducked at this, but laughed and coughed, smiling when a shell landed far east of the fort.

"Blind Arkies," someone shouted.

They fell quiet. Men dropped their crutches, leaned against the log wall and gaped at the forest. Cresting the stubble of oak, elm, and hickory, the sun's pale light, found among the trees the chests and legs of horses facing the fort. He counted ten. They edged forward. He lost count, dozens, hundreds. Men around him adjusted their bedpans, wiped their mouths with the corners of blankets.

The cannon stopped. A shout sounded from the wood. One thousand cavalry stepped into the sunlight of the meadow. Black pits were the horsemen's eyes, faces as shadowed and malleable as burlap. Cloaks spattered, mottled, bark rather than cloth. Soot streaked hands and foreheads, bare feet red and raw in the stirrups as if the cavalry had burned their way here instead of riding. Rifles, scythes, rakes, hoes, pitchforks, an agrarian nightmare of gigs and shotguns tilted at the ground. Belts bristled with knives, pistol butts. A yellow vapor purled from them and foam caked the chest of every mount.

Next to Leighton, a man in a cane-bottomed wheelchair set his revolver in his lap and commenced to pray in furious noddings.

The wounded grabbed their rifles, started peeling at the white cartridges, tamping their guns. Leighton felt a tap. The boy with a smashed lower jaw stood holding a cartridge out for him. Leighton took the cartridge, bit the top and handed him the opened package. The boy nodded, patted three revolvers he had loaded himself.

Across the meadow, the cavalry whirled and formed an even line while one rider rode before them. The rider waggled above his head a blackened sword. The rider's lips moved, and he tossed his hair. The cavalry bellowed a raw vowel in answer.

Several of the wounded fired their pistols.

The patient next to Leighton shouted for them to stop. Shambling about, he called for a line of fire. As if healed, the men moved forward with a swift grace, placing the rifle muzzles against the wall, pressing their cheeks to the stocks.

The shouting patient borrowed a crutch and held it high. "Wait on them." The wounded watched him, eyes blinking over the stocks.

In the meadow, the rider circled the sword above his head. The riders' chests rose as if they took one great collective breath, and then from them came the high trickling sound, but now it was a shout, a bouncing horrendous note Leighton imagined only savages could make, the sound of men preparing to leap off a bridge above a valley spiked with pines, a sound as brutal and heedless as the edge of a hatchet.

Horses and riders nodded, surged, and the meadow exploded with hoof and mud, the high yowl lofting above the pounding. Leighton cringed. The patient still held the wavering crutch. The mass of cavalry grew until Leighton could almost discern individual faces, sodden and bewhiskered, eyes black, lips and cheeks blue, pounding, heaving, steeds gaunt, skeletal miracles of hide and power.

Down came the crutch. Great spikes of flame, the staggered fire of one hundred fifty erupted, a blast as if the patients tore the very cloth of morning to leave nothing but smoke and concussion.

Leighton whooped. Nothing like it. Jesus.

Cavalry tumbled, horses running askew, men thrown and trampled. But still coming. Leighton expected them all to fall, but the wood before him spattered. Bullets thumped into the logs. Something tugged at his coat. He turned expecting the jawless boy holding a cartridge. Nothing. Pistols fired along the length of the wall. One of the riders loomed up, leering, screaming, his face bulging into a fist of holy rage. He lurched over and stabbed a hickory pike into the neck of the man in the wheel chair. The patient gagged and bucked. Pistol fire peppered the rider, who fell. The shaft of the pike remained propped against the wall, its carved point securely sunk through the dead patient's neck.

Blue and silver smoke covered the line of patients. They rose and lurched, black shadows around which smoke and sunlight quivered, the flare of pistols flashing like summer lightning deep in clouds. The shadows shuffled and loaded, bandages and blankets swishing. Metal clanking, men breathing, quick tears of paper, the spat of the powder, all performed without speaking, rote motions in the piles of smoke. Leighton had felt such a moment before when the drill teams on the cliff hit exact stride, four teams grunting and shifting, the sledges ringing. The patients stood to the wall, arms drawing the ramrods into the air, sliding them down, steadying pistols, faces becoming gray ovals, indistinct. Their motions were a reverie of union, a purified human effort that vented bursts of fire.

The smoke thinned. The horsemen were gone. All across the meadow, dark lumps squirmed and smoked. Against the woods, the cavalry circled and formed. Through a divot in the wall, Leighton saw a man raise himself to crawl on his elbows, his hands and forearms shattered. His face was white and blue, eyes bulging. The patients watched the forming cavalry. One jerked the pike from the dead patient's neck. He flung the pike over the wall. Another patient wheeled the chair with its corpse back behind the ammunition wagons. In the meadow the wounded horseman quit crawling and collapsed. He lay on his side staring at the wall.

Any of these men he fired at could be Greevins. Or Charley, or Hoyt, or Ferguson.

The cavalry achieved their line. The horses shook their heads. Up went the black sword. Up went the crutch. The cavalry came, men rocking in the saddles, elbows flapping like wings. Leighton beaded. In the nub at the end of his muzzle he caught one single horseman. The circle of the horseman's mouth, the whiskers, the mustache, all became distinct. The iron nubbin of the gunsight erased a portion of his chest then his head as he came riding. Leighton trembled. The rider's shout, that heedless vowel, rose above the hooves. He rode alone, leapt over downed horses and men alone, broke from the thundering pack with just his sword lowered at the wall, and he was screaming. A sword against five weeks worth of powder and shot.

The crutch wavered an instant, but held. Exhaling slowly, he hooked his finger over the trigger. The man's oval mouth bobbed in his sights, squalling, face red. Down came the crutch. Leighton fired. The man dropped from the horse, which swerved away from his tumbling.

Hours of it—cavalry reforming, invalids reloading. At the crest of one charge, Leighton's head was banging, and the hooves and stinking hides of horses sailed above the patients, and suddenly horses and riders staggered inside the fort. Like hornets, the invalids swarmed them. Leighton gripped the gritty hem of a rider's coat and pulled him down only to have the horse nip a chunk from beneath his shoulder blade.

"Damn you. God damn you," the Arkansawyer hollered as the invalids finished him with the butts of their rifles.

When the fracas eased, the patient leaned his crutch on the wall and bound Leighton's wound. Rolling an extra bandage the patient crammed the cloth in Leighton's mouth. Then he helped him reload and heave his rifle back to the top of the shattered wall. Leighton howled and bit with fury on the bandage in his teeth.

"One more is all they got. I swear it," the patient said.

The sunlight seared the meadow and forest with its winter white. When the smoke dissipated, the meadow, stilled with frost, the brambles, covered in blue crystal, became intensely serene.

They charged the fort again and again. The invalids killed them long into the evening until finally the horsemen shuddered and rode away.

III

Beside the stone outline of Heron's rifle pits, Leighton bartered. From the army, he brought home bedraggled horses, mules with the grass staggers and a decent pair of drafts, which had been worked to the point of suffering spinal compression. They limped around with one leg stiff from forearm to pastern. The driver in charge of them claimed no experience with animals bigger than a dog, and insisted he was merely a poetaster from Connecticut. He showed Leighton a little book to prove this. He lost his hand at Prairie Grove, but insisted on serving as best he could. The army did not have the time that Johnson Davis did, and so Leighton began to build the stock from what might have otherwise become horsemeat if worked much longer. For opportunities such as these he kept a constant watch, and when he and Johnson grew a crop of vegetables, he asked the poetaster out for dinner and some of the last of the port. Leighton treated the poetaster as if he were a very remarkable and interesting person all through the evening. And in a way that grated Leighton, he could see in the poetaster a cultivation he would never have, the knowledge of museums with polished marble, lectures by men with minds ablaze, languages and statues, paintings by Spaniards, college walls draped with ivy. As the poetaster spoke, Leighton sensed his hills and stone crowd around him, a squadron of shoulders hunched in ignorance and distrust. When he left, Leighton read the poems to Judith in the twilight, and they both became quiet and teary.

One morning that summer a man accompanied Greer to Leighton's house for one of the musters. He wore the uniform of a unit from Indiana, said his name was Delderfield. Greer left them, and Delderfield rode with Leighton toward town. He was a plump man, and his shirt and peacoat were exceptionally wrinkled. At the wrists, his cuffs were stiff with red mud, and there was a red dust covering his cheeks, as if he had slept in a puddle. Leighton worried that Delderfield might be here to question him about some aspect of his father's crime, or worse the Texans. Maybe he was someone Heron sent.

Delderfield coughed into his hand. "There's a fellow I know named Gronnen. He's stationed in St. Louis in Gratiot Prison."

Leighton stared at him. It was seven a.m. or earlier, and already the air was hung with humidity that brushed his face like the patina of steam around a boiler. Beads of sweat shimmered at Delderfield's hairline.

At a darkening in the woods, Delderfield halted. He turned in the saddle and reached into his saddle bag. Leighton touched the butt of his rifle hooked at his side.

Delderfield drew out a lump wrapped in a towel, handed it to Leighton. In the trees, an insect awoke, began to sizzle. "I didn't ever see you," Delderfield said. "That Greer kid knows how it is." He pulled his horse away and veered south on Ozark Road. "Be good to that kid." He hunched his back and gave the horse heel.

Leighton watched him go, then unwrapped the parcel. The towel swaddling the parcel was so greasy, it felt soaked with water. It stunk powerfully like a hospital—urine and quinine and bear oil. Inside was a tarnished brass student lamp. He lifted the top of the lamp. It was empty, save for a paper rolled into a little tube. He unrolled it.

Inside was a letter on fine linen paper. The handwriting on the letter was Morkan's. Leighton steadied the horse, whispering to it.

LEIGHTON:

A GOOD MAN WHOSE NAME I HOPE I LIVE TO TELL HAS LET THIS MESSAGE GET TO YOU. I AM CONSUMPTIVE, BUT AM ALIVE AND HERE. THE WAR HAS TO BE OVER SOON; EVERY DAY MORE AND MORE ARE HERE, THEN

BOUND FOR PRISONS FURTHER NORTH. MARRY WHEN
THIS IS DONE.

The handwriting changed and Leighton squinted. It was not
Morkan's writing.

SON, I HAVE FAILED A MAN WHO BEFRIENDED ME—YOU
REMEMBER THE PREACHER OVERBO? I MUST HAVE YOU
KNOW, OVERBO AND ANOTHER DIED FOR MY FAILINGS.
I WILL NOT LET YOU IN MY PASSING LIVE IN THE LIE
THAT MANY ARE MAKING FOR ME. NO MATTER THE RE-
PORT I AM NO HERO. THERE ARE SOME LIES YOU LIVE
IN, AND SOME THAT YOU END. IF A MAN CAN LEARN IN
A PLACE LIKE THIS, SON, KNOW THAT I'VE FOUND A
MAN'S SOUL IS NOT MADE BY WHAT HE EMBRACES BUT
IN WHO HE EMBRACES, WHO HE DEFIES, WHO HE FAILS.
I PRAY THAT I WILL LIVE TO EMBRACE YOU.

YRS.
MICHAEL MORKAN

P.S. I TOOK DOWN THIS LAST FOR HIM AND I DON'T
BELIEVE HE'LL DIE. BUT I WILL WATCH HIM FOR YOU.
THIS HERE TOOK HIM ALL OF A MORNING.

THEY WILL NOT EXCHANGE HIM. DO NOT UNDER ANY
CIRCUMSTANCES COME TO ST. LOUIS.

JULIAN GRONNEN

Leighton read the letter again and again. He touched the envelope to his nose. It smelled of bear oil and potatoes. If he could roll the letter back in the lamp. He wished he had never seen it, and almost would rather assume that Morkan was dead somewhere, hung for treason. The letter was worse than hope.

That day, his Home Guard unit rode the western outskirts of town, passed several hours looking for a cave and a system of tunnels Southern sympathizers were rumored to be building, a phantasm, another story for the Guard to chase. When they found nothing, the men rested in the shade of a grove of bois d'arcs, letting the most intense heat of the day pass. Grasshoppers popped and clicked in the tall switch grass around them. They were close to the old battlefield, where all the war started. It dwindled to this then, cavorting and sweating on mindless excursions. Rumor told there was a sinkhole nearby—he remembered the teamster Peterson talking of one—that was full of the bodies of the Federal dead. The young men talked feverishly of this hole while the older men tried to sleep under the trees.

Nathan Greer sat down beside him. "It's too hot even for whiskey," he said. Greer's father managed a mill before the war, and most of Springfield thought the Greers lazy simply because they kept strict milling hours, and would not start the mill for small orders at a moment's notice.

Greer was young, maybe two years younger than Leighton, but already he knew when to drink whiskey and when to abstain. Heavy like Dewey, he was red headed, with freckled skin that was always pink and sunburned. With his bright green eyes, if he were a heavyset young St. Louis girl from Kings Highway, Leighton would have been enthralled. Greer looked at Leighton, his frown growing serious.

"You can tell me, 'cause I don't care at all about them," Greer whispered. He jutted his chin to indicate the other Home Guards. "This morning. That was from your father, wasn't it?"

Leighton nodded.

"My father didn't go to war," Greer said. "I wish I knew something I could tell you to do. But I don't know. I would if I knew. I promise I would."

Leighton nodded. He waved Greer away, pulled the brim of his cap low across his eyes. Should he be in mourning, he wondered? He was elated that Morkan could be alive, terrified that this hope might be taken from him. Even in the sunlight that turned the switch grass to blazing amber, he felt a pallor of darkness flickering over the ground.

Leighton's commander, Corvin Looney, was the Morkans' tailor before the war. He fought at Wilson's Creek and at Pea Ridge, the battle that drove Price deep into Arkansas. By August, just to avoid the drudgery of guarding the forts and escorting garbage, he began to invent his own bushwhackers to hunt after, and this ensured at least four days of riding through the country under the flag of John Barleycorn. Unless there was rain. If it rained, the Guards dashed for cover, and sat on their horses drinking and jawing. The horses' necks smoked with rain water. Looney ordered the Guards to wait until the roads became muck. Then the tailor called off the hunt. Everyone returned home.

When Looney's Home Guards accomplished nothing by late September, a general assigned Lieutenant Avery Kreft to guide them far south to where Kreft learned of a group of bushwhackers. The Guards' mission was to find and capture the group's leader and kill anyone with him.

When Looney explained this, the name Kreft froze the livery stable where the Guards mustered. Leighton paused in the midst of bartering chaw for cigars. He usually waited for the outskirts before he started drinking, but this morning he uncorked his flask of whiskey there in the stable. Over the stink of animals, he smelled the lime up from the teal pool. He made a point never to look at the quarry when the Guards met here.

That May, he witnessed Kreft bearing the severed head, the blood-streaked hands and feet of a bushwhacker named Grist through the streets of Springfield. A crowd of Unionist women had rollicked behind Kreft cheering, tapping at the body parts that dangled like a stringer of fish from Kreft's saddle. His smug face glowed behind a book. Before the war he studied at Springfield's Men's Academy and gave lectures in Minneapolis, St.

Louis, and Chicago on Latin grammar, American Transcendentalism, and the Necessity of Abolition.

Kreft met the Guards at dawn. He rode a burly, white horse with a gray stripe on its muzzle. Beneath the blue wool uniform and black cap, the Lieutenant's pale skin and long blond hair shone. Today, he wore a blond mustache, swooping in wings above his thin lips. He scowled at each Guard. Looney saluted. Kreft snorted and raised a copy of *Caesar's Gallic Campaigns.*

Leaving Springfield, the Guards rode past work crews of mostly Federal regulars and freed Negroes, or refugees from the hills. The war is won. And yet, the Federals finished five forts and were still digging in as if the war could return. He and these dozen men were riding into the wilderness to capture or kill Missourians who were convinced the war remained. How could he ever tell his father the story of the war, when its course made so little sense, was only a string of deaths and privations? He wished he could write him a letter full of the glorious prose from the Memphis paper, the patients firing, their gowns flapping like the tunics of Athenians on the plain at Marathon.

The Guards traveled south into the forested White River Hills. In the trees, cicadas had made a full hatch. Black and orange bugs about the size of Leighton's thumb buzzed and rattled, brayed on the limbs. There were thousands of them, and their noise reminded Leighton of a saw that ripped but could never finish the actual cutting. The giddiness of the bugs amused, then saddened him. They twirled dead in every puddle.

Along the road, the Guards passed blackened chimneys, entire hamlets scorched to leave only rock-bordered squares. Even this opulence, the forest's teeming green leaves, the shirring of the bugs was suspect. The war left Springfield and everything around it in ruins. Now, the Guards brought the war here. They were usually boisterous after three hours' ride, but this morning they were silent. All but Kreft rode drinking and hunched.

The trunks of the oaks became thinner and more closely spaced. These gave way to dense runs of pine, the height of which made Leighton gape. This forest—pine and hardwood— had never been cut. In the green shadows, the stillness hung palpable and close as a curtain. The charred remains of settlements became more infrequent, and the Guards often halted on seeing ruins and were quiet for some time after.

Kreft rode point. He glanced up from his book only when turning the page with a stiff index finger. Looney rode behind Kreft, and Leighton followed the commander. Behind Leighton was Nathan Greer. They came upon another scorched square in the midst of which sat a sawhorse untouched, a magical gray survivor. Looney laughed at this and lit a cigar, passed Leighton his flask. Greer smiled. Leighton's cheeks were warm, and he felt drunker than the outing warranted.

"Now that there is enough to reassure a man of the coming of the Lord and sure afterlife," Greer said, pointing to the sawhorse. He took the flask.

"That's a stretch," Looney said.

Leighton used Looney's cigar to light one of his own. "No, wait. The work in it does." He puffed and smiled. This would be a good ride after all, and that fool Kreft with his Caesar had no more idea where bushwhackers were than the bugs did.

Looney fetched the cigar back. "Oh, don't be an ass. It's a sawhorse." Once he got drunk, he sat up straight and actually looked like a commander.

"You can't deny a man built it. There it stands, a record of him," Leighton said.

Looney poked his cigar at it. "What if it were a jakes?"

"If that's what a man built." He shrugged.

Greer nodded with enthusiasm.

Looney shook his head. "That man's as gone as the shed that sawhorse set in." He regarded the forest around him with a long frown. "I seen Browner's store turned to fire wood, Jerzitt's, the wagon company." His face reddened. "My shop. My damn shop." He drew a furious puff on the cigar and pushed his spectacles back on his nose. "There ain't any afterlife."

Leighton stared at him. When he drank Looney's whiskey, it burned against his ribs. These men made better talkers than the miners, and they thought nothing of showing Leighton disrespect. On the street, before the war, Leighton, being Irish and Catholic, would never have spoken to Greer, and Looney would have acknowledged Leighton with solicitous grace. "Way I see it," Leighton said, "there's four ways to an afterlife. There's work, like I said."

Looney snorted.

Greer slapped the commander's back. His red hair bobbed. "Hell, the rich kid may be wearing one of your coats, tailor."

Leighton waved his cigar. "Second is children, and you can't deny that. Third is memory of your loved ones."

"Now wait." Looney slowed. Others passed them. "You don't know a thing about children."

"I know all about being one."

Looney blinked at this.

"Do you know anyone better to remember Michael Morkan?" Leighton asked. The ploy was unfair. Respect for Leighton's loss might prevent Looney from refuting the point. "So long as I'm alive, so long as I remember," he whispered, "my father's living."

"Memory is an afterlife?" Looney asked. His eyes were narrowed. He had warmed to the argument. This was not just jawing.

Leighton nodded. "I solemnly believe."

Greer scratched his chin. "But if you can love someone and make them immortal, what keeps you from hating someone into an afterlife?"

Leighton smoked. "Probably no difference."

"What's the fourth?" Looney asked.

"Our deeds. Beyond works. I mean actions. Say I kill somebody."

Looney moved forward in the saddle, and they all three hastened to keep with Kreft. "But if no one remembers it?" Looney asked.

"The dead man does," Leighton said.

"Not very well." Looney drank.

Greer laughed, and Leighton smiled.

"But." Leighton held up a finger. "Say someone tells one of my deeds. Say I kill a man and someone tells of it, and others remember it. I'm immortal time and again."

"What if that someone's lying while he's telling? Then where are you?"

"Still immortal. Just lied about."

Greer and Looney laughed, but even so Leighton beamed. He felt he won something surviving Looney's scrutiny. They caught up to Kreft. There were two stories Leighton heard about Kreft's killing of the bushwhacker Mulcifer Grist. The first story told of Kreft waiting mounted in an open field near Grist's lair. When the bushwhacker took his morning jaunt, Kreft fired once in the air for Grist's attention. Then, bushwhacker and Federal galloped towards each other, revolvers snapping until Grist fell, shot through the heart. Grist's finger still thumped and squirmed against the trigger even as Kreft hacked through the bushwhacker's dead fist.

The other story told that Kreft shaved his mustache the morning he killed Grist. He wore a riding skirt and lacy blouse, kept his face hidden in one of his books. The bushwhacker tipped his hat to the passing lady. Kreft aimed from behind the bush-whacker and shot Grist five times in the head and back. Kreft saved one bullet for the horse. Then, in the summer sunshine, a thin, golden-haired woman, a lover of literature, a murderer named Kreft whacked with a hatchet a bushwhacker's ankles, wrists, and larynx. Leighton watched Kreft lick the tip of his finger and turn another page.

"Isn't that so, Lieutenant?" Leighton called. "Our town will hardly forget your brave killing of Grist and bringing him to us. Is that not immortality?"

Kreft frowned. "Your need for immortality," he said, "is con-gruent with your over-loud voice." He did not lower the book.

They camped at sunset in a clearing made by two burned cabins. They did not build a fire. Kreft insisted this was enemy territory, very much the haunt of Sam Davies, the man they were after. A pack of fool targets around a fire was what made filth like Davies trouble for the Union.

"These very houses right here belonged to families who had no stake in the war." Kreft frowned and smoothed his mustache. "Innocents. These are Sam Davies' prey."

Kreft left the clearing to scout, and Looney was beset by complaints. It was Looney's habit to billet at the homes of pro-Union families when in the field, and the Guards considered sleeping in a clearing in unfamiliar forest without fire or fresh water to be extreme hardship.

Leighton stayed quiet through this grousing. The trunks of the trees became dark gray pillars. The raspings of the cicadas remained so constant, their noise was now a wind that rose and fell. Dark hills loomed and vanished into one another. Looney referred to these as balds, and in the waning light, when individual trees blended to shadow on the round slopes, some hills appeared to be the stubbled tops of skulls.

Greer used his saddle blanket as bedding and his wool jacket as a pillow. Leighton sat next to him against a tree. The stars burned a crowded blue hole above the clearing.

"Phew!" Greer said, jerking up from his bedding. "Horsies!" He slapped his saddle blanket, raising dust that made him sneeze. He shook his head and recovered. "You reckon Sam Davies burned them houses?" he asked.

It was dark, and the scorched squares were not visible. Yet there remained the notion—*the people are gone*—and that stunned him. If he squinted, he could see three blackened steps that led to nothing. He imagined the man who had set them was proud to have sandstone steps instead of wood. The steps faced west and were probably warm in the evening, a fine place to sit. There was no one to enjoy them.

"I said, 'do you reckon . . . .'"

Leighton patted his arm. "I have no idea, Greer. Someone burned them."

Greer was quiet. "How can you leave it at that? It's got to be one or the other: Davies or the Federals."

"No. Owners could have done it themselves if they didn't want either side to use their place and were leaving." Rumors said families did that quite often in Arkansas.

"But you still don't know, and we ought to."

"It's not our place to know. Be respectful and get some sleep."

Greer muttered for a while, but was soon breathing short and shallow. Leighton felt ridiculous pontificating to him, as if anything was really won in the argument with Looney. Ought we to know the real situation, to know who really burned those houses? If the wind blew exactly right, he thought he could smell ash. Kreft told them something they could know. But what he said were stated as facts: Sam Davies burned this. The people were still gone.

In his sleep, Greer jerked and cried out. Then he murmured something—an apology? an explanation? Leighton leaned so close to him, he could smell the hardtack in his teeth and the mint leaves the boy chewed to calm his stomach.

"Was it one of them falling dreams, Greer?" Leighton asked.

Greer gave no answer.

Kreft woke them up well before sunrise. The woods kept so silent in the cold before dawn that when a green meteor sliced above the clearing, Greer swore he heard the meteor sputter like a fuse.

They rode deeper into the woods. The path cut along ridges, switched back and looped for no conceivable reason. They rode single file, Kreft still on point, today reading something called *The Life of the Gracchi*. Drinking decreased, though every Guard was smoking or chawing. At times the forest grew so dense, their caravan appeared dark green, webbed with yellow veins of sunlight.

They entered a valley made by two balds and bottled by a steep ridge. Triangles of sweat-matted hair clumped on the neck of Leighton's horse. The men were grumbling at Looney. One horse lost a shoe, and that rider clung to Greer's back. Leighton was watching an astonishing purple lizard flick its rainbowed tail when a puff of dust erupted on a boulder beside his horse and something went whining off into the trees.

Leighton's horse reared. Looney and Kreft leapt to the ground. Greer's horse threw its extra rider. Behind Leighton, riders spun and struggled to keep their mounts.

Kreft unhooked his rifle and moved toward the ridge, prodded the white horse in front of him as cover.

Leighton hugged the neck of his horse and urged it to pick its way toward Looney, who was following Kreft. A flash of smoke rose from a shadowed cave in the ridge at the end of the valley, and again a bullet went popping through the trees.

Kreft and Looney gained a deep sinkhole in the valley floor, and Leighton, Greer and three other men joined them.

The remainder of the unit scattered and disappeared among the boulders and pines. Every few seconds, Leighton could see blue Federal hats poke from the brush, then vanish.

In the sinkhole, the men were breathing hard. Greer and Leighton's horses rubbed together, and Greer was gripping Leighton's sleeve, jerking it and smiling. Leighton leaned forward so he could hear Looney and Kreft.

"May be just an old homesteader," Looney said to Kreft.

Kreft was watching the ridge with half-lidded eyes and a frown of grave boredom. "Commander Looney, you have received fire. By definition, this situation is belligerent. Treat it accordingly."

Greer spat, wiped the back of his hand across his lips. "Is it Sam Davies?"

Kreft jutted his chin, turned and regarded each man in the sinkhole. "The cave in that ridge is known to be one of his crannies."

One of the Guards drew his revolver and fired at the ridge. The horses lunged and men cursed. Looney grabbed the Guard by the collar and shook him.

Metal glinted from the cave. A pistol fired, but the bullet sang far west of the sinkhole. It appeared that whoever was in the cave could not see the Guards in the sinkhole and was firing blindly. The ridge was stable lime of moderate quality, and Leighton knew the cave could be just an eroded depression between rock faces, or an immense cavern. Kreft cornered one man, or maybe dozens waited in ambush.

One of the Guards west of the sinkhole fired as did Greer and others. The shots were answered by at least five separate puffs of smoke from the cave. Despite Looney's hisses and waves, a general firefight ensued until the Federals all spent six shots and were crouching and scuttling to stuff the little paper cartridges in their chambers. Greer whined and cursed though no more shots came from the cave. Leighton drew his gun, expecting the opponents to dare a more open vantage. Nothing occurred. Great piles of blue smoke crowded the valley. Greer dismounted, and with his revolver raised, he left the sinkhole, knees bent as if stalking a possum. He ducked into brush nearby.

The wind shifted, and was cool from the northwest. Wind drove the smoke against the ridge, obscuring the cave.

Kreft coolly regarded Looney, then the Guards. He kept his rifle trained on the cave, though he had yet to shoot. "It appears, commander, we have an aperture from which protected shootists can deal fire at roughly the western half of this valley." He scanned the Guards, some of whom were finished loading and were peering from the brush. "Your horses are shaken by gun fire. Your men have rifles, yet they insist on piddling fire with cavalry revolvers. It seems obvious you and your men have been doing next to nothing for the cause of the Union. My report to follow this...."

Kreft's words were lost in another melee of shooting. Leighton's horse shook and stamped, and Leighton jerked its reins down. Looney whapped a Guardsman in the back. "Cease fire," he shouted. "Cease. God damn you."

Wide-eyed faces poked up in the brush.

From the cave there was silence.

Leighton glared at Kreft's pale cheek pressed to the rifle stock, the Federal's tiny eyes open in the smoke. A man like Kreft could ruin the Guards. Looney's men weren't out here for the Union. They were from the Ozarks, and Washington was Liberia for all they cared. Kreft glanced at Leighton.

"How do you know that cave doesn't have a back exit?" Leighton asked.

Kreft's eyes widened, and for once, he did not appear smug.

Looney nodded at the Lieutenant. "Well?"

"We'll take a detachment behind the two hills." Kreft pointed at the balds. "We must not be flanked, and our quarry shall not escape."

Smoke diminished but still bunched against the cave. Leighton figured the northwest wind must have driven some of the smoke within or a ventilation shaft near the back was drawing smoke in just as it would air from the outside. Kreft mounted. He nodded at Leighton, who nudged his horse.

The lieutenant was hard to keep up with. He and Leighton circled behind the eastern bald and dashed through the brambles at its base, Leighton hugging his horse's neck. At each darkening in the trees, at each lurch of shadow, he closed his eyes and ground his teeth, sure that Kreft rode them into an ambush, men bristling with pistols. Kreft huffed his mount northward up the back of the ridge, his eyes scanning every cranny. Soon they were on top and could see the sinkhole below where Looney peered up.

Leighton dismounted and, glancing behind him, crouched near his horse well back from the precipice. Kreft knelt at the edge of the ridge. He turned to Leighton and smiled. "Maybe there is no back to your cave?"

Leighton watched the forest behind them. Any branch or combination of bush, vine, and leaves formed an arm, a leveled rifle. When the wind stirred, the forest shuddered and crept. "Maybe not big enough to crawl through."

"You were sharp to ask about a back exit," Kreft said. He motioned for Leighton to join him at the precipice.

Leighton felt suddenly proud that Kreft would consider him wise. He wondered if the Lieutenant might tap him as a Guardsmen worthy of respect.

Trees struggled to grow on the ridge, and some died and fell to gather in black bunches against scrub cedar, which flourished. Kreft and Leighton picked their way to a better vantage where one of these brush piles made for cover directly above the cave.

From the edge Leighton could see each of the Guardsmen scattered across the valley. They rose and ducked behind brush and boulders. Greer smiled and waved at Leighton. Most of the Guards managed to keep their horses, but three horses were grazing far up the western bald in the afternoon sun. The ridge overhung the cave too far for Leighton to actually see the bush-whackers. The ridge was roughly thirty-feet high where he and Kreft lay above the cave. Down in the valley the Guardsmen began firing, this time using rifles and revolvers. The air below the ridge whined with bullets, and gunfire shot in tongues from the cave. A horse fell, then rose shaking.

"I'm hit." Greer stood and wailed. "My foot." He hopped to the sinkhole.

Looney waved to him to get down. A shot cracked from the cave, and Greer froze, stood holding his chest, his mouth open, eyes wide. He stared at Looney, at the cave, then up at Leighton. From a distance, he looked as if he were about to ask a question.

"Idiot." Kreft grunted.

"He's just a kid," Leighton said. He stood and shouted Greer's name.

Kreft grabbed the arm of his coat and jerked Leighton downward.

Leighton pulled away from Kreft, but crouched again and yanked at the hair above his forehead. "Nobody showed us what to do when we're shot."

Kreft shook his head. In the valley, Greer plunked to his seat. Holding his hand out from his chest, he stared at his bloodied palm.

Kreft elbowed Leighton. "You're loud enough. Tell the vermin they are surrounded." He pointed to the edge of the rock.

Leighton crawled forward. He laid flat against the ridge, smelled moss and soil. He glanced behind him at Kreft, who sat picking at his mustache. Leighton wanted a cigar and a drink. Greer was sobbing.

"You are surrounded," he yelled. The Guardsmen in the valley raised their guns and whooped.

"Identify your unit," Kreft hissed.

Leighton turned to him. "You sure?"

Kreft scowled and jabbed a finger at the valley.

Leighton sighed. "We are Corvin Looney's Federal Greene County Home Guards," he shouted. Greer slumped, his crimsoned palms open in penance.

The Guards in the valley whooped again. Two fired at the cave.

There was quiet. No return fire. Smoke piled toward the cave, and Leighton could see wisps of it being sucked inside.

"How many are you?" A nasal voice, high-pitched came from the cave. Leighton recalled the voices of hill people.

When Leighton leaned forward, Kreft grabbed at him. "Seventy-five men," Leighton yelled.

Kreft nodded and grinned. He was lying right next to Leighton now, and his cheeks assumed a light that Leighton took for glee. "Good. They're fools to ask and fools to believe."

The wind blew. When Leighton cocked an ear at the cave, he thought he could hear whispering far below, a sharp discussion. But this was likely a trick of the wind. Leighton marveled at the rustling that carried all through the valley and over the balds. He no longer felt the urge to glance behind him. This place was the greenest, darkest forest he'd seen. He tallied the immense value of the timber around him. Thousands of feet of perfect lumber, years of fuel for a kiln. A strange place to shoot at one another. A solemn place for Greer to be sitting, a stunned child staring at his hands. Beneath trunks a boiler-width across, over a fecund mat of leaves and needles, strange for the tailor Looney to be crawling, bandages wadded in his fists. He remembered reading that the Mormons called a place like this Eden before his fellow Missourians massacred them.

"Tell them any that are willing to give up will be unharmed and escorted to Springfield," Kreft said.

Pleased, Leighton yelled this. His voice echoed off the valley.

There came the hill voice. "Not any of us needs to go to Springfield. Thank you."

Leighton laughed. Kreft gritted his teeth, narrowed an eye at Leighton.

Leighton shrugged. He knew no reason to shoot at the men in the cave. The other Guards now were all watching Greer and Looney. Their guns were still drawn. Even if the Guards were led by an abolitionist lecturer, they were shooting only because they had been shot at. They had no idea if they were shooting at fellow Missourians or Arkansawyers. He looked at Kreft, saw a knot of bone move above the Lieutenant's cheek. This was nobody's war but Kreft's and people like him. Greer was hugging Looney and bawling, his face purple beneath his red hair. His sobbing and babble echoed off the balds and ridge. The situation was inscrutable: they were all shooting because they were shooting. The sun lanced in golden rods through the columnar pines. This was the sort of garden where God left man.

"Tell them we have artillery and will use it," Kreft snapped.

Leighton yelled this.

"Come ahead and use it, then," the hill voice replied. "Don't mind us."

Leighton distinctly heard laughter from the cave. He glanced at Kreft, who flushed. Kreft wormed forward on his elbows, revolver drawn for a shot.

Leaving Greer in the arms of another Guardsman, Looney rode up the eastern bald. He dismounted. His face was gray and wet. "Why don't you ask who these fools are?" He directed this at Kreft.

"They are Davies and his band," Kreft said, still scooting around on the bluff. "And they know I am with you."

Leighton snorted.

"Why else do they not surrender?" Kreft asked.

"They're holed up in a cave," Leighton said.

Kreft scowled. "Well, Commander Looney, prepare your men for an extended stay. We have ample ammunition and supplies. We'll wait them out."

Looney's eyes widened. "Lieutenant, my men are accustomed a little more to billeting. It's almost October."

Kreft stood in Looney's face. "Commander, your missions for months have been to capture and rid our state of these violent elements. Your men are nothing but worthless Paw Paw Militia. And I won't be surprised to find among you traitors of the same ilk as those we have surrounded."

Looney drooped, but Leighton stiffened.

Kreft edged forward. "These are filth below us," he said. His face was purple, his teeth clenched.

Looney backed away and sat down. He kneaded his brow.

Kreft glanced at Leighton, then glared. Here in Kreft, in his blond hair and pink-rimmed eyes, his pale Northern skin was the face of all of Morkan's captors. His stare made Leighton's breath catch.

"Lieutenant." Leighton hesitated. "The war's over here." Though it was a lie, he said it as he might say a prayer, a chant against oblivion: Yea, though I walk through the valley of the shadow. "You're on the wrong side of the river."

Kreft laughed. "Gentlemen, I will wait here alone if need be."

Leighton shook his head, and Kreft and Looney began the same argument. Leighton crawled to the edge of the ridge, rested his chin in his hands. Greer was now flat on his back and very still, a Guardsman tending, touching his chest with just the tips of his fingers. After a moment, the Guardsman covered Greer's face with a blue field cap. Leighton pressed his cheek against the cool stone. If Thou shouldst retain our iniquities, O Lord, he thought, then more than watchmen for the dawn I will wait.

A shot popped from the cave, and the Guardsmen opened fire. Again, smoke clustered against the ridge to be sucked into the cave. Leighton regarded the brush on the ridge. At the quarry, they would have burned the brush out, let it fall burning to the pool in the quarry pit. There was enough here for an enormous fire.

Kreft and Looney were still arguing when Leighton turned.

"Let's smoke them out," Leighton said.

The two men stared at him. "How?" Kreft asked.

Leighton showed them how brush propped against the scrub cedars could provide a fire. The cedars would burn through. They were small and dry enough, or they could be axed. A bonfire could be dropped right in front of the cave. The wind still blew from the northwest, and was becoming cold.

Kreft frowned, but nodded. Looney called for four men to ride up to them. Once the men were picked, the brush was easily hacked and piled against two small scrubs rooted at the edge. Leighton ordered the Guards to gather extra brush to be dropped on the fire. The men brought lantern oil from their saddlebags and soon soaked a patch of the brush. With a few sparks from a flint, some coaxing of the tinder, the brush grew to a whirling fire.

Looney strutted and extolled the idea. There was certainly no way to bring fire from the valley to the cave without being shot. Even Kreft smiled as the brush emitted thick gray loops of smoke. Looney and the four men rode back down into the valley. Kreft and Leighton sat waiting with the axes.

Leighton laid down and leaned over the edge again. "If you'll give yourselves up," he yelled, "if you'll come on out, we'll take you to Springfield, no harm." He coughed. The left side of his face stung and tingled from the fire. The smell of cedar enlivened him like whiskey. From the flames, he lit a cigar. The cigar smoke made his chest ache. At least this way, no one else would die.

The cedar gave, and the fire shifted. Leighton jammed the ax against the burning brush. Kreft joined him. With a shove, the cedar cracked and most of the fire tumbled over the bluff. They watched it scrape against the rocks, land, and scatter. For a moment, the blackened logs only glowed. But then, blue wisps of smoke curled off the brush and groped for the cave. The Guardsmen cheered.

Kreft drew his revolver, but Leighton grabbed his wrist.

"Don't be an ass," the Lieutenant said. "They'll try to put it out."

Leighton began dumping massive armloads of leaves and pine needles, some of which actually reached the smoldering brush. The wind increased, and flames grew. He dropped down branches.

Then, from the cave, a crouching figure ducked between rocks. Kreft rose.

Leighton removed his cigar. "Do you surrender?" he shouted.

The bushwhacker lunged for the brush, and Kreft and the Guards in the valley opened fire. The bushwhacker fell, began crawling back toward the cave. Firing in the valley quit. Steadying his revolver across his wrist, Kreft squinted and shot the bushwhacker, who collapsed.

"God damn it," Leighton said. "He was done trying."

Kreft frowned. "You best speed this up."

Leighton took a flask of lantern oil from his saddlebag, uncorked the top. He heaved the flask at the brush, a long stream of oil twirling from the top of the bottle as it descended. With a whoosh of air, the brush burst in an orange ball, smoke billowing black, then gray again.

Smoke poured off the brush and rushed up toward them, enveloping the cave.

Leighton and Kreft stepped to one side.

"Ready your men, Looney," Kreft shouted.

With the smoke covering the cave, Looney moved all his men into the sinkhole. In a short while, figures came hurtling from the cave, coughing. Leighton could hear them choking, arms waving above their heads. Five, seven, eight of them, some tumbling to the ground having run in blindness through the fire, slapping their hands to their pant legs and vests, the others stumbling, squawking, "Don't shoot. She's done! That's enough!" He saw, thank God, Looney wave his arms to have the Guards hold their fire.

The flare of Kreft's revolver left his eyes blinking. Kreft fired again. Leighton saw two bushwhackers falling, others turning to stare at the fire droppers. One held up his white palms in the green-gray light of the forest. His mouth opened in a plea, Kreft's revolver flared, the mouth exploded red, the head whipping back, man spinning.

Leighton drew his revolver, cocked and jammed it in Kreft's ribs and a revolver stubbed his own ribs, Kreft's gun, the Lieutenant's eyes glowering. They held each other gun to rib to gun.

Kreft smiled. "Who," he asked, "does not sometimes envy the good and brave?"

The Lieutenant's eyes locked with Leighton's. The brown of Kreft's irises dulled, the striated color deepening as it compressed the black pupil. Leighton could hear the bushwhackers below pleading, some wailing.

Kreft pushed the pistol deeper into Leighton's flesh.

Leighton bit down on the cigar, its end tilting up. "*Te absolvo*, brother." He lowered his gun.

Kreft turned back to the valley. Some of the bushwhackers made it to the woods and disappeared. One was crawling. He reached the sinkhole's edge. Kreft beaded and dropped him. Leighton shot Kreft twice in the head.

The sun began to set when Leighton examined each of the bushwhackers. The men he found had dirty faces. Their hair was matted and full of lice. One was very old, and his beard grew in a long, white spike to the middle of his chest. All were hill people. Their skin was tanned. Knots of muscle dotted their scrawny frames. The youngest was trying to grow a mustache. Another kept a well-trimmed beard. The fourth was clean-shaven with a

261

stern jaw and brown eyes, a face so handsome Leighton could only glance at him.

The Guards did not speak to each other, but wandered the valley drinking to themselves. Soon it was very quiet, and the cicadas resumed.

After the fire died, Leighton followed Looney into the cave, and they searched by lantern. There were several bottles of whiskey, an enormous smelting pan that stunk strongly of sulfur. There were molds and many lead bullets, big loaves of smelted lead, wood and coal stacked in piles. On a little table far in the back were tintypes of plump, naked women hugging and fondling jackasses and hounds with stiff erections. A scrap of paper was pinned flat. Leighton removed the scrap from the rotting felt top of the table. On the front of the scrap was the label for a brand of nerve pills. On the back was a note. The penmanship was quite good. It read:

22 SEPTEMBER 1863
DEAREST MADEMOISELLE MARLENE YARBERRY,

IF I COULD GET YOU TO COME UP TO YELLVILLE ON THE
TENTH OF OCTOBER TO SEE ME AND BRING MY OTHER
HORSE THAT WOULD SURE PLEASE ME.

ALWAYS YOUR SERVANT,
GENE VALANCE

The Guards spent the night in the valley, their eyes wide open in the dark, their fingers oily and cold from clutching their revolvers. The next morning, Looney asked some of the men to drape a body either on back of the saddle or to ride without a saddle and drape a body in front. In the sinkhole they left two dead horses. After a vote, Looney took Kreft's white stallion. Leighton removed his saddle, and Looney helped him wedge Kreft across the withers of Leighton's horse. After much fighting and circling, they managed to twine the dead Guardsman Greer to the loin and hip of Looney's new horse.

Looney sat stiffly with Greer face down in back of him. The tailor's eyes were red, his face marred with soot. With the first light of dawn behind him he appeared battle-worn, a worthy commander on his white steed.

"Look each of you into the other's eyes," he said to his men. "That man dead on Morkan's horse died by a stray ball in a fire-fight."

The Guards shifted in their saddles, their faces taut.

"I'd a killed him, too," one said, "if I's up there. The sumbitch."

Looney circled his horse slowly to catch their countenances. As his horse moved, Greer's red hair bobbed where he lay. One of his hands was hardened in a fist. "Any man that has a different idea, speak up."

No one spoke. The sun fingered its way through the pines, and when it struck the men, their faces seemed etched in chalk.

Leighton rode the day in a fury of drink, often imagining Kreft might rear up from where he flopped and strangle him. Sometimes, he whispered to Kreft that he was dead and deserved it. For hours, he dozed with his palms braced against Kreft's spine.

Late that night, they rode into Fort Ozark with six stinking corpses. The pickets on Ozark Road did not challenge them, only stood and gawked. The commander of the fort greeted them in his nightshirt, a candle held high and wavering. He smiled and patted the Guards' legs. His men brought lanterns. None of the dead were Sam Davies. The dead were men of no renown whatsoever. Looney reported Lieutenant Avery Kreft as killed in the line of duty and cited Kreft's bravery. Then Looney officially resigned his commission as Commander. Looney's Federal Greene County Home Guards were disbanded and Leighton and its members were distributed among other Home Guard units, which drank, and billeted, and stayed under trees in the winter rain.

IV

WITHOUT MORKAN, THE FARM SUPPLIED TASKS AND crises at a terrific pace. The back fences were down, a fox was raiding the chickens, someone was felling hickories near the property line with Weitzer's. The cows needed treating for hollowtail. Johnson lost a finger and the skin of his forearm to the sow and was down with fever. Yet, when Leighton peeled potatoes beside Judith in the kitchen, a calm assurance moved over him, almost as if carried on the scent of her sweat, so different from a man's stink, a smell like fresh cut grass and corned beef. Her cheeks filled out again, her body thickened, and that was somehow heartening, like seeing soil rise up black and grainy when tilled. She worked without pay, and he kept a tally of the weeks, intending to reward her someday, telling her so once a week. They both worked with the gruff sloppiness of the weary. Years later he would remember the spring of 1864 as a time without time, a dazed procession of work and drudgery. Despite not knowing of his father's fate, he counted the small blessings. At least his Federal service kept soldiers from storming the house for food and fodder. At least some of the oxen and drafts were replaced. At least the muskets were still here, the Belgian shotgun, and the currency waited in the springhouse.

In the evenings, they sat on the front porch together, Judith in one of the high-backed chairs from the library, Leighton on the steps.

"I feel like a queen sitting in these here," Judith said. She draped her wrists over the arms of the chair, and holding her head high, she did look formidable if not regal. "You reckon Miss Charlotte felt like a queen on this front porch?"

Leighton shook his head. "I imagine you're the first to feel that way."

Her eyes were closed and a smile rounded her cheeks. The wind was bringing the smell of some new flower Leighton could not identify. Judith seemed to bask in it, like a barn cat in the sun. On the horizon, a tendril of black smoke explored the twilight—something more being burned; one more thing overturned.

"This time's going to teach you peace, Leighton. Not much matters. Dying matters a little. So avoid it. You got to learn to be still. You got a lifetime to go, and if I see straight, you going glide through it like a gar in the shadows. So mean and true, it can't be nothing but exactly what it is."

He leaned his back against the right leg of the chair, his shoulder against her knee. Her calf went stiff at his side, and he could feel her weight shift away from him in the chair. Maybe he was too old to be near her for comfort? He sat quietly waiting, wanting.

He patted her shin, taut as armor. "Judith, I want you here," he said. "All my life."

"We see," she said, suddenly tense. "We see."

When she finally relaxed and moved her leg to better support him, he felt so relieved his eyes stung.

"Remember, Leighton, I am your Judith. We get each other through this if you are My Leighton."

My Leighton. Her childhood name for him not only at play, but also whenever she saved him from his own impetuousness, from his own urges and mischief.

He let loose a long, slow breath. And when she sensed him fully at ease, his urge passed, she pinched his ear lobe and pulled it gently until, laughing, he swatted at her hand. Together, they watched swallows chitter and arc through the sky, swooping like the tips of arrows.

One of the horses swallowed a rotting hedge apple and lay on its side wheezing sure to die. Johnson arrived with the board Leighton ordered from the saw barn. Following him, to Leighton's surprise, was Cora Slade. In her hands she bore the drenching bottle and dill plants loaded with seed which she must have uprooted from near the hog pens. She hung back.

"Johnson?" Leighton asked.

The Negro knelt with the board. Under the horse's neck beneath the lump of the hedge apple, Leighton slipped a flat lime tablerock mossy enough to give cushion. He set another heavy boulder waiting beside the horse's neck. Johnson glanced back at Cora and spoke at a whisper. "She come up when I was cutting this. She seemed to know everything about you."

She wore a white cotton dress with a butternut hem, and she had muddied the knees. With her head bowed she appeared heavier than he remembered. "We may just need a nurse up here, Cora Slade."

Lifting her head, she strode up the hill and with each step the light in her eyes returned and the old mirthful smile Leighton remembered lifted her face.

"If you'll have this good man fetch me a bedpan full of vinegar?"

Johnson left them.

"What on earth, Leighton?" she asked. She knelt as well but began clawing at the ground. She prized up a long, square piece of flint and spat on it, kneaded dirt off with her thumbs. She cocked her chin at Leighton's contraption. "This will be a treat to see."

He scowled at her. "May kill it. It's a good horse. Was Johnson's horse, named Half Dollar." He placed a knee on the board and balanced the wood against the hedge apple now become a fulcrum. Too stunned and starved for air, the horse lay still, resigned.

With a pestle of flint already shining with spit, she found her a flat piece of jasper and was clearing it in the same way. "Half Dollar?" she asked.

A woman helping him, so different than Judith, who moved in such old, familiar routines. This woman overturned things, inserted herself between people. Johnson returned with a wash basin stinking with cider vinegar.

"My Pa told Johnson he wouldn't give a half dollar for it," Leighton said. He lifted the round boulder above his head and with a roar, he brought it down hard on the board.

Cora and Johnson jumped. There came a crunch, and Half Dollar's eyeballs bulged and he gave a little squeak. Everyone, even the horse, kept still. Gingerly Leighton lifted the board. There beneath the horse's frothy gray skin, the hedge apple had snapped. With a gulp and another roll of its eyes, one of the small pieces crawled down his neck. The horse breathed, one eyeball now watching Leighton closely.

"Mother Mary," whispered Cora. Then, recovered, she motioned Johnson to hurry and hand her the basin. "Strip the dill with me here, will you two?"

The smell of dill seed enveloped them as they stripped the brown and white little teardrops. She began crushing them between her rocks. "Don't fret the weedy part, gents. By God, he is a horse, after all." What she crushed she swirled in the vinegar, the she poured the contents into the grimy, brown drenching bottle and shook it.

"Now get his head up, and someone lay on him. He's going to hate this, but it will numb him and help break that up." Johnson wrenched the horse's head up and his mouth open while Leighton sat on his girth.

She pushed the bottle deep in the horse's throat and poured. The horse struggled, gargling the stuff. With a grunt she jammed the tilted, glubbing bottle down his gullet. He lurched, and threw Leighton off, stood and kicked. Leighton dove for Cora and tackled her round the waist.

Half Dollar stopped, bowed his neck to swallow. Then he wagged his great head snorting and blowing vinegar, dill, and slimy orange bits of hedge apple over the two of them. Johnson nabbed his halter laughing.

It took a moment before Leighton realized he still held Cora around the waist. He eased off, eyeing her. She was smiling, leaning back on her hands, watching Johnson lead Half Dollar away, her dress spread round her legs. What a bright woman.

"I thank you," Leighton said. "It's a relief to save a horse once in a while."

"I haven't seen you on that lovely one, the gray walking horse." When he said nothing she caught on that the horse was gone. "Oh, I'm sorry. Stolen?"

He shook his head.

In her hair was a rosewood clip with an ivory filigree, and at its apex the iron H, Hoerkstroetter, the jeweler Morkan shopped at for Charlotte. Leighton felt that black spirit well at his throat, as if he had stumbled on something both intimate and purloined. "Why are you here?"

Her smile vanished. She frowned. "Is there any word of your father, Leighton?"

"I had a letter from him. Smuggled. He was ill." In his mind he could hear the horse gasping again and he could see his father struggling for air. "Why?"

"Leighton, I am weak. I am having trouble waiting." She touched his hand. "Will you go and get him? Can you?"

He pulled his hand from under hers very slowly.

"Did he ask you to wait for him?"

Her face paled, lower lip bulged as she swallowed. He knew then that he had deeply hurt her. She buckled her jaw, brushed the dirt from her dress. "I believe he asked us both to wait."

In early April, a knock came at the front door. It was mid-morning, so if there was a call to muster, then likely it was very serious. He was patching the base of a wall with a mortar of slaked lime, water, and sand. In the spring sunlight pouring through the open windows, the house appeared dingy to him, tattered at its edges, as if he kept cattle there all winter. Through one of the windows he spied a soldier at the front door. The soldier's coat was dusty, and Leighton noticed his sleeves and hat bore a crimson stripe. Leighton fixed his Home Guard cap on his head, unwrapped the whipcords that held the door. He was able to salvage the one the Federals smashed capturing his father, though it bore an enormous bowl shaped dent waist high. It wobbled open.

The soldier standing there had a slim face, a waxed mustache. The crimson rim of his cap was set off by a single thick, black eyebrow that stretched across his forehead in a taut line. He had a pair of white gloves folded in his right hand. On one glove, the tips of three fingers were yellowed from tobacco.

Leighton saluted. "Lieutenant."

"At ease," the lieutenant said. He blinked at Leighton, craned his neck to see inside the house. "Is the young master Morkan in, please?"

"I am."

The soldier smiled. "I apologize. The field cap threw me. Federal, I see."

Leighton asked him in, hollered for Judith to get them some water. They sat in the parlor. Leighton's chairs were still greasy and the fabric stunk powerfully of woodsmoke. The lieutenant noticed this—his dark eyebrow formed a slight *V*, his nose wrinkling. Nevertheless, he placed his gloves on the arm of the chair, rested his hat on top of them.

Leighton nodded at the hat. "Artillery, sir?"

"Of a sort, yes. I'm actually attached to a prison in Illinois. I interrogate officers."

Leighton stared at him. Judith arrived with two glasses, handed one to the lieutenant. He took it, his eyebrow rising. He cupped the glass in both hands, touched the base of it to his forehead. "Oh, you have a superbly cool well." He drank the water. "Let me guess, a well house of stone, set into the side of a hillock? A shaft down to the sweetest limestone spring in Missouri?"

Leighton shrugged. The soldier was either very thirsty or was jesting, was probably from some big city, Chicago, say, where they already had running water in each house. "It's just an old springhouse."

Nodding, the lieutenant sat up straight. "I know your father. I defended him at his trial. My name is Browning, Lieutenant Browning."

"He told you about me, then?"

Browning nodded. Leighton hesitated a moment, then realized Browning would not have come alone if he meant to arrest someone.

"Is he well?"

"Gratiot is a difficult place." Browning said this matter-of-factly. He sipped his water. He was poised, and his uniform, though a little dusty, was so crisp that Leighton felt a twinge of dislike for the man. Browning reminded him too much of Kreft.

"I take it you failed in your defense."

Browning's eyebrow jolted, and his eyes, a bright hazel, widened. "You are very like him. I've certainly felt this bluntness before. Your father is a man of limited words, but when they arise, they are truth. They cut to the chase."

Leighton leaned back in his chair. The woodsmoke smell still made his eyes ache. "Strange," he said. "My father was known in town as a man of politic words, not verbose, but certainly a salesman, capable of boasting with the best drummer." Leighton paused. Browning watched him with unblinking eyes, his head cocked slightly as if he were listening and thinking intensely. "Are you sure you have the right Morkan? It is so often misspelled *M-O-R-G-A-N*. Like the workhorses."

"And you have his humor." Browning set the glass of water aside, reached in his coat pocket and pulled out a satchel and a little booklet of rolling papers. "May I?"

"If you roll me one."

Browning quickly rolled two cigarettes, losing only a little tobacco from the ends. He leaned forward in his chair, handed the cigarette to Leighton, struck a match to both of their cigarettes.

The smoke made Leighton's throat ache sweetly. His temples throbbed.

"Understand, Master Morkan, Gratiot is swamped with prisoners now. The war is going terribly for the south. Chattanooga has fallen. General Sherman is in Georgia. The army of Virginia is dug in and attritting. Little Rock has fallen. Mississippi is deserted. The prisoners come in trains so loaded they practically sway on the tracks."

Leighton snorted.

Browning frowned. "What I am saying is, there is a great likelihood that the significance of the case against your father has dwindled considerably in the minds of the officers running that prison." He stared at Leighton, and the corners of his eyes wrinkled. "I believe I can convince them to release him, to remand him to custody at home."

Leighton's arm trembled. The cigarette made his head feel stuffed with air. He sat forward. "In all seriousness?"

Browning smoked and held his cigarette in his fingertips, glancing at it as if it were a shard of silver to be admired. He sat forward. "It may be difficult. Your father was not a model prisoner. He resisted interrogation; from what I gather, he protected several men who were attempting escape."

Leighton sat back in the chair, held the cigarette away from his face.

"He is an honorable man," Browning said. "When I defended him, I felt he was even noble."

There it was, just as his father warned him, not a compliment but a solicitation. He was pleased to have recognized it, but unsure if his instinct were right. "Your offer to do this is so generous when I have nothing," Leighton said. He pinched the bridge of his nose, sat very still and feigned a moment of sadness. "I'm overcome that you'd seek me out and offer your help like this. It has been such a hard war. There's been so much deceit in this town."

When Leighton looked up, Browning was perched on the edge of his seat, his brow wrinkled. "I apologize," Browning said. "I'm afraid while I am at your service, it may take coin to grease the bars, so to speak."

Leighton was quiet for a moment. "I am destitute."

Browning smiled. "Trust in me, Leighton. Remember I defended your father. I know you to be a resourceful young man. I'm here interrogating two officers in the stockade. I will leave Friday for Illinois with them, then return to Springfield again I imagine in June, a regular sort of cycle. I'm thinking nine hundred dollars would be all anyone in St. Louis could need to free him."

On his return from the quarry, Leighton had counted the coin in the strong box, found it to be just under nine hundred. Browning had hit the number so exactly, Leighton was speechless for a moment. The lieutenant was smug, but surely not so smug as to have extracted that number from Morkan, then come here to speak it. "That's more than everything I could sell on this farm."

Browning leaned forward. He reached out to Leighton, touched the arm of Leighton's chair. "We'll work together. I have friends. They'll lend us money on his behalf. And he must have friends here. Get with them. Get what you can." His eyes narrowed, his forehead wrinkling with what appeared to be concern. "He really is very ill. We need to get him home."

"Ill?"

"Consumption."

Leighton bowed his head. Then after a moment, he nodded.

Browning finished his water. He looked at Leighton. "Say, now, take me on a tour of the lands, please. Morkan told me so much about each aspect of the farm, I feel as if I've already been here."

Leighton rose. He showed Browning the stock barn, the hog pen, the hen house. At each, Leighton was Spartan in answering Browning's questions. Browning watched him, eyes narrowed under the thick eyebrow.

They passed the springhouse, and Leighton waited, but was stunned when Browning asked nothing more about it. Browning even wrinkled his brow as if annoyed that Leighton stopped so long in one spot with nothing to say.

Leighton led him into the patchwork of garden plots behind the house, pointed out Johnson Davis's cabin, where the Negro was splitting wood. Eventually, Browning remounted, thanked Leighton for his hospitality. Leighton thanked him for his news.

"Look, Lieutenant, may I ask a frank question?"

Browning nodded.

"What's in it for you if you get my father free?"

"Certainly no monetary reward. It may take nine-hundred to a thousand dollars to move things in St. Louis." Browning paused. His horse stepped high, bouncing him. At least it was an old sorrel, nothing so fancy as Kreft's white Arabian, or the Walker Heron stole. "Call my offer, if you will, an atonement for my own sins."

Leighton led him to the gate. "My father, I'm sure, appreciates all you are doing."

"Leighton." Browning frowned. "I know these days trust is terribly hard to come by. I'll prove myself to you."

After staring a while, Leighton saluted. Browning eyed him, his horse prancing; then he smiled, swung his horse toward Springfield.

Leighton let him have an hour's ride. Then he removed the strongbox from the springhouse, took it upstairs to his bedroom, and tucked it in the highest corner of his wardrobe. Johnson Davis rigged up the battered old stone wagon, and Leighton and Judith drove to town. After Browning's visit, Leighton worried about what exactly Browning's connection was with troops in town. He wanted to take Judith along so that a visit to Correy would appear a natural part of a stop for goods.

The wagon moved with a nauseating lurch. The rehabilitated drafts suffered the barn skitters, and tended to stop and paw the ground, rolling their eyes. Leighton stopped the wagon at Correy's house, set the brake.

Correy answered the door, stood blinking at Leighton.

"May I come in?"

Correy nodded.

The interior was clean now, spare to the walls, modestly lit by a small lamp. A big, pink ceramic cross was nailed to the wall. "What can I do for you, Leighton? There haven't been any sales."

"Something very strange has happened."

Correy's face remained flat for a moment. "What's that?"

"A lieutenant came out to the house this morning, wearing what I thought was an artilleryman's uniform from that Iowa battery. Hazel eyes. Brown hair. One big, black eyebrow. Said his name was Browning. Defended my father at trial in St. Louis. He's willing to go back there, too, on the chance that by now the Yankees have lost some of their fire to keep my pa. He said it would cost money there."

Correy blinked at him. He motioned to the bench set against the square kitchen table. They sat.

"All I need to know, Correy, is whether or not this Browning can do anything." If he told him all his suspicions he worried that Correy might make assumptions. "I'll ask my folks in the know, but you know people at the prison, and in it. Browning said he was here interrogating officers. I'd appreciate it if you

273

could find out all you can about him before I commit any money to him."

Correy sat quietly for a moment, pushing his tongue against his lips as if he were dipping snuff. "Leighton, I hate to be around that prison for any reason." He ran the back of his knuckle across his wet lip. A clock ticked like a twig snapping. "But for you, and for Morkan." He nodded.

Leighton stood. "Why don't we meet at the Quarry Rand, say in a week?"

"Did this Browning say Morkan was alive?"

Leighton nodded. "He's ill, but alive."

Correy rose, led Leighton to the door.

"I promise my father will appreciate this," Leighton said.

"He has to come out alive to keep that promise," Correy said glumly.

Early that next week, Correy sent a note with one of the Home Guards from Leighton's unit. When the Home Guard left, Leighton slit the wax on the note, opened it.

14 APRIL 1864
LEIGHTON:
BROWNING IS REAL. HE MAY BE ABLE TO DO SOME-
THING.
ELIJAH CORREY

Leighton went to muster that day, his mind in a tangle. Browning had been solicitous, had all the markings of someone out to swindle him. Yet Correy confirmed that the possibility was there, that Browning could save Morkan. The April wind whooped through the trees, bore down so hard on him and the riders in his unit, it became maddening, as if the earth were furious at them and wanted them cleared from her table. They camped that night and met a payroll wagon in Marshfield and escorted it into Springfield, rifles ready at their hips. The wind was infuriating then, as they wended through the trees and bramble that had taken over the few remaining oak savannas. They could hear nothing but its howl as it moved branches and newly opened leaves into phantoms of bushwhackers in ambuscade. Despite the Federal dominance in town, the surrounding countryside felt as if it belonged to another nation.

In town he asked his commander about Browning, and his commander led him to a whiskey barrel bar in a shed that used to house a knifemaker's outfit. Though the lathe and belts were all pilfered, soldiers leaned on the dusty tables and turning benches, complained to the barkeep of foundry sand blackening their uniforms. Someone capped the rod of a drop forge in the corner with a captured hat from Marmaduke's cavalry, the Confederates that assaulted the fort during the Battle of Springfield. The forge was transformed to a steely Rebel dwarf sulking in the shadows, furious hands stiff at his sides.

Leighton's commander introduced him to a sergeant named Orville Lawrence who was a guard at the prison in the Men's Academy. After drinks, Lawrence confirmed there was a Browning out of Illinois working at the prison, a fat guy, with blond hair, a beard.

That Wednesday, he went to Correy's again. The foreman was sitting on his porch steps. He smelled of horse shit, and his dungarees and boots held clumps of brown dung and hay.

"Don't you look down on me, Leighton Morkan. Cleaning a stable ain't as bad as riding with their payrolls."

Leighton sat on the step with him. "Tell me which Browning you mean?"

"The one at the prison." He stared at Leighton.

"What'd you find out about him?"

Correy's brow furrowed. "That he was who he said he was."

"Did you meet him?"

"Hell no, Leighton. If I can help, I don't go near them people."

Leighton lifted his cap and ran a hand through his hair. "Report I got from an Orville Lawrence is that Browning's a different fellow from the one that came to the house. And my visitor knows a little too much about the family to be just an old guard at the prison here."

Correy's face grew red. "If I get you all in dutch again, I swear to God I'll hang myself."

"Nonsense."

Correy sat for a long time, staring exhaustedly at his boots. "What's your visitor aiming to do?"

"Swindle me." Leighton stood from the step. "You still willing to go to St. Louis?"

"Right this minute?"

"After I reckon with my visitor." Leighton fixed the blue cap on his head.

"You know where I am if you need me," Correy said. His eyes were as dark and hollow as his cheeks. "Maybe I can get help from the real Browning. I wouldn't be any too pleased if someone was using my name that way."

"Be careful if you do seek him out," Leighton said.

Correy blushed again, but nodded.

Leighton did nothing to gather money. Friday, he and Judith were out in the yard hoeing. Clouds bunched up from the west to clutter the sky, and their shadows coursed over the ground, focusing sunlight into solid diagonals of brilliance like pipes of yellow glass on the horizon. Judith was humming an old lullaby of his mother's, and every once in a while she lifted a bit of dirt on the blade of her hoe, dribbled it over Leighton's brogans. Disgusted he butted her with the handle. In a fit of her screeching and both of them cackling, he tackled her but could not push her burly form to the ground. They grunted, laughed, and circled the garden until Leighton caught himself, released her, and brushed his dungarees. As he watched her catch her breath he could still feel the warmth and moisture of her breasts where they had dappled his wrists. His heart worked like a piston. "Judith, Judith," he said, and her face darkened.

Then he saw Browning coming up the hill, holding his crimson-trimmed hat to his head in the wind.

Judith lost her smile.

Leighton stuck his chin at the house. She lifted her dress and left her hoe at the edge of the garden.

Browning reined his horse. He smiled down at Leighton. His pants and coat were rumpled. "The quarryman's son is a farmer?"

"Who are you?"

He dismounted, pulled out his tobacco pouch. "I'm Lieutenant Micah Browning, cousin of Cyrus Browning, attached to the 5th Illinois. My cousin and I are down here to interrogate two officers and determine whether we should leave them here for exchange or take them back to Alton."

Leighton rested his hands on the end of his hoe, leaned his chin over them. "I didn't get any money. I don't have anything for you."

Browning's face fell, and above his dark eyebrows, his forehead creased. He pulled at his bottom lip.

"I'm sure hoping you can still help me," Leighton said, then wanted to kick himself. His voice let his sarcasm through too clearly.

Browning looked up. He glanced at Leighton's belt, then drew his revolver. "Take me to your springhouse, and we'll see about funding."

He jabbed the gun at Leighton, who raised his hands.

"You need a drink?" Leighton asked.

"This is no time for humor." They began walking for the well. Leighton cursed himself that he left his coat in the house, and in it the pepper-box. "I know you've got a strong box and I figure eight hundred some dollars, currency," Browning said.

Leighton stopped. Browning jabbed him in the back. A cloud scudded across the sun, darkening the ground. "It's not in the springhouse."

"I see. Take me to it."

They ascended the stone stairs, walked through the front room of the house. Leighton's mind raced. Where could he take Browning so that he could turn on him, get the gun from him or get something to kill him with? He thought of leading him into the cellar, taking a lantern, whacking him with that.

Inside, he hesitated at the stairs, and Browning lunged forward, stabbed the gun in his back. "I will shoot you just above both kidneys and you will bleed and call for your mother and maybe even your father and then die in terrible pain, living just long enough to tell me where your precious money is." Browning jabbed the gun into him. "But sadly, there will be no time to get a priest to settle your little soul."

Leighton headed up the stairs, noticed his coat was fallen from the banister to the floor beyond his reach. He clenched his fists—the pepper-box lay on the floor in his coatpocket. There would be no getting at it. They walked the stairs, Browning's boots thumping behind him. They entered his bedroom, stepped to the wardrobe. He opened the wardrobe, figuring he might be able to strike Browning with the box. He was trembling.

Browning stabbed the gun against the back of his neck. "Slowly. Very carefully."

Leighton lifted the box, felt the great weight of it shift and strain his wrists, all that coin, everything he had. His teeth were clenched, his eyes stinging with anger and tears.

He turned slowly to Browning, whose dark brow was so bunched it appeared to be a scar. A shadow moved from the door, something metal flashed in its hand—Judith. She pointed the pepper-box, her pink tongue stuck between her lips, one eye screwed so tightly, Leighton almost laughed. Leighton's eyes must have given her away, because Browning turned. When he did, she fired. The pistol coughed all four barrels into him.

He fell back against Leighton, who brought the strong box down on the revolver, knocking it from his hand. Leighton cracked Browning across the forehead with the box, and the coins spilled over the floor in a shining cascade.

Browning was dead. Leighton froze, the strong box still open in his hand, the coins glittering against the brown puncheons.

The pepper-box thumped to the floor. Judith covered her mouth with her hands, her eyes traveling from the coins to Browning to the coins again.

Leighton knelt beside Browning, bowed his head.

"You lied to me," she said in a dismayed whisper. "You lied to *me*."

"Judith, I would tell you. . . ." He raised a hand to quell her protests.

". . . I would tell you this isn't my money to give, but that's only half true. It's my father's, and it's all the family has."

"And they's plenty of it you could pay me and Johnson and Isaac."

"I owe you both one hundred and eighteen weeks. I have every intent to pay."

She was seething, her fists clenched. "I just near died for you."

"I have to have seed money to start up the quarry with. Without it. . . ."

Judith leapt on him, bowled him flat, knocked his breath away with her knee in his chest, tore at his hair. He got a grip on her neck and squeezed. As they rolled they thumped Browning aside, Leighton struggling to keep his grip on her neck and avoid her blows, the coins sliding and ringing, biting impressions in his back. When she landed a punch to his jaw, he roared, and was able to roll with her sideways and crack the back of her head against the door frame. Her eyes widened and blinked. He cracked her head there again. Her arms fell limp; her eyes rolled back in her head for a second. She groaned.

"Think about what you're doing, damn it," he said. "We need each other."

She breathed deeply, held her eyes shut. Her breath came through her tight lips in a whistle. "Think what you done."

He slowly rose, then began to gather the coins, plunk them in the strongbox. She lay with her cheek to the puncheons, her eyes narrowed on him, mean as a wounded cat's. She glanced at the dead man.

"What am I going do about him? Ain't the Federals going hang me for this?"

Leighton shook his head. "He's no Federal. He's been sleeping in them clothes off in the woods somewhere. Look at the ticks on him. He's nothing but a thief."

Near the last of the coins, he set aside fifty dollars worth of eagles and Indian heads. He scooted the pile over to Judith. She blinked at it, raised herself on her elbow.

"Don't you tell Johnson," Leighton said. "You do and I swear, that day, you're all off my land."

She scooped the coins toward her. "I ain't never going forget what you done. Liar."

After a moment, Leighton nodded at the dead man. "And I won't forget what you've done for me."

That evening by dusk, she recovered fully, save for a visible knot beneath the short hair at the back of her head. Without speaking, they removed Browning's uniform. Leighton was convinced Browning thieved the uniform from an Iowa artillery unit. Staring at Browning's hazel eyes, Leighton knew this man had at least seen his father, had either been in prison with him or interrogated him. At one point, while Judith was getting the man's britches off, Leighton shook the corpse so violently it gave three agonal gasps that made him and Judith leap back from the body.

"Finished?" Judith asked him, once they both had their breath.

He turned away for a moment and Judith completed her task.

Together they carried the body in a wheelbarrow down toward where the creek on Weitzer's land widened into a deep swimming hole. Bumping along the rock roads, with the trees greened, the air warm and loud with birds, streaked with the yellow and peach of early sunset, the corpse's white hands dangling, Leighton laughed aloud at one point. Nothing fit. Browning's head bounced and made the barrow thump like a cracked bell. Judith covered her mouth with her hand.

They dumped him in the Weitzer's swimming hole face down. For a moment, they stood watching the water curl over his head, drive silt around him. A tiny goggle-eye darted among the strands of Browning's hair, nipped them as the strands waved. If he was found, Leighton figured he would be considered a bushwhacker, a spy, a thief shot, stripped, and rightly left for dead. His uniform was stolen from an artillery unit Leighton was certain he did not belong to. A star glared above them, and the water, once it stilled, reflected this single blue point, the purpling sky, and two squat shadows.

"Guess I'm a Morkan now," Judith said.

"Why?"

"Saved the money, didn't I?"

Leighton snorted. "Yes you did, Judith. You sure did."

They left him among a babble of frogs, walked the hill together, and as they did, Leighton could hear coins clicking in the
pouch Judith kept between her breasts.

For a time, Judith and he were cold toward one another,
hardly speaking, avoiding work that put them in the same room
or in the same section of the garden or barn. But, as spring
turned to summer, the collusion of dumping the body, the fact
that Judith heard turkey buzzards squabbling in the Weitzer's
woods, and the conspiracy of hiding Judith's pay from Johnson
and Isaac drew them back together. They became a brother and
sister once more, two who spoke in a strange set of private jibes
and endearments, who not only knew the family's latest secrets,
but were now the perpetrators of all the deeds that require secrecy.

V

CORREY CAME UP THE HILL AND RIDING BEHIND HIM
was a heavyset blond soldier. Leighton's arms were caked with
gray mortar to the elbow, and as the riders approached he stood
by the front porch in his shirtsleeves with his hands palm up.
Judith stood beside him, her thick arms and round face coated
with mortar as well.

Frowning, the heavyset man removed his cap. He fidgeted on
his mount as if something about Judith and Leighton disturbed
him. Even Correy looked at the two with his brow creased.

"Leighton, this here's Cyrus Browning," he said.

Leighton nodded at him. Judith moved so close, he could
feel the soft warmth of her hip pressing against his own. With
her hands held out from her sides dripping with mortar like his,
her gray streaked face set firmly at Cyrus Browning, she filled
Leighton with a fierce strength.

"I'd ask you in," Leighton said, "but we had some trouble
with your cousin."

Cyrus dismounted with a grunt. "That's what I'm here about.
To restitute you for another man using my name." He tied his
horse at the porch rail, then stood before Leighton. His eyes
narrowed at Judith when she did not move off.

"I don't need your money," Leighton said.

Browning frowned. "That's not what I mean. In September,
I go back to St. Louis and report at Gratiot before going on to
Alton." He ran the back of his sleeve across his brow. "I will do
everything I can to get them to release your father."

"Costing what?"

"Your time. Your horses. And probably you'll need a wagon
to get him home in."

"He's ill?"

Cyrus's face went flat. "Every prisoner in Gratiot is ill." After a moment, Cyrus looked down at his feet and took a deep breath. "Young Morkan, if you can trust that fellow there." He pointed at Correy. "I want you to trust me. I am sorely sorry for what has happened, and whether you believe it or not, the United States is sorry. War is one thing. But personal treachery is more than should be tolerated."

"See you in September," Leighton said. "And I don't have to trust you. There's miles and miles between here and St. Louis for us to get to know one another."

Cyrus frowned. "You know you are addressing a Federal officer."

Leighton said nothing.

Cyrus fixed his campaign hat back on his head and untied his horse. Once he'd heaved his body on to it, the saddle leather crunching, he turned to Leighton again. "Tell me, whatever happened to that other Browning, the imposter?"

Judith tensed, but Leighton patted her arm. "He's moved on," he said.

After a moment watching Leighton, Cyrus nodded. Then he and Correy turned for the road.

On a rainy afternoon near the end of August, Correy and Cyrus Browning returned and dismounted at the barn door where Johnson and Leighton were working. Correy wore a Federal uniform, and his tack was all U. S. issue. Cyrus looked officious in his blues.

"Despite my being with you, young Morkan, this could turn ugly either way. Get on your blues, but pack a set of old farm clothes and I have a gray coat for each of us."

Judith stood behind him, holding her dress up from the mud, breathing hard. "Come in. I got your uniform," she said.

She followed him to the house, watched him scrub his hands at the trough. In his room she motioned to his pressed tunic and breeches, his boiled and pressed shirt. She stood with her back to him as he slipped out of his work clothes.

"Is all that all right? I got that together right? You missing anything?" she asked.

He was preoccupied with the buttons of the tunic, his thumb and finger running over the imprint of the eagle, the tiny letters **U. S.** He remembered Heron thieving in the alley so long ago twisting buttons off the dead Kansan. Donning the uniform, he felt like a thief. What war had he fought to deserve this garb? One battle when he killed a Rebel. One skirmish when he killed Kreft. He pulled the campaign coat over him, and the tag— **"AVENGE OUR HOLY UNION"**—scratched against the back of his tunic. In his coatpocket was a letter from General Eggbert B. Brown commending his service in defense of that Union in the "Quinine Brigade" and with Corvin Looney in the capture of a guerilla leadworks. The letter went on to commend his honorable transfer to his current Home Guard unit.

Judith brushed his fingers aside, buttoned his campaign coat, then stood holding his arms. Even in the gray light from the windows, her round face shone. Her dark eyes focused on his chest, worry pinching their corners.

"I'll be back," Leighton said. "With him."

"'Less you're lying to me," she said, very quietly, smiling.

"Do you think I can trust him, this Browning?"

She shrugged. Then she stepped back from him, stooped, and shook something loose from the neckline of her dress, a hemp cord, her satchel of money. Lowering her chin to her chest, she lifted the cord over her head.

She held the pouch of coin out to Leighton. He hesitated, then took her hand and closed her fist around the satchel. Already the strong box full of money was wrapped in a canvas satchel and tucked beneath the wagon seat. "No," he said.

He took her face in his hand, her soft chins slick with sweat against his callus. She tensed, but then the gentleness of his grip overcame her. Her bosom pressing against him, his hand clutching her thick arm, they stood so close together, a prayer could not have slipped between them. "There is no coin from anywhere could pay for what I owe My Judith."

The sob she caught in her throat rang on the stone beneath them and up the stairs and claimed the entire house for one, still moment. She steadied herself. Then she assessed him head to toe with those black eyes. "Come back. Whole. Even if it's just you."

Telegraph Road was awash with mud, and the dark skies poured on the wagon and its two outriders. At night, they camped under the wagon and even when the rain stilled, only Correy and Leighton whispered together. Cyrus Browning lay on his saddle blanket snoring with his back to them.

"Is he really doing what he says, Correy? Restitution?" Leighton said, staring at the spot where Cyrus's snore ground away rising and falling.

"We both are. Him and me."

Leighton surveyed the pitch black of the woods around him, the maddening downpour of rain against the wagon bed above them. He risked lighting a cigar. "I want you to do this only because you think it's right."

Correy pulled the horseblanket close. "Just let me do it. Who cares for the why?"

"I do," Leighton said. "Please, don't do this out of any sense of owing us something. If you're doing that, I want you to turn back."

"If he's alive, it's not so much the both of you I will owe."

Leighton waited.

"You see, Cora . . . we been thrown together. And times were bad."

"Correy," Leighton said very softly. "He asked her to wait for him."

Correy gripped Leighton's hand stuck in the cold mud. "I know. She knows."

When Leighton said nothing more, Correy settled the blanket around himself as if to sleep. After a long time he asked, "What would you do if the war was over Leighton?"

"Get restitution for every dime Browning's army took from my father and me." He smoked. "Bust and cook that old fort's stone into cement." He was quiet awhile and the rain diminished. He put out his cigar. "Keep Heron the Hell away from me I guess."

"If you get your pa back, will you run the quarry?"

"I'd give anything to have just half a day of him bossing me and that quarry."

When Correy said nothing for a long while, Leighton nudged him with his toe. "Will you do something for me, Correy?"

"What? Anything, of course," he said sleepily.

"Marry her. And don't hurt her."

When the clouds broke, the sun made the forest and road steam. In the heat, they rode with their coats stowed and their tunics undone.

Cyrus pressed his horse to keep even with Leighton and the wagon. His eyes scoured the woods ahead. "If guerillas find us, you let me do the talking. I bluffed my way out of many a tight one." Cyrus rode with his back straight, a gloved hand planted on his fat thigh.

"If you get us killed, how'm I to get restitution from you?" Leighton asked.

Glaring, Cyrus nudged his mount ahead of the wagon.

That afternoon they were fording a creek when a dozen horsemen came stepping down the creekbed. They wore Federal coats, but their hair was long and ragged, their beards unkempt. Like Ferguson and Bert, they bristled with pistols and knives.

Leighton halted the wagon and Correy and Cyrus moved their horses next to him.

One of the horsemen edged his mount forward and peered into the wagon bed. Leighton noticed two bullet holes in the chest of the horesman's Federal tunic, shots that would have killed him. He wore captain's bars.

"What you been hauling?" The captain's eyes were gray and so level and lifeless they might have been ingots of solder.

"Lime, captain," Leighton said.

The captain glanced at Cyrus, then at Correy. "What for?"

Cyrus was about to speak, but Leighton spoke first. "For the dead, sir."

The captain ran his thumb along his bottom lip. Behind him, his men shifted in their saddles. "Which dead?"

"We buried both, sir."

Sitting back, the captain looked to his cohorts. "What about them?" He nodded at Leighton and Correy and Cyrus.

The shortest of the riders spat brown tobacco juice in a drop so quick, Leighton almost missed it. "Skelp them."

"Aw, shit," said another.

The captain held up a hand. "You're a Federal Home Guard, ain't you?"

Cyrus Browning moved in the saddle, its leather creaking. Correy, too, shifted. Along the horsemen's tack were draped hemp necklaces bearing tufts of hair and grayed flesh, a Negro's thumb, a small ear, still pale, on which there hung a delicate golden hoop and the blue flash of its diamond singlet.

"I am a Federal Home Guard because I had to be. My father is Michael Morkan, the man who gave General Price black powder from his quarry." Leighton pictured in his mind a gar moving through the darkest hole of water.

The captain stroked his chin. "And where you going with a empty wagon?"

Cyrus sat up straight in the saddle, placed his gloved hand on his thigh. "We two captured this wagon and him as a teamster and are going to find Captain William Clarke and his unit."

The woods were so quiet that when the wind stirred it blew a heavy drop down from the oaks, popping the leaves as if a bullet were skipping through them. A few of the horsemen jumped at this, then steadied. They turned their eyes on Cyrus.

"We wear these uniforms only as a safeguard against Yankees," Cyrus said.

The captain scanned the faces of his men, faces that gave no hint of their intentions. Grimy skin, unblinking eyes. "Captain Clarke requested a wagon?"

"Anything for the Cause," Cyrus said.

Leighton saw Correy shiver.

Parting his coat at the waist, the captain casually drew a knife, and stepped his horse over to Cyrus Browning. The knife shimmered blue, but the captain kept his eyes on Leighton. "Master Morkan, why is this here fellow lying to me?" He put the knife beneath Cyrus's chin. When his horse stamped, the blade's tip lifted the fat beneath Cyrus's beard.

"How can you tell he is?" Leighton asked.

A few of the horsemen narrowed their eyes at Leighton. One grinned, his teeth as brown and filthy as an old hound's. From the tip of the captain's knife, a streak of blood scurried down the blade. Cyrus's eyes danced.

The captain paid this no attention, his gray eyes glimmering for a moment on Leighton. "You tell me how lucky it would be for a fat fool like this to swipe a pair of pants that fits him just right?"

"Am I lying to you?" Leighton asked.

The slightest grin broke the captain's face, and he removed the knife from Cyrus's neck. In a flash, his horsemen in the front rank all had revolvers drawn and cocked. Their attentions seemed focused on Cyrus.

The captain moved his horse until he was within inches of Leighton. He looked down on him. "Where are you going with a empty wagon? And two trembling Yankee cowards for company?"

"I'm going to bargain to get my father out of Gratiot before he dies of consumption."

The captain regarded Leighton for a bit, then raised his eyebrows at his men. Their faces showed no hint of any leaning.

"For the true word of an honorable man bravely given in the face of sure death and disaster"—He paused and methodically wiped his blade against his britches—"I normally wouldn't give a squirt of piss in a hand sieve." He replaced his knife in its scabbard.

His men began to grin. The short one bounced in the saddle as if something delightful were about to begin.

"But this afternoon, I am filled with a spirit akin with the afflicted, with the put upon," the captain said. He swung his horse to move in rank with his men. "Gentlemen." He bowed in the saddle. "I give you your lives."

"Aw, shit," one of his men said.

They turned their horses and proceeded down the stream.

Cyrus turned stiffly in the saddle, the water dancing yellow bands of light across his sweat-soaked back. He watched the riders disappear, his chest jerking and falling. At his collar, sweat and blood made a chain of red.

"Mr. Browning, you all right?" Leighton asked.

Blinking, Cyrus nodded.

"Can I trust that you will be a better performer when we reach Gratiot?"

Cyrus's face fell and reddened.

"I don't mean to shame you," Leighton said. "I just want to know."

"I'll be fine."

The St. Louis they came to was like nothing Leighton remembered. The roads were clogged with cavalry and wagon trains, squads of blue soldiers. A man in a poplin suit tried to convince them to buy canvas hoods soaked in cedar shavings and brine against the yellow fever. At every corner, a dutchman was in charge, directing traffic, scouring each civilian's baggage. In the dripping alleys, crowds of refugees huddled holding out pots and cups and filthy hands for alms.

Down toward the River, then onto eighth, McDowell's Surgery School finally came into view, its domed turret now soot-streaked, its high windows barred. Unlike any street near the River, Gratiot was a puddle of quiet. The urine and death reek of the prison made Leighton's head pound.

"Where's that fellow with the hoods?" Correy asked.

Cyrus halted them. He put on his dress coat, nodded at them to do the same. "Now I will handle all this. Let's swing round here to the old loading dock."

A brick arch ushered them into a mud-bottomed portico where the smell of rotting food overcame the stink of the prison. In the cool shade stood two guards, and between them the gray wraiths of a dozen men in chains. With a pang, Leighton remembered his father's miners on the cliffs covered in sweat and lime dust. He scanned the faces of the chained men, but saw no one he knew.

Cyrus traded salutes and talked for a long time with an officer at the dock.

Correy leaned toward Leighton. "He know what he's doing?"

Leighton shrugged. "At least he's among his kind of soldier." He scowled at the guards watching the prisoners scoop garbage onto wagons.

Cyrus rode back to them. "Correy, I want you to stay with the wagon. I got an idea, Leighton. It might make a difference if you were to come with me."

Leighton glanced at Correy, then reached under the wagon-seat and drew out the strongbox with all its currency.

The officer Cyrus spoke with led them up a flight of stairs, past the heat of a kitchen, then up two more flights. They came to a tall walnut double door, and the officer stepped inside. Though the hall was clear, the walls hummed with a constant murmur. Periodically a shout or cry rose up.

After a long time, the officer stuck his head out and called for Cyrus. Rising, Cyrus told Leighton to wait just a bit. He stepped behind the door. The weight of the metal strongbox creased Leighton's thighs. Carrying a bushel basket, a prisoner shuffled by, shackles ringing—the basket was filled to its brim with human hair. An hour passed.

Finally the door opened, and Cyrus ushered Leighton into a cluttered office dominated by a desk piled high with papers. When Leighton stepped into the office, a plump colonel with a mustache sat behind the desk. Leighton saluted, and the colonel motioned him to a leather chair.

Leighton sat, the coins scraping slightly in their box.

"Leighton, this is Colonel Tuttle," Cyrus said. "Show him your service papers."

Tuttle fixed a pair of spectacles on his nose and examined Leighton's papers with pursed lips.

"What happened to the other Browning?" the colonel asked.

"He's dead, sir," Leighton said.

Cyrus jolted, stared at Leighton.

"You kill him?"

"He came to rob my home and used an assumed name, which I imagine he swiped from our Lieutenant Browning here."

"You are a man of more candor than your father." Tuttle ruffled Leighton's papers again. "Your service record is encouraging. I'll level with you. Your father is an unrepentant traitor.

He has protected tunnelers, spies, and Rebels of all ilk." Leighton wondered if this were sleight of hand.

The colonel removed the spectacles and rubbed his red eyes. "I would hang him, but he is about to die. If you remove him, he will likely die. Yet that is what Lieutenant Browning has asked of me."

"I would like to take him home, sir," Leighton said.

"Why should I reward you for killing a Federal officer?"

"Pardon, sir. That officer was a thief. And in a month, you will give me a body."

Tuttle chuckled. "True." Replacing his spectacles, he stuck his chin at the box in Leighton's lap. "Show me what Nimms died for."

Leighton fingered the latch on the strongbox, felt the dent where he had struck Nimms's head. How the coins had spilled at Judith's feet, a cascade of lies!

He opened the box and set it on the desk before Tuttle.

Craning his neck over the papers piled on his desk, Tuttle reached into the box. "And you'd give this up to get a dead man back?"

"With all due respect, sir, it is on your desk."

Tuttle pulled one of the eagles up, turned it side-to-side. When lamplight flashed on the gold, Leighton saw the red sunset on Morkan's spectacles the night the Federal army left Springfield. All lost. All for naught. The war is won and there are no winners.

Tuttle tucked the eagle in his pocket, then removed his glasses and folded them against his chest. "You are a fool." He closed the strongbox, still full, then pushed it across the desk to Leighton. "I'll have orderlies bring him down to you."

Two hours passed as the three of them waited in the loading bay under the brick arch. Leighton trembled, kept a boot planted against the strongbox.

Finally the swinging doors on the dock opened. Two orderlies carried a stretcher between them and on it lay a gray slip. Not Morkan, not his father, but a pencil sketch of a man, his eyes feverish and bright.

At the bottom of the stairs, Morkan tumbled off the stretcher and tried to crawl back into the prison, scrabbling at the ground of the loading dock while Leighton held his waist. He didn't protest or grunt, only clawed at the dirt, his eyes bulging. He was so thin, Leighton felt the balls of his squirming hips rotating in the palms of his hands. The two of them struggling together brought even the garbage detail on the dock to a halt. Filthy soldiers and shackled prisoners paled. Morkan collapsed, gasping, coughing blood. With a sad face, Tuttle's adjutant saluted Correy and Leighton, then turned back up the stairs.

Correy and Leighton set him in the wagon, swathed him in army blankets, and pulled him through the streets of St. Louis.

Once they cleared town, Correy rode far behind the wagon, shaking. Cyrus moved his horse beside Leighton, and cleared his throat several times, but then said nothing, only stared at Leighton, then at the road.

"I want you to know, Lieutenant Browning, how much I appreciate your arranging this. Truly I want to thank you." He could say no more, and sensing this, Cyrus nodded. Cyrus slowed his horse, fell behind and said some words to Correy, then turned his horse back toward the road to Gratiot.

As he and Correy rode southwest, Leighton stopped the wagon often just for the reassurance of hearing Morkan's breath rise and fall like a whispered question. In his numb hands, the reins to the drafts felt like two warm knives.

At the house, Johnson and Judith met them on the front porch. Leighton, Correy, and Johnson took Morkan down from the wagon. They brought him into the house, laid him on the stone floor. Then Johnson and Leighton went to fetch a cot from the sleeping porch. Correy took the horses to the barn.

Judith brought warmed water, a towel. Together, the men lifted Morkan and set him on the sleeping cot. His forehead was damp and warm. For a long time Leighton touched Morkan's forehead and stroked his face, let his hand drop, then fell to stroking the face again. The rough of Leighton's fingers caught on Morkan's whiskers. Beneath the beard, his cheeks had the slack give of a bag of dry sand. Leighton bit his lower lip, turned to Correy who was standing on the front porch. "Get Cora," Leighton said. "She'll know how to nurse him."

Correy took Johnson's Half Dollar and rode for Cora.

Judith toweled Morkan's neck and mouth, chest and arms. Though her cheeks were wet, her eyes held his gaunt face in a look of genuine care.

Leighton swallowed, his eyes burning with tears. This was his father, and he looked to be a hundred years old. Here lay the life Heron held against him, claimed as dead and not dead. Leighton's own suffering at the quarry and all through the last three years buried the grief Morkan's death would bring. Johnson took the back of Judith's head and pressed her forehead to his chest, held her against him, her neck twitching next to the old Negro's blue suspender. The very strangeness of the sight calmed Leighton, made him realize the magnitude of what he could have lost. This moment, before the war, would have required rigid dignity. He knew he should not show his grief to the two Negroes. Offer it up. Instead he stood and embraced Johnson and Judith, bowed his head. For just a moment, he took his solace in that circle of family they three had been, a circle they would never have again. The war, he knew, would now overturn even the bonds it had forged. It had brought Morkan back.

Correy arrived holding Cora's hand. She wore a coatee and a pink dress with black ribbons and buttons as if Correy had surprised her on her way to Mass. Her cheeks seemed round and she had stoutened in the hips. Despite the chill air, she was sweating. Over her shoulder she bore a cowhide satchel dappled with blood traces and offal splashed at her while nursing. When she spied Morkan, she did not halt. Over her face and body came a leveling seriousness Leighton had seen soldiers assume in battle once they sighted the enemy. She cast aside the coatee, knelt, then stiffened her index and middle fingers. She thumped Morkan's chest, which was white and pitted, the bones in the center of his chest protruding like a pale spider.

She kneaded his neck, scowling. Then she parted his lips and swabbed her fingers inside his mouth. When she lifted her fingers, they were spotted with blood. She backed away and hung her head.

"Will he live?" Leighton asked.

She took a deep breath. "I tell you, Leighton, in this war I seen men with a head cold fall dead, and I seen skinny little boys with every limb lopped off, but in heart and mind they was living like fury—I don't know what for. Anyhow, well, you thump his chest and tell me."

Leighton stooped and stiffened his fingers. When the backs of his fingers struck Morkan's chest, there was a thickness behind the noise they made, as if beneath his ribs and sternum a layer of clay hardened. Leighton rested his palm flat on Morkan's chest and glanced up at Cora.

"It is consumption, Leighton."

Suddenly Morkan's chest rose and he caught a deep breath. "Damn it," he mumbled. Weakly but insistently, his hands pushed Leighton's palm from his chest.

Leighton let his hand drop. He grinned at Cora. "He'll live to whip our asses and lend us money."

Cora bit her chapped lip but smiled. "For now. Leighton, that ain't going away."

Cora relaxed inch by inch. She glanced around the house she hadn't seen since Charlotte's death, so long ago. When her eyes met Correy's Leighton saw the old brightness flicker across them, like a star on the surface of a pond. She reached a hand out to Judith, whose eyes widened.

"Would you like to learn a bit of nursing, love?"

Judith hesitated, glanced at Leighton, then nodded.

In the kitchen, Cora removed her satchel and opened it, drawing out a long canvas bag. "You must be Judith," she said. "Michael spoke of you and what a help you are."

Her voice brought to mind Mrs. Charlotte's voice so strongly, Judith cringed and her mouth went dry.

"Now, don't be frightened, love. There's nothing mysterious in what we're about to do." She untied the top of the canvas bag and poured out twelve brown lumps, like flower bulbs, some with veins of twisted black that ran between them joining the bulbs as if by cables. "Do you have an itty bitty knife? Pocket knife will do."

Judith found one while Cora washed one of the bulbs. "Judith, these are the corms of a swamp orchid, brown stems with white little bell flowers, the puttyroot." With the knife she bared an end of the root. "What do you grate horseradish with?"

Judith stared.

"Never mind. The knife will do. Watch now." She shaved the end in small sheets.

"Look like milk coming out."

"More like glue. I have seen Indians fix crockery with it." Sticky with paste, the cuttings she stacked then diced. "It will be tedious, but see how the fluid gums it together. That helps. You try."

Judith cut with care. She glanced up, still cutting, and Cora could see that she would do fine at this. "You the lady Mr. Michael used to see."

Cora blushed but nodded.

"And now you with another."

With small white fingers Cora held to the countertop, which was really a long butcher's board ending in a slops trough—a man had designed this kitchen. Poor Charlotte. Poor Judith. From memory so long ago she saw Michael tying his brown Walker in Elijah's yard, and pushing his hat low to his head, crossing to her doorstep.

The Negress arranged the puttyroot in a tight square on the countertop with two quick flicks of the blade. She set the knife aside.

"What you gone do if he wakes up and still loves you?"

At this Cora snapped from a reverie to stare Judith in the eyes. Mr. Michael's gal had a face made for mirth, but when it was hardened it was no sight to see.

"Why do you deal me pain?" Cora asked slowly and quietly, so that Judith knew she was in control of herself when she very well might choose not to be. "Why hurt me when I am standing here teaching you?"

Judith returned her challenge with such a placid face, Cora felt effrontery, for the Negress clearly meant to be woman of this house. "When you crossed the threshold," Judith whispered, "I feel in myself there walks pain into my house. Even when she

295

bearing light and penance, there steps pain through my front door."

Cora breathed deeply through just her nose, and Judith could feel the woman wrestling with her angel inside.

Judith spoke very softly, and dared to put her hand on Cora's to settle the nurse and pin whatever devil she brought. "I love that Leighton in a way you won't never understand. Now hear me through. Leighton, he love that dying man. A thorn in Old Marse Morkan's side mean a knife in My Leighton's heart."

Reeling a moment ago, Cora felt herself bobbing to right. Through the Negress's touch—this was the longest any black had held her skin—she felt a current of power and care and tenderness. Breathing deeply again, she said, "Please get us a tea strainer."

Judith fetched a tiny iron-mesh ball on a chain. With the knife she scraped the oozing root into the ball.

"Mix it with sassafras if you have it. It will not taste good. No sugar, though," Cora said. She touched the back of her hand to her lips wet with sweat.

Judith bobbed the ball in hot water. "I appreciate your teaching me," she said. "You understand why I say what I say?"

Cora regarded her with a flicker of a smile. "You know, Judith, I came close to being the woman of this house, God rest Mrs. Charlotte. I understand you perfectly."

"I be obliged, then, if you teach me all I need to know. And you best to know thereafter, you will feel the dust of this circle protecting me and mine."

Afternoons flies buzzed at Morkan's face, and Leighton stirred them with a wide fan Judith used to shoo flies from summer dinners. When Morkan struggled up from the cot, he hacked gray and crimson clots. Leighton held Morkan's arm, which was thin as a rod in a sheath of leather. In the close humidity of the privy, Morkan clutched at his chest, and Leighton supported him, lowered him to the privy seat. Morkan became less a being and more an article, a scarecrow Leighton dragged from privy to bed.

Leighton hunted squirrel and hare each morning and boiled the meat, serving Morkan a broth dotted with flecks of the catch. He even shot and boiled a jay once, and his father ate the bitter meat with the same glassy eyes, not speaking or knowing his son.

Judith watched Morkan while Leighton hunted, and often sat with Leighton on the porch when he returned. Despite Morkan's state, they did not speak above a whisper in his presence, and then mostly of his illness. His predicament drew them together in a bond of worry. "We sound like two old grandparents," he whispered.

Judith glanced at him, then back at their charge. Her smile was as disturbing as it was lovely.

Evenings, Morkan ranted, and then Leighton bent to each word. Often Morkan clutched at his son's shirt.

"Can't get pilings down." His eyes rolled and his forehead beaded with sweat. "Stinkstone. Pounding like fury."

Every sentence Morkan spoke wavered with intensity and desperation. He called rolls pausing after each name for the answer, his mouth twisting, eyes squinting in confusion when no one replied. Often he whispered lists of machine companies and suppliers and what was owed them—"$4, Scranton $17, $2.50, $943, Jennings, Independent $110, Berkmeier"—prices, wages, material in no predictable order. But Leighton weighed on these words, nodded and answered the glassy-eyed man as if a conversation existed, as if the cracked lips were divulging vital knowledge. There was a second narrative, too, something that had nothing to do with the quarry, a babble of rats and mud, of Horatio, the Holy Roman Empire, and Tuttle. One evening Morkan bolted upright in bed, shouting hang me, hang me. Even after Leighton calmed him, stroking his forehead, Morkan's coughing was profuse.

There were no musters. Some evenings Correy came late and spent the night. He often brought liquor, sometimes brought honey and flat cakes. He was still a stable hand for the Federals, but now attached himself to a blacksmith as an apprentice. Some nights his face was full of soot, and his clothes stunk of the foundry. They talked often of Greevins and how much they missed him or of Heron and how much Leighton dreaded him. They never once spoke Cora's name. After Correy fell asleep, Leighton watched the Federal campfires, which grew in number until they were unreadable, no shape at all.

On a morning late in September, Morkan mumbled about vagrants and overhead conveyance systems. His chatter grew far less intense, more like any sleeper's mutter, and his color returned. He no longer woke sopping with sweat, and he had regained a little weight. Leighton listened to him, but could not make sense of his dream ramblings, so he stood on the porch and watched for Correy. When Morkan spoke Leighton's name, the word melded in one of the frantic roll calls. His father coughed and called his son again. Leighton turned, and Morkan was sitting up on the cot, thin arms folded over his chest. Leighton bent to him, and his father's eyes gleamed.

Morkan stroked his son's hair, his head bouncing slightly as he laughed. Tears shone on his cheeks. Leighton fetched him some water. He drank heartily.

He looked around, dabbed his lips with the blanket. "A wagon?" he asked.

Leighton nodded, his voice catching. "We brought you. Correy and me."

Morkan blinked at him. "A man now." He coughed twice, cleared his throat. He closed his eyes for a minute. Leighton gave him a kerchief and he cleaned himself up. "Why the hat? Thought you were a prison guard." His breath after each sentence popped and caught like a stuck valve.

Leighton took the Home Guard field cap off his head. "It's the Federal Greene County Home Guards. They're like Enrolled Militia. We just don't have to do as much."

Morkan's eyes were wide, and he appeared shocked.

"Had to," Leighton said.

Morkan's face fell. After a moment he said, "I understand." The grooves in his cheeks darkened. His chin jutted in a frown of such deep remorse, Leighton was stunned.

"I got your letter."

Morkan looked up at him. "Prayed I would never be brought home to you."

Leighton shook his head. "There's no undoing it. Welcome home."

Morkan raised his shaking fingertips to cover his eyes. After some time, he looked up at Leighton again. "Years they took. From me and you." He held out his hand and Leighton clasped it.

They were quiet for a time, and Leighton pulled one of the high-backed chairs next to the cot. Outside evening was coming on, but the air remained warm. Each shallow, liquid breath Morkan took was the warble of a bird to Leighton. He told Morkan of the Texans, Bert's death and the stolen stock. He told him nothing of the feast of deer, or of the jewels lost. Leighton shut the front door and got Morkan an extra blanket and another pitcher of water. He told him of the Home Guards, and Greer's death, but when he came to the conclusion of the story, to Kreft's slaying, he stopped short of telling his father, realizing that according to the story the town had, Kreft was a hero due his adulation. That story, for Leighton's sake, for Morkan's sake, had to remain a fact.

"There were eight or so of them killed. They'd been making bullets." He drank his sassafras. "We lost Greer and that Lieutenant got hit by a stray bullet and he died."

Morkan stared at him a long time, his eyes narrowing, and it was obvious to Leighton that his father knew there was something more.

After a bit, Morkan said, "Deserved it."

Leighton shrugged, relieved there was nothing more to say.

"And Heron came, Da. He took over the quarry for two seasons and made me help him at the stone."

Morkan sat up very straight, his eyes burning. "We still have the quarry? They didn't take it because of me?" He cleared his throat, trembling. "Heron don't have it?"

Kneeling to him Leighton touched his arm, felt the spongy give of his father's wasted skin on the bare palm where his callus had not grown back. "It's ours still."

Morkan nodded, but his yellow skin flushed. "The bastard." He dabbed his lips with the blanket.

Leighton waited for his father to cool down. "In prison, was there anyone who interrogated you who you told about the money in the well?"

Morkan bowed his head. He was so thin in the face, the nub of his chin protruded like a scabby saddle horn. Finally Morkan nodded.

"Did he have thick eyebrows, hazel eyes?"

Judith entered the room carrying a fresh chamberpot.

"Nimms," Morkan said. "Yes. Was he here? They sent him. I have no idea where he's gone."

"He came here," Leighton said. "He called himself Browning."

He sat up and gripped Leighton's hand.

Judith set the chamber pot next to Morkan's cot.

"He's dead," Leighton said.

She glanced at Leighton.

"Someone in town shot him for a thief," Leighton said.

Judith relaxed and touched Leighton's arms with just the tips of her fingers.

Morkan smiled. "Well, my God." He shivered, put his hands under the covers and closed his eyes. "What about Widow Slade?" he asked.

"Rest yourself, Da."

His eyes popped open. "What about Cora?"

Leighton hung his head, and took a deep breath. "In the time you been gone, we didn't have any news on what had happened, you see. Only the one letter."

Morkan sat up slowly, inching his way along, gripping the sides of the cot.

"She and Elijah Correy have grown mighty close."

Morkan's stare was for a moment the bleary-eyed remnant of his former stupor, and Leighton clutched his shin, fell to his knees, wrapped his arms around Morkan's legs as if to hold him together.

Morkan blinked at him, then reached in his ragged shirt, into the pocket. A sad, puzzled look came over his face.

"Judith, fetch Da's truck, will you?" Leighton said.

With a scowl Judith returned holding Morkan's belongings, all he carried when he was released from Gratiot. Morkan placed the tiny bundle in his lap. From it he fished a soiled tintype, stared at it, then handed it to Leighton.

Cora, done up like a queen of France, a silly painting of a palace behind her. At the corners, the metal was green and black and bore Morkan's fingerprints as if ancient tabs of leather framed the little portrait. Half the tintype was shorn away— some companion had been severed from poor Cora irretrievably. "It bore me through," he whispered.

Once he was sleeping, Judith straightened the blanket at Morkan's neck. "Listen at him breathe."

Leighton nodded. "It sounds awful. It sounds beautiful."

Judith whispered, "I sure think it's good you don't tell him about Browning."

The following afternoon, Correy arrived and was overjoyed, then suddenly apprehensive to see Morkan sitting up and making sense. They chatted awhile.

Then Morkan said, "Elijah Correy, you have done much for me."

Correy bowed his head and held his temples in his fingertips.

"I have one more thing to ask of you."

"Ask it." Correy's voice broke with emotion.

Leighton turned away.

"I ask that you let me see Cora Slade one last time if I make it to my feet."

The house was so silent and still, a shift of wind sent a crackle through the air.

Correy nodded. "Yes. Of course. You must settle that between the two of you."

Morkan frowned at him, and his face was the face of the old quarrymaster. "That is right, settle. What she chooses." A line had been crossed, now a price exacted, a penance paid. "You grant me that, our part is settled between you and me."

Correy folded his hands before his waist, clutching his Federal cap like a mourner at a grave. He nodded.

They all three talked until late, and Morkan took his first sip of port in three years. It made his head spin, but sang as sweet as any freedom he had imagined.

VI

MORKAN'S REVIVAL WAS SLOW, BUT BY MID-OCTOBER
he shuffled on his own. Though his cough subsided, any amount
of laughter or a talk by the fire caused him to wheeze and spit.
A changed man, he could spend a whole hour watching trees
in the wind or red paper wasps sucking water from the husk of
their nest and spitting the water down in iron beads. He was
quiet, idle. When his health improved, he could not sleep in
the cot, and Leighton often caught him sleeping on the floor of
the mud room, where the kitchen stove kept things warm, and
the clay and moss made the floor soft. When Judith offered to
leave him sheets and pillows there, Morkan snapped at her, then
flushed with embarrassment. After that, she left a blanket and
an old feather pillow on one of the benches each night. Mornings Leighton found him leaning on the sill of the front window
downstairs, holding his hands outside the window.

Often in the early evenings, Morkan, Leighton, and Judith sat outside on the porch as Indian summers warmed the
air. Leighton smoked cigars. Watching his father bask in the
light of the setting sun, watching Judith rest against the door
frame, fanning her glistening neck, he was filled with comfort,
and a sense that they had survived all the terrors that war could
visit on them. Enough leaves were down that Rockbridge road
made a muddy red ribbon through the trees. Everything seemed
promising, like a new day was ready to begin the instant the war
was over.

The war dragged on elsewhere, but it was done with Springfield. After careening through the Ozarks with 12,000 cavalry late in October, Price was clobbered near Kansas City. The
dreamer and general faded into Indian territory and at last left
for Mexico. The Home Guards never mustered again. With the

provosts in charge, the city afforded such an air of stability, a man named Justinian Ziggler, who'd been a telegraph operator with Shane Peale, set up a little paper called the *Daily Leader*. It was on this front page in the spring of 1865 that Leighton read to Morkan of Lee's surrender, of the new all-Republican legislature meeting in St. Louis, and a new Constitution for the state. And on the 16th of April he read to Morkan that an actor managed to shoot Lincoln in a theater in Washington.

Morkan let out a slow, tight breath. "Lord."

Leighton was unsure whether Morkan was expressing surprise or relief. "That's a lot of hate."

"I knew men in prison would have lined up to shoot that bullet."

Eventually Morkan grinned, clapped his hands together once. "Well, we ought to open the quarry. There's no use moping about Dixie or even Abe dying."

"Opening the quarry may take some doing," Leighton said, but he too was smiling.

They rode into town, both of them on old Federal horses Johnson saved from ruination. When they reached the outskirts, they could hear the sound of hammers and saws. Several young boys were tearing down the burned facade of Parham's Saloon, and next to the scorched foundation was a stack of new lumber. Both the Morkans stopped and smiled at this. Despite the surrenders, Leighton wore the blue coat and cap of the Federal Home Guards. Looking around, Morkan saw dozens of others in the same garb. Morkan wore a black mackinaw and a slouch hat. He kept a thick, red beard, which hid the thinness of his cheeks. He looked like a foreman, maybe even a laborer in a stolen coat, rather than the quarry master.

Leighton rode up to Billy Breen, a carpenter he recognized who appeared to be the crew chief at Parham's. Breen, too, kept on the blue coat, the Federal hat.

"Billy," Leighton said.

Billy grinned, dropped the nails he was holding between his lips into his hands. "Morkan," he said to Leighton.

"Give us a week and we'll have whitewash," Leighton said to him, leaning down from the horse to shake his hand.

Billy laughed. "Aw, it'll be thin as ever, I'm sure."

"Maybe," Leighton said. "But where else you going to get it?"

As the two chatted about the new saloon scheduled to go in at Parham's, Morkan shifted his legs in the saddle. He was disgusted that after only a few minutes of riding, his groin and thighs ached fiercely. Watching Leighton talk with another veteran, he soon forgot the pain. A delight overcame him. His son wore the Federal blue, as did the carpenter, the laborers sweating at the framing. Like the streets outside Gratiot, Springfield crawled with blue, and Leighton was a passport.

Leighton rejoined him. "Breen'll spread the word. Looks like we got a whole town to rebuild." He sat high in the saddle, his chin set confidently. The wool of his coat shone like the throat of a grackle. "They need mortar and gravel and cement."

"Good thing you wore that coat."

When Leighton squeezed his arm, Morkan was struck by the power in his son.

Even through the gates, the quarry appeared dismal. Green clumps of scrub cedar dotted the jagged cliffs. Morkan gaped at Heron's pile of stones for rifle pits gleaming above the cliffs.

"Look at the stone that son-of-a-bitch would have thieved," Morkan said.

Leighton dismounted and was sawing through the gray rope that bound the gate. "It's still on our land," Leighton said, flexing and shaking his wrist to relieve it. "If we cut and sell it as flagstones or little tombstones, we'll make a killing seeing as it's already free of the cliff. What do you say to that?"

"I'd say I know my son talking when I hear him," Morkan said. He was glad Leighton remained intent on the rope. He felt foolish touching his eyes with his cuffs.

The rope parted and drooped. Leighton swung the wrought iron gate wide. Chickweed spread its green wire all across the lot. Morkan eased his horse through the gates, then wadded his slouch hat against his thigh.

Leighton felt a sense of triumph and elation when Morkan finally passed through the gate. Their war—the Morkan's war—might finally be won. Not by an army or a rebellion, but by the Morkans enduring like stone. As the gaunt form of his father crossed under the stone archway on the roan's rickety back, Leighton drew his hat from his head and crushed it against his chest.

The lot was rife with chert and messy piles of overburden. The cliffs were green and brown with moss. Gone was the stock barn save for its stone foundation.

Morkan whistled.

"Some serious sweat to make here before we pound any lime out of this," Leighton said.

Morkan dabbed his lips with the collar of the mackinaw. For the first time in four years he felt like he was his own man again—not a pawn of Tuttle's, nor a ward to his son, but Michael Morkan, the quarry owner. "If I was a Saxon hayseed Rebel, I'd whoop at the top of my lungs right now."

Leighton stared at him. "Let's not do that. I've heard plenty of it."

Morkan grinned. Leighton tied the horses. His father dismounted with a stiffness that made him seem ancient. The office listed, walls slumping beneath its tin roof. Inside was a shambles, but Leighton brought a clipboard and paper from home. He toured Morkan around the quarry, pointed out tools that needed purchasing, structures that needed rebuilding.

By evening they took their schedule of priorities and needs to The Quarry Rand. When they entered and Morkan removed his slouch hat, Shulty's jaw dropped. He came around the corner of the bar, his face wrinkled in a huge grin, his eyes watering. Several of the soldiers and patrons at the bar watched him, whispered questions to one another, then their eyes widened once a local told them who Morkan was.

Shulty slapped Morkan's back. "The ghosts are walking now that all this fric-a-frac is over. It is sure good to see you, old man." He seated the two of them down to a table in the corner. "My God! Danny! Get us three porters."

Danny Montbonne Beauchamp came to the table with three glasses full of porter so dark it appeared black. She was taller, but her arms still looked taut as a young boy's. Her dress was exceptionally frilly and yellow.

The men drank. To Morkan, the porter tasted as hearty as a slice of hot bread, so thick and perfect.

Shulty patted Morkan's arm, and frowned, his voice falling to a whisper. "Have you seen that new Constitution?"

Morkan shook his head.

"Well, I think you better be concerned with it. It took me quite a hearing and a chunk of change to a damned Republican barrister to convince the loyalty committee that accepting Rebel currency wasn't any treason." His voice fell to a whisper. "It's something you need to be concerned about over there." He nodded toward the quarry.

"No, sir," Morkan said. "I've done my time. I've crawled in shackles and mucked in dung. They can ask no more of Michael Morkan."

Shulty cocked his head. "The hell they can't, Michael. This legislature's a mean pack of them, I'm telling you."

They drank in silence for a moment.

"Now, I have been getting a lot of questions from laborers about whether you all will open that quarry," Shulty said. "I seen you in there today. Give me the skinny."

Before Morkan could speak, Leighton answered the bar-keep. "We'll need clean up hands real soon, tomorrow even, so drop the word."

Morkan raised his eyebrows at Leighton. Leighton blushed.

"Only tell the best of them, Shulty," Morkan said. "It appears to me there's a lot of loose wheels around town."

"Yeah, there are," Shulty said. "You remember old Hurley Crane? Well, Wednesday last some bastard popped him with a shotgun, took his horse, and left Hurley for the maggots. And him still in the Federal army. There ain't any law and order, save for Shane Peale, and that boy's too busy telegraphing yet for," his voice dropped to a whisper, "for Billy Yank and these goddamn Republicans."

Morkan and Leighton grunted, both sensing the conversation might touch off opinions they would rather keep to themselves.

When they finished their porters, they ordered a dinner of beans and rye bread. They ran down the list, and Leighton informed Morkan of the current costs of materials and where things might be bartered for. With it being spring they could corral the stock. No need to build a barn. Most important was to get the mill and the kilns going, get lime crushed and burned as soon as possible and so get cash flowing in. All the while as Morkan laid out these plans, Leighton took notes, the steel pen digging deep into the paper. For a moment, Morkan remembered Nimms writing in the Morocco book. His breath caught, and he stared, glassy-eyed for awhile. Waiting for Morkan to resume, Leighton tapped the pen on the tabletop.

As they rode home, Morkan sat high in the saddle, a strange smile on his face. "Leighton, listen. Back there with Shulty? When he started about Peale and the Republicans, you didn't say a thing. Why?"

Leighton's slanted eyes widened and blinked, the eyes of Charlotte, and he looked like her now, just before she fell ill—thin, ruddy in the face, the jet black hair limp. The war had ravaged his son, Morkan saw, sure as disease.

"Well, it's something I've followed while you been gone. At least Correy says so. I listened at Shulty saying that, and I thought, my pa wouldn't give any opinion about this, even to Shulty, even if Shulty spoke poorly of a friend. I might tell the friend. But no need for a barkeep to know how I feel on it. He's liable to tell just about every drinker he can."

Morkan nodded. They loped along in the twilight, which was pink and red as the meat of a melon. "You've had all this a long time on your own. Do you think you can work again with me? Can you stand me being in charge once in a while?"

Leighton gave his horse's ear a long steady pull. The beast pealed back and wiggled its black lips, leering at Morkan and rolling its eyes.

The next day, a rider, Shane Peale, and a fat little man in a dark suit waited at the gate to the quarry. Peale was a guard for the provost's office and the fat man probably worked there as well, Leighton guessed. The two rose and beat dust off their britches. The rider pushed his hat back, and there on Morkan's old chestnut Walker sat Heron.

The fat man cleared his throat and Peale shouldered his rifle. Leighton squeezed the leather satchel at his side, felt the lumps of coins brought from the currency he and his father managed to rescue, that Judith saved. A bribe might soon be in order. But Heron loomed there. Leighton reached in his coat pocket and drew out two cigars, offered one to Peale who took it. He extended the other to the fat man, who was engrossed in unfolding a document. After a moment the fat man frowned at him, so Leighton lit the remaining cigar for himself. Heron crossed his arms over his chest.

The fat man rattled the parchment before Morkan. "Michael Morkan, by commission of Governor Fletcher and the Loyalty Committee provided in the Constitution of 1865, I hereby command you to take the Ironclad Oath of Loyalty and sign it here in the presence of these witnesses."

Morkan blinked at him. "Why?"

The fat man licked his lips. He had enormous eyes, and his face was clean-shaven and pale as a mole's. "For traitorous acts, including the wanton giving of aid and support to persons engaged in hostilities against the government of the United States of America."

Morkan looked at Heron, then blinked at Leighton who shrugged and nodded. Morkan raised his right hand.

"Repeat after me."

The oath was long and tangled with therefores and heretofores and forced Morkan to claim that he was familiar with all elements of the new Constitution. Morkan repeated everything, his Irish accent and the fat man's drawl droning in the April sun. Leighton watched a flight of doves bolt from the quarry cliffs. Even over his cigar he could smell the lime. The chestnut Walker wagged its head nodding at Morkan's familiar voice.

Morkan finished the oath, cleared his throat firmly. The fat man offered a pen, and Morkan signed holding the parchment against his knee. Leighton and Shane Peale signed in turn as witnesses. Then the fat man handed the document to Heron.

Heron folded the paper closed. On his head he wore the same field cap as Leighton's, save that a gold band set his off. His uniform was black and crisp. He rolled his hand at the fat man, urging him forward.

The fat man turned and drew a new document from his vest. "So, Michael Morkan." He rattled the document. "By Articles 26 through 34 of the Constitution be it known that as a traitor you will be allowed neither to conduct any business transactions in currency, notes, barter, or kind, nor to hire workers for transactions or constructions or excavations; neither to submit options for contract, lease, or sale of goods and property, nor to supervise work in any way on the property at the confluence of Summit and State Streets, said property consisting of one office, one stock barn, one smithy, one derrick, steam engines, two kilns, one mill, and all other implements useful in the work of quarrying, grinding, burning, and blocking limestone."

The fat man took a breath. His eyes scanned the document again, his lips mouthing the words.

Morkan wavered a second in the saddle. To come this far to freedom, to regaining what he had, and now Heron could keep him from his living. "What was the oath for, then?" he asked.

The fat man scowled. "Being a traitor."

"So despite taking it, I can't do my work."

Heron stepped the Walker forward. "You want I should read it to you?"

Leighton took the cigar from his mouth. "What's that say about keeping books?"

"The pup doesn't speak for this concern, does he, Michael Morkan?

"Any word he gives you comes from my mouth. Sure as any word I give comes from his." Morkan said this with cold resolve, disease never cracking his voice.

Leighton regarded his father a moment—ragged mackinaw, long, thin hands easy on his hip where a gun might be. Beneath the wide-brimmed, black slouch, his winnowed face reminded Leighton of the horsemen who rampaged from the winter woods to storm the forts of Springfield. As never before Leighton felt himself beside a comrade in arms.

Wagging a finger, the fat man read the parchment again. "That would be committing transactions to paper."

Leighton extended his hand, and the fat man released the document. "No," Leighton said. He pointed at the parchment. "I make the transactions. He records them."

Heron looped the reins to the Walker and pulled it close to Leighton. "Where did you come by the uniform of a Federal home guard? Did you kill some poor citizen and thieve it?"

Watching Heron's hands and chest, Leighton reached slowly inside his coat. Heron popped a hand on his hip and brushed his coat aside to show the butt of a pistol.

Leighton grinned—for the first time he saw fear in Heron. "Troubles?" he asked. When Heron tensed a notch, Leighton said, "Got service papers to show you, Colonel."

Out of his coat pocket, Leighton pulled his service letter from General Eggbert B. Brown, the letter that helped free his father. He opened it, held it to Heron.

Taking it, Heron stroked his beard and read. "Battle of Springfield," he murmured. "Quinine Brigade. Served with Avery Kreft."

Heron sat back, his eyes widening. Heron's face grew placid and lost all its smugness. "After working here, you joined the Federal Army," he spoke slowly, "were wounded, and fought in the most remarkable crack brigade west of the Mississippi?" He paused and stared at Leighton.

"My father went to prison. I went to war. Even after the likes of you. Straighten your fellows out here. And let us into our quarry."

Hearing Leighton, Morkan felt pride's arrow push from his heart to his forehead.

"I suppose your service does make you something other than a traitor," Heron said. "But you have another problem. For the time being you have only one real customer—the provost's office. And I am its sole purchasing officer."

"Have you built you a railroad from Rolla?" Leighton asked. "Have you cut you a canal to White River?"

Heron scowled.

Leighton extended his hand, and Heron returned the service letter. "Begging your pardon then, Colonel, but you have no other quarry."

Heron backed the chestnut off and sat up straight in the saddle. "Well, pup, it may be a long time before we see any significant building, or before we resume on that courthouse after all." Nudging his horse, Heron pulled right up alongside Morkan. "And for you, I suggest you follow the ban that officer read. For I'll be here, or someone like me here every morning there is daylight. Peale, you make sure this traitor does no working. We'll see what Colonel Phelps advises about traitors keeping accompts."

When he turned to follow Heron, the fat man was beaming, the top of his head glistening like a warm sausage.

"I'm real sorry, Leighton, but I'm supposed to stay here," Peale said.

Leighton pulled the cigar from his mouth, snapped its coal off with a flick of a finger. "Do what you have to, friend."

"Mr. Morkan, will you do only the books for now?"

A group of men was gathering and pointing at him and Leighton and Peale. Dozens of men came, men in grimy coats and battered hats.

"Mmm, aye. Only the books," Morkan said.

In the quarry yard Morkan dismounted and stood close by Leighton. "Reckon Heron will be at that all day, keeping good men from rightful work?"

Leighton nodded. He saw a terrible threat to the quarry in Heron's words and in the shadow his father cast now. Crushed underfoot, the chickweed smelled heady as a strong spice. The face of the cliffs was rough and irregular, showing that it was mined without regard to quality of stone or natural seam.

Leighton opened the office door, crossed the floor and propped the slat windows wide to the morning sun. A brown dust hung in the air of the office. The floor was covered with a black filth, tin cups, strips of clothing. Leighton could have the floor scoured. It might have to become his office. The stove was ripped from the wall. The pipe dangled, and he could hear a starling spitting and burbling at its top.

"They can't be here daily," Morkan said.

Leighton turned to him. "I've been with these people. They have noses and ears everywhere." He leaned back against the desk and crossed his arms. "If Michael Morkan fails to hire a man, that man will turn right around and tell every Federal the traitor Morkan's running the quarry." Leighton rolled the cigar between his fingers, head bowed. His heart was thumping. This was his father he was lecturing, the man who built this place. "If it's not the men you don't hire, it'll be Heron or the Loyalty Committee checking on you. You'll be shut down for good. Won't matter if I say I'm running this."

Morkan was craning his neck, looking back toward the gates.

"What are we going to do?" Leighton asked. "What if he is in charge at the provosts and doesn't buy anything? Da?"

"How much you reckon those fellows with nothing to do will hire for?"

Leighton shrugged.

"Ugly as it may seem, your accountant recommends you hire them at next to nothing, less than a waterboy before the war. And pay them twice a month, not daily."

"Jesus," Leighton said. "That'll be as bad as the Federals did to me working me here and moving that stone and not paying a shinplaster for it."

"And they did that, didn't they?" Morkan said. "So there'll be no problem. It's what they expect." He saw Leighton's face darken. "Listen, Leighton, I didn't come through this to lose your quarry to the likes of that man."

Standing from the desk, Leighton's face flattened. With his one eye lazy, with the slant of the two of them, he looked as if he had been brained with a shovel. "My quarry?"

Morkan cleared his throat. "Let's not kid ourselves, Leighton. Consumption doesn't go away. I'll be a dead man in a year, maybe more, but still. Whose quarry do you think this has been all along?"

"Ours."

Morkan was quiet awhile. "All you been through and all you seen, and still you have a streak of good in your heart? I admire you. But I can't take this with me."

The men were kicking stones in the lot now, spitting tobacco, swearing, waiting with their hands in their pockets. Peale checked their service papers one-by-one.

"What if they find better wages?" Leighton said very quietly.

"Raise them when it comes."

"It sounds awful."

"Temporary," Morkan said.

"What will you do if they say you can't run the books?"

"I expect that's what they will say." Morkan bobbed his eyebrows. "And then I'll be free to campaign widely and publicly for civic improvements."

When Leighton made his offer two of them walked back up the trail to the gate.

"That ain't a living wage," said a man who stayed.

Leighton put his hands on his hips, the tip of the cigar pointed airward. "I ain't asking you to live. I got work is all. And that's more than you got, fellow."

The men frowned and glanced at each other.

"And I'm not paying today. You come back every day for two weeks and I pay after second Saturday's work."

"Shit," one said. He crammed his hat back on and turned to the gate. The others grumbled. Then, to Morkan's relief, they followed Leighton to the tool shed on the cliffs and set to work with shovels, wheelbarrows, and bare hands. By noon, the man who cursed and left returned looking red faced. He brought with him five others.

The next morning, Heron and three mounted Ohio troops waited at the quarry gate. Almost forty laborers waited behind them kicking at the gravel and jawing. The Morkans arrived in the stone wagon Leighton had driven to St. Louis. In its bed were two casks of powder and a whole regimen of carpentry tools. Behind the wagon waited their Federal horses, a roan, another draft horse and a bony pair of oxen.

Morkan climbed down from the wagon.

"Michael Morkan," Heron said. The men at the gate grew still. "The Loyalty Committee has determined that accompts are business transactions, and you are thus precluded from the conduct of such by Articles 27 and 29 of the Constitution of the State of Missouri."

Morkan's face and neck reddened. At the gate the men squinted at him and glanced at one another. A few smiled.

Heron shifted in the saddle and stroked the neck of Morkan's Walker. "I would very much like to hear that oath of loyalty once more."

With Heron reciting, Morkan began. His accent made the word *heretofore* shudder, and the men at the gate cupped their hands at their ears, whistled and jeered. But Morkan never slumped. His eyes glowered at Heron until the troopers silenced the men. When Morkan finished, he unclenched the fist he hid in the pocket of his mackinaw.

"Pup, I wish you the best of luck running your new quarry," Heron said. He and the troopers headed to the shade on the other side of the street.

Leighton sat slumped on the seat, the reins loose in his hands.

Morkan put his back between Heron and the troopers watching. "Sit up proud, Leighton," Morkan said. "Don't look me in the eye."

Leighton sat straight and still.

"You know how to run this," Morkan said. "Get the house in order."

Leighton snapped the reins and took the wagon through the gates.

Trailed by at least one trooper, Morkan rode the town for several hours and recruited men and stock saying only that a young man at the quarry was buying and hiring. As the day wore on he wavered. Looking a horse in the mouth, talking with a soot-faced blacksmith's helper, he imagined he was aiding his son and their cause, and this heartened him. But stumbling into an alley to cough and spit, he saw his assigned trooper lean against a rain barrel to watch him, and he felt like an outlaw, a derelict. Still, he reminded himself, in the pockets of his trousers there might be nothing save grit, but Leighton, his son, walked the cliffs of the quarry.

At the end of the day, he waited outside the courthouse and caught Colonel Phelps leaving. The trooper stepped forward.

Phelps waved him off.

"Michael Morkan?" Phelps asked. He was as tall as Morkan and unbent by the war, his beard pepper-gray and as well kept as a baronet's hedge. With his long face and blue eyes, he made Morkan think of well-intentioned ministers, the old fellows who poked around the Irish quarters in St. Louis, striving to convert ratty Catholics.

"Colonel Phelps, sir, it is good to see you." He shook Phelps hand.

"I don't reckon it is entirely," Phelps said with a pained smile.

"Ah," Morkan said, raising a finger, "I don't come bitter about the new constitution. I come as a citizen to make sure that a spirit of civic improvement is encouraged at the highest levels. And that would be you, Colonel."

"It was always John before," Phelps said. He motioned for Morkan to follow him to the livery. "But then, things have changed."

They were out of earshot from courthouse followers. The trooper lagged as well.

"John, we need to see that courthouse finished, don't you think?"

Phelps halted at a stall and a dark bay circled to the door, sputtering. Phelps watched Morkan with a stony face and blank eyes.

Morkan patted the thick neck of the horse. "My son served in the Quinine Brigade. It's my son runs that quarry."

Phelps bowed his head. "This is not a world of my making. It is not up to me."

"You mean to tell me Marcus Larue Heron from Brittle Band, New Hampshire, is entirely in charge of Greene County, Missouri's rebuilding?"

Phelps nodded. "I am sorry." He paused. "I dislike someone not from this community. . . . Well, we all must put up with some 'outsiders' for awhile, Michael. I remind you, you played no small part in why we must."

With the help of a hostler, Phelps readied his tack. "And Michael." He stopped and cinched the girth. "I wouldn't bandy Leighton's service. To praise him invites scrutiny. And I have already bested Heron on Leighton's age of majority. You are all in jeopardy."

Phelps mounted, ducked the livery doors, and rode stately into town.

Late that night, Leighton arrived home. Morkan met him in the mudroom. Leighton's face glowed, and lime remained at the roots of his hair and beard. In the candlelight he appeared blue.

Morkan set a toddy down beside him carefully as one might set a charge in a hole. "How's it fare?"

Leighton plunked his brogans beneath the opposite bench. The tongue of one crumpled as it fell. The other remained taut and stiff with gray and black clusters of stone.

"Fares hard." Leighton sipped the toddy. He leaned his head back against the cedar paneling and closed his eyes, cradled the toddy in his lap. "The men don't like it any at that pay. We got the mill going. I don't even need oxen. I got workers enough to trod the thing in a circle."

Morkan frowned, so sickened he had to wait before he spoke again. "Leighton, you understand we got to generate cash."

Leighton's jaw stiffened. "Bet we pay a price doing it."

"We won't get any help from Phelps," Morkan said. "Heron is in charge and without him, well, there's the lifeblood. I never could make that place work on little contracts alone. I needed that flow of county money."

Rubbing his face, Leighton gave the mudroom the glassy-eyed look Morkan saw on him whenever the war haunted him.

"Leighton, when I talked with Phelps he said something that disturbed me. He asked that I not praise your service record overmuch to keep off Heron's scrutiny. Why would he say a thing like that? You've told me what all you did and it all sounded fine."

Leighton was quiet for a long time. "Heron doesn't need to know that Nimms came here."

317

When Morkan lowered himself to the bench, he gripped Leighton on his way down. "Phelps knows?"

Leighton shrugged. "Tuttle did, though."

"Nimms wasn't shot in town was he?"

In the kitchen Judith clattered a pan against the griddle.

"Missy, we live here," Morkan called. Though his tone was jocular, his eyes were on Leighton, level and serious.

Leighton fretted at his palm where the callus was gone. "Died by my hand. Here."

With his collar at his lips, Morkan waited.

Leighton's voice was a whisper, "And Kreft died at my hand as well. Those men with us, Looney's men banded together. We have held our word since, so far as I know."

"Well, even so, it was an accident?"

The eyes Leighton turned on his father were as lightless and cold as the pool at the base of the cliffs.

VII

EVENINGS THEY FOUND MACHINE PARTS, FEATHERING drills, engraver's tools and all manner of truck that the two of them had spirited home. Often there was such a haul they took a stone wagon. They rode together, separated when they met the guards at the gates.

One morning they rounded a corner on Weitzer's land and were met by a short, grungy gunman with two pistols drawn. From his mouth dangled the long stem and red starbust of a fire pink. No mask. Along his cheek a scalloped powder burn shone.

"Raise them hands, now."

Morkan raised them and glanced at his son.

"Raise that gun up there, Reb," Leighton said.

"You just go to hell, now," the gunman said. The fire pink dropped from his mouth. "I'll shoot every part of you." In his fuming he did raise the gun at Leighton.

Seeing the lead noses of bullets, Leighton slowly raised his hands.

"That's the ticket." He poked his gun at Morkan. "You, scarecrow. Put them feet on the ground."

Morkan dismounted.

"And, real slow, hand me what's in that satchel swinging on your belt."

Bulging at Morkan's waist was a leather pouch with a set of washers to the steam derrick and its pressure hoses. "You low-down. . . ."

"Save it, Pa," Leighton said.

Morkan handed the gunmen that pouch.

The gunmen shook it, beaming when its heft rang and jingled. Taking Morkan's horse by the halter, he whooped and mounted.

"You want this other horse," Leighton said, pointing at the dray.

The gunmen wrinkled his nose. He whooped again and dug his heels into Morkan's poor old roan and galloped off south.

Morkan stood with his head bowed, trembling, his collar to his lips. Leighton gripped the wagonseat, and let his heart slow.

"Could have got us killed, Leighton." Morkan said. "Why the hell did you ask him to raise his gun there?"

"Sometimes the scoundrels don't even have the cash to load a weapon."

Morkan groaned, but walked around the dray and took Leighton's hand to climb into the seat. "Let's get moving. I'd rather be in town in the midst of a crowd and hope he's miles away."

They clipped along in silence.

"So it has come to this, gunmen on the roads thieving."

"He won't have any valves leaking," Leighton offered.

"There's one thing I must know." Morkan said. He gripped Leighton's belt to steady himself in the wagonseat. "Why's it always my horse gets stolen?"

Leighton hired a new accountant, Emil "Randy" Odem, a Federal veteran who had lost an arm to the elbow at Iuka, Mississippi. With complicated straps, Leighton helped Odem fasten a wooden stake with a squared end to his stump each morning. On this squared end, Odem fitted all manner of implements including a stout clipboard for accompts, and even a beer stein he used as a coffee mug. He dragged the implements along in a child's cart.

Around ten a.m., women came in a line. Leighton and Odem met them by the scales where a pile of new-kilned lime waited. Lime-water for cold storage, cleansing teeth, lime for the privy, lime for the bugs, for the ditches, for fertilizer, for patching drafts and drying canker sores. One Negress in a checkered gingham showed Leighton ten boils bigger than strawberries on the back of her boy's head. A farm wife with thick, pink arms confessed that without a swilling of lime-water and crushed mint her husband's breath would be downright searing.

Leighton had missed this part of quarrying when he was on the cliffs before the war, this lovely, brawling gaggle of females. He tried not to accept vegetables or meats as trade in kind, but the women brought them—lettuce, potatoes, walnuts from last year, dried corn, pickled bream reeking of dill even through the wax seals. They brought lard oil lamps, guns, spurs, books of poesy, knock-kneed oxen, china, pewter, samovars, portraits of Franz Sigel.

Judith took special delight in coming once a week, though the household never needed lime in that quantity. Upon her arrival, the women, even the whites, parted at Leighton's command. Lifting the sides of her dress sewn with new and multicolored alterations to accommodate her regained opulence, she was a glorious pattern book of fabric, a rainbow rustling. She stood at the head of the line, stouter than ever before and glowing with sweat. With all the women waiting, she took her time chattering to Leighton while one of his men brought the cask of choteau up from the office. Leighton handed the box of worthless powder into her hands and she paid him nothing. Then amid the scowls and curled lips of the waiting women, Judith thrust out her ponderous bosom and strutted past the lot of them with her head held high. The white ladies felt sure she was a kept woman; the Negresses gossiped enviously at her soft life and increasing size. Leighton brought the cask back empty the next day and always wondered what Judith did with the sulfurous waste stone. Soon every Negress bought a weekly cask and it became a profitable mystery. One admitted sheepishly to him that other than making her skin more dry and yellow, she knew no reason to buy the stuff, except that it brought Judith such great prosperity.

Through niggardly trades, Leighton gained three draft horses, half a dozen more oxen, and three wagons from families in straits. He knew Federal supply officers well enough to purchase powder at superb prices. The officers reasoned powder would go bad, anyhow, waiting for the next war. After shooting two scabby oxen, he ordered much longer yolks with extra crossbraces made. He hitched these yolks to three of the wagons. When laborers finished shoveling stone into these, they grabbed the braces and heaved back on them like oarsmen, bracing the load down the ox trail to the stonebreakers waiting with their hammers and then to the mill where oxen and men turned a monotonous circle and the great rollers scraped and thumped keeping time. At least once a day, a man was injured and so lost his job and sometimes a limb to the wagon wheels. Leighton brought the sick call set from home, figuring no one who died at the farmhouse could have been saved anyway.

Late one night, Judith was mashing Morkan some puttyroot tea when Leighton came in with one of the ledgers.

"It's not working, pa." He ran his finger down the columns. "The cash is going. We'll end up just like that Burns fellow you bought it off of."

Morkan scanned the columns.

"Something has to be done about Heron or we lose the quarry," Leighton said.

"Cut the pay. Or cut the numbers."

"Did already." Leighton's eyes appeared frantic and they were ringed with black. "We need Heron to move on. Or we need him to die."

Morkan pushed the ledger sheet back to Leighton. "The idea!" But when Leighton frowned, Morkan said, "Well, you are certainly the man for that."

Leighton's jaw was clenched so tight his chin thrust forward like a hoof. "It can't be me." He gathered the ledger and left the kitchen.

From a dark corner at The Quarry Rand, Morkan watched the round rump of a songstress as she plodded among the patrons. She waved a fan and sweated while she sang. A big woman, she was drunk and bumped into tables. Men raised their mugs as she approached. Her voice was so lovely, though, her melody made their eyes mist if they didn't watch the comedy and pain of her lumbering. A thin man in a jade coat took a beer from Danny Beauchamp and slurped it as he scanned the room. Spotting Morkan, he stepped quickly to him, set his beer on Morkan's table and stuck out his hand.

"I'm Justinian Ziggler. *The Daily Leader.*" His curly black hair barely hid the pencil at his ear, and his hands were dark with printer's ink. "Thanks for sending for me."

"Michael Morkan," Morkan said.

Ziggler sat down. Squirming, he fished in his coat pocket and brought out a folded newspaper. "I'd be happy to get your thoughts on a column of mine." He extended Morkan the paper.

Morkan took it and squinted. Ziggler fetched a candle from another table. After lighting the candle and scooting it toward Morkan, he sat and fussed with a pipe.

Morkan looked up, and with the candle wavering, his eyes felt scorched and dry.

"On page three," Ziggler said, puffing.

Morkan fixed his new specs on his nose, then opened the paper.

It was a long piece about war debt. Holding the paper with a serious face, Morkan ran his eyes along the page for a long time as if reading. Then he set the paper down slowly. "Damned insightful," he said. "It is a fortunate thing you came to this town, Mr. Ziggler. You're shining a literary light and politicians are cringing from it, I'll wager."

Ziggler took the pencil from his ear and touched the lead to the tip of his tongue. "Why would you, a traitor and Confederate sympathizer, want to call on me? Clearly from what you just read you can see where this newsman stands."

Morkan licked his lips. "Don't you look around you, Mr. Ziggler, and long for a finished courthouse, for flagging to carry mourners to a real cemetery for the fallen heroes? One filled with monuments?"

Ziggler squinted at him. "I swear to god. You hillbillies don't even read my paper when you read my paper."

Morkan pressed the newspaper flat against the table.

"If we are wallowing in war debt, where in the world do you come off crying for business in the name of civic pride?"

Morkan scowled. "Mr. Ziggler, without a courthouse, without roads, without progress, where will you come up with the revenues to pay that debt? Not from old Rebels like me."

Ziggler was quiet.

"What if I were to tell you the provost's chief purchasing officer is deliberately thwarting progress by refusing business with the town's one quarry?"

Ziggler watched him with a bland expression, then pushed his chair back from the little table. "You know, Morkan, I can tell at one time you really had it, could probably sell sweat to a nigger." He rose. "But like the rest of your stinking Rebs, you're singing songs like Claibe Jackson is still waltzing in Jeff City, and naming your damn children Sterling after that fool Price." Downing his beer, he plunked the mug on the table. "Face it. You're nobody now. And there's nothing you can do if one of us wants your quarry."

When he left, Morkan held on to the table and watched him go. Behind him, in the warm, orange light, the songstress sang.

Many times Morkan drew up a well of strength to go and see Cora, only to find that fortitude vanish in light of what might happen to his son and the quarry, and in light of what he felt happening in his lungs. If it were consumption she would know for sure. Aiding his son was somehow easier if the only diagnosis he faced were Judith's, one he could doubt.

Failure and boredom made him long for his real work. From Isaac, he borrowed old buckskin leggings, a coat so weathered it held the texture of burlap, a vest died pink with sumac, and a shirt as brilliant yellow as a field of goldenrod. It was all garb from Lovell, the previous owner of the farm. Johnson helped Morkan tie a red bandanna over his hair and under his chin.

Finished, Johnson backed away from him. He chuckled.

Morkan raised an eyebrow, invitation enough for Johnson to speak.

"You look like a filthy old Delaware trader."

Morkan grinned.

He rode in and stowed his horse at the livery. Morkan passed below the weather-ravaged archway and joined a small queue of men waiting to be signed on.

The man who met the queue wore the same sort of Federal cap and peacoat as Leighton. Just above his eyes was a strap that bore an armature. On the end of the armature was a set of three monocles, and one monocle hung over his right eye. A long walnut cudgel was fastened to his elbow, and on this a clipboard was stuck. With the monocles flashing the blue limestone, the straps of his prosthetic creaking, he seemed more a mechanism than a man. He had to be the invalid Odem Leighton spoke of hiring.

Odem worked his way down the line, scratching each laborer's name on the clipboard. Each laborer showed Odem a set of papers. He came before Morkan.

"Lafêtê," Morkan said.

"Lafayette," Odem said, scrawling.

When Morkan produced no papers, Odem glanced up from the clipboard. In the monocle, the eyeball was as twisted and fat as a snail. "Your discharge or current service papers, please."

Morkan shrugged and smiled. He launched into French without hesitating. "Give me a minute," he said. "Before I was a furrier I was a stonemason in Normandy."

Odem blinked at him. "Pardon but I don't speak it."

When Morkan reached for his vest, Odem stepped back and whipped a Colt from his belt. Behind its glass, the snail of his eyeball jigged. The line of men fell away. Then Morkan raised his hands, nodded his chin at his vest. Odem inched forward, keeping the Colt on him. He patted Morkan's chest, then reached in the vest pocket. With a quick grab, he snatched out a canvas roll tied in ribbon. He handed this to Morkan who untied it. When the canvas unfurled, there hung the shining chisels for scoring monument facings.

Odem whistled low. "You're hired, Lafayette."

Down Summit Street came Heron riding Morkan's chestnut Walker. With the traces looped in his hands, he sauntered the Walker to Leighton.

He wore civilian clothes, a fine linen suit, a collarless boiled shirt. His graying beard, once long and black, was now trimmed to so sharp a point it seemed his chin was hung with an iron wedge. "I thought I would have you ruined by now," he said.

Leighton fixed his Federal hat tightly on his head. "Here I am." Behind him came the crack of black powder.

Heron's eyes danced above his smile. "I would like to see your books and make sure no traitors are keeping them."

Leighton escorted him to the office. Bending to a drawer in the desk, he removed a ledger. Beside the ledgers, amid dusty but well-ordered files, was a leather pouch and in it the slip of callus fallen from his palm, now dusted with the pyrite the pouch used to hold. Across the dead skin, he imagined the pyrite's sparkle as he snapped the ledger open.

"I have heard rumor that these men, Federal veterans all, are paid fortnightly at a dime a day. Is that true?"

"Ready for your audit, sir."

Heron ran his eyes over Leighton, especially his cap. "To my displeasure I have discovered that your name is on the deed to this quarry, right alongside your father's."

Leighton kept his face still. "Good business practice. Even for a quarrymaster, a quarry offers many ways to die."

Heron unbuttoned his coat to show the butts of his pistols. Then he sat very still. "You trouble me, young Morkan. I see more and more young men like you, men for whom threats, even unto death, trip so easily from their tongues. It's as if nothing really matters to you."

"Business matters to me, sir."

Heron snorted. "I think a lot more matters to you." He watched Leighton for a bit. "Did you know that I am a writer?" He paused and looked beyond Leighton, eyes aglow as if focused on a golden horizon. "I am now completing a major memoir of my service for the Union, and a refutation of the malignment of General John C. Frémont." Heron began a monologue about the glories of the war in the West. Many minutes passed with Heron talking. Outside, another blast thumped and cracked along the cliffs, louder and sharper than need be. Watching Heron's lips prattle words of courage and honor, Leighton curbed a desire to leap up and fire the new blaster. Such palaver.

Finally he could take no more and asked again, "The accompts?"

The light fell from Heron's face, and his eyes narrowed. "You are the first veteran I have met who does not heed a story that affirms the valor of his service."

Leighton shrugged. "Send me the book."

When Leighton led him from the office, a blast shook the air behind them. Leighton cursed. The blaster was using too much powder—four plumes of dust rose in the air, and Leighton and Heron were pelted with stone.

Up on the cliffs, the blaster weaved when he stood from behind the blast ditch, but the powder monkey did not rise. Leighton hustled to them and Heron followed.

The powder monkey, a big-nosed kid named O'Reilly, lay with his eyes wide. Crimson surges of blood escaped from his neck where a stone ripped a hole. Leighton grabbed the blaster by the collar of his shirt.

"Get Odem and the sick call set, and you get back up here." Leighton shook him with each syllable. The blaster scrambled down to the office. Kneeling to O'Reilly, Leighton pulled his own shirt off, wadded it, and held it tightly to the boy's neck. He was about the age Greer was when he died. Instantly the shirt turned dark red, grew sopping and warm in Leighton's fist. Heron stood with his arms crossed at his chest.

Leighton stroked the boy's hair back from his eyes. With the rhythm of the boy's heart, with each gush, the shirt seemed to shrink. Blood swathed Leighton's thighs. He could feel O'Reilly's pulse, sure and strong as the beat of a drill down the cliff where the work did not stop. The heart took no notion that all was at an end.

Odem arrived, his stump showing from his short sleeve, the sick call set cradled in his good arm. He set it down and opened its gilded doors, which flashed gold in the sunlight. The blaster stood gaping. A cutter followed Odem up, a tall, rangy man dressed in old Indian garb. Leighton stared at him—the nose, the eyes beneath the lime-dusted scarf that swathed his head and the bandanna covering his mouth. Then Leighton knew it was Morkan. Damned Heron stood next to him. If Heron discovered Morkan there, covered in lime dust, the quarry might be lost.

O'Reilly gurgled and tried to sit up.

"Get down here," Leighton said to the blaster.

Odem cuffed the blaster in back of the head. Then, once the man knelt, Odem set the chrism in his hands, and handed Leighton the tiny platter with the host.

The blaster shuddered. When O'Reilly's mouth opened, a bubble of blood like a red sac swelled at his lips.

"Put that oil on your thumb," Leighton said to the blaster. He glanced at Morkan and Heron but was relieved to see them both focused on O'Reilly's dying.

In the blaster's shaking hands, the crystal stopper on the holy chrism rattled. Then Leighton grabbed the blaster's wrist. "Stick your thumb out." When he did, Leighton pressed the blaster's oiled thumb against O'Reilly's clammy forehead. From O'Reilly's singed shirt, there came the smell of burnt powder like tar and beneath this the powerful salty stink of blood. Slowly Leighton forced the blaster to make the sign of the cross. "Never forget this," he whispered to the blaster, his teeth clenched.

When he turned the trembling blaster loose, he took the wafer from the platter. So old, it was yellow and brittle as plaster, the tiny cross in its middle like the shadow of a fossil after eons of weathering. It was not forgiveness; it was penance, for Leighton, and the blaster. "Just take this on your tongue, O'Reilly." For an instant, holding the consecrated host, Leighton's mind cleared of the quarry, of his father, of Heron, of the war. There was only O'Reilly slipping away and the white wafer and the ritual of hope, of sacrifice. "I'm sorry," Leighton whispered to O'Reilly.

At his lips, O'Reilly's blood gripped the wafer, then darkened it as the boy expired.

After a time, Leighton stood, left his shirt on the ground. Holding his face in his hands, the blaster was still kneeling beside the cadaver.

"All my teaching has failed," Heron said. "You can't respect them *and* treat them to hard labor and rough wages. You'll die of it."

Leighton stood with his stained palms held out to Heron.

Heron turned his gaze on Morkan. Then he curled his lip at him. The elaborateness of Morkan's costume now struck Leighton—the yellow shirt, the berry red vest, the deerskin leggings. Spectacular sleight of hand.

"Mr. Odem will escort you to the gate," Leighton said to Heron.

"I see I need only wait," Heron said.

With Odem leading, Heron walked the ox trail down to the pit. The blaster followed and Leighton and his father were alone with the cadaver.

Leighton stared at Morkan. "If he knew you were here."

Morkan raised an eyebrow at Leighton. He knelt to O'Reilly, held the back of his hand to the boy's lips, then bowed his head.

"He's right about one thing," Morkan said. "You can't work these men like this and try to care for them. You'll lose your mind." With just his fingertips Morkan touched O'Reilly's face. "I am so sorry for asking this of you, Leighton."

"I am asking you something worse," Leighton said slowly. "You need to leave here and decide."

Morkan pushed O'Reilly's eyes closed. Leighton fetched a keg of quick lime. Without speaking, they doused the cadaver with handfuls of the frigid powder.

"Pa, if he were gone, you could come back here to stay. Think on that."

"Leighton, how can a murder be an answer to this?"

When Leighton looked at his father, Morkan sensed an entirely new kind of scrutiny. "You know I've had to kill more than horses since you been gone."

Morkan wandered the new shops and monger's barrows downtown, squandering a few of the eagles left from what Weitzer relinquished. Looney's Tailors opened above Rathbun's General Store, and Morkan received a note in the middle of June inviting him for a fitting.

In a loft above the general store, Looney nailed down two battered old church pews for customers to wait on. At the end of one pew spread a brown and crimson stain, blood from the years when the churches held no worshippers but housed scores of wounded. Morkan sat on the opposite end of the pew. He listened for a minute to Looney's voice coming through the open transom that topped the fitting room door. The tailor was cajoling someone into letting him make a vest. "It's just the best tweed I seen. Better than before the war."

"Shit," his customer said.

Morkan opened the *Daily Leader* and read a long, dramatic story of the Swamp Fox's surrender. The windows to the loft were tall, and there was so much dust on them that the afternoon sun appeared tan. Beneath them, traffic stirred more dust into the air. Lovely traffic—he spotted a phaeton, two carryalls, a caisson someone converted to carry passengers. Criers with vegetables called, and a whole wagon patch of melons stunk sweetly across Mount Vernon Street. The town was a leaf unfurling.

The fitting room door opened and Peterson, the teamster who first met them with the news after Oak Hills, walked out, stopped and blinked when he saw Morkan.

Gripping the pew, Morkan rose.

Peterson raised his arm, and where there should have been a hand to wave, there was nothing.

They stood for a moment, staring at one another. When Looney poked his head into the alcove, he lost his smile, lowered his gaze.

"It is good to see you, Peterson." Morkan said. He cleared his throat.

Peterson nodded. "Heard you can't run your quarry. Heard the boy runs it now."

Morkan frowned, nodded. "He's quite a businessman, yes."

"Heard you gave the Rebs powder when they come. Heard we kept you in prison a good long time." His voice was acidic and he smiled at each bit of woe he dropped.

"There wasn't much good to it."

Morkan was about to ask Peterson how he fared after Oak Hills. But then Peterson said, "Gratiot. Ain't that a shame, now." He fixed his hat on his head and descended the stairs whistling.

Once he was gone, Looney looked up. "Never you mind him, Michael Morkan. Just come on in here."

Looney stooped to avoid the ceiling joist that struck the fitting room into two compartments. He pulled the measuring tape off his neck and asked Morkan to stand straight and still.

With gentle taps of his fingers, he raised Morkan's right arm and measured, reminded him that his right cuff was one-quarter inch longer than his left, that the war did not change the solid things.

"Changed Peterson."

Looney bit his bottom lip, circled the tape around Morkan's neck. The tape made his throat itch. Looney grinned. "It didn't change the length of his cuff, though."

Morkan coughed, smiling.

"Michael, I didn't call you in here for business."

Morkan waited. Looney went on measuring, dropping the tape from Morkan's hip down to his ankle. "You two, you and Leighton, have a problem." Looney was whispering. "And it's become my problem as well."

Looney paused. He looked Morkan in the eyes, a level stare, a face Morkan had never seen on the tailor.

"Leighton told me about it," Morkan said. "About Kreft."

Looney took a breath, and then he nodded. "Any one of us up there who could have would've killed that man. Course, I can't imagine you'd hold any onus on Leighton for it, considering what you been through."

Morkan felt his knees give a little, and the tape went slack. His voice fell to a whisper. He wanted to plumb Looney, to understand his son. After a moment he said, "It is still hard for me to imagine that he killed a Federal officer while on duty."

Looney's jaw buckled. "I have gone to great lengths to keep that within the circle of my men. But now, Mr. Morkan, we have someone spading the graveyard dirt."

Downstairs, Rathbun's laughter rang alongside the cash register.

"Heron interviewed me twice now, and talked with others from my old unit."

Morkan held his collar to his lips.

"Morkan, Leighton and I are in a tight spot. You see, we are citizens, with honorable Federal service records. We can conduct business, rebuild our lives, provide for our loved ones. And we cannot do anything to jeopardize that."

At Looney's shirt pocket there glinted the silver eyes of seven needles.

With delicate fingers he wrapped his tape round Morkan's neck. "You on the other hand." He let the tape go slack, and jotted the measure on his little pad.

"I didn't fight in this war. I didn't kill people."

The tailor moved very close to Morkan, his chin nearly rubbing Morkan's own. Down in Rathbun's a woman argued prices. "Would you come through it only to lose all you have to an outsider who did kill people, who would have killed your son in that quarry if he could have?"

Morkan began to protest.

"Listen to me," Looney said, whispering again. "A tailor makes a fine alibi, and the provost's purchasing officer is often on desolate roads between one job or another."

Morkan clenched his jaw.

"I hear you and Leighton encountered the pleasure of meeting a horse thief. I believe Heron deserves to meet one as well."

"This is no way to settle. . . ."

"No way to settle? When did the war end here?" Looney shook him by the arm. "Who declared peace in the Ozarks. Heron is no Ozarker. You see that. He's a carpet-bagger. And, Michael, he's not going stop. He'll take your quarry and ruin Leighton."

Morkan closed his eyes.

Out in the street, a crier hawked subscriptions for daily delivery of ice.

Looney rolled his tape slowly. "Name the day and I will schedule you a final fitting. You'll wear your alibi."

In Correy's eyes, the orange glow of the coke flashed as if reflected on the surface of a slough. With his cheeks sunken, his lips pursed, he appeared much older than the young drill foreman Morkan remembered. Seated in the clutter of the smithy hung with its brands and tongs, his gaze locked on the fire while back of the furnace the kid at the bellows wailed away.

"That boy'll burn that coke right out'n thar," Morkan hollered, disguising his voice to sound like the old blacksmith who was Correy's mentor. Correy jolted from his reverie.

Behind the furnace the kid's soot black face peered around at Correy and Morkan who were laughing. The kid held the bellows open in confusion and fear, then gave the bellows one last spurt. The furnace crackled.

Correy spat toward him, then yelled words so muddled Morkan had to think them apart. "Get out of there now, Dean, you little bastard."

Dean scuttled away.

Correy threw down his filthy glove and clasped Morkan's hand. "Skulkin' round here secret as a mason," he chided.

Morkan smiled, but saw Correy's smile fade.

"Correy?" Morkan asked.

Correy licked his lips to clear some of the spittle off them. Sam Slade suddenly came to mind, how the old drunk's lips were glossy and wet when he was sailing a sea of liquor. "When you come to, you asked if you could see Cora."

"Yes, I did."

"I would ask that you go ahead and do so."

"Why?"

Correy planted his hands on his hips and was suddenly fierce and challenging in a way Morkan had never known him to be.

"Because I aim to marry her," he said. "Yet she asks after you."

Correy touched his lip with the knuckle of his thumb. Then his voice fell and his shoulders relaxed a little. "Michael, I feel she yearns to make peace within herself."

Morkan bowed his head. "I will go and see her."

Correy hesitated, then patted his old employer's shoulder. They were equals now, or maybe Correy was above him. Correy could work. His hat was no Federal's though. It was the hat of railway firemen and blasters, a rounded peak with a bill worn at the back, shining with coal dust. "What will you do if she doesn't want to marry?" Morkan asked.

"Well, if she refuses me after you see her and she turns you away, which she will, I'll know I have only me to blame."

They were quiet and wind stirred the tongs, which rang like sour tuning forks.

"Why aren't you working at the quarry?" Morkan asked. "Leighton would take you as a blacksmith. No more helper's wages."

Correy shrugged, ran his fingers among the brands so that they wobbled like pendulums from their pegs. "Wages are bad I hear. Might as well learn. And really, Leighton knows his business."

Morkan frowned. "I'm worried, Correy."

Correy scuffed the heel of his boot into the dirt floor of the smithy.

"Heron has his eye on squeezing us out of the quarry," Morkan said.

Fetching his glove, Correy lifted one of the brands and hooked it over the fire, moving as slowly and deliberately as if he were at gunpoint. There was a pile of canvas satchels fanned over the anvil.

They both watched the brand brighten from blood red to orange.

"Correy, I've learned something about Leighton that could lose him the quarry."

Correy did not look up from the fire. "Then you best hide it with all you got."

After Morkan said nothing for a long time, Correy pulled the brand from the furnace, held it glowing over the canvas bags. He stared at Morkan. "If you'd of seen him going to St. Louis for you, you'd never let another man touch a hair on his head." Raising the brand, he pressed the canvas with it, and the fabric sizzled and smoked. When he raised the brand, it left the scar **US**.

"That was war, Correy. This is peace."

"Says who? Where's peace round here?" Correy plunged the brand on another bag. Blue smoke swirled around them. "Heron's a Federal anyway." His voice fell. "After what they done to you, don't you want to see ever one of them suffer?" Spit escaped his mouth, and for an instant he recoiled.

They stared at one another for so long Correy put the brand back in the fire. The cuff of his glove stuck out like a funnel. He wiped his lips with this, and left a black streak at his mouth. "Sound bitter, don't I?"

Morkan shrugged.

Correy hefted the brand. "He risked his life going to Gratiot. Took that money there, and would have give ever eagle to get you back."

Watching Correy, Morkan could see determination in his ravaged jawline, could see how staunchly Correy believed in Leighton. "But I can't."

Correy raised his eyebrows. "You and me, Morkan, we never raised a gun in this for either side. But you made Leighton do just that. He stuck around for you to keep that quarry." Correy turned and stamped the brand against the next bag with more force than necessary. "Ask yourself again if you can't."

It took some days' courage, and Morkan could not fathom why. Surely a talk with Cora could be done as cold as the business of sacking a waterboy or hiring a driller. But somehow in her wronging him, in their wronging each other, the sight of her, the notion of sitting in a room with his old love towered over any interview of his life. Watching Judith slice the puttyroot, breathing some uncertain flash of the air near his former sickbed, he sensed Cora had been here.

Her house never seemed smaller and he took no precaution to tie Half Dollar at Correy's. Still he hesitated on the doorstep and was about to go, when the door opened, and Cora stood with a dustbin piled high.

Her eyes went wide. Her hair she kept longer—it was bound in a leather thong at the back of her head. On her pale face the two mysterious hands of smallpox still rested. She appeared rounder in the face and arms, and he wondered if worry and idleness drove her to eating as it had done to Charlotte, who grew uncomfortably stout once they moved to Springfield. Then it occurred to him in a swift rush of sadness that she very well might be with child.

335

Cora recovered. "Half Dollar," she said. The horse pricked its ears. She tossed the dust off the stoop then turned to Morkan. "Thought I heard a gasping old horse out here."

Morkan pulled his collar to his lips to avoid the dust floating southward. "I can't tell you how much I've missed real, quality sassing."

A hand on her lips, she dropped the dustbin and sobbed once. Then she threw her arms around him and drew his cheek to her soft, full neck. She was crying, laughing, and against him he felt her slightly rounded stomach, and he knew she was to be a mother.

She drew him inside the house. Trunks yawned in the middle of the floor; Sam Slade's old iron bed was gone; the wallpaper border was steamed down in half the room.

"Packing once more?"

"Not for any long trek, I tell you. Not this time." There was still laughter in her voice. She fanned herself with her hand, her face growing hot and red. "Pardon me. You know me, Michael. Never an ounce of fat. But now I'm puffing up like a muffin." Then she stopped, and all the happiness that had been in the air seemed to drop to the floor and dissipate.

Morkan struggled for words.

"How is Leighton?" she asked.

"He does fair." Her sleeves were bunched far up her arm, and her dappled skin there was so beautiful to him it was a sorrow to behold. "I have an awful decision . . . ." He stopped and considered that already he visited enough trouble on her just being present. "Something I may have to do for him."

She bowed her head, and when she did her chin doubled. Though she should have appeared cherubic, matronly, and secure in so much new life coming, she seemed to him to be scared and alone. "Well, you had two of us waiting on you here in Springfield, Michael Morkan." She smoothed her apron against her belly. "One of us did not wait so well." Then her eyes met his, and they held no joy. "But your son waited for you loyal as a Templar in a castle afire."

He traced the lock on a trunk with his finger. "I may well die for helping him."

Her voice came out cold as ashes. "Are you still a man that clings to middle ground, even after all you have seen, and all you lost?"

When he said nothing, they were a quiet a long time, and he realized she had hung the truth out between them as glaring and incontrovertible as a soiled bedsheet from the window of a bridegroom's chamber. Had he only married her, had he only let her follow the army to St. Louis, and him and his son with her.

After a painful long while he said, "I want to thank you for coming to the house. I know it was you had to teach Judith all her nursing."

"That Judith, she is something."

"Well, she holds a very dire vision of me." He stooped and folded a blouse from a pile, wanting his hands busy. "I wonder, what was your diagnosis?"

She looked down and her face darkened. Then she raised her eyes, and they were not wet, but clear. She opened her arms to him. "Come here," she said. "Gather me in."

When he hesitated, she took his hand and pulled him to her. She placed one of his hands at her waist and pressed another into her hip. Forcefully she drew his head down until his lips touched her round shoulders. Then she clung to his neck, and she moved them in a slow waltz step. He stiffened at first, too surprised. Then his fingers glided tentatively. Finally his hands clutched her and admired her arms and back and hips in nearly their old accustomed fashion, save that a terrible time was passed, her body was changed, and his body was blasted. When she felt a tear touch her scalp, she pushed him away.

Her fingertips lingered on his shirtpocket where something cold and metallic lurked beneath the fabric over his heart. Then it hit her what the metal was. She took a breath. "That there, Michael, is the last dance we will ever have. And not for any reason of morality." She looked at him, and her face grew calm and almost cold. "Tell me true. You feel that dance in your heart. But you don't feel it anywhere else. Am I right?"

He paused and indeed his heart was warm, but the rest of his body was numb and hollow and asleep. When he touched his lips, he felt a whisper of blood there.

"I'm very sorry, Michael."

He felt tricked, cheated of something dear. She had danced with him as a nurse, not a lost lover. But this notion subsided. There was no way to tell for sure, and it was too terrible to ask.

With her arms across her chest regarding him, she stood proud, stout, a life renewed within her.

"Oh, Cora," he said. "I suppose I will die wondering what a happier world it would have been had I taken your advice, those years ago."

Her staunch pride melted, her face softened, and there she stood, his old Cora in the twilight. "It will long be bittersweet for me to wonder as well, Michael Morkan."

She showed him to the door. Half Dollar stuck his head under the eve and snorted as if he remembered her. She hugged his neck, gave it a firm pat. Morkan took the halter.

"Cora Correy," he said with a joviality only he could muster at a time like this. "Sounds like a blue spring flowing in Antrim."

Cora blushed and when she did the small death hands of the pox that had touched her face became part of a ruddy and healthy complexion. She throbbed with life at the ready, like bottomland soil just turned. Beside her he felt like a husk, the spirit long since departed. "It sounds funny, don't it?" she asked.

Morkan laughed, his collar to his lips. "You'll do it proud. No one will mock it."

In a clearing on a ridge where three dogwoods now grew, Morkan and Leighton had buried Charlotte and put a cast iron bench there one All Hallows Day. Over her resting place they lowered a long tablet, seven foot by four foot. Leighton beveled the edges smooth to frame a long-stemmed rose Morkan carved. Her headstone bore a mare taking a final rest before foaling—horses such as the one she had given Leighton were her life's passion.

CHARLOTTE MORKAN, BELOVED WIFE AND MOTHER

the stone read in Leighton's script, noticeably Leighton's for it was so plumb and precise.

Morkan lowered himself to the bench. Since seeing Looney a week had passed. Gill-over-the-ground foamed blue and purple at the tablet's edges, and the tablet and stone were now dappled yellow, black, and green.

He clasped his hands and spoke with his lips against his fingers. "Well, old girl, I have promised you not long, not long." He steadied himself, hands gripping the warm iron bench. "But if I do what's asked of me, I have to say, old girl, not ever." He nipped the tablet with the toe of his boot. "This might very well be goodbye."

From the clearing, as he and Leighton had planned, she could admire the gray columns of the house, its dark eyes, the beard of its stone stairs. In their marriage he could count on one hand the number of times he had knowingly, willfully disappointed her.

As evening came on, the sky turned from silver to a foreboding Federal blue. Wind snaked through the wildflowers and stirred the leaves of the dogwoods in some teetering assessment. Coming fast with lead gray clouds, a cold front chilled the air.

He did not hear Judith arrive. She dropped a coat about him. "Come down to dinner," she said. She learned her English listening to Charlotte and warbling Irish women in St. Louis. Often something tumbled from her mouth that made Morkan shiver with grief at the sound of that old voice lost. "Lean on me, now. It's dark."

They picked their ways down the ridge and through the forest trails to the house, and he did lean on her often when there was no need.

At the kitchen she sat him down to stew, then began the monotonous slicing of puttyroot for the tea that held his lungs together.

"No Leighton yet?"

Judith stopped mashing for a moment. "He's working awfully hard."

The Irish voice again. Morkan set his spoon beside his bowl as carefully as one might lay down a fuse. Clasping his hands, he rested his forehead against his fingertips. A pot scraped on the griddle and Morkan heard the rasp of Judith's knife sweeping the root into the strainer.

Her apron rustled—she wiped her hands, then left him for a minute.

When she returned, she paused beside him until he raised his head up. In her arms there glowed the Belgian double-barreled shotgun. Someone had sawed it short.

Judith set the gun on the table, the breech open, the blueing shining across the barrels. "That tailor brung you a nice new suit."

The water whistled. The suit was poplin, a fine summer tan. In its pocket he found a note telling him that Heron rode in to the provost office each morning from a bordello off the road to Pleasant Hope. "Any day they ask, that's your fitting." It was not signed.

"Judith why do I have to do something terrible to keep what's rightfully mine?"

With care, Judith poured the tea. "Leighton never had time to ask that question when that man from your prison come to visit."

Another debt to a good son. If you never truly take a side in war, he wondered, how do you say now the war is won. Morkan took the tea from her. "Tell Johnson to come very early."

"Johnson's not coming. I do it." She crumpled the note and tossed it in the stove.

Before dawn, the cold front loosed a steady rain over the hills. Judith dressed him as the Delaware trader, and placed on his back a long poncho of Leighton's from days with the Home Guards. Leighton had not yet risen.

"Deliver the suit this morning to Looney's. Tell him I come today for the fitting."

Judith nodded and looked him up and down. "If he kills you, he ruins us all." She pulled the lime-stiffened bandanna up to cover more of Morkan's face.

As Morkan rode for town on one of the quarry's new, unbranded nags, wisps of clouds crawled the deep green of the hillsides. A cool, light rain, ideal weather for cement to set, Morkan thought, or for a heart to harden.

In a grove where Greer's Mill Road met the lane to Pleasant Hope, Morkan dismounted and unwrapped the shotgun. He slapped the surprised horse on its rump. With its wet tail down, it shivered and trotted for the quarry or for home.

Clearing his throat Morkan scanned the road. In the murk of dawn, there was no one. He hid the gun beneath the poncho and fretted that the rain would be too heavy to keep powder dry. In the lane he practiced walking with a limp to distract from the stiffness of the gun. He stuck close to the overhanging boughs of oak and hickory. With every step, he felt delirium coming, felt the blood in his lungs begin to hang and rattle.

Just when Morkan felt the road falter, hooves pattered in the rain. Heron rode hunched on Morkan's old Walker, struggling to light a cigar. The horse stopped when it smelled Morkan. Heron looked up, a flame in his hands. He tossed the tinder away.

"Ain't you the Delaware I seen at the quarry? No working in the rain?"

Morkan wavered a moment and Heron positioned the heel of his hand on his pistol. Heron glanced down at his horse and wrinkled his brow, patting its wet neck.

"Fired me," Morkan said. He leaned forward, pulled the bandanna down, hiding his face. He cleared his throat and spat on the chert of the road. As he did he cocked both barrels beneath his poncho. In his gray sputum on the orange and yellow chert, there ran a livid thread of crimson. "Too sick."

Heron's hand slipped from the pistol to rest on the saddle horn. "You know there will come a time when I run that quarry. Then I'll have the Delaware cut stone as long as he wishes. Sick or not."

Morkan sighed. Then he drew the shotgun up, letting the ragged poncho part. Heron froze.

"Lovely picture," Morkan said. "Hold it in your mind. Think on nothing else."

"Michael Morkan," Heron said quietly. Behind him the rain hissed.

The first barrel blasted him loose of the saddle. With a lunge the old brown Walker charged and swept Heron off, thudding him to the roadbed. The horse bolted away.

341

Heron lay face down in the dirt, gasping, one hand scrabbling for the pistol pinned beneath his hip. His back was likely broken low on his spine, for he could not turn. Along his teeth a red line of blood began floating.

Morkan pressed the muzzle against the back of Heron's skull. For an instant he thought this last shot would be easier—the deed was near done; the man was mortally wounded. But the trigger seemed welded fast. "I don't have any desire to do this."

"Then don't," Heron said. For just a moment he stopped searching for the pistol and rolled his silver eyes up at Morkan, pleading.

Morkan pulled the trigger and finished him, then snuck away into the woods.

That afternoon, Danny Montbonne Beauchamp led Morkan to a corner table where the sun broke through and glared yellow. Feeling dizzy, he wondered if she were leading him to his established spot so as to fix him, a sputtering star cornered in a violent galaxy. After he was seated, she returned with a glass of port that seemed thick as medicine. Once swirled, it left a crimson film clinging to the inside of the glass.

"That is some suit you have there, Mister Michael," she said.

He pinched the sleeves as if just realizing he was clothed. He reached in his coat for an eagle, but Danny winked at him. "Mr. Michael, you're on Mr. Leighton's tab."

When he laughed, only a slight catching in his throat made any sound. "Danny Beauchamp, you are an astute woman."

She did a curtsy, bowing her head and flipping her frilled dress. Morkan warmed as if he already finished the port—the silly joy of youth was a grand thing to see.

Looney had rags to dry him with. Morkan had left the gun in a sink hole that was filling with water. The coat fit him exactly. In the fitting, they never spoke, Morkan and the tailor, only tugged at the fabric.

"Hold out your hands," Looney said when they were done.

A pair of shoes, galluses the tailor gave him. A shirt boiled and brilliant white.

Looney poured a droplet of oil onto Morkan's palm, then one onto his own.

Looney rubbed his hands together, nodding to Morkan to follow. Then the two of them patted their necks, touched their collars.

Now, Morkan shone like a banker about to foreclose.

Outside Shulty's windows, a belch of black smoke squirted up in a column from The Mistress, fired and chugging once more. There were only five other patrons in the bar. Three were men Morkan's age. The youngest, with a face so woolly he appeared feral, sat in the corner near Morkan, rubbing his sooty fingers around a beer mug. He wore a frayed peacoat with the collar turned up. He muttered resolutely to himself, his eyes bulging now and again. At the same table was a gray haired man, his face thin and sun-wrinkled. His beard grew in a gray fluff that fell to the middle of his chest, and he pulled and twirled it there, holding his drink and smiling a broad smile at Morkan. He was beatifically drunk.

Morkan flashed a grin at the gray haired drunk, but felt his smile quickly fade. In the quiet, he heard a thunk from the quarry, powder going off, a bench being blasted. The powder thunked again, sounding very much like distant cannon. The young man in the peacoat shuddered and ducked. The gray haired drunk swatted him on top of the head. They blinked at each other, then toasted one another and drank solemnly. Here I am to fade among the dislodged and unkempt, Morkan thought. The gray haired drunk squinted at Morkan.

The door opened, and Leighton stood glancing about the bar with his slanted eyes. He nodded when he saw Morkan, waved at another man across the bar as he walked to his father. Leighton wore an old coat of Morkan's, the sleeves rolled in thick donuts. The lapels were thinner than anything in fashion, and the coat's tails were so filthy with lime and Portland cement, they hung stiffly at Leighton's sides. His face was grim, his shoulders slumped.

Seeing him cross that room of castoffs, Morkan's throat bound tight and he was filled with a terrible joy. He had freed his son. His chest rattled when he breathed.

Leighton sat down so hard, Morkan's port bobbed in the glass. When he removed the Federal cap, now mottled gray with lime, the cap left an indent all around his glossy black hair. Beneath Leighton's beard, Morkan saw the face of a thin, exhausted child.

"Hell of a suit there," Leighton said. "Where'd you fetch the cash for that?"

"Looney tailored it on credit."

Leighton fell quiet and watched his father with Charlotte's eyes.

"Tired?" Morkan asked.

Leighton nodded. "You don't look so good, Pa. Let's get you something hot."

Morkan looked away, and was glad when Leighton finally set to yelling for Danny. She brought him a stout and placed a bowl of stew before both of them.

Morkan stared at the stew for a moment. Danny halted, her eyes on him.

The gray haired drunk behind Morkan sat far forward and tapped Morkan. Leaning into the table, Leighton moved his hand to his coat. Morkan stiffened.

"Say. Say, 'scuse me?"

Morkan didn't turn. "Yeah."

The gray haired drunk pulled his chair beside Morkan, raised his open palm to Leighton, who waited, his jaw set squarely so that Morkan could just see the white tips of his teeth. His son's face at that moment was more chilling to Morkan than anything the drunk could have done.

"Ain't you the fellow. . . ." The drunk's voice fell to a level that was suddenly quiet and sober. "Ain't you that fellow gave Pap Price all that powder before Lexington?"

Danny's back tensed and her chest rose as she inhaled. She glanced at Morkan, then at Leighton.

Morkan turned slowly to the drunk, whose head weaved a little, but whose chin and jaw rose in what appeared to be inebriated pride.

"Ain't you that man? I saw you in the Men's Academy?"

Morkan's heart tightened. The drunk could easily be a prisoner's murderous cousin, a thief, some zealous ex-Confederate, a Union scout.

Leighton's eyes fastened on the gray haired drunk. The darkness beneath those eyes, the slight bulge of his lip told Morkan that his son undoubtedly had the pepper-box out, leveled at the drunk, and that he would kill the drunk without hesitating. For the first time, Morkan realized his son was someone not to be crossed, that the war had left him capably dangerous in a way Morkan never needed to be, in a way Morkan would never need to be again. Leighton's stare was death's assurance plain as a sickle's edge. The drunk's woolly partner swung forward in his chair, his big eyes bulging at Leighton.

"Of course he is, Yancey," Danny whispered. "He's a hero." When she touched Yancey, the gray haired drunk, her arm was shaking. "You let me get you all a round of whiskeys. Have you a drink together."

Danny returned and set the tray down, quickly poured four whiskeys in shot glasses three fingers' deep. Still eyeing Yancey, Leighton relaxed in increments. Yancey and his woolly partner each took a breath, and it was plain to Morkan that they saw in Leighton the cold sort of killer that rode them down all through the war. As Morkan watched his son, the child he saw behind the mask of Leighton's beard and bruised eyes astonished him and became as rare and precious as a seam of gold in a granite wall.

Yancey and the woolly drunk took their whiskeys, as did Leighton and Morkan. Yancey bit his lip. He spoke quietly. "They beat you pretty thorough, but I saw how you held." He stuck his chin at Morkan. "Story I got says you held out the whole war in Gratiot." Yancey's eyes were teary. "Never told them a thing."

Morkan stared at the whiskey in his hand, the blue sheen along the rim of the glass. When he looked up, Yancey raised his glass to him.

"God bless you, sir," the drunk said, tipping the glass upwards.

"In all your troubles," the woolly man said, raising his glass as well.

When Morkan sat long enough for things to become awkward, Leighton raised his whiskey to the men. "The war was hard, fellows. You'll have to forgive my pa."

Danny tapped the tray against her dress, then left with her brow creased. The two drunks nodded, and with Leighton they finished their whiskeys before Morkan brought his to his lips. They were silent for a time. Leighton's spoon scraped against the bottom of his bowl. Morkan could feel his son watching him, waiting to see if Morkan could bring himself to correct Yancey about Gratiot, about his heroism. Or maybe the boy understood what had happened today.

Shane Peale pushed the door open and stood blinking for a moment. He scanned the entire bar, spotted Morkan and Leighton, but kept glancing about as if making sure all was calm. He walked over slowly, nodded at Leighton when he stopped before the table.

He looked at Morkan. "Where you been today, Michael Morkan?"

Leighton glanced at his father, then at the deputy. "Is there something I can do for you, Shane?"

Peale frowned and shook his head.

"Been at the tailor's all morning," Morkan said. He plucked his new suit happily at the lapels. "I swear, though, Peale, he's lost his touch in the war. It never took Looney so long to fit a suit. I was just telling Leighton. . . ."

"Heron's been found shot dead on the road to Pleasant Hope."

Morkan took a breath. Leighton's face hardened, and his eyes fixed on Morkan's. Then his eyes grew serene. Far too much killing and mingling with both sides steeled his son in fires Morkan could never imagine. Even now, with catastrophe approaching, there was in his face a surety of purpose as obdurate and honed as the tip of an iron chuck. In a gruff voice Leighton said, "Peale, go you to Looney's. You'll find my pa's been over there wasting money all morning, and now he's been wasting it here."

Peale's brow wrinkled.

For the first time, Morkan felt victory coming, felt it like a sediment in his chest, a base that dried him, cured him, and left him hollow of vengeance, hollow and, to his surprise, at peace. His own name, Morkan, was no longer lost in the war and its winning, no longer vanquished like McBride, like Price, like Overbo. But more important, his son was saved, and the quarry, the boy's living, was saved. What father wouldn't go to Hell for that? He dabbed his lip with his collar. "I am mighty sorry, Peale."

When Peale had been gone a while, Yancey leaned forward again. "Still, after all this time, they trouble you?" he asked.

Morkan stared at his son, who regarded him with a look of wonder Morkan had not seen since the boy was new to the stone.

"Well, sir," Yancey said. "It sure is fine to drink with you."

Leighton finished the stew. "Going or staying?" he asked Morkan.

Morkan sat, the sun cutting a yellow square across the lap of the poplin suit. "Staying," he said after a moment.

Leighton cocked his chin behind Morkan at Yancey and his partner. Morkan frowned, shook his head. Leighton rose.

"Say," Morkan said. He spoke low. "Leave me a couple of eagles, will you?"

Leighton stopped, blinked at him. He opened the coin pouch at his belt.

"I could stand them a round or two," Morkan said, so quietly he was sure Leighton hadn't heard him, until he looked into his son's eyes. Instead of victory there was a loss in them, a final sizing up. Leighton was leaving his father behind in whatever place Morkan could save for himself, the place men like these two would make for him. And his time was short. The coins shone in Leighton's palm. The skin there was raw, devoid of the callus that marked the two of them, father and son, as lime miners.

Morkan placed his hand in Leighton's for a moment. On his fingertips the warm skin of Leighton's palm mingled with the electric cold of the lucre.

Leighton squeezed his hand, met his eyes. "I'll swing back," Leighton whispered. "Take you home." Then he cast the gold pieces on the table and left for his quarry.

Leighton eased the trowel between the bricks, placing mortar in the hole left for the white piece of limestone that marked the hearth as one built by a Morkan.

Behind him Cora Correy leaned against the doorjamb to the new home Elijah Correy was building her. She was heavy and very pregnant now.

"Keep working, please, Leighton," she whispered. "The watching does me good."

Leighton picked mortar up on the tip of the trowel and smiled at her. Seeing her content there made him want to marry.

"Is it hard working now with Michael gone?" she asked softly.

"No, ma'am. Not the working that is." He scraped more carefully—this chimney and hearth fell together by the old magic. He wanted no flaws. With the quarry growing steadily busy, this might be the last one he set himself.

"You know, Elijah says you are better at all this than Michael was," she said, a hand stroking her stomach absent-mindedly. "And what you have added to the courthouse is something to behold."

Leighton cradled the white stone, cool, smooth, and heavy. With a shudder of grief he sensed his father's hands on it, then recalled his own hands on the icy lines of his father's headstone, the white of the three dogwoods under moonlight.

"I heard in Gratiot he built a tunnel that freed a dozen men. That true, Leighton?"

When he set the hearth stone it made a sound like dirt gasping free of a shovel.

"You shouldn't listen to stories, dear," he said, and caught his Irish accent echoing off the timbers of the ceiling. "They'll upset you in your condition."

As he gathered his tools and rolled the drop cloths, she stood at the hearth admiring the white stone and his masonry.

"Patience, now," he said. "Give yourself seven days before you build a fire. Then it will keep mother and many a child warm."

She blushed. So Irish, that voice, so very much like his father's. What a son he might have been to her. His boots rang as he left. Watching him build awed her—he worked with the gentleness and reverence of a priest preparing the altar for the Host. Such power, standing by her new fireplace filled her with the feeling that this was forever, this home was forever, this town forever, her family, her child, her love was forever. On the one white stone, as cold and sparkling as if it were a gem cut from winter snow, she ran her fingers over the blue, chiseled name

MORKAN.

Author's Note and Acknowledgements

THIS IS A WORK OF FICTION. EACH CHARACTER IS FULLY a creation of the author's imagination, and no character is meant to represent any person living or dead. With history, the author has taken liberties throughout.

Readers desiring more history about the Ozarks, St. Louis, and Springfield are directed to the many books that inspired this novel, among them Elmo Ingenthron's *Borderland Rebellion*, William Garrett Piston's and Edwin C. Bearrs's books on the Battle of Wilson's Creek, Bell Irvin Wiley's two volumes on the common lives of soldiers, Louis S. Gerteis's *Civil War St. Louis*, Michael Fellman's *Inside War*, Halbert Powers Gillette's *Handbook of Rock Excavation*, and above all Lynn Morrow's and James Keefe's, *White River Chronicles of S. C. Turnbo*. Too numerous to mention are the many other books I marketed for University of Arkansas Press and University Press of Mississippi. I learned much from each of them and owe their authors thanks as well.

I am grateful to, and readers desiring more history are recommended to, Missouri's many and vibrant local historical societies, to *The Missouri Historical Review*, to the exceptional park rangers at Wilson's Creek National Battlefield and the battlefield's manuscript collection, and to the helpful librarians at the Shepherd Room in the Springfield-Greene County Public Library, where this book began. Also allow me to recommend the Western Historical Manuscript Collection in Rolla, one gatekeeper of which was kind enough to read a part of this when I started, and even more considerate to tell me exactly what he thought.

Thanks to the Arkansas Arts Council and the Mississippi Arts Commission, both of which gave me fellowships. The Mississippi Arts Commission has twice generously funded my work. This book would never have come to polish without the editorial input of Speer Morgan and Evelyn Somers of the *Missouri Review*. Greg Michalson saved this book by saying no to it at length and twice. Portions of the manuscript first appeared in the *Missouri Review,* the *Ontario Review,* and the *South Carolina Review.* A novella-length excerpt was a finalist for the Pirate's Alley/Faulkner Society Novella Competition. To those editors, staff, and society members, I am grateful. Thanks to Donald Hays, John Williams, William Harrison, Joanne Meschery, Miller Williams, and especially to James Whitehead. Thanks go to my steadfast critic and faithful friend, Randolph Thomas, and to Susan Perabo, Jay Prefontaine, Chris Kirk, Brad Barkley, Sidney Thompson, Elizabeth Oehlkers Wright, John Baken, and Michael Carragher for their reading and help. Bless Tom Franklin and John Evans for trying to get me published when no one else would listen. Thanks to Michael Heffernan, the Irish Catholic who led me to Father Mark Wood and Brother Christian Guertin. I will always be beholden to Donald Harington, whose constant encouragement and example kept me writing. I could not imagine a better editor than Donald Holliday or a better press and staff than that at MCP. I thank St. John, Evangelist, Patron Saint of all writers and those in the book trade, for all his intercession and prayer.

About the Author

Photograph by Melody Golding

BORN AND REARED IN SPRINGFIELD, MISSOURI, STEVE YATES is an M.F.A. graduate from the creative writing program at the University of Arkansas. His fiction has won two fellowships from the Mississippi Arts Commission and one from the Arkansas Arts Council. Portions of *Morkan's Quarry* first appeared in *Missouri Review, Ontario Review,* and *South Carolina Review.* A novella-length excerpt was a finalist for the Pirate's Alley Faulkner Society William Faulkner / Wisdom Award for the Best Novella. Yates has published short stories in *TriQuarterly, Southwest Review, Turnstile, Western Humanities Review, Laurel Review, Chariton Review, Valley Voices, Harrington Gay Men's Literary Quarterly,* and many other journals. He is assistant director / marketing director at University Press of Mississippi in Jackson, and lives in Flowood with his wife, Tammy.

353

CPSIA information can be obtained at www.ICGtesting.com
Printed in the USA
LVOW08*0128250315

431738LV00003B/6/P